Raves for M

Elemental

Phoen

"It's not lighthearted fluff, but rather a dark tale full of the pain and devastation of war, the growing class struggle, and changing sex roles, and a couple of wounded protagonists worth rooting for." —*Locus*

"A classic good/evil struggle marked by ventures into witchcraft in this satisfying story of a young woman's aspirations and struggles." —*The Bookwatch*

The Gates of Sleep

"Putting a fresh face to a well-loved fairytale is not an easy task, but it is one that seems effortless to the prolific Lackey. Beautiful phrasing and a thorough grounding in the dress, mannerisms and history of the period help move the story along gracefully. This is a wonderful example of a new look at an old theme." —*Publishers Weekly*

"With colorful characters, Lackey makes her variation of the Sleeping Beauty story great fun to read." —*Booklist*

"A lovely variation on a familiar fairy tale." —*Locus*

The Serpent's Shadow

"This is rather a departure from recent form for Lackey, which her characteristic carefulness, narrative gifts, and attention to detail shape into an altogether superior fantasy." —*Booklist*

"The author of the popular Valdemar series turns her hand to historical fantasy in this intriguing and compelling recreation of England in the waning days of its imperial glory." —*Library Journal*

"This new novel is one of (Mercedes Lackey's) best." —*Science Fiction Chronicle*

Novels by MERCEDES LACKEY available from DAW Books:

THE HERALDS OF VALDEMAR
ARROWS OF THE QUEEN
ARROW'S FLIGHT
ARROW'S FALL

THE LAST HERALD-MAGE
MAGIC'S PAWN
MAGIC'S PROMISE
MAGIC'S PRICE

THE MAGE WINDS
WINDS OF FATE
WINDS OF CHANGE
WINDS OF FURY

THE MAGE STORMS
STORM WARNING
STORM RISING
STORM BREAKING

KEROWYN'S TALE
BY THE SWORD

VOWS AND HONOR
THE OATHBOUND
OATHBREAKERS
OATHBLOOD

BRIGHTLY BURNING
TAKE A THIEF
EXILE'S HONOR
EXILE'S VALOR

VALDEMAR ANTHOLOGIES
SWORD OF ICE
SUN IN GLORY
CROSSROADS*

Written with Larry Dixon:

THE MAGE WARS
THE BLACK GRYPHON
THE WHITE GRYPHON
THE SILVER GRYPHON

DARIAN'S TALE
OWLFLIGHT
OWLSIGHT
OWLKNIGHT

Other Novels:

JOUST
ALTA
SANCTUARY

THE BLACK SWAN

THE ELEMENTAL MASTERS
THE SERPENT'S SHADOW
THE GATES OF SLEEP
PHOENIX AND ASHES
THE WIZARD OF LONDON

And don't miss:
THE VALDEMAR COMPANION
Edited by John Helfers and Denise Little

*Forthcoming from DAW Books

MERCEDES LACKEY

Phoenix and Ashes

The Elemental Masters, Book Three

DAW BOOKS, INC.
DONALD A. WOLLHEIM, FOUNDER
375 Hudson Street, New York, NY 10014
ELIZABETH R. WOLLHEIM
SHEILA E. GILBERT
PUBLISHERS
http://www.dawbooks.com

Cover art by Jody A. Lee

DAW Books Collectors No. 1306

DAW Books are distributed by Penguin Group (USA).

First Paperback Printing, October 2005

1 2 3 4 5 6 7 8 9

DAW TRADEMARK REGISTERED
U.S. PAT. OFF. AND FOREIGN COUNTRIES
—MARCA REGISTRADA
HECHO EN U.S.A.

PRINTED IN THE U.S.A.

To Janis Ian; amazing grace

Acknowledgments

When I needed to populate the village of Broom and Longacre Park, the denizens of the Dixon's Vixen bulletin board sprang to my aid by volunteering to be scullery maids, war-heroes, or villains as I chose. So if the names of the inhabitants are not consistent with the conventions of 1917, that is why.

And

Thanks to Richard and Marion van der Voort (www.atthesignofthedragon.co.uk), who vetted my historical and colloquial accuracy.

And

To Melanie Dymond Harper, who, when I lost my map and pictures of Broom, went out into wretched weather to recreate them for me.

1

December 18, 1914
Broom, Warwickshire

HER EYES WERE SO SORE and swollen from weeping that she thought by right she should have no tears left at all. She was so tired that she couldn't keep her mind focused on anything; it flitted from one thought to another, no matter how she tried to concentrate.

One kept recurring, in a never-ending refrain of lament. *What am I doing here? I should be at Oxford.*

Eleanor Robinson rested her aching head against the cold, wet glass of the tiny window in the twilight gloom of her attic bedroom. With an effort, she closed her sore, tired eyes, as her shoulders hunched inside an old woolen shawl. The bleak December weather had turned rotten and rainy, utterly un-Christmas-like. Not that she cared about Christmas.

It was worse in Flanders, or so the boys home on leave said, though the papers pretended otherwise. She knew better. The boys on leave told the truth when the papers lied. But surely Papa wouldn't be there, up to his knees in the freezing water of the trenches of the Western Front. He wasn't a young man. Surely they wouldn't put him there.

Beastly weather. Beastly war. Beastly Germans.

Surely Papa was somewhere warm, in the Rear; surely they were using his clever, organized mind at some clerking job for some big officer. She was the one who should be pitied. The worst that would happen to Papa was that he wouldn't get leave for Christmas. She wasn't likely to see anything of Christmas at all.

And she *should* be at Oxford, right this minute! Papa had promised, promised faithfully, that she should go to Oxford this year, and his betrayal of that promise ate like bitter acid into her heart and soul. She'd done everything that had been asked of her. She had passed every examination, even the Latin, even the Greek, and no one else had ever wanted to learn Greek in the entire village of Broom, except for little Jimmy Grimsley. The boys' schoolmaster, Michael Stone, had had to tutor her especially. She had passed her interview with the principal of Somerville College. She'd been accepted. All that had been needed was to pay the fees and *go.*

Well, *go* meant making all sorts of arrangements, but the important part had been done! Why hadn't *he* made the arrangements before he'd volunteered? Why hadn't he done so after?

Hadn't she had known from the time she could read, almost, that she all she really wanted was to go to Oxford to study literature? Hadn't she told Papa that, over and over, until he finally agreed? Never mind that they didn't award degrees to women now, it was the going there that was the important part—there, where you would spend all day learning amazing things, and half the night talking about them! And it wasn't as if this was a new thing. There was more than one women's college now, and someday they *would* give degrees, and on that day, Eleanor meant to be right there to receive hers. It wasn't as if she would be going for nothing. . . .

And it wouldn't be *here.* Not this closed-in place, where nothing mattered except that you somehow managed to marry a man of a higher station than yours. Or, indeed (past a certain age) married any man at all.

"Oxford? Well, it's—it's another world . . . maybe a better one."

Reggie Fenyx's eyes had shone when he'd said that. She'd seen the reflection of that world in his eyes, and she wanted it, she wanted it. . . .

Even this beastly weather wouldn't be so bad if she was looking at it from inside her study in Somerville . . . or perhaps going to listen to a distinguished speaker at the debating society, as Reggie Fenyx had described.

But her tired mind drifted away from the imagined delights of rooms at Somerville College or the stimulation of an erudite speaker, and obstinately towards Reggie Fenyx. Not that *she* should call him Reggie, or at least, not outside the walls of Oxford, where learning made all men (and women!) equals. Not that she had ever called him Reggie, except in her own mind. But there, in her mind and her memory, he was Reggie, hero-worshipped by all the boys in Broom, and probably half the grown men as well, whenever the drone of his aeroplane drew eyes involuntarily upward.

And off her mind flitted, to halcyon skies of June above a green, green field. She could still hear his drawling, cheerful voice above the howl and clatter of his aeroplane engine, out there in the fallow field he'd claimed for his own, where he "stabled" his "bird" in an old hay-barn and used to land and take off. He'd looked down at her from his superior height with a smile, but it wasn't a patronizing smile. She'd seen the aeroplane land, known that in this weather he was only going to refuel before taking off again, and pelted off to Longacre like a tomboy. She found him pouring a can of petrol into the plane, and breathlessly asked him about Oxford. He was the only person she knew who was a student there, or ever had been a student there—well, hardly a surprise that *he* was a student there, since he was the son of Sir Devlin Fenyx, and the field, the aeroplane, and everything as far as she could see where she stood belonged to Lord Devlin and Longacre Park. Where else but Oxford was good enough for Reggie Fenyx? Perhaps Cambridge, but—no. Not for someone from Warwickshire and Shakespeare country. "I want to go to university," she had told him, when he'd asked her why she wanted to know, as she stood looking up at him, breathless at her own daring. "*I* want to go to Oxford!"

"Oxford! Well, I don't know why not," he'd said, the first person to sound encouraging about her dream since her governess first put the notion in her head, and nearly the only one since, other than the Head of Somerville College. There'd been no teasing about "lady dons" or "girl-graduates." "No, I don't know why not. One of these days they'll be giving out women's degrees, you mark my words. Ought to be ashamed that they aren't, if you ask me. The girls I know—" (he pronounced it "gels," which she found fascinating) "—work harder than most of my mates. I say! If your parents think it's all bunk for a gel to go to university, you tell 'em I said it's a deuced good plan, and in ten years a gel'd be ashamed not to have gone if she's got the chance. Here," he'd said then, shoving a rope at her. "D'ye think you can take this rope-end, run over to *there,* and haul the chocks away when I shout?"

He hadn't waited for an answer; he'd simply assumed she would, treating her just as he would have treated any of the hero-worshipping boys who'd come to see him fly. And she hadn't acted like a silly girl, either; she'd run a little to a safe distance, waited for his signal after he swung himself up into the seat of his frail ship of canvas and sticks, and hauled on the rope with all her might, pulling the blocks of wood that kept the plane from rolling forward out from under the wheels. And the contraption had roared into life and bounced along the field, making one final leap into the air and climbing, until he was out of sight, among the white puffy clouds. And from that moment on, she'd hero-worshipped him as much as any boy.

That wasn't the only time she'd helped him; before Alison had come, she had been more out of the house than in it when she wasn't reading and studying, and she went where she wanted and did pretty much as she liked. If her mother had been alive, she'd likely have earned a scolding for such hoydenish behavior, but her mother had died too long ago for her to remember clearly, her father scarcely seemed to notice what she did, and she had only herself to please. Reggie had been amused. He'd ruffled her hair, called her a "jolly little thing," and treated her like the boys who came to help.

In fact, once after that breathless query about Oxford, he had given her papers about Somerville College, and magazines and articles about the lady dons and lecturers, and even a clipping about *women* who were flying aeroplanes—"aviatrixes" he called them—with the unspoken, but clearly understood implication that if anyone gave her trouble about wanting to go to Oxford, she should show them the clipping as well as give them his endorsement of the plan to show that "nice girls" did all sorts of things these days. "Women are doing great things, great things!" he'd said with enthusiasm. "Why, women are doctors—I know one, a grand gel, married to a friend of mine, works in London! Women *should* go exercising their brains! Makes 'em interesting! These gels that Mater keeps dragging round—" He'd made a face and hadn't finished the sentence, but Eleanor could guess at it. Not that she had any broad acquaintance with "ladies of Society," but she could read about them. And the London newspapers were full of stories about Society and the women who ornamented it. To her way of thinking, they didn't seem like the sorts that would be terribly interesting to someone like Reggie. No doubt, they could keep up a sparkling conversation on nothing whatsoever, and select a cigar, and hold a dinner party without offending anyone, and organize a country weekend to great acclaim, but as for being interesting to someone like Reggie—not likely. Even she, an insignificant village tomboy, was more interesting to him than they were ever likely to be.

Not that she was all that interesting to someone like Reggie. For all that she looked up to him, and even—yes, she admitted it—was a bit in love with him, he was as out-of-reach as Oxford was now. . . .

In fact, everything was out of reach now, and the remembered sun and warmth faded from her thoughts, replaced by the chill gloom of the drafty attic room, and the emptiness of her life.

Nothing much mattered now. The war had swallowed up Reggie, as it had swallowed up her father, as it had smothered her hopes. The bright and confident declarations of "Home by Christmas" had died in the rout at Mons, and were buried in the trenches at Ypres, as buried as her dreams.

She had thought she was through with weeping, but sobs rose in her throat again. *Papa, Papa!* she cried, silently, as her eyes burned anew. *Papa, why did you leave me? Why did you leave me with Her?*

For it wasn't the war that was keeping her from Oxford, anyway. Oh, no—her current misery was due to another cause. Surely Papa would have remembered his promise, if it hadn't been for the manipulations of Alison Robinson, Eleanor's stepmother.

Two more tears oozed out from under her closed lids, to etch their way down her sore cheeks.

She wouldn't be able to treat me like this if Papa hadn't gone. Would she?

Horrible, horrible woman. She'd stolen Papa from her, then stole her very life from her. And no one else could or would see it. Even people that should know better, who could *see* how Alison treated her stepdaughter, seemed to think there was nothing amiss. *If I hear one more time how lucky I am that Papa married her and left her to care for me while he's gone, I think I shall be sick. . . .*

The day she first appeared had been, had Eleanor only known it, the blackest day of Eleanor's life.

She pounded an impotent fist against her thigh as she stifled her sobs, lest She should hear. . . .

Papa had gone on business; it had seemed just like any other of dozens of such absences. Eleanor was accustomed to Father being absent to tend to his business from time to time; most fathers in Broom didn't do that, but Charles Robinson was different, for he was in trade, and his business interests all lay outside Broom, even outside of Warwickshire. He was a man of business, he often told her when she was old enough to understand, and business didn't tend to itself.

Although her father never flaunted the fact, she had always known that they lived well. She'd had a governess, when most children in the village just went to the local school. Miss Severn had been a *good* governess, one, in fact, who had put the idea of Oxford into her head in the first place, and good, highly educated governesses were (she knew now) quite difficult to find, and expensive.

Besides that, they had maids and a cook—well, there were others in Broom who had "help," but not many had maids that lived in, or a cook at all. And they lived in one of the nicest houses in Broom. "The Arrows," a Tudor building, was supposed to have been there at the time Shakespeare passed through the village after a poaching expedition, got drunk and fell asleep under the oak tree in front of the tavern.

But her papa hadn't made much of their prosperity, so neither had she. He socialized with the village, not the gentry, and other than visits to Longacre to see Reggie fly, so had she. They weren't members of the hunt, they weren't invited to dinners or balls or even to tea as the vicar was. The governess, the special tutoring later—this was, to her, not much different from the piano lessons the butcher's and baker's daughters got.

In fact, she hadn't really known how prosperous they were. Papa's business was hardly glamorous—he made sacks, or rather, his factories made sacks. All sorts of sacks, from grain-bags to the rough sailcloth duffels that sailors hauled their personal gear in. Well, someone had to make them, she supposed. And from time to time, Papa would visit one or another of his factories, making sure that everything was operating properly, and look over the books. His trips always happened the same way; he'd tell her and Cook when he was going and when he would be back and they'd plan on simple meals till he returned. He would drive their automobile, chugging and rattling, to catch the train, and at the appointed time, drive home again.

But last June something different had happened.

He'd gone off—then sent a telegram that something had

happened, not to worry, and he would be back a week later than he had planned and he'd be bringing a grand surprise.

She, more fool, hadn't thought any more of it—except, perhaps, that he was buying a new automobile. That was what he had done when he'd gotten the first one, after all, come back a week later, driving it, all bundled up in goggles and hat and driving-coat, and full of the adventure of bringing it all the way from London.

And he came back, as she had half expected, not in the old rattle-bang auto, but in a sleek, long-bonneted thing that purred up the street.

The problem was, he hadn't been alone.

She had been with him. And right behind them, in their own car, *They* had come.

She had come arrayed in an enormous scarlet hat with yards and yards of scarlet scarves and veils, and a startling scarlet coat of dramatic cut. Father had handed her out as if she was a queen, and as she raised a scarlet-gloved hand to remove her goggles, he had said, beaming with pride, "And here's my surprise! This is your new mother—" he hadn't said "stepmother," but Eleanor would never, ever call that horrible woman "Mother" "—Alison, this is my daughter. And look, Eleanor, here are two new sisters to keep you company! Lauralee, Carolyn, this is your sister Eleanor! I'm sure you're going to be the best of friends in no time!"

Two elegant, languid creatures descended from the rear of the second automobile, wearing pastel blue and lavender versions of *her* getup, and removed their goggles to regard her with stares as blank and unreadable as the goggles had been.

Broom had never seen anything quite like them. They looked as if they had come directly from the pages of some London quarterly. Only *she* smiled, a knowing little smile, a condescending smile that immediately made Eleanor aware of her untidy hair that was loosely tied with a ribbon like a child's, her very plain linen day-dress, *not* in vogue and *not* new, of her uncorseted figure, and her thick, clumsy walking shoes. The two girls raised their heads just a trifle, and gave her little patronizing smirks of their own. Then all three had sailed into the house without so much as a word spoken.

And with a shock, Eleanor had found herself sharing the house and her papa with a stepmother and two stepsisters.

Except—from the moment they entered the door, there wasn't a great deal of "sharing" going on.

The first sign of trouble came immediately, when the girls inspected the house and the elder, Lauralee, claimed the second-best bedroom—Eleanor's room—as her own. And before Eleanor could protest, she found herself and her things bundled up the stairs to an untenanted attic room that had been used until that moment as a lumber room, with the excuse, "Well, you'll be at Oxford in the autumn, and you won't need such a big room, now, will you?" Followed by a whispered "Don't be ungracious, Eleanor—jealousy is a very ugly thing!" and a frown on her papa's face that shocked her into silence.

The thing that still baffled her was the speed with which it had all happened. There'd been not a hint of any such thing as a romance, much less a marriage, *ever!* Papa had always said that after Mama, no woman could ever claim his heart—he'd gone a dozen times to Stoke-on-Trent before, and he'd never said a *word* about anything but the factory, and she thought that surely she would have noticed something about a woman before this.

Especially a woman like this one.

Oh, she was beautiful, no question about that: lean and elegant as a greyhound, sleek dark hair, a red-lipped face to rival anything Eleanor had seen in the newspapers and magazines, and the grace of a cat. The daughters, Lauralee and Carolyn, were like her in every regard, lacking only the depth of experience in Alison's eyes and her ability to keep their facade of graciousness intact in private.

Eleanor only noticed that later. At first, they were all bright smiles and simpers.

Alison and her daughters turned the house upside down within a week. They wore gowns—no simple "dresses" for them—like nothing anyone in Broom had seen, except in glimpses of the country weekends held up at Longacre. They changed two and three times a day, for no other occasion than a meal or a walk. They made incessant demands on the maids that those poor country-bred girls didn't understand, and had them in tears at least once a day. They made equally incredible demands on Cook, who threw up her hands and gave notice after being ordered to produce a dinner full of things she couldn't even pronounce, much less make. A new cook, one Mrs. Bennet, and maids, including a lady's maid just for Alison called Howse, came from London, at length, brought in a charabanc with all their boxes and trunks. Money poured out of the house and returned in the form of tea-gowns from London and enormous hats with elegantly scrolled names on the boxes, delicate shoes from Italy, and gloves from France.

And amid all of this upheaval and confusion, Papa beamed and beamed on "his elegant fillies" and seemed to have forgotten Eleanor even existed. There were no tea-gowns from London for Eleanor. . . .

Not that she made any great show against *them.* She looked like a maid herself, in her plain dresses and sensible walking shoes. They didn't have to bully her, not then, when they could simply overawe her and bewilder her and drown her out with their incessant chattering and tinkling laughter. And when she tried to get Papa alone to voice a timid protest, he would just pat her cheek, ask if she wasn't being a jealous little wench, and advise her that she would get on better if she was more like *them!*

She might have been able to rally herself after the first shock—might have been able to fight back. Except that all those far-off things in the newspapers about assasinations and Balkan uprisings that could never possibly have anything to do with the British Empire and England and Broom—suddenly did.

In August, the world suddenly went mad. In some incomprehensible way, Austria declared war on Serbia, and Prussia joined in, and so did Germany, which apparently declared war on everybody. There were Austrian and Prussian and German troops overrunning France and England was at war too, rushing to send men to stop the flood. And though among the country-folk in Broom there was a certain level of skepticism about all this "foreign nonsense," according to the papers, there was a sudden patriotic rush of volunteers signing up to go to France to fight.

And Papa, who was certainly old enough to know better, and never mind that he already had been in the army as a young man, volunteered to go with his regiment. And the next thing *she* knew, he was a sergeant again, and was gone.

Somehow Oxford never materialized. "Your dear father didn't make any arrangements, child," Stepmother said, sounding surprised, her eyes glittering. "But never mind! This will all be over by Christmas, and *surely* you would rather be here to greet him when he comes home, wouldn't you? You can go to Oxford in the Hilary term."

But it wasn't over by Christmas, and somehow Papa didn't manage to make arrangements for the Hilary term, either. And now here she was, feeling and being treated as a stranger, an interloper in her own house, subtly bullied by glamour and not understanding how it had happened, sent around on errands like a servant, scarcely an hour she could call her own, and at the end of the day, retreating to this cold, cheerless closet that scarcely had room for her bed and her wardrobe and desk. And Papa never wrote, and every day the papers were full of horrible things covered over with patriotic bombast, and everything was wrong with the world and she couldn't see an end to it.

Two more tears burned their way down her cheeks. Her head pounded, she felt ill and feverish, she was exhausted, but somehow too tired to sleep.

Today had been the day of the Red Cross bazaar and tea dance. Organized by Stepmother, of course—*"You have such a genius for such things, Alison!"*—at the behest of the Colonel's wife. Though what that meant was that Eleanor and the maids got the dubious privilege of doing all of the actual work while Stepmother and "her girls" stood about in their pretty tea-gowns and accepted congratulations. Eleanor had been on her feet from dawn until well past teatime, serving cup after cup of tea, tending any booth whose owner decided she required a rest, watching with raw envy as her stepsisters and other girls her age flirted with the handsome young officers as they danced to the band Stepmother had hired for the occasion. Dances she didn't know—dances to jaunty melodies that caused raised, but indulgent eyebrows among the village ladies. "Ragtime"—that's what they called it, and perhaps it was more than a little "fast," but this was wartime, and beneath the frenetic music was an unspoken undercurrent that some of these handsome young men wouldn't be coming back, so let them have their fun. . . .

Eleanor had cherished some small hope that *at last* someone who knew her would see what Alison was doing and the tide of public opinion would rise up to save her. Alison, after all, was the interloper here, and with her ostentatious ways and extravagance, she had surely been providing more than a little fodder for the village cats. But *just* when she was handing the vicar's wife, Theresa Hinshaw, a cup of tea, the woman abruptly shook her head a little, and finally *looked* at her, and frowned, and started to say something in a concerned tone of voice, out of the corner of her eye she saw Alison raise her head like a ferret sniffing a mouse on the wind, and suddenly there she was at the woman's elbow.

"Mrs. Hinshaw, how *are* you?" she purred, and steered Eleanor's hope away into a little knot of other women.

"I was wondering why we haven't seen Eleanor about," the vicar's wife began.

"Yes, she used to run wild all about the village, didn't she, poor thing," replied Alison, in a sweetly reasonable tone of voice. "A firm hand was certainly wanted *there,* to be sure. You'd never guess to look at them both that she's the same age as my Carolyn, would you?"

Eleanor saw Mrs. Hinshaw make a startled glance from the elegant Carolyn, revolving in the arms of a young subaltern, to Eleanor in her plain frock and apron and ribbon-tied hair, and with a sinking heart, saw herself come off second best.

"No, indeed," murmured Mrs. Sutherland, the doctor's wife.

Alison sighed heavily. "One does one's poor best at establishing discipline, but no child is going to care for a tight rein when she's been accustomed to no curb at all. Keep her busy, seems to be the best answer. And of course, with dear Charles gone—"

The vicar's wife cast a look with more sympathy in it at Eleanor, but her attention was swiftly recaptured by Lauralee, who simpered, "And poor Mama, not even a proper honeymoon!" which remark utterly turned the tide in Alison's favor.

From there it was all downhill, with little hints about Eleanor's supposed "jealousy" and "sullenness" and refusal to "act her age"—all uttered in a tone of weary bravery with soft sighs.

By the time Alison was finished, there wasn't a woman there who would have read her exhaustion and despair as anything other than sulks and pouting.

The music jangled in her ears and made her head ache, and by the time the car came for Alison and her daughters (*"Dear little Eleanor, so practical to wear things that won't be hurt by a little wet!"*) and Eleanor was finished with the cleaning up and could trudge home again, she felt utterly beaten down. Her aching legs and feet were an agony by the time she reached an unwelcoming home and unfriendly servants. Alison and the girls held high celebration in the parlor, their shrill laughter ringing through the house as they made fun of the very people they had just been socializing with.

She got plain bread-and-butter and cooling tea for supper in the kitchen—not even a single bite of the dainty sandwiches that she had served the *ladies* had she eaten, and of the glorious high tea that the cook had prepared for Alison and her daughters there was not a scrap to be seen. And by the time she went up all those stairs to her freezing-cold room, she'd had no strength for anything except hopeless weeping.

What does she want from me? The question echoed dully

in Eleanor's mind, and there seemed no logical answer. She had no doubt that Alison had married Papa for the money—for her all her airs at the tea, there was nothing in the way that Alison behaved in private that made Eleanor think that her stepmother found Papa's absence anything other than a relief. But why did she seem to take such pleasure in tormenting Eleanor?

There didn't seem to be an answer.

Unless she was hoping that Eleanor would be driven to run away from home.

Oh, I would, but how far would I get? If that was what Alison was hoping, the very nature of this area—and, ironically, the very picture that Alison had painted of her stepdaughter today!—would conspire to thwart her. Eleanor wouldn't get more than a mile before someone would recognize her, and after that carefully constructed fiction of a sullen and rebellious child that Alison had created, that same someone would *assume* she was running away and make sure she was caught and brought back!

And if Alison had wanted to be rid of her by *sending* her away, surely she would have done so by now.

She'll never let me go, she thought bitterly. *Not when she can make up lies about me to get more sympathy. And who believes in wicked stepmothers, anyway?*

She must have dozed off a little, because the faint, far-off sound of the door knocker made her start. At the sound of voices below, she glanced out the window to see the automobile belonging to Alison's solicitor, Warrick Locke, standing at the gate, gleaming wetly in the lamplight. He looked like something out of a Dickens novel, all wire-rimmed glasses, sleek black suits and sleek black hair and too-knowing face.

Oh. Him again. He seemed to call at least once a week since Papa had gone. Not that she cared why he came. It was odd for him to come so late, but not unheard-of.

Someone uttered an exclamation of anger. It sounded like Alison. Eleanor leaned her forehead against the cold glass again; she felt feverish now, and the glass felt good against her aching head. And anyway, the window-seat was more comfortable than the lumpy mattress of her bed.

Her door was thrust open and banged into the foot of the bed. She jerked herself up, and stared at the door.

Lauralee stood in the doorway with the light behind her. "Mother wants you, Eleanor," she said in an expressionless voice. "Now."

Eleanor cringed, trying to think of what she could have done wrong. "I was just going to bed—" she began.

"Now," Lauralee repeated, this time with force. And then she did something she had never done before. She took two steps into the room, seized Eleanor's wrist, and dragged her to her feet. Then, without another word, she continued to pull Eleanor out the door, down the hall, and down the narrow servants' stair.

The stair came out in the kitchen, which at this hour was empty of servants—but not of people. Alison was there, and Carolyn, and Warrick Locke. The only light in the kitchen was from the fire on the hearth, and in it, the solicitor looked positively satanic. His dark eyes glittered, cold and hard behind the lenses of his spectacles; his dark hair was slicked back, showing the pointed widow's peak in the center of his forehead, and his long thin face with its high cheekbones betrayed no more emotion than Lauralee's or Carolyn's. He regarded Eleanor as he might have looked at a black beetle he was about to step on.

But Alison gave her a look full of such hatred that Eleanor quailed before it. "I—" she faltered.

Alison thrust a piece of yellow paper at her. She took it dumbly. She read the words, but they didn't seem to make any sense. *Regret to inform you, Sergeant Charles Robinson perished of wounds received in combat—*

Papa? What was this about Papa? But he was safe, in Headquarters, tending paperwork—

She shook her head violently, half in denial, half in bewilderment. "Papa—" she began.

But Alison had already turned her attention away towards her solicitor. "I still say—"

But Locke shook his head. "She's protected," he said.

"You can't make her deathly ill—you've tried today, haven't you? And as I warned you, she's got nothing worse than a bit of a headache. That proves that you can't touch her directly with magic, and if she had an—accident—so soon, there would be talk. It isn't the sort of thing that could be covered up."

"But I can bind her; when I am finished she will never be able to leave the house and grounds," Alison snarled, her beautiful face contorted with rage, and before Eleanor could make any sense of the words, "you can't touch her directly with magic" her stepmother had crossed the room and grabbed her by one wrist. "Hold her!" she barked, and in an instant, the solicitor was beside her, pinioning Eleanor's arms.

Eleanor screamed.

That is, she opened her mouth to scream, but quick as a ferret, and with an expression of great glee on her face, Carolyn darted across the room to stuff a rag in Eleanor's open mouth and bind it in place with another.

Terror flooded through her, and she struggled against Locke's grip, as he pulled her over to the hearth, then kicked her feet out from underneath her so that she fell to the floor beside the fire.

Beside a gap where one of the hearthstones had been rooted up and laid to one side—

Locke shoved her flat, face-down on the flagstone floor, and held her there with one hand between her shoulder blades, the other holding her right arm, while Alison made a grab for the left and caught it by the wrist. Eleanor's head was twisted to the left, so it was Alison she saw—Alison, with a butcher's cleaver and a terrible expression on her face. Alison who held her left hand flat on the floor and raised the cleaver over her head.

Eleanor began screaming again, through the gag. She was literally petrified with fear—

And the blade came down, severing the smallest finger of her left hand completely.

For a moment she felt nothing—then the pain struck.

It was like nothing she had ever felt before. She thrashed

in agony, but Locke was kneeling on her other arm, with all his weight on her back and she couldn't move.

Blood was everywhere, black in the firelight, and through a red haze of pain she wondered if Alison was going to let her bleed to death. Alison seized the severed finger, and stood up. Lauralee took her place, holding a red-hot poker in hands incongruously swallowed up in oven-mitts. And a moment later she shoved that poker against the wound, and the pain that Eleanor had felt up until that moment was as nothing.

And mercifully, she fainted.

She woke again in the empty kitchen, her hand a throbbing sun of pain.

Like a dumb animal, she followed her instincts, which forced her to crawl to the kitchen door, open it on the darkness outside, on rain that had turned to snow, and plunge her hand into the barrel of rainwater that stood there, a thin skin of ice forming atop it. She gasped at the cold, then wept for the pain, and kept weeping as the icy-cold water cooled the hurt and numbed it.

How long she stood there, she could not have said. Only that at some point her hand was numb enough to take out of the water, that she found the strength to look for the medicine chest in the pantry and bandage it. Then she found the laudanum and drank down a recklessly large dose, and finally took the bottle of laudanum with her, stumbling back up the stairs to her room in the eerily silent house.

There she stayed, wracked with pain and fever, tormented by nightmare, and unable to muster a single coherent thought.

Except for one, which had more force for grief than all her own pain.

Papa was dead.

And she was alone.

2

March 10, 1917
Broom, Warwickshire

THE SCRUB-BRUSH RASPED BACK AND forth against the cold flagstones. Eleanor's knees ached from kneeling on the hard flagstones. Her shoulders ached too, and the muscles of her neck and lower back. *You would think that after three years of nothing but working like a charwoman, I would have gotten used to it.*

The kitchen door and window stood open to the breeze, airing the empty kitchen out. Outside, it was a rare, warm March day, and the air full of tantalizing hints of spring. Tomorrow it might turn nasty again, but today had been lovely.

Not that Eleanor could get any further than the kitchen garden. But if she could leave her scrubbing, at least she could go outside, in the sun—

But Alison had ordered her to scrub, and scrub she must, until Alison came to give her a different order, or rang the servants' bell. And if Alison "forgot," as on occasion she did, then Eleanor would be scrubbing until she fainted from exhaustion, and when she woke, she would scrub again. . . .

The nightmare that her life was now had begun on the

eighteenth of December, two years, three months, and a handful of days ago, when Alison Robinson hacked off the little finger of her left hand, and buried it with spells and incantations beneath the third hearthstone from the left here in the kitchen. Thus, Alison Robinson, nee Danbridge, had bound Eleanor into what amounted to slavery with her black magic.

Magic. . . .

Who would believe in such a thing?

Eleanor had wondered how Alison could have bewitched her father—and it had turned out that "bewitched" was the right word for what had happened. That night and the nights and days that followed had given her the answer, which only posed more questions. And if she told anyone—not that she ever *saw* anyone to tell them—they'd think her mad.

For it was madness, to believe in magic in these days of Zepps and gasworks and machine guns.

Nevertheless, Alison was a witch, or something like one, and Warrick Locke was a man-witch, and Lauralee and Carolyn were little witch's apprentices (although they weren't very good at anything except what Alison called "sex magic" and Eleanor would have called "vamping"). Alison's secret was safe enough, and Eleanor was bound to the kitchen hearth of her own home and the orders of her stepmother by the severed finger of her left hand, buried under a piece of flagstone.

She dipped the brush in the soapy water and moved over to the next stone. Early, fruitless trials had proved that she could not go past the walls of the kitchen garden nor the step of the front door. She could get that far, and no farther, for her feet would stick to the ground as if nailed there, and her voice turn mute in her throat so that she could not call for help. And when Alison gave her an order reinforced by a little twiddle of fingers and a burst of sickly yellow light, she might as well be an automaton, because her body followed that order until Alison came to set her free.

When her hand had healed, but while she was still a bit

lightheaded and weak, Alison had made her one and only appearance in Eleanor's room. Before Eleanor had been able to say anything, she had made that *gesture,* and Eleanor had found herself frozen and mute. Alison, smirking with pleasure, explained the new situation to her.

Her stepdaughter had not been in the least inclined to take that explanation at face value.

Eleanor sighed and brushed limp strands of hair out of her eyes, sitting back on her heels to rest for a moment. Under the circumstances, you would have thought that the moment would have been branded into her memory, but all she could really remember was her rage and fear, warring with each other, and Alison lording it over her. And then a word, and her body, no longer her own, marching down to the kitchen to become Mrs. Bennett's scullery maid and tweenie.

Perhaps the eeriest and most frightening part of that was that Mrs. Bennett and *all* the help acted, from that moment on, as if that was the way things had always been. They seemed to have forgotten her last name, forgotten who she really was. She became "Ellie" to them, lowest in the household hierarchy, the one to whom all the most disagreeable jobs were given.

The next days and weeks and months were swallowed up in anger and despair, in fruitless attempts to break free, until her spirit was worn down to nothing, the anger a dull ache, and the despair something she rose up with in the morning and lay down with at night.

She even knew *why* Alison had done this—not that the knowledge helped her any.

She, and not Alison, was the true owner of The Arrows, the business, and fourteen manufactories that were making a great deal of profit now, turning out sacks for sandbags to make trench-walls, and barricades, and ramparts along the beaches . . . for in all of her plotting and planning, Alison had made one tiny mistake. She had bewitched Charles Robinson into marrying her, she had bespelled him into running off to be killed at Ypres, but she had forgotten to get him to change his will. And not even Warrick

Locke could do anything about that, for the will had been locked up in the safe at the Robinsons' solicitor's office and it was the solicitor, not Alison, who was the executor of the will. There was no changing it, and only because Eleanor was underage was Alison permitted to act as her guardian and enjoy all the benefits of the estate. *That* was why she had been so angry, the night that the death notice came.

And after Warrick Locke investigated further, that was why she was forced to keep Eleanor alive and enslaved. Because if Eleanor died, the property went to some impoverished cousin in the North Country, and not Alison at all. Periodically, Eleanor was called into the parlor and given paper and pen, and wrote a letter under Alison's sorcerous dictation to the solicitor, directing him to give Alison money for this or that luxury beyond the household allowance. Alison fumed the entire time she was dictating these letters, but Eleanor was far, far angrier.

There were times when Eleanor wished she could die, just out of spite. . . .

She had eavesdropped on as many conversations as she could, which wasn't as difficult as it sounded, because Alison and Locke discussed such matters as if she wasn't present even when she was in the same room. She knew that her stepmother was something called an "Elemental Master" and that her power was over earth. What that meant, she had no real notion, but that was probably why Alison had buried Eleanor's severed finger. She knew that Warrick Locke was an "Elemental Mage," and that his power was also over earth, and that he was nothing near as powerful as Alison was. Lauralee and Carolyn were one rank below Warrick, evidently.

That Alison had far more power even than she had demonstrated against Eleanor was not in doubt. Eleanor had overheard plenty in the last three years, more than enough to be sure that the two of them were up to a great deal of no good. But of course, they wouldn't care what she heard; even if she could get out of the house, who would believe her wild tales about magicians?

For that matter, she hardly knew anything of what was going on in the world outside this house—just what she could glean from the occasional newspaper she saw. In the early part of the war, she had been able to get more information by listening to the servants, but—well, that was one way in which the war had affected *her.* There had been nine servants in the Robinson household—three more than the six that Eleanor and her father had thought sufficient—at the time when her father was killed. A man-of-all-work, a gardener, a parlormaid, three house maids, the cook Mrs. Bennett, and two ladies' maids, one (Howse) for Alison herself, one shared by Carolyn and Lauralee. Now there were two, Eric Whitcomb from the village who had returned from the war with a scar across the front of his head from some unspecified wound, and rather less than half his wits, and who did the gardening, the rough work and heavy hauling, and Alison's maid Howse. All the rest of the work was done by Eleanor. No one outside the house knew this, of course. Alison's status would have dropped considerably.

The man-of-all work had gone first, not so much out of patriotism (for after March of 1915 as the true nature of the slaughter in the trenches became known, it became more and more difficult to find volunteers) than because he had caught wind of conscription in the offing, and at the same time, was given the opportunity to join up with a regiment that was going somewhere *other* than France. "I'm off to the Suez, lovey," he'd told the downstairs house maid, Miranda Reed. "I'll bring you back a camel. I'll still be PBI, but at least my feet'll be dry."

Miranda had wept steadily for two months, then turned in *her* notice to go and train as a VAD nurse ("It can't be more work than this, and I'll surely get more thanks," she'd said tartly on departing). The next to go had been the parlormaid, Patricia Sheller, after her brothers were conscripted, leaving no one to help at her aged parents' London shop, and it wasn't long before Katy Feely, the stepsisters' maid, followed, when the work of the upstairs maid was added to her own load—she claimed she too was going to be a VAD nurse, but it wasn't true. "I've had enough of those cats, Mrs. Bennett," Katy had whispered to the cook in Eleanor's hearing. "And enough of this grubby little village. I'm off! There's heaps of better positions in London going begging now!"

By then, even married men were being conscripted, and Mrs. Bennett's son had been killed, leaving a wife and two tiny children with a third baby on the way; Mrs. Bennett turned in *her* notice to go and help care for them.

The result had been a sea change in how meals were dealt with in this household. Alison could compel Eleanor to cook—but she couldn't compel Eleanor to cook *well.* And it appeared that no matter how great Alison's powers were, they weren't enough to put the knowledge of an expert cook into Eleanor's mind, nor the skill of that cook into her hands. Eleanor hadn't done more than boil an egg and make toast in her life, and cooking was an undisclosed mystery to her. So for one week, Eleanor labored her way through the instructions in the cookery books, but the resulting meals were anything but edible. After that week, Alison gave up; the White Swan had supplied most of the components of luncheon and dinner to the household from that time on, while Brown's Bakery provided bread, crumpets, scones, muffins, cake and pie for afternoon tea.

The rest of the help had followed when Alison proved disinclined to pay for their meals from the pub as well as hers. Kent Adkins the gardener and Mary Chance the other maid vanished without bothering to give notice.

Eleanor still wasn't more than an adequate plain cook, and she took a certain amount of grim satisfaction in the fact that no more dishes with fancy French names graced Alison's table unless they came ready-made out of a tin. She could not bake much of anything—her bread never seemed to rise, and her pie crust was always sodden. She *could* make ordinary soup, most eggy things, toast, tea, and boil veg. She could make pancakes and fry most things that required frying. Anything that took a lot of practice and preparation came from the Swan or out of hampers from

Harrods and Fortnum and Mason, things that only required heating up before they were presented at table.

There was rationing now—sugar, according to complaints Eleanor overheard or saw in the newspaper, was impossible to get, and the authorities were urging meatless days. There were rumors in the newspapers that other things would soon be rationed—but none of that touched this household *as* privation. However it happened, and Eleanor strongly suspected black-marketeering, there were plenty of good things stocked away in the pantry and the cellar, including enough sugar to see them through another two or three years, and plenty of tinned and potted meats, jams and jellies, honey, tinned cream, white flour, and other scarce commodities, enough to feed a much larger household than this one. Not that Eleanor ever saw any of that on *her* plate. Rye and barley-bread was her lot, a great many potatoes roasted in the ashes or boiled and served with nothing but salt and perhaps a bit of dripping, and whatever was left over from the night before put into the ever-cooking soup-pot, sugarless tea made with yesterday's leaves, and a great deal of sugarless porridge. In fact, the only time she tasted sweets now was when an empty jam jar came her way, and she made a little syrup from the near-invisible leavings to pour over her porridge or into her tea.

She glanced at the light coming in through the door; almost teatime. This, of course, was Howse's purview, not hers. There was a spirit-kettle in the parlor; Howse would make the tea, lay out the fancy tinned biscuits, bread, scones, crumpets, tea-cakes, butter and jam. If toast was wanted, Howse would make it over the fire in the parlor. And then Howse would share in the bounty, sitting down with her employers as if she were their equal. Thus had the war affected even Alison, who, Eleanor suspected, had learned at least one lesson and would have done more than merely sharing meals in order to avoid losing this last servant. A lady's maid was a necessity to someone like Alison, who would have no more idea of how to put up her own hair or tend to her wardrobe than how to fly an aeroplane. The laundry could be sent out, prepared foodstuffs brought in, and Eleanor's strength was adequate to the rest of the needs of the household, but if Alison and her daughters were to keep up their appearances, and to have a chance at ascending to the social rank they aspired to, Howse must be kept satisfied. And *silent,* where the true state of the household was concerned.

Eleanor sighed, and stared into the flames on the kitchen hearth. There was a patent range here too on which most of the actual cooking was done, with a boiler and geyser in back of it that supplied hot water for baths and washing, both upstairs and down, but Eleanor liked having an open fire, and wood was the one thing that Alison didn't keep her from using. Since the spell that bound her was somehow tied to the kitchen hearth, it would have seemed more natural for Eleanor to hate that fireplace, but when she was all alone in the kitchen at night, that little fire was her only friend. In the winter, she often slept down here now, when her room was too cold for slumber, drifting off beside the warmth of that fire, watching the glowing coals. Now and again, it seemed to her she saw things in the flames—little dancing creatures, or solemn eyes that stared back at her, unblinking. The truth also was that no matter what she did around the fires, she never got burned. Leaping embers leapt *away* from her, smoke always went up the chimney properly, even when the north wind drove smoke down into the parlor or Alison's room. No fire ever burned out for her, and even that ever-cooking soup-pot never scorched. Her fare might be scant and poor, but it was never *burned.* Which could not always be said of Alison's food, particularly not when she or Howse undertook to prepare or warm it themselves, at the parlor hearth . . . and though Eleanor kept her thoughts to herself, she could not help but be glad when hard, dry, inedible food and burned crusts came back on the plates to the kitchen.

Sometimes Eleanor wondered why her stepmother hadn't simply done to Howse what she had done to Eleanor and turn *her* into a slave, but even after three years, she didn't know a great deal more about magic than she'd learned on that December night. Alison clearly *used* it, but she had never again performed a spell or rite where Eleanor could see her. Perhaps the reason was no more complicated than that while crude, unskilled work could be compelled, skilled work required cooperation. . . .

And even as she thought that, Eleanor realized with a start that she had been sitting on her heels, idle, staring into the flames on the hearth, for at least fifteen minutes.

The thought hit her with the force of a hammer blow. *Could Alison's magic be losing its strength?*

With a mingling of hope and fear, and quietly, so as not to draw any attention to herself, Eleanor climbed carefully to her feet and tiptoed to the kitchen door. The high stone wall around the garden prevented her from seeing anything but the roofs of the other buildings around her and the tops of the trees. There was a wood-pigeon in the big oak on the other side of the east wall, and the cooing mingled with the sharp metallic cries of the jackdaws. She stood quietly in the late afternoon sunshine, closing her eyes and letting it bathe her face.

Then she stepped right outside onto the path between the raised herb beds, and had to bite her lower lip and clasp her hands tightly together to avoid shouting in glee. She was outside. She was *not* scrubbing the floor—

But as she made a trial of approaching the garden gate, she found, with a surge of disappointment, that she could not get nearer than five feet to true freedom. The closer she got to the big blue wooden gate, the harder it was to walk, as if the air itself had turned solid and she could not push her way through it. This phenomena was not new—unless Alison was there and "permitted" her to approach the gate, the same thing had always happened before.

Still, to be able to break free from the spell *at all* was a triumph, and Eleanor was not going to allow disappointment to ruin her small victory. And after a quick, breathless, skipping run around the dormant garden, she was not going to allow discovery to take that victory from her, either. She went back to her scrubbing. Except that she wasn't scrubbing at all. She was sitting on her heels where she could quickly resume the task when she heard footsteps and simply enjoying the breathing space.

The sound of high-pitched voices in the parlor told her that the ladies were having their tea. Just outside the door, starlings had returned to the garden and were singing with all their might. The kitchen was very quiet now, only the fire on the hearth crackling while the stove heated for dinner. Alison's mania for forcing her to clean meant that the kitchen was spotless, from the shining copper pots hanging on the spotless white plaster walls to the flagstone floor, to the heavy black beams of the ceiling overhead. It looked very pretty, like a model kitchen on show. But of course, no one looking at a model kitchen ever thought about the amount of work it took to make a kitchen look like that.

She stared into the fire, and thought, carefully. If this glimpse of limited freedom wasn't some fluke, if incomprehensible fate had at last elected to smile on her—well, her life was about to undergo a profound change for the better.

Her stomach growled, and she smiled grimly. Yes, there would be changes, starting with her diet. Because one of the things that the spell on her did was that it prevented her from going into the pantry late at night to steal food.

In many households, the food was kept under lock and key, but Eleanor's father had never seen the need for that. He felt that if the servants needed to eat, they should feel free to help themselves.

Alison hadn't felt that way, but the pantry still had no lock on it, and while Mrs. Bennett had lived her, it hadn't needed one. The cook had kept a strict accounting of foodstuffs, but that wasn't why there was no pilferage. Mrs. Bennett had kept everyone so well fed that none of the other servants had seen the need to raid the stores.

With Mrs. Bennett gone, however, Alison had changed the spell that bound Eleanor to keep her from the stores. Howse, of course, never appeared in the kitchen, and wasn't going short either, since she shared Alison's meals.

But Eleanor had heard all the servants' gossip, before

they'd given notice, and she knew all the tricks for stealing food now that she hadn't known back before Alison came. So if she had even one chance at the pantry—well, she knew how and what to purloin so that even if Alison inspected, it would not be apparent that anyone had been into the stores.

What a thought! No more going to bed hungry—or feeling sick from eating food that had "gone off" and been rejected by Alison because that was all that there *was* for her to eat. Or at least, there would be none of that *if* she could bend the spell enough to get into the pantry at least once.

And suddenly, with a great leap of her heart, she realized that within a few days or a week at most, she would have the house to herself, as she always did in spring and fall. The annual pilgrimage to London was coming, when Alison and her daughters went to obtain their spring and summer wardrobes. Always before this, she had found herself restricted to the kitchen and her own room entirely for those few days. But perhaps *this* spring—

The sound of fashionable shoes with high heels clicking on hard stone broke into her reverie, and she quickly bent to her scrubbing. When Alison appeared in the doorway, striking a languid pose, Eleanor looked up, stony-faced, but did not stop her scrubbing. But she was much more conscious of the fire on the hearth than usual, and to keep her face still, she concentrated on it. The warmth felt—supportive. As if there was a friend here in the room with her. She concentrated on that.

Alison wore a lovely purple velvet tea-gown with ornaments of a cobwebby gray lace, with sleeves caught into cuffs at the wrist. As usual, her every dark hair was in place—and there was a tiny smile on her ageless face. She made a tiny gesture towards her stepdaughter, and Eleanor fought to keep her expression unchanging, as she saw, more clearly than she ever had before, a lance of muddy yellow light shoot from the tip of that finger towards her, and briefly illuminate her.

But she also saw, with a sense of shock, something entirely new. As that light struck her, there appeared a kind of cage of twisted and tangled, darkly glowing cords that pent her in. The cords absorbed the light, writhed into a new configuration, then faded away, and Eleanor sat up straighter, just as she would have if she had felt the compulsion to scrub ebbing.

"That's enough, Ellie," Alison said. "The laundry's been left at the tradesman's entrance. Go get it and put the linens away, then leave the rest for Howse."

"Yes, ma'am," Eleanor said, casting her eyes down, and thinking, wishing with all her might, *Tell me you're going to London! Go to London! Stay for a long time, a fortnight, or more! Go to London!*

And she bit her lip again to stifle the impulse to giggle, when Alison added thoughtfully, "I believe we'll be going on our London trip in two days, if the weather hold fine. You'll be a good girl while we're gone, and do all your work, won't you, Ellie."

"Yes, ma'am," she replied, getting to her feet, slowly, and brushing off her apron, using both actions as an excuse to keep her head down.

"Go tend the laundry." And once again, out of the corner of her eye, she saw a lance of grayish yellow light strike that tangle of "cords" and make it visible for a moment, saw the cords writhe into a new configuration. But this time she felt something, the faint ghost of the sort of compulsion she usually experienced, driving her towards the hall and the tradesmen's entrance. She allowed it to direct her, because the last thing she wanted was for Alison to guess that her magic was no longer controlling her stepdaughter completely.

As she folded and put away the linens, though, she wondered—what had happened? And why *now?*

I'd better take advantage of it while I have the chance, she decided, finally. *Who knows how long this respite will last?*

The usual chores occupied her until dinner, more floor-scrubbing, bath-drawing, tidying and dusting and dish-washing, while Howse tended to her own duties, and Alison and her daughters went out to pay calls or do their "work." It wasn't what Eleanor would have called work—

sitting in meetings debating over what sort of parcels should be sent to "our boys in the trenches," or paying visits to the recovering wounded officers in the hospital to "help" them by writing letters for them or reading to them. Alison and her daughters did not deign to "help" mere unranked soldiers.

Eleanor heard them return and go upstairs to change for dinner. That was when she prepared what she was able to cook, then laid the table and waited in the kitchen until summoned by the bell. Then she served the four courses to the four diners in the candlelit dining room with a fresh, white apron over her plain dress. It was ham tonight, from the Swan, preceded by a delicate consommé from a tin, a beetroot salad, and ending with a fine tart from the Browns' bakery. Though this was one of the more difficult times of the day, as she served food she was not allowed to touch and watched the girls deliberately spoil what they left on their plates with slatherings of salt and pepper so that she could not even salvage it for herself, tonight she comforted herself with the knowledge that *her* dinner was not going to be as meager as it had been for far too long—

While Alison and the girls were lingering over their tart, she went upstairs and turned down the beds, picked up the scattered garments that they had left on the floor and laid them ready for Howse to put away. She swept out the rooms for the last time today, then went back down to the kitchen to wait for them to leave the table. When she heard them going back up to their rooms for the evening, she went into the dining room again to clear the table and return the ham and a few other items to the pantry. But she smiled as she did so, because once she had closed the pantry door, she made a little test of opening the door again—and found that she could.

Ha!

It was her turn to linger now, and she did so over the dishes, over cleaning the kitchen, until she heard all four sets of heels going up the stairs to their rooms. Then she waited, staring into the fire, until the house quieted. Oddly, tonight there seemed to be more than a *suggestion* of creatures dancing in the flames—once or twice she blinked and shook her head, sure she had also seen eyes where no eyes could be.

And then she stole to the pantry, and opened it again. There was a faint feeling of resistance, but nothing more. And the culinary Aladdin's cave was open to her plundering.

Now, she knew this house as no one else did, and she knew where all of the hiding places in it were. One, in particular, was secure to herself alone. There was a hidden hatch under the servants' stair that for some reason her father had never shown Alison. Perhaps it was because Eleanor had been the one to discover it, and as a child had used it to store her secret treasures, and sometimes even hid in it when she had been frightened by storms. The hatch disclosed a set of narrow stone stairs that led down into a tiny stone cellar that *he* thought was a priest's hole, perhaps because of the little wooden crucifix, about the size to fit on the end of a rosary, they had found on the floor of the place. Eleanor had always thought it was a place where Royalist spies had hidden; perhaps it had served both functions.

Here Eleanor kept those few things she didn't want to fall into Alison's hands, such as most of the books that she had been using to study for the Oxford entrance examinations, other volumes she managed to purloin in the course of cleaning, and her mother's jewelry. Alison and her daughters didn't know about the jewelry, and never missed the books, which didn't much surprise Eleanor, as they seemed singularly uninterested in reading. Now the place was going to serve another purpose, as the repository for her stolen bounty of food, in case Alison managed to strengthen her magic, and there was not another chance for a while.

For the next hour or so she went back and forth between the pantry and the closet, never carrying much at a time, so that if she heard Alison or the girls coming, she could hide what she had. Jam, jelly, and marmalade, two bags of caster-sugar, some tinned meats and bacon, tinned cream and condensed milk, and many more imperishable things went into that cellar that night. She was very careful not to take the *last* of anything, and in fact to take nothing that was not present in abundance, removing items from the back of the shelf rather than the front. By the time she was finished, she had a small wealth of foodstuffs hidden away that made her giddy with pleasure.

Then she cut herself a generous slice of ham and a piece of buttered white bread to go with her soup, cut a little slice of the tart, and added milk and sugar to tea made with fresh leaves. And she had the first filling meal she had gotten since Mrs. Bennett left. She felt *so* good, and *so* sleepy with content, in fact, that she didn't bother to go up to her own room. Instead, she cleaned up every last trace of her illicit meal, and pulled the pallet she used in cold weather out of its cupboard, spreading it out in front of the fire.

And as she fell asleep, she smiled to think she saw sleepy eyes blinking with contented satisfaction back at her from the coals.

3

March 10, 1917
First London General Hospital

AT THIS TIME OF DAY, the ward was full of people; relatives hovering over their boys—though some of the boys were almost old enough to be Reggie's father, had Devlin Fenyx still been alive. Reggie was in the officers' wards, which meant that he had the luxury of being in the hospital building, and not outside in a tent as the enlisted men were. He usually didn't have any visitors, since his mother was afraid to travel alone and to her, "with a servant" qualified as "alone." Today, however, was different. Two of the men from 11 Squadron were on leave and had come to visit.

"Dashed handsome young fillies they've got hovering about you, Reg," said Lt. Steven Stewart, enviously. One of the "handsome young fillies"—a VAD called Ivy Grove—clearly overheard him. She blushed, bit her lip, and hurried off. Small wonder; almost any pilot got the hero-treatment from the women, and Steven was an infernally handsome fellow, who still hadn't shaken the "Oxford manner."

Reginald Fenyx could not have cared what the VAD nurses—or any others—looked like. All he cared about was that they were *there*, they talked to him, kept his mind on other things during the day—that they noticed when he was about to "go off," and came over on any pretext to keep the shakes away. Because when they were gone—

Tommy Arnolds, Reggie's flight mechanic and a wizard with the Bristol aircraft, wasn't nearly as subtle as Steven was; he stared after Ivy's trim figure with raw longing. He was a short, bandy-legged bloke, but what he could do with a plane was enough to make the pilot lucky enough to get him weep with joy when he took a bird that had been in Tommy's hands up. "Blimey," Tommy said contemplatively. "Wish they'd send a trim bit like *that* over, 'stead of those old 'orses—"

"They do send the trim bits over, Tommy," Steven said, fingering his trim moustache with a laugh. "But the old horses keep them out of *your* way. Your reputation precedes you, old man!"

Reggie managed a real smile, as Tommy preened a little, but his heart wasn't in it. They'd generously spent five hours of leave time here with him, but there was a limit to their generosity.

"And speaking of trim bits—" Steven tweaked the hem of his already perfect tunic. Steven, like Reggie, did not have to rely on the fifty-pound uniform allowance for *his* outfitting, and like Reggie had been before the crash, he was never less than impeccably turned out. "If Tommy and I are going to find ourselves a bit of company on this leave, we'd better push off. Can't have the PBIs showing up the Flying Corps, what?"

"Thanks for turning up, fellows," Reggie said, fervently. "Give my best to the rest of the lads. But not *too* soon."

"You can bet on that!" Steven laughed, and he and Tommy sketched salutes and sauntered out of the ward, winking at Ivy, the VAD girl, as they passed her, making her blush furiously.

Reggie lay back against his pillows, feeling exhausted by the effort to keep up the charade that he was perfectly all right, aside from being knocked about a bit. It was grand seeing the fellows, but—it was easier when people he knew *weren't* here and he didn't have to pretend. He had more in common with the lad in the next bed over, a mere second lieutenant by the name of William West, for all that West was PBI and Reggie was—*had been*—a pilot, a captain, and an ace at that. All the shellshock victims were in this end of the ward, together. Sometimes Reggie thought, cynically, it was so that their screaming in nightmares and their shaking fits by day wouldn't bother anyone else.

There weren't many shellshock cases in the Royal Flying Corps, anyway. The pilots and their support crew were well behind the lines, out of reach of the guns and the gas. That was the lot of the PBI—the "Poor Bloody Infantry," upon whose lines in the trenches the pilots looked down in remote pity, chattering and clattering through the sky.

Or we do just before Archie gets us, or the Huns shoot us down— Reggie amended, and then the first sight of that azure-winged Fokker interposed itself between him and the ward, and the shaking began—

He clawed at his bedside table for a glass of water, the paper the lads had brought him, anything to distract himself. But then, before he could go into a full-blown attack, something altogether out of the ordinary distracted him. Because, coming towards him down the aisle between the beds, accompanied by his usual medico, Dr. Walter Boyes, was another doctor, but this time it was someone he recognized.

"Captain Fenyx—" Boyes began, quietly, so as not to disturb West, who had subsided into a morphine-assisted sleep, "—I believe you already know my colleague."

"I should say so!" he exclaimed, sitting up straight. He had never been so pathetically glad to see anyone in his life. "Doctor Scott! Maya! I had no idea you were on the military wards!"

"I'm not," the handsome, dark-haired, dark-eyed woman said, with a smile. Her exotic beauty was more than enough to make even the stark white hospital coat and severe black skirt look out-of-the-ordinary. "Good heavens, Reggie, can you see the War Department unbending enough for that? Now, if I were unmarried and prepared to volunteer for Malta, they would take me, and they *might* even allow me to practice in Belgium or France, but here? Oh, they *would* accept me as a VAD aide, of course. But because I'm married, they won't take me any other way. Heaven forfend that Peter might have to supervise the household once in a while."

"Well—when you put it that way—" He shrugged. The War Department was full of idiots, everyone knew that. Unfortunately, they were the idiots in charge. Maya Scott and her fellow female doctors, few though they were, would have made a big difference to the wounded. And if they were worried about the morals of the patients being corrupted, or even those of the other military doctors, wouldn't a married doctor be "safer" rather than more dangerous? "But why are you here, then? Surely not just for me?"

"Entirely just for you; I've been sent by a higher power." A little smile curved her lips, suggesting that this was a joke. "Walter is a friend of mine; he worked in our charity clinics before the war," she continued. "I didn't know you were here until Lady Virginia got hold of me two days ago; she gave me your doctor's name, and that was when I went hunting for him and you."

Ah, that explained "higher power." His godmother was a force of nature.

"I would have been here sooner, but until I got hold of Walter, I wouldn't have been allowed near you." It was her turn to shrug. "I'm a female, not your relative, your fiancée, nor a nurse, you see. Never mind that I'm a doctor; evidently it is expected that you would immediately corrupt my morals, or I yours. Fortunately, Walter has made all smooth. *He* is allowed to bring in anyone he likes as a consulting physician, so long as I don't expect to be paid."

In the course of that exchange, Reggie and Maya communicated something more, wordlessly. A lift of an eyebrow on Reggie's part towards Dr. Boyes—*does he know?* The tiniest shake of the head from Maya, confirming his initial impression—*no.* So, Doctor Walter was neither an Elemental Mage himself, nor was he among the few who were not Mages that nevertheless knew of the existence of Mages and magic.

Doctor Maya, however, *was* an Elemental Mage. In fact, she was an Earth Master.

"Walter, can the patient leave his bed?" she asked in the next moment. "I'd like to talk to him privately."

"I don't want him to put weight on that leg yet, but yes," Doctor Walter replied, and sent the VAD girl for a wheelchair. Then he added, in a hushed voice Reggie was sure he was not meant to overhear, "If you can get something out of him about his experience—"

"That's what I'm here for," Maya said soothingly. "I haven't seen a great *many* shellshock cases myself, but I've gotten some. Nurses are coming back to us in sad condition, particularly the ones who've been on transports that were torpedoed, or shelled while working near the lines or riding with the ambulances. His grandmother and Lady Virginia DeMarce, his godmother, thought he might be more willing to unburden himself to someone he knows."

Reggie almost laughed with pent-up hysteria. Someone he knew! Good God, if that was *all* it was! If they only knew, all those medicos—if they only knew!

But the chair arrived, and he levered himself into it, wanting nothing more than to be out of this ward, quickly, where he could finally talk to someone who would at least *understand.* Because he was not "just" a victim of shellshock. Oh no. That was only the smallest of his problems. . . .

It was an unseasonably warm day, he discovered, as Maya wheeled him briskly and efficiently out into the hospital garden. That was a relief, for she was able to find a little alcove where they could be quite private, and park him with his back to a wall. He blessed her exquisite sensitivity, but she *was* an Earth Master, after all, and a Healer to boot, and sensitivity came with that description.

"Well, Reggie," she said, the moment she settled down across from him, with their knees practically touching. She took out a bit of paper from her pocket and consulted it. "I'm going to make this easier *and* more difficult for you. I have been studying Doctors Freud and Jung's works, and as you heard, I have already seen several normal cases of shellshock. I did my studying of your case before I arrived, so let me tell you quickly what *I* know, then we'll get to what I *don't* know. I know you were shot down, your observer was killed—" she looked at the paper in her hand "—Erik Kittlesen, wasn't it?"

He nodded, numbly, both desperately grateful that he wasn't actually having to tell all this himself, and appallingly afraid of what he was going to have to say when she started asking questions.

"You came down close to the Hun side in No-Man's Land. Some of the Huns came to get you out of the wreckage, and a barrage hit, killing everyone but you. Then one of *our* parties got you out, dragged you to a bunker, and *another* barrage hit, burying you in the bunker for two days until another rescue party dug you out. Is that the long and the short of it?"

He nodded. His mouth felt horrible dry, and when he licked his lips, he fancied he could still taste that horrible substance that passed for air in the trenches and the bunkers—a fetid murk tainted with the smell of past gas attacks, and thick with the stench of death, of blood and rotting flesh, rats and foul water.

"Now comes the hard part," she said, and reached over to take his unresisting hand. "Now I ask you questions. And Reggie, you *must* answer them. I can't help you if you don't, or won't."

Once again, he nodded, feeling his throat closing up with panic, and the sting of helpless tears behind his eyelids.

"Why did you get shot down?" she asked implacably. "You are an Air Master, one of the most skilled I know. We both know it wasn't luck that was keeping you in the sky, *particularly* not given the horrid old rattletraps you were often given. So what happened?"

"I went up," he croaked. "And—Maya, this is a damned wretched thing to say, but—look, the only way I was ever able to face what I was doing was to never, ever think about the Hun as anything other than a target." He made a sound like a laugh. "Actually, I was Erik's only chance to go up at all, which was why I was in a two-seater instead of flying solo as usual. Everyone knew that even though Erik crashed more birds than he flew, anything he aimed at, he hit—he even took down a Hun with a half-brick, once! He'd crashed his plane as usual; the only things available were my usual bird, which was having a wonky engine anyway, and the two-seater. They knew if he was in the observer's seat, I could concentrate on flying the bird and he could concentrate on what he was good at. But if it hadn't been for me, he wouldn't even have been up there that day."

Maya nodded. "I see why you feel doubly responsible." *Pilots were not in such plentiful supply that Erik would not have been up on his own.* He knew that; he'd been told that too many times. She didn't say it, because she must have known that he'd been told it and didn't believe it, and he was grateful that she didn't say it aloud again because she understood it wouldn't help. There were a great many things in this war that people understood, but didn't say aloud. It was probably the only way most people kept from going mad.

But of course, I'm already mad . . . or getting there. . . .

"But *why* were you shot down?" she persisted, as if she knew that this was where the first crack had appeared in his armor. Maybe she did.

"Because—" he swallowed. "Because this time, when I went up, there was someone I'd never seen before up there to stop me. Bright blue Fokker. Maya, *he* was one of us. He was an Air Master too. And—" he shook his head. "and I felt something. From *him.* Not his thoughts, more like what he was feeling. He was—he was in mourning." He closed his eyes for a moment, to fight down his own tears. Words were totally inadequate to what he had felt in that single moment. Mourning? It was deeper than mourning. It had been self-revulsion, hatred for what the man had been doing, and a terrible, terrible sense of loss. The Hun hadn't only been mourning what he had to do—he was in mourning for the loss of everything he cared for. "He was—" Reggie groped for words. "flying with sorrow, the deepest, blackest sorrow I ever felt in my life. And it was because by doing his duty, which was the honorable thing to do, he was being forced to kill us, who should have been his comrades. Because his beautiful blue heavens were filled with a rain of blood, and his beautiful blue wings belonged to the Angel of Death. He knew he would never, for however long he lived, fly in skies free of blood. His world was shattered, and he'd never really feel happiness again."

Maya's fingers tightened on his. "Vishnu preserve us," she replied, her voice full of the shocked understanding he had hoped to hear.

"I—couldn't shoot him. He couldn't help but shoot me. I—" he shook his head. "I didn't evade. He got Erik first, then my tank, and then my engine. He got Erik, and I felt him die, and it was my fault—my fault—"

Once again her fingers tightened on his, but she did *not* say, as so many fools had, that it wasn't his fault. "You made a mistake," she said instead. "At some point, Reggie, you have to stop paying for it, and forgive yourself. But only you can decide how much payment is enough." Then her voice strengthened. "You were shot down. Your collarbone and your knee were both shattered, your ribs were cracked, and I think only your Mastery saved you from worse. Then the Huns came to get you out before your plane went up in flames. Something happened then, too, didn't it?"

"*A* Hun came to get me out," Reggie corrected. "A young fellow came pelting out regardless—I suppose our boys must have seen what he was doing, because they held their fire. He came pelting out, into No-Man's Land, over the wire, and hauled me out while the bird was burning. And he went back for Erik, and—" he swallowed "that was when the shell hit. Young fellow, he couldn't have been sixteen. Maybe less." He felt his throat closing again at the thought of that earnest young face, at the young voice that told him *"Stille, stille, bitte. Ja, das ist gut, stille."* "The boys that came after me found some bits of his things, a letter from home, a picture of his mother. His name was Wilhelm, that's Hun for William, like West in the next bed over from me in the ward. PBI, like young Willie, too. Wilhelm Katzel. That's *two* fellows that died because of me, in less than five minutes."

She nodded, but said nothing for a moment. "I think," she finally said, "When this is over—you should tell his mother how brave he was."

That was not what he was expecting to hear. "How will that help?" he asked angrily.

"I don't know," she replied, not reacting to his anger at all. "But I do know that it won't hurt. It will let her know he hadn't lost his decency or his honor in this vile slaughter, and that's something for her to hold onto. This war has made beasts of so many—perhaps it will comfort her to know that her Wilhelm was still a man."

It was not the answer he had been expecting, and he flushed a little. But she was right. She was very right.

But of course, the worst was yet to come.

"That isn't where the real trouble lies, though, is it?" she continued. "Oh, it's horrible, and you are burdened terribly with guilt, but that isn't the worst." She tugged a little on his hand, forcing him to look up, into her eyes. "The worst came when you were safe, didn't it? In the bunker. Buried alive."

He almost jerked his hand out of hers, and began to shake uncontrollably. "How did you—"

"Reggie, I'm an *Earth Master.* The ground in France and Belgium is *saturated* with blood," she said, with a thin veneer of calm over her words. "I *know* what that attracts. There are monsters in the earth of France, Reggie, and they are fattening and thriving on that slaughter—and when that shell hit that bunker, they had a tidbit of the sort they could only crave and dream about in their power. Air and Earth are natural enemies, and they had *you* in their territory, in their grasp, to do with what they wanted." His vision began to film over as panic rose in his chest; he clutched her hands, as though clutching a lifeline, as she put into words what he could not. "They had you, Reggie, their greatest enemy, a Master of Air *and* a Master of the Light, helpless, on *their* ground." He couldn't see, now, as all the memories came flooding back. He heard his breath rasping in his throat, his heart pounding, and could not move for the fear. Dimly, through the roaring in his ears, he heard her ask the question he did not want to answer.

"What did they do to you, Reggie? What did they do?"

Maya Scott sat with her husband in a place in the Exeter Club where—before her marriage to Peter Scott—no woman had ever been before. It was a lovely day outside, still; the windows stood wide open to the warm air, and the sun streamed down onto old Persian rugs, caressed brown leather upholstery, and touched the contents of brandy bottles with gold.

"So," said the Lord Alderscroft, often called the Old Lion—older now than when she had first met him, and aged by more than years. "You've seen the boy."

She nodded.

Lord Alderscroft sat like the King on his throne, in his wingback chair in his own sitting room in his private suite on the top floor of the Exeter Club, and raised a heavy eyebrow at Maya. "Your report, please, Doctor Scott?"

Maya never sat here without feeling a distant sense of triumph. It had been her doing that had broken down the last three barriers of the White Lodge housed here in the Exeter Club—of gender, lineage, and race. She would have failed the Edwardian tests on all three counts; female, common, and of mixed Indian and British blood. But King Edward was gone, and King George was on the throne, and after the defeat of her aunt, there was not a man on the Council who felt capable of objecting to her presence. And truth to tell, they *needed* her. They had needed her before the war. She was one of a handful of Earth Masters who could bear to live and work in the heart of a great city.

Now they needed her—and the other women they had admitted to the White Lodge—more than ever. The war had been no easier on the ranks of the Elemental Masters than it was on the common man.

Today, however, triumph was not even in the agenda.

"He's in wretched shape, my lord," she said slowly. "It is not helping that so many physicians and most officers, all of whom should know better, are convinced that shell-shock is just another name for malingering. Even as *he,* himself, acknowledges that he is not well, there is the subconscious conviction that if he only had an ounce more willpower, he would get over it and back to the fight. I can tell him differently until I turn as blue as Rama; until he believes it in his heart, he will continue to berate himself even as he suffers."

Lord Alderscroft—who, not that long ago, would have agreed with those physicians and officers—sighed heavily. He knew better now. All Elemental Masters knew better; the war was hellish, but it was worse on the minds and nerves of Elemental Masters. The truth was, most of the Masters that had gone into the trenches, *if* they survived the senseless, mindless way in which the War Department threw away their lives, were there for less than six months before their minds broke. "So he is in no fit state, as Doctor Boyes reports, with a ripe case of shellshock as well as physical injuries. And as if that were not enough, then there is what he faced, in the earth."

She shook her head, and swallowed, as her husband closed his hand over hers. She had closed herself off as much as she had dared, but as a Healer and a physician, she had needed to know something of what he had experienced.

She had been ready for it, and of course, it had come at second hand, but it had been too horrific for anyone to really understand without sharing it.

She gave Peter a faint smile of thanks. "You do not wish to know the details, my lord. Horrors. That is enough, I think. The inimical forces of all four Elements can terrify, but I think that those of Earth are most particularly apt at destroying the mind with fear. They swarmed him and tormented him from the moment the earth was shattered around him to the moment that the rescue party broke through and got him out. The records say he was more dead than alive. I am not at all surprised. What I am surprised at is that he has a mind left at all, much less a rational one."

"Well," Alderscroft rumbled, his face creased and recreased with lines of care, "We humans have taught them about torment and horror all too well, have we not?" He sighed again.

"Do not lay too much upon the shoulders of mere mortals, my lord," Maya replied, grimly. "Recall that it is Healing that is in the Gift of the Earth Mages and Elementals. The converse is harm, and it is naturally true of the dark side of that Element." She thought with pity of the poor fellow, who she last recalled seeing as a bright young Oxford scholar, utterly shattered and weeping his heart out, bent over her knees. It was a state she had wanted to bring him to—for without that initial purging, he could not even begin to heal—but it had been painful for her to do so, and only the fact that she had done it before, to others, even made it possible for her to carry it through. But she was a surgeon, and surgeons became hardened to necessity after a time. You could not cleanse a wound without releasing the infection. You could not heal the mind without letting some of the pressure off. "The larger consequence for *us,* my lord, is that he has cut himself off from any use of his powers."

Lord Alderscroft closed his eyes. "I feared as much. And we cannot afford that. Too many of us are gone—"

"Nevertheless, he has closed off his mind to his power," she replied. "And it is of no use trying to get him to open it now. *He* tells me that the things that attacked him destroyed his Gifts, and he believes it with every iota of his being."

"And that isn't true?" A second figure stepped away from the shadows beside the fireplace; another nobleman, Peter Almsley, lean and blond, nervously highbred, and the Scotts' best friend. He was in a uniform, but he was on some sort of special duty with the War Department that kept him off the Front. She suspected that special duty was coordinating the magical defense of the realm. Certainly Alderscroft wasn't young enough anymore to do so.

She closed her eyes for a moment. Even if Fenyx never flew again, *he* could be put to doing what Almsley was doing—with more effectiveness. The Air Elementals actually controlled winds and weather to some extent, and if an Air Master could see to the *physical* defenses of the country—

She did not shudder, she had endured worse than bombardment by Zepps and Hun aeroplanes, but—it was hard, hard, to hear the drone of those motors in the sky, in the dark, and look up helplessly at the ceiling and wait for the first explosions and wonder if you were sitting on the target, or if you would be able to scramble away to somewhere safer when you knew where the bombs were falling. And if the latter—who, of your friends, *was* sitting on the target. If Reggie could be persuaded—

She shook her head. "There is nothing wrong at all with his Gifts," she said, decidedly. "But I think that, in those dreadful two days underground, he understood instinctively that his very power was what attracted the Earth creatures to him, and that if he closed that power off, they would cease to torment him. At some level deeper than thought—Doctor Freud would have called it the *id*—in the most basic of his instincts, he walled that part of himself away. And now he truly does not believe it exists anymore."

"So you can get him back—" Alderscroft began, eagerly, looking optimistic for the first time this interview began.

But she shook her head emphatically. "Not I. This is too complicated a case for me. Doctor Andrew Pike in Devon is the man you need—"

But Almsley groaned. "Not a chance of a look-in there, Maya. Not now, not *ever.* It's one thing to unburden his weary soul to you, my heart—but if you call in the good Doctor Pike, or worse, send the boy to him, our Reggie will have to admit that he's gone balmy, and that he can never do."

Maya looked from Almsley to Alderscroft and back again, and felt like stamping her feet with frustration at what she read there. Men! Why did they have to be so *stubborn* about such things?

"Maya, think," her husband said, quietly. "If he's sick with guilt over the idea that he's malingering, what do you think the mere sight of Andrew Pike at his bedside do to his feelings about himself?"

Defeated, she could only shake her head.

"Going 'round the bend is just not the done thing, my heart," Almsley said sadly. "It's what your dotty Uncle Algernon does, not an officer and a gentleman. Andrew could probably have him right and tight in months, but that doesn't matter. If he saw Andrew, he'd be certain that we all think he's mad, and if he's mad, he's broken and useless, and worse, he's a disgrace to the old strawberry leaves and escutcheon. If he's gone mad, he might just as well die and avoid embarrassing the family."

She leveled her gaze at Alderscroft. "Then you had better hope he can get well and work his way through his troubles on his own," she said, doing her best to keep accusation out of her tone. "But *I* don't think that he will. Not without a powerful incentive to break through that wall of fear that keeps him away from his power, and I can tell you right now that duty, honor, and pride are not powerful enough. Duty, honor, and pride aren't enough to get him through the shell-shock, much less break through to his Gifts again. Furthermore—"

Should she tell them?

She was a physician; she had to.

"Furthermore, I consider that without Doctor Pike's help, there is a real possibility that he may do away with himself if he can't manage to get himself through. Because I am not sure he can live with the pain, the fear, and the conflicts inside himself as he is now."

There. She'd said it.

She expected them to look shocked, to protest. They didn't; they only looked saddened and resigned.

"It won't be the first one we've lost that way," Almsley said softly, revealing the reason for their reaction. He turned to Alderscroft. "What do you think, send him home on recovery leave?"

Almsley hadn't asked her, but she answered anyway. "At least if he is at home, he will be in familiar surroundings and far away from anything military. It might help."

Alderscroft nodded his massive head, slowly. "Get his grandmother to keep an eye on him; I think it's the best we can do. I'll talk to some people, and get him leave to recover at home." He turned back to Maya. "Thank you, doctor. You have been of immense help; more than you know. I only wish it were possible to take more of your advice. I promise, we will see to it that everything that *can* be done, will be. And it will not be for lack of—flexibility—on our part."

That was a dismissal if ever she had heard one, and reluctantly, she allowed her husband to assist her to her feet and took her leave.

But it did nothing to end her anger—which was the only way she could keep her own profound depression at bay. *I hate this bloody, senseless, useless, stupid war.*

4

March 14, 1917
London

THE ROBINSONS HAD TAKEN THE first train to London, set themselves up at the Savoy Hotel, and gone straight out to take care of the most urgent need for all three of them—new wardrobes. But their visits to the first three fashion houses—their usual haunts—were less than a success.

"Have you ever seen such ugly colors?" Carolyn complained (rather too loudly) to her mother, as she and her sister followed hard on their mother's heels out to the pavement in front of the third. "Drab brown, drab olive, drab navy and drab cream. Khaki, khaki, khaki! And nothing but tweeds and linens! And for spring and summer! What about silk? What about muslin? Do they think we're all Land Girls?"

Her mother shrugged. "We'll try another atelier, dear," she said, with a glance up the street, looking for a taxi. "Someone who isn't trying so hard to be patriotic and dress us all in uniforms."

"I don't see why one has to be plain to be patriotic," Lauralee pouted. Her sister sniffed.

"Plain? Made up like a Guy, more like!" Carolyn exclaimed. "I don't want to look like I'm in uniform and I don't want to look like a—a suffragette! I want—"

"Leave it to me, girls; I have some notions," Alison replied, and spied a free taxi in the same moment. Taxis were thin on the ground in London now, but Alison had no intention of subjecting herself to the Underground or the 'buses. It didn't take much more than a lifted finger and a spark of magic to summon it, as it passed by five other people trying to hail it, including one disgruntled cavalry officer.

She leaned over and gave the driver—a very old man indeed—an address that made him look at her in surprise. But he said nothing, and she took her place beside her daughters. It was pleasantly warm; unpleasantly enough, they were all three wearing last year's spring gowns. This would never do.

To the surprise of her daughters, the establishment that the taxi left them at was *not* any of the usual fashion houses Alison patronized. She ignored their surprise, for it was painfully clear to her that the usual establishments would not do this year. There was probably a good reason why all the houses that *she* could afford to patronize were using domestically produced fabrics this spring, and it was a reason she should have anticipated, given the start of rationing.

She would have to resort to another ploy—though the rather grubby theater district was not a place one would normally go to find one's wardrobe. She opened a door with the cryptic words *Keplans Haberdashery* painted on the frosted glass. The girls followed her up a narrow, rather dirty wooden staircase with no small trepidation; she smiled to herself, knowing what awaited them at the top.

She and the girls emerged from this place feeling a glow of triumph. Here, at least, fashion was not being subjected to patriotism. But then again, the ladies who frequented this dressmaker absolutely required every aid to seduction that fine clothing could provide, for most of them had "arrangements" with the gentlemen of Whitehall, the City, and both Houses of Parliament—arrangements that did not include wedding rings. As a consequence, they were unlikely to sacrifice beauty for the appearance of respectability. Alison knew of this place from her early days as one of the demimondaine—but of course, unlike the rest of her sisters-in-sin, she'd had the means at her disposal to ensure she *got* a wedding ring before too long into her arrangement.

This particular dressmaker spent half the time creating costumes for the theater, and half dressing the kept ladies of the town; but because she did the former, she had a huge storehouse of fabric to pull from. After the third house had disappointed, Alison had come to the reluctant conclusion that it was possible the war and the Hun submarine blockade had begun to affect even those with money to spend on London dressmakers. This dressmaker had only confirmed that, as she had pulled out roll after roll of silk and muslin with the comment, "You won't see *that,* thanks to the Kaiser." Silks came from China by way of Paris; muslin from India or the United States. Both had to come by way of the ocean, and between ships being sunk, and ships being commandeered to bring over military goods—luxury goods probably still *were* coming, but now their prices had gone beyond the reach of a minor industrialist's widow.

Of course, even in Broom, one didn't go to a *theatrical costumier* for one's wardrobe—but Alison had a way around that. When the dresses arrived in their plain packaging, she would have Ellie cut the labels out of last year's gowns and sew them into the unlabeled new ones. Perhaps it was a bit foolish to do so, but after all, the laundry *was* sent out—and the laundress would take note if this year's gowns had no labels anymore—or worse, had labels from *Keplans Haberdashery* rather than a fashion house that was cited in the London society pages.

Half of keeping up appearances was in attending to details.

Alison smiled, as the girls chattered happily on the way back to the Savoy. There was a slight drawback to patronizing Miss Keplan. They would have to stay in London for nearly a week to accomplish all the fittings, whereas the establishments they usually used had mannequins and fitting-dummies made to all three women's measure. Still, the results would be worth the extra days. The girls would look like butterflies among the caterpillars at every garden party and fete this spring and summer. Men responded to these things. They would outshine much prettier girls, just because their frocks were prettier. With any luck, one of them, at least, would catch someone with a title, money, or better still, both to his name.

Robinson's fortune was reasonable, and since by magically enhanced maneuvering, Alison had secured the monopoly of supplying sacks for sandbags to the army, it was not likely to run out any time soon—but Alison was weary of being reasonable, weary of Broom, weary of being the leading light in a claustrophobically tiny and insignificant social sphere. She had wearied of it very soon after ascending to the throne of unofficial queen of Broom. She had much larger ambitions.

Alison aspired to Longacre Park.

It was not a new desire. As a scrawny adolescent, hard-eyed with ambition, she had aspired to the circles of those who feted royalty. She would gather with other spectators on the pavement whenever a grand party or ball was being held, and vow that one day *she* would be among such invitees. When she had been taken up by an aging courtesan with enough of the gift of Earth Magery to recognize it in another, she had seen it as a first step to those circles and deserted her dreary working-class family, even though all such a relic of Victoria's time could hope for was the company of prosperous shopkeepers and minor industrialists.

But Alison had bided her time, and ensnared the first of the unmarried gentlemen moderate means to cross her path, sacrificing wealth temporarily for respectability. She had slipped up a trifle, allowing him to get her with child twice—well, he was more virile than she had thought. She had rid herself of him soon enough, which left her a comfortably off widow, and had laid the foundations for better conquests by learning the lessons that would fit her for the circles of the exalted, while at the same time mastering her Magery. Etiquette, elocution—especially elocution, for Bernard Shaw was right, the wrong accent guaranteed failure at this game—she had instructors for everything. A good nanny for the children and the proper boarding schools gave her the time she needed to attain full command of Earth Magic at the same time.

That had been at the hands of a *male* Earth Master, of course, and a suitably old one, who flattered himself that the attentiveness of this attractive widow was genuine and not inspired by the desire to have all of his secrets. Strange how male mages never seemed to learn from the lesson of Merlin and Nimue. A female would not have been so easy to manipulate, nor so hopelessly naive. She had learned all he had to teach, and then—well, he got his reward, and had not survived the experience. He had, however, died with a look of incredulous pleasure on his face. She had owed him that much. She wondered what the coroner and undertaker had made of it. And had made of the fact that he might have been sixty, but when he died, he had looked ninety.

"Mama, we're here!" Carolyn called out, shaking her out of her reverie. She followed the girls out of the taxi, paid and tipped the driver, and entered the hotel.

No one took any note of them—well, no one except a couple of young officers in the lobby who gazed at the girls appreciatively. She repressed a grimace. Had the family been of note, there would be concierges and porters swarming about them, eager to know their slightest whim, even with the hotel staff so seriously depleted by the war—

Well, if she had anything to say about it, they would be swarmed, one day.

They entered the elevator, and with a nod and a shilling to the operator, ascended to their floor.

Which was not the *best* floor. Respectable, and the denizens of Broom would have been overwhelmed by the elegance, but it was by no means the best the Savoy had to offer. And that rankled.

But she would not show that before the girls. They required ambition, and they had it, but it must be unclouded by envy. Envy would put disagreeable lines in their faces. They must be like athletes, or perhaps warriors, with their eyes and minds firmly fixed on the prize. They must be ruthless, of course, but they should never waste time on so unprofitable an emotion as envy.

The girls fluttered into the salon, still chattering about the gowns. They understood completely that they must not say *where* the gowns were coming from, of course, but they were bewitched, properly bewitched, by the pastel silks and delicately printed muslins that had been spread out for their approval, and the elegant copies of the gowns that the other fashion houses were showing. As Alison had well remembered, the dressmaker was a very clever little woman; within days of new gowns being shown for the season, *she* had sketches of every one of them, and was making copies.

And the gowns that *she* copied were not those of the houses that Alison could afford to patronize. Oh no. These were the gowns that would make their appearance on the lawns of stately homes like Longacre Park. . . .

For the truly, fabulously wealthy, and the extremely well-connected, were no more affected by the blockade than the theatrical dressmaker was. In the case of the latter, it was because she had an entire warehouse of fabrics stockpiled, and besides that, access to dozens, perhaps hundreds of old gowns and costumes that could be remade. In the case of the former—well, where the habitués of the Royal Enclosure were concerned, a bolt or two of fabric could be brought over, somehow. . . .

Well, perhaps this would be the year. And if the faintly frivolous gowns caused a stirring of dismay at the Broom cricket games, or the country club tennis matches, well, perhaps the owners of the gowns could move into territory this summer where their appearance would harmonize with the surroundings, rather than stand out from them.

She shook off her reverie. There was, of course, more to this biannual visit than just the replenishing of a wardrobe. She had other calls to make while she was here.

"I'm going out, girls," she called out to them. "Have your dinner sent up. And you are *not—*"

"On any account to stir from these rooms," they replied in chorus, and ended with a giggle.

"Practice your charms," she said, with a lifted brow.

"Oh, Mama—" Lauralee objected. "They're so much more difficult here!"

"All the more important that you learn how to set them here," she replied severely. "You have no more magic than the old woman who taught me—but if I have anything to say about it, you'll learn how to make much better use of it than she did." A thought occurred to her that would give them malicious amusement, and would set their minds on the proper task. "Our windows overlook the street. Why don't you exercise your skills and your minds by making unsuitable persons conceive of a passion for one another?"

"Oh, Mama!" Carolyn exclaimed, delight sparking in her eyes. "May we?"

"I would not have told you to do so if I did not mean it," she replied, with a little smile of her own. "Make me a thorough report when I return."

She telephoned the Exeter Club as they set themselves and the small bits of apparatus they would need at the window. There would be no need to find taxis for this visit. Lord Alderscroft would send a car. This was, after all, the business of the War Office.

Maya narrowed her eyes suspiciously as she watched Lord Alderscroft's visitor. He had not invited her into his own rooms; instead, they were meeting in the same Aesthetic public dining room that she had been taken to the first time she entered the doors of the Exeter Club.

What she had not known then was that one of the mirrors was one-way, and hid a tiny spyhole. She didn't think that anyone had been watching her that time, but even if they had been, they hadn't learned anything they couldn't have learned by watching her openly.

Alderscroft wanted her assessment of someone he wanted to keep an eye on Reggie Fenyx. It was another Earth Master. And already Maya disliked her.

"Really?" the elegant woman said, her eyes widening slightly. "Young Fenyx is so badly off as all that?"

No, Maya did not like Alison Robinson; she did not trust Mrs. Robinson one tiny little bit. She had no reason for these feelings, other than her instinct, though, which was not enough to give as a reason to Lord Alderscroft, who distrusted feminine intuition.

Were the rumors true that far too many people that Alison Robinson was intended to keep watch on died instead? And was that enough of a reason for suspicion? Of course, they had all been spies for the Hun, and there was never any reason to point to Alison Robinson as the cause of their deaths but—

But—

Maya toyed with her tea on the other side of the one-way mirror, listened as Alderscroft assigned Alison Robinson to keep an eye on Reginald Fenyx, and reflected with some relief that this was a perfectly absurd assignment. After all, someone like Mrs. Robinson, the widow of a mere small manufacturer, was *not* going to have entree into—

"But Lord Alderscroft," Alison said, smiling, "This is really quite impossible! I have no entree into such exalted social circles! Why, I should not be able to do more than glimpse the young man at a distance! The closest approach I could manage would be in the autumn, as the hunt goes by, if he even participates in the hunt at all! You know I have no objection to doing anything you and the War Office might ask of me, but really, dropping me behind enemy lines and asking me to pass myself off as a *kleine hausfrau* would be simpler!"

"Ah, erm—" Alderscroft coughed. "Well, perhaps I should—"

"If I am to carry out this assignment, you shall have to manufacture an appropriate background for me," the wretched woman went on, to Maya's dismay. "You'll have to find an impoverished line in Burke's with a daughter called Alison of the proper age, one that might well have decided that ungenteel comfort was preferable to leaking roofs and no proper plumbing. And then you'll have to arrange a proper introduction to his mother, by letter if nothing else."

"That will take time, I'm afraid," said Alderscroft, sounding apologetic.

"I can wait," she replied gaily, with a delicate little laugh. "After all, a job worth doing is worth doing properly. Thank you, my lord. This is much preferable to investigating the occasional foreigner on a walking tour through Shakespeare country." That sweet little laugh grated on Maya's nerves. One Earth Master to another—that woman was altogether too well shielded. But then, London was unbearable for an Earth Master without being shielded . . . and although it would have been much more *polite* to forego her shields within the Exeter Club, she wasn't a member of the Lodge, so she couldn't know that it was safe to do so. So that was no good reason to mistrust her, or at least, it was not a reason that Alderscroft would accept.

The creature was back to harping on that introduction. Maya had seen more than her share of social climbers in India, and she knew another one the moment she saw her. Though she might not be able to *read* Mrs. Robinson, she didn't have to in order to recognize those signs.

Doesn't she have daughters? Oh yes . . . planning on marrying into the family, are you, my dear? If you can manage it, that is. Well, there was the one saving grace of Reggie's condition; he was so heavily blocked that the Robinson woman could run him down with a locomotive-sized love spell and he'd be impervious to it. He was, in fact, the mirror *opposite* to an Elemental Master now, he was powerfully *un*magical. She could throw spells at him for a week, and all that would happen would be that they would be swallowed up without a trace. And as for simple vamping—

Our Reggie's had every sort of woman there is fling themselves at his head by now. He's not going to think much of a couple of provincial belles hanging out for a title and a fortune. And if you can't recognize that, dear lady, you are an utter fool.

And sure enough, she was back on that so-precious introduction again. "It probably should be a letter, Lord

Alderscroft," she was saying, with a melting smile. "Or better still, two—one to Lady Devlin directly and one I can hand-carry. Say that—oh, I am too diffident to push myself on her, but would she please look me up as I'm too terribly alone down there in the village?"

Maya gritted her teeth. *Oh, please rescue me from these wretched peasants, she means.* And she knew that Alderscroft's subconscious would recognize her tone and the cadence of her speech as well as her words and respond to it *in spite* of the fact that he knew she was as common as a dustbin. That was because she *had* the proper accent, and the proper manner, and everything in his upbringing and training was screaming out to his subconscious that here was gentry. For one moment she hated Alderscroft, his automatic response to the proper turn of phrase, his automatic assumption that anyone born to the strawberry leaves was "one of us" and deserving of special treatment and protection.

For one moment, she hated them all, and felt a powerful sympathy for the socialists and the Bolsheviks, and it was very tempting to think about throwing a bomb or two into the Royal Enclosure at Ascot, just to shake them up a bit. Certainly you could fire a cannon off through there and never hit anyone who would be missed by society—

But then good sense overcame her, and she sighed, and acknowledged that there were aristocrats who were good stewards, and useful. And as for the rest, she forgave Alderscroft and his set for being idiots, and went back to paying attention to the conversation.

Well, there was one thing that being born a half-caste in India was good for, and that was in knowing what *wouldn't* work with the British aristocracy. Though she might very much *like* to point out to the old lion that the Robinson woman had played him like salmon on her line, it would do no good at all.

No, she would simply tell Alderscroft that the woman was heavily shielded and couldn't be read—that she certainly had ulterior motives for wanting that introduction and remind him of the two daughters looking for husbands—and that Fenyx's own grandmother would do a *much* better job of keeping an eye on him than any stranger ever could.

And then she would go confide her *real* feelings to her husband Peter—who would certainly, at that point, take them to his "Twin." And there was no one that Peter Almsley did not know among the Elemental Mages inside the peerage. Almsley's grandmother, who was herself a powerful Elemental Master, almost certainly knew Reggie's aunt, who was another. And when *those* two heard what she had to say. . . .

Now Maya smiled for the first time since she began listening to the conversation, struck by the mental image of a herd of water-buffalo surrounding an injured calf to protect it from a tigress.

The tigress had no notion of what she was about to face.

Alison was pleased with herself. Despite some setbacks, this trip to London had been unexpectedly productive. She sat down at the little desk in the sitting room of their suite to catch up on her correspondence, while the girls unpacked the day's purchases.

"Mama," said Carolyn, idly tracing the line of the fringe on the new shawl she had purchased that morning, "What do you know about the Americans getting into the war?"

Alison looked up from the letter she was writing to Warrick Locke. "The Americans have no intention of entering the war, child. President Wilson is a pacifist. If the sinking of the *Lusitania* did not accomplish it, nothing will. Why?"

"Well," Carolyn persisted, with a small, sly smile playing about her lips, "It's just that—you had rather they didn't, wouldn't you?"

"It would interfere greatly with my plans, yes," she said sharply. "And it would probably interfere with our income as well. Why do you ask?"

"She asks because she's been meeting with that American boy from the embassy in the tea room," Lauralee interrupted, frowning with jealousy at her sister. "And she doesn't want to get in trouble over it, so she wants to make you think she's been doing it for—"

"Lauralee—" Alison held up a warning hand. "First, do *not* frown. Frowns do not improve your looks, and cause wrinkles. Secondly, let your sister answer for herself. Carolyn?"

"He *is* the ambassador's son," Carolyn protested, pouting prettily, in a way that Alison approved. "And you *know* Mama has been busy, and you *know* we've been hearing rumors in the hotel! I thought I ought to find out at first hand!"

"And it has nothing to do with the fact that he's tall, and blue-eyed, and looks like—" Lauralee muttered, sullenly.

"And don't allow jealousy to show, Lauralee," Alison reproved absently. "It gives one jowls. What did the young man tell you, Carolyn?"

"That the President will *certainly* enter the war next month!" Carolyn said in triumph. "He's going home to enlist! So are most of the young men on the embassy staff!"

Alison's lips tightened. This was no part of her plans. At the moment, the war was at a stalemate—both sides were worn out and weary, and the conflict might well drag on for years, which was very good news for the Earth Elementals that *she* favored, and for her plans concerning Reggie Fenyx. For the latter, she planned more fear—her Elemental creatures making his life a never-ending round of attacks of terror—until the one girl who could drive them away appeared in his life. At which point, he would probably marry her on the spot. Or at least be willing to.

But to complete the plan, she would need time. Time for the boy to heal physically enough to be sent home on recovery leave. Time for Lord Alderscroft's introduction to bear fruit. Time for her spells to work, time for Carolyn—or Lauralee—to be the answer to his prayers, time for him to propose and for a proper society wedding. And then more time, for she did not intend for him to survive the war, and he would have to recover from his shellshock and go back to the Air Corps, and if the Yanks entered the war—

America was full of brash young men who were perfectly willing to fling themselves into combat. America was wealthy; within months she could turn her factories from making frying pans into making cannon and machine-guns. And America had immense, untapped resources on her own soil; she did *not* depend on ships to bring those resources to the factories. If America entered the war, it could be over within a year.

Unless—

She couldn't *stop* them. But she could add a new enemy to the equation . . . one that should add to the attrition in the trenches, and slow the number of troops coming over.

"Carolyn, dear, I believe that we ought to hold a little farewell dinner for all those fine young men at the embassy," she said, in a tone that made Carolyn's eyes narrow. "We ought to thank them for being *so* willing to serve. Invite them to a little supper tomorrow night."

Lauralee also caught the scent of something in the air. "Mama—" she began, then shook her head. "Come along, Carolyn. Let's go write invitations. I think there are six or seven of them, including the ambassador's son, Mama."

"When you are finished writing the invitations, make the supper arrangements with the Savoy chef," Alison replied, already unpacking what she needed from her trunk. "You should know what to do already."

"Yes, Mama," her daughters chorused, and Alison smiled with content. Well-trained and obedient, everything a mother could ask for.

By the time that all the arrangements were complete, and the invitations sent to the embassy by messenger, Alison was ready. Her implements—deceptively simple ones—were set out on the thick silk cloth that she used as her portable Working table. It already had the runes and circles of containment embroidered into it, dyed with blood—hers, and others. She spread it out over the table they used when they dined en-suite, summoned the girls, doused the electric lights, and lit the candles she had unpacked.

"This may be one of the most underrated incantations in our arsenal, girls," she said, as the two of them moved closer to stand on either side of her. "And yet, it requires surprisingly little power, especially here, in the city. We are going to call an Earth Elemental. The trick to this is that you have to remember to be *very* specific about what you want from this entity. You already know that one of the great Gifts of the Earth Mage is to heal—but the converse is also true. Watch."

With the precision of a surgeon, Alison placed a deceptively plain bowl (made of clay dug from a graveyard and fired in the same fire as a cremation) in the center of her Working cloth. Into it she dropped a tiny bit of rotting meat (she always kept some sealed in a small jar with her when she traveled), and several more equally distasteful ingredients, burying them all beneath a layer of dirt dug from the piles of tin-waste near a mine. Then she closed her eyes, held her hands over the bowl, and let the power flow from her, into it, chanting her specific invocation under her breath and concentrating with all of her might, and the sullen ocher-colored energies flowed out of her fingertips and into the bowl, pooling there in the candlelight.

Carolyn gasped, and at that sign, she opened her eyes.

The Earth Elemental standing in the now-empty bowl might not look like much—it was a squat little putty-colored nothing, with the barest suggestions of limbs and a head, the sort of crude and primitive object that might be found in an ancient ruin. It looked utterly harmless—but properly used, it was one of the most powerful of all of the inimical Earth Elementals, because it was one of the most insidious.

It was called a *maledero*, and it brought, and spread, disease.

"I need an illness," she told it. "One that spreads in the air. It should *seem* harmless, but kill. I don't want it to fell everything that catches it, no more than one in four, but no less than one in ten. It should bring death quickly when it does kill, it should lay out those it does not kill, and it should be hardest not on the very young nor the very old, but those in the prime of life. It should spread rapidly, and be impossible to stop, because by the time victims are dying, it should have passed on to others."

The putty-colored thing smiled, showing a mouth full of jagged and rotting teeth, while above the mouth, a pair of bottomless black eyes looked at her. "How if it spreads through a sneeze?" it suggested. "If it be spread by any other means, this might be countered."

She nodded. "Ideal. There will be six young men here tomorrow night for dinner before they journey homewards. You will infect them, and *only* them, and you will lie dormant within them until they have ended their journey in a place where there will be thousands of young men like them. Then you will release yourself, and be free to spread as far as you please, across the whole world, if you like—*except* to myself and my daughters."

"Easily done," the thing croaked, and it—divided, right before their eyes, into six identical creatures, each one-sixth the size of the original. "We pledge by the bond," they chorused.

Alison nodded, and tapped the side of the bowl with her willow-wand. "Then I release from the bowl. When you have infested the young men, you will be released from the room."

She inscribed the appropriate sigils in the air, where they glowed for a moment, then settled over the six creatures and were absorbed.

"When you have come to the place across the sea where thousands of young men have gathered to train as warriors," she continued, still inscribing the sigils of containment in the air, "You will be free to infect and spread as far as you please, save only myself and my daughters," she wrote her own glyph and those of Carolyn and Lauralee, and the sigil of prohibition on top of those three names. All this sank down to rest briefly on the little Elementals, before being absorbed into them. The flow of power was minimal—one of the reasons why this was such a useful conjuration.

"And now, you may conceal yourself within this room,

until the vessels have come," she concluded, breaking the containment with a flourish of her wand. The entities gave her a mocking little bow, and faded away.

The girls looked at her, wide-eyed. "Did you just—create a disease?" Lauralee gaped.

She shrugged. "It is better to say that I altered one to suit our purposes. It will probably be a pneumonia or influenza, but when it is released, it will be something quite different from any other of its kind. It will certainly be bad enough to decimate the ranks of the Americans long enough to keep them from winning the war in a few months. And that is all that we will need." She smiled at her girls, who stared at her, wide-eyed. "I doubt it will kill one in four of those that are really healthy; the Elemental I conjured is not strong enough for that. But it will cause a great deal of havoc. That is something else to remember. Sometimes you do not need to confront your enemy directly; you only need to interfere with him."

She began putting her supplies away; neither girl offered to help, as was proper. She would not have allowed them. They were *never* to touch her Working materials.

That, after all, was how she had managed to get control over her teachers.

"And now," she added brightly, putting the last of her equipment away and locking the little trunk in which it was kept. "I believe it is time we went downstairs to dine."

5

March 14, 1917
Broom, Warwickshire

WHEN ELEANOR WAS CERTAIN THAT Alison and the girls were on the train to London, the first thing she did was to go straight to the kitchen, throw open the pantry doors and plan herself a feast.

Brushing aside Alison's magically laid prohibitions like so many cobwebs, Eleanor could not help but gloat. She felt the barriers, certainly, but she was able to push right through them. And the irony of it was, there had never been any good reason to make the pantry off-limits while the Robinsons were gone, nor to restrict Eleanor to the foodstuffs that Alison allowed her to keep in the kitchen. When they returned, there were things in here that would have had to be thrown in the bin because they were spoiled, that Eleanor could perfectly well have eaten while the others were gone. It made no sense, no sense at all.

It was all just spite, just pure meanness.

She surveyed the shelves, and decided that she would clean out her ever-simmering soup-pot and give it a good scrubbing before starting a new batch, while she ate those things that would go bad before long. And she could include the end of that ham in the soup.

It wasn't all cream for her, though; most of Alison's magics still worked. Before she had done much more than empty out the soup-pot into a smaller vessel to leave on the hearth, and fill the pot with soapy water, the compulsions to clean struck her. Up the stairs she went, discovering that she still had to sweep and dust, air the rooms out and close them up again, mop and scrub down the bathroom. True, she didn't have to spend as *much* time at it, nor work quite as hard, but she couldn't fight the compulsion off altogether. And although she tried, she discovered that she couldn't leave the house and garden either, even with Alison gone. But after some experimentation, she had the measure of the compulsions. She finished everything she needed to do in the upstairs rooms by luncheon, which meant that she would have the rest of the day free for herself.

The first thing that she did was to make herself a *proper* luncheon, and to read while she ate it; she chose a book from the library, a room which had been mostly unused since her father died.

She ate in the library, too, in defiance of crumbs—after all, *she* was the one who was going to be doing the cleaning-up—curled up in her father's favorite old chesterfield chair with her feet to the fire she built in the fireplace.

After she had finished eating, the compulsions urged her into work briefly, but she discovered that she could satisfy them merely by making a few swipes with a dust-mop and the broom in each room so long as they were *visibly* clean. By this time her soup-pot had soaked enough, so she gave it a good scrubbing inside *and* out, and put beans to soak in it. She returned again to the library with a tray laden with teapot and the cakes that would have gone stale, there to lose herself in a book until the fading light and growing hunger called her back to the kitchen and that feast she had promised herself.

Then—luxury of luxuries!—she drew *herself* a hot bath, and had a good long soak and a proper hair-washing. Baths were what she got at the kitchen sink these days, and often as not, in cold water. She used Lauralee's rosewater soap, knowing from experience that it was something Lauralee wouldn't miss, whereas if she purloined Alison's Spanish sandalwood, or Carolyn's Eau de Nil bars, they *would* be missed. After a blissful hour immersed to the neck in hot water, and an equally blissful interlude spent giving her hair the good wash she had longed for, she emerged clean and scented faintly with roses.

Her hair wasn't very long, though it was unlike the girls' ultra-fashionable bobs—Alison hacked it off just below her shoulders on a regular basis—so it didn't take long to dry in front of the kitchen fire. She slipped a bed-warmer into her own bed to heat it while she dried her hair, and after banking the fires in the kitchen and the library, and making sure the stove had enough fuel to last through the night and keep the hot-water boiler at the back of it warm, she went to bed at last feeling more like her old self than she had since before her father had left on that fateful trip.

She fell asleep at once, relaxed, warm, and contented.

She hadn't expected to dream, but she did. And her dreams were—rather odd. Full of fire-images, of leaping flames themselves, of odd, half-fairy creatures whose flesh glowed with fire and who had wings of flame, of the medieval salamanders that were supposed to live in fires, of dragons, and of the phoenyx and the firebird. They weren't nightmares, nothing like, even though she found herself engulfed by fires that caressed her like sun-warmed silk.

In fact, she found herself *wearing* the flames, like an ever-changing gown. In her dreams, she found these mythical beings welcoming her as a friend, and in her dreams, that seemed perfectly natural and right. They were lovely dreams, the best she'd had since before Alison came—and she didn't want to wake up from them.

The compulsions broke into those dreams, jarring her awake her at dawn.

Full of resentment, she resisted them for a moment, pondering those dreams while they were still fresh in her mind. What on earth could they mean? That they meant *something,* she was sure.

And once or twice, hadn't she felt a sense of familiarity

about them? As if the things she did and saw were calling up an echo, faint and far, in her memory?

Finally she could resist the compulsions no longer, for her legs began to twitch, and a nasty headache started just between her eyebrows. She knew those signs of old, and got reluctantly out of bed to start her round of morning chores.

At least she was going to get more to eat this morning than a lot of tasteless porridge.

The sun was just coming up over the horizon, and distant roosters were crowing, as she began the day. This was the day of the week when Eleanor usually did the heavy laundry, the sheets and the towels, and her own clothing, and there was no real reason to change her schedule. Usually she looked forward to the day, as she often got a chance to wash up in the laundry-water, though the lye-soap was harsh enough to burn if she wasn't careful.

She went out to the wash-house in the little shed at the back of the garden to fire up the wash-boiler out there, a huge kettle built right into a kind of oven, pump it full of cold water, and add the soap. She returned to the house and collected all of the linen before breakfast. A glance up at the sky told her that the day was going to be fair again—a good thing, since it meant she could hang things out in the sunlight, and wouldn't have to iron them dry. With even Howse gone—Alison wouldn't have traveled a step without her maid—there was less of the wash than usual, but Eleanor was feeling unusually energetic. Perhaps it was simply that she wasn't forced to do her work on a couple of spoonfuls of unflavored oat-porridge and a cup of weak tea.

She actually enjoyed herself; the winter had been horribly, dreadfully cold, and doing the household laundry had been nothing short of torture. Today—well, it was cold, but briskly so, and it was grand to have the sun on her back as she pinned up the sheets and towels. By mid-morning, it was all washed and wrung dry and hanging up in the garden, and Eleanor was scrubbing the kitchen floor, exactly as she usually did on wash-day, though it wasn't often that she was done this early.

And that was when a knocking at the kitchen door startled her so much that she yelped, and dropped the brush into her bucket of water with a splash.

She stared at the closed door, sure that what she had heard must have been some accident of an echo—someone out in the street, perhaps, or knocking at one of the neighbors' gates.

But the rapping came again, brisk and insistent.

Who could be knocking at *this* door? Surely no one knew that she was here—

It must be a tradesman. Or someone about a bill. It couldn't be a delivery; Alison was punctilious about canceling all deliveries when she expected to be gone. The old cook had been quite incensed about that—"As if *we're* of no account and can live on bacon and tinned peas while she swans about London!"—but she had even done so back when the house was full of servants.

Not that I would mind if there had been a mistake! A delivery of baked goods would be jam on top of the cream. . . .

The knocking came again. Whoever was there wasn't going away. She got to her feet, and slowly opened the door.

There was a woman there—perhaps Alison's age, or a little older, but she was nothing like Alison. Her graying brown hair was done up in a knot at the back of her head from which little wisps were straying. Friendly, amber-brown eyes gazed warmly at Eleanor, though the focus suggested that the gaze was a trifle short-sighted. Her round face had both plenty of little lines and very pink cheeks. She was dressed quite plainly, in a heavy woolen skirt and smock, with an apron, rather like a local farmer's wife, complete with woolen shawl wrapped around herself. She smiled at Eleanor, who found herself smiling back.

"Hello, my dear," the woman said, in a soothing, low voice that tickled the back of Eleanor's mind with a sensation of familiarity. "I'm Sarah Chase."

Sarah Chase! Eleanor knew *that* name, though she had never actually met the woman. Sarah Chase was supposed—at least by the children of Broom—to be a witch!

Not a bad witch, though—she didn't live in a cobwebby old hut at the edge of the forest, she lived right in the middle of Broom itself, in a tidy little Tudor cottage literally sandwiched in between two larger buildings. On the right was the Swan pub, and on the left, the village shop. Any children bold enough to stand on the threshold of the door and try to peer into the heavily curtained windows never were able to see anything, and the extremely public situation meant that their mothers usually heard about the adventure and they got a tongue-lashing about rude behavior and nosy-parkers. No one in Eleanor's circle of friends had ever seen Sarah Chase, in fact—

But here she was, standing on the threshold, a covered basket in one hand, the other outstretched a little towards Eleanor.

"Well, dear," the woman prompted gently. "Aren't you going to ask your godmother inside?"

Godmother?

Her mind was still taking that in, as her mouth said, without any thought on *her* part, "Come in, Godmother." And the village witch stepped across the threshold and entered the kitchen like a beam of sunshine.

For the third time in her life, Eleanor's life turned upside down.

She sat, in something of a daze, on a stool beside the kitchen fire, where her prosaic soup-pot full of beans and the end of the ham simmered, and listened to impossible things.

Things which she never would have believed—if her finger wasn't buried beneath the hearth-stone.

Sarah looked perfectly comfortable in the sunny kitchen with its blackened beams and whitewashed walls. Eleanor never even thought to invite her into the parlor. But then, these were not particularly discussions for the parlor.

Eleanor was hearing, for the first time, that the woman

her father had thought he had married was no more than a fraction of what she actually *was.*

". . . so your father never knew, of course," Sarah concluded. "Never knew that your mother was a Fire Master, or that we were such friends, she and I, never even knew such a thing as magic existed at all." Her cheeks went pinker, and she gave Eleanor an apologetic little shrug. "That's the way of it, usually, when one of Us marries one of Them, Them as has no magic. We generally keep it to ourselves, for more often than not it does no good and a great deal of harm to try and make them understand. The ones with minds stuck in the world they can see are usually made very unhappy by such things. Either they think *they* have gone mad, or they think their spouse has, and in either case it only ends in tears and tragedy." She nodded wisely. "Like the Fenyxes. Him and his father, *they* have the magic—or Lord Devlin did before he died, but Lady Devlin, she's got no more idea than a bird."

Eleanor gaped at her. This was somehow harder to believe than that her own mother had magic. The Fenyx family? Were what Sarah called Elemental Masters?

Sarah went right on, not noticing Eleanor's state of shock—or else, determined to get out everything she needed to say without interruption. "So we met here, of a night, or of an afternoon, over cups of tea as two old friends from such a small place often do, and your father would look in on us and laugh and ask us if we were setting the world aright, and of course, we never told him that we *were*—in small ways, of course, but small ways have the habit of adding up."

"You were—setting the world aright?" Eleanor repeated, and shook her head. "But how—"

"A little magic here, a little magic there; hers more than mine, you understand, since I'm but a mere Witch, and she was a Master. But—oh, she would speak to the Salamanders of a night, and find out whose chimneys were getting overchoked with soot, and I'd have a word with the owner of the house by-and-by, and Neil Frandsen would come along and clean it, and there'd be no chimney fire, do you see?"

Eleanor blinked again. "Is that the plumber, Mr. Frandsen? The man that cleans chimneys with a shotgun?"

Sarah threw back her head and laughed. "Oh, aye! But less often then than he does now, I'm afraid—he was nimbler when he was young; now he don't like to go atop the houses much. But you see what we did? And there was other things—*never* a house-fire have we had hereabouts once she came into her powers, nor a barn-fire, and no accidents with fire either. If a cottager's baby tumbled *into* a fire, it tumbled right back out again, with just enough scorching on his smock to make his mama take better heed. No fires from a coal hopping out; no curtains blowing into candles nor gas-flames. Sometimes it isn't so much doing things that's important as it is keeping them from happening." She sighed. "I remember how she used to put you in your cradle next to the fire, or once you were old enough, just on a blanket. No worries you'd be burned, of course—the Salamanders used to frisk and play around you, and you'd laugh and try to catch them with your little hands. Clear enough it was, you'd taken after her. And then—she died."

"She drowned," Eleanor whispered, and shuddered. All her life, the one thing she'd been afraid of was water. Sarah nodded.

"The enemy Element," Sarah said sadly. "The Element that hates hers; the river flooded, you see, and to this day, I don't know if it was accident or an enemy. She could have told me, but—well, the river flooded and washed out the bridge as she was trying to get across to get home to you. Her allies had no power to save her. And your father, well, he couldn't bear to look upon me, who was her close friend, so I stayed away. And you seemed to be flourishing, and I heard about you going up to university and all, and I thought, well, well enough, I'll leave her be, and when she starts to come into her power, I'll send to the Fire Masters who've people at Oxford, and they'll take on the teaching of you. So much more clever than I, those dons and scholars—"

"But *She* came." Eleanor's voice cracked.

"Then *She* came." Sarah's voice hardened. "My Element, but a Master, more powerful than me, and better connected by far. In magic as in everything else, it's who you know that gets you places, and what you've got." Sarah grimaced. "She's trusted by them as should know better, but don't; there's no help there—yet. I could no more stand against her than your mother could stand against the flood. But *you* are coming into *your* powers, and I can set your feet on the right path, and you can break her, if you grow strong enough. And this is where I can make a start—"

She got up out of the chair where she was sitting and walked over to the hearth. She stared down at the hearth-stones for a moment, then bent, and traced a symbol with her index finger on one. It glowed for a moment, a warm, lovely golden-amber, before sinking into the stone.

"Blast her," Sarah muttered under her breath. "She's stronger than I thought."

"What?" Eleanor asked.

"It's a spell that will answer to Fire as well as Earth; it's what She did to bind you here. I know a counter that will work within her spell to free you from this house and hearth for a few hours at a time, though you won't be able to go farther than, say, Longacre," the witch said. "You'll have to learn how to work magic of your own to make her spell answer to you, how to bend it to your will for a little—we'll start you learning Fire magic now, if you're ready, but definitely before she comes back."

"I—Sarah, I don't know, this all seems so—" She was going to say, "impossible to believe," but at exactly that moment, something looked at her out of the hearth-fire. She looked back, feeling her eyes widen as she recognized the fiery-eyed lizard of her dreams.

"Well, and there you are," Sarah said, with triumph, following her startled glance. "Salamander. Sure sign of you coming into your powers, no matter what *she's* done."

"You can see it too?" she asked incredulously.

"Well, of course. I can *see* the Elementals, and if they feel like it, they might help me out, but I can't command them, not even Earth. I'm not a Master," Sarah said; wistfully, Eleanor thought. "But you can command the ones of Fire; because you're a Fire Master, you'll have their respect, and because of your mother, you already have their loyalty, and the only way you'd lose that would be to do something they didn't like."

"What do you mean, *I have their loyalty?"* Eleanor asked incredulously.

"Hold out your hand," Sarah replied. "To the fire, I mean. You'll see."

Dubiously Eleanor did so, and before she could pull away with surprise, that same something leapt out of the flames and began twining around her hands like a friendly ferret. It *looked* like a lizard made of flame, and it felt like sun-warmed silk slithering through her fingers and around her wrists.

"It's not burning me—" she gasped, staring at the creature in fascination.

"And I'll wager you've never been burned in your life," Sarah replied triumphantly. "Have you?"

"Only—" Eleanor began, then stopped. She *had* been going to say, "only when Carolyn cauterized my finger," but then she realized that she had not actually been *burned,* not even then. The bleeding had been stopped, and the wound sealed, but no more, and it hadn't been a burn that had caused her so much pain, it had been the wound itself and the fever that followed. "—ah, I haven't," she admitted, watching the Salamander weave around her outstretched fingers.

"What—what does all this mean?" she asked at last.

"That I need to begin teaching you what I can, and there is no time like the present. Unless you had something planned?" Sarah tilted her head to the side. "A garden party, perhaps?"

That brought a smile to Eleanor's face, and a rueful shrug. "So long as my stepmother isn't here—"

"We must take advantage of that. Let your friend go back to his fire and we'll begin."

By nightfall, Eleanor knew a hundred times more about magic than she had before Sarah knocked on the door. She knew about casting circles of protection and containment, a little about summoning, and something about the Elementals of her own Element, although the only one she had seen as yet was the little Salamander, the weakest of the lot. And she was far more tired than she would have thought likely. It wasn't as if she'd been *working*, after all, just sitting and walking about the kitchen, nothing more.

"It takes it out of you," Sarah said solemnly, as the two of them worked on a little supper in the evening gloom. "And you're lucky that woman is of another Element, or she'd know when you were working, as she'd be able to cut you off from your power. As it is, she's strong enough to bind you and command you."

By this point, Eleanor had gotten well past the suspension of disbelief and was at the point where she would have accepted the presence of an invisible second moon in the sky if Sarah had insisted it was there. Part of this was due to fatigue, but most of it was simply that she had taken in so many strange things that her mind was simply fogging over.

"Why am I so tired?" she asked, setting down plates on the kitchen table, while Sarah ladled soup into bowls and cut slices of bread for both of them.

"Because the power you've been using to cast circles and all has to come from you yourself, lovey," Sarah replied.

Eleanor frowned, and rubbed her temple with the back of her wrist. "But I thought magic just was—magic!"

"Something out of nothing, you mean?" Sarah laughed. "Not likely, my girl. The only time you get power at no cost to you is when your Elementals grant it to you, or you take it from someone else. And I'll give you a guess where your stepmother gets much of *hers* from."

Eleanor sat down in her chair. "She'll be back in a day or two—and what will I do then?" she asked. "How am I going to see you, or keep learning?" It was a good question; what *would* she do? She was kept busy from dawn to dark and then some; how could she ever get time to continue learning and practicing?

"Does she lock the doors?" Sarah asked. "You'll wait until the house is asleep, and then you'll draw the glyph and bend her spell and come to me for an hour or two." She smiled slyly. "You do the cooking, don't you? Well, one advantage of being a mere Witch is that *I* don't rely on power to do everything. I'll give you some things to put in their food that will send them to bed early on the nights you're to come, and keep them there a-snoring, and they'll be nothing the wiser!"

Eleanor blinked. "Is that safe?" she asked, dubiously. "I mean, what if they—taste it, or something?"

"They won't. And I'll have a charm on it to make sure they eat enough of it to do what I want." Sarah seemed quite confident that she could do exactly what she claimed. Eleanor wasn't nearly as confident—but then, she didn't have anything to lose by trying, either. "Now, you eat," Sarah continued, "so you get your energy back, and we'll practice those shields and wards again."

Eleanor sighed, and applied herself to her food. She wanted to protest; she hadn't had a moment to herself all day. When she hadn't been learning the "shields and wards" that Sarah thought were so important, and which didn't seem very much like magic to *her,* she'd been taking in the laundry, putting it away, and tidying up. She had been so looking forward to another afternoon in the library—but the promise that she might be able to break herself free of Alison's magic was so tempting that she hadn't so much as whispered a complaint.

As if she had heard all those thoughts, Sarah looked up from her dinner and smiled at her. "I know it's hard, my dear," she said, in a kindly voice. "Cruel hard on you, it is. But I'm having to teach you the hard way, to bring up the protections and take them down without leaving a trace for your wretched stepmother to find. Until you can do that, you daren't even try to work magic here, for she *will* know, and that will be no good thing at all."

Eleanor shuddered at the idea of her stepmother discovering such a thing.

"And you *should* shiver," Sarah said, noting it. "Do believe me in that. It would be very, very bad for you. She would bind you in so many spells that you would scarcely be able to walk without being under compulsion, and *I* should not be able to do a thing about them. Never forget that *she* is a Master, and until you have Mastery of your own, she can bind you by that finger beneath the hearthstone to whatever she wills."

Eleanor glanced over at the hearth, and shuddered again. "I won't forget," she said, quietly.

"Then eat," the witch replied, "And we'll work tonight until you're too tired to carry on."

And so they did, though to her credit, Sarah Chase helped with the washing up before they did. Over and over again, Eleanor spun out the cinnamon-tasting, warm-red power of the Element of Fire from the crackling blaze on the hearth, and built it into an arching dome around herself, then sent the power back into the hearth and erased all traces of the energy from the very air around her. She wondered now why she had never noticed the power before this, though; although it was easier to see amid the flames of the real fire, there were wisps of it everywhere, like the last breath of fog above the grass on a spring morning, or the trailing bits of smoke above a chimney. There were other colors of power there too, now that she knew what to look for—a warm amber glow that was somehow as sweet as honey that seemed to surround Sarah Chase like sunlight, a hint here or there of a thread of blue or a flicker of green—but none of them called to her as that scarlet flame did.

There were several Salamanders in the hearth-fire by now, and she felt their presence as a friendly and encouraging warmth. That helped her when she faltered, right up to the point at which she ran out of energy altogether, and simply sat right down on the hearth and looked up at the witch with pleading in her eyes. "I can't," she said, plaintively. "I—"

"Ah, then we're finished for now!" Sarah exclaimed. "The one thing your mother always told me is that Fire is the most dangerous of the Elements; handle it carelessly at your peril, is what she said!"

"She did?" Eleanor glanced at the hearth; three little Salamanders coiled quietly amid the flames and blinked slow and sleepy eyes at her. They didn't *look* dangerous—

But then, neither did a bull, until you got into the field and it charged you.

"She did." Sarah offered her hand; Eleanor took it, and the witch pulled her to her feet with surprising strength. "You sit at the table for a moment, until you're feeling livelier, then get yourself to your bed. I'll be back tomorrow at the same time, unless *she's* come back by then. And in that case—well, I'll leave you a note in the wash-house. Oh, and any time yon Salamanders want to frisk about you, let them. They'll do a bit of slow healing on you when they do. Give them a month, maybe two, and they'll heal those scullery-maid's hands of yours."

Eleanor nodded. Of all the places in and around The Arrows that Sarah could get to, the wash-house was the safest to leave any such thing; Alison hadn't so much as set foot in it in all the time she'd lived here.

"Now, I'll let myself out, don't get up," Sarah concluded cheerfully. "Maybe have yourself a cup of tea and a bit of toast before you go to bed." She picked up her basket, wrapped her shawl around her shoulders, and suited her actions to her words, slipping out into the night-shrouded garden and closing the door after herself.

Eleanor simply sat, and looked back at the hearth-fire again. The Salamanders were still there, still watching her, reminding her of nothing so much as a tangle of kittens.

If kittens could be made of flames.

"Why didn't I ever see you before?" she wondered aloud.

She was shocked to her bones when the one in the middle raised its head, looked straight at her, and answered her.

Because She *was there, and you had not fought her power.* Just a touch of scorn came into the creature's tone. *Why should we show ourselves to one who would not fight for her own freedom?*

It was a good question. "But I thought that I had—" she replied, slowly.

All three of them shook their heads negatively. *Hating someone is not fighting them,* the middle one pointed out. *You pushed, but pushing is not fighting, and you gave up too soon. Yesterday, you* fought. *That was good. If you fight, we will help. But remember that if Earth can smother Fire, Fire also can consume Earth.*

Before she could say, or ask, anything else, the Salamanders faded into the flames, and were gone.

6

March 18, 1917
London

THE ONE DISADVANTAGE OF BEING in London was that even the meals at the Savoy were subject to rationing and shortages. However, if one was forced to pay lip-service to rationing and shortages, at least the Savoy had excellent chefs, who could make a great deal out of very little. While breakfast was something of a disappointment when compared to the same meal served three years ago, it was still superior to virtually anything being served anywhere else in the city.

Still, as Alison regarded her plate with mild disapproval and wished—for just this moment of the day, anyway—that she were back in Broom, the thought of her well-stocked pantry brought something else to mind. This was the first time that Alison and the girls had stayed in London so long since the cook had left. Eleanor was certainly breakfasting on crusts by now. The thought made her smile a little; the wretched girl was such a source of unnecessary complication that not even her usefulness as a servant outweighed it.

After breakfast, as Howse put the finishing touches on her hair, Alison wondered briefly if she ought to do something about the girl back in Broom. It wouldn't do for her to starve. And all alone for so long—was it possible she might be able to get into mischief? Would anyone think to check the house and find her?

Then she dismissed the thought. The girl had plenty of food in the way of potatoes, turnips, dried beans and black bread, and she couldn't get out of the house and garden. No one knew she was there alone, so no one would come looking for her. In fact, Alison was not entirely sure anyone in Broom still remembered her, except vaguely; other concerns occupied Broom now, as they occupied most of Britain. There wasn't a family in Broom that didn't have at least one member fighting, wounded, maimed or dead; most had several. Fully half the jobs in Broom that had once been taken by men were now being filled by women. On consideration, Alison doubted very much that anyone in the village ever thought about Eleanor, even to wonder what had happened to her.

Besides, there were a great many things that could be done here that could not be done in Broom. Warrick Locke was very useful with his black-market connections, enabling her to get hold of all manner of goods that were otherwise unobtainable, having them shipped home in discreet parcels marked as "hessian," "beans," or "oats," or other things that were not in short supply. And it was not only convenient to meet her solicitor here, it was safer. There were no prying eyes noting how often the man came to see her and how long he stayed. Meetings that happened too often made tongues wag in Broom, and she had the image of a respectable widow to maintain if she was to remain the top of the social pyramid.

Not that the thought of taking Locke as a lover ever crossed her mind. *If* she ever took a lover, and that was *not* likely, it would be someone who she could not buy with other coin, and the situation would have to have a great deal of advantage in it for her.

Mind—once she got access to the social circles of Longacre Park and the Hall—

Well, that was for the future, and Warrick was still very

useful. In fact, she had a meeting scheduled with him this morning, at a working-class pub where no one knew either of them. So long as no Zepps or aeroplanes appeared to drop bombs on Southwark, things should go smoothly.

She frowned into her mirror again, as Howse handed her the neat, mauve velvet hat she wanted, and she pinned it on. One true disadvantage of being in London—it was within range of the Hun's Zeppelins and 'planes. That *was* an annoyance, though Alison was sure enough of her power that she was not concerned that *she* would fall victim to a Hun bomb. But bombing raids threw such terror into the populace that getting around in the vicinity of one afterwards was a great trial, and one not compensated for by the abundance of energies released by death and fear afterwards.

She took herself downstairs, after warning the girls to remain in the hotel. Since the American boys had left, and her girls didn't find walking or taking the 'bus or Underground amusing, even Carolyn was inclined to obey without an argument. There were plenty of officers frequenting the tea-room and bar of the Savoy; if they wished to flirt, all they had to do was go downstairs.

Since Alison had arranged last night with the concierge to procure a taxi, there actually was one waiting for her without the need for magic. Though the ancient cabby looked at her a bit oddly when she gave the address, he made no comment.

The taxi deposited her on the doorstep of the pub without incident, although the arrival of the taxi itself caused a little stir among the local loungers; these days it was not the usual thing to see a taxi in Southwark. Locke was waiting for her, however, and escorted her into the pub and a private parlor he had arranged for as per her request, and the short-lived moment of interest faded once they were inside.

The private parlor was quite small, scarcely larger than the booth whose high-backed seats framed a window that didn't appear to have been washed for a decade, and looked as if it dated back at least two hundred years. The wood of the walls and the booth itself was nearly black with age, but the place was comfortable enough. They placed an order for luncheon; fish and chips seemed to be the only thing that was available, as the girl said, apologetically, over and over, "Sorry, miss. Rationing."

"Robbie's got my motor car," Locke announced as she settled herself in the ancient leather of the seat. "I'll have him drop you either back at the hotel or somewhere across the river where you can get another taxi, as you prefer."

She nodded. "Now what was it you wanted to see me about personally?" she asked, with some suspicion. "If it's about those American boys at the embassy, they've gone."

Locke shook his head; his thick glasses glinted in the dim light. His poor eyesight was what had saved him from the front; he was the next thing to blind without his spectacles, and though he might have been accepted at this point had he volunteered, he was hardly inclined to do so. No one even gave him so much as a sour look, with his disability so clear for anyone to see, and *he* saw no reason to throw his life away in the trenches.

For which Alison was grateful. It would have been impossible to find another solicitor she could have let in on her secrets, much less one as well-connected. In fact, if he was ever called up in despite of his eyesight, she had a little plan in mind to take out his foot or his knee, thus rendering him completely useless as a soldier. It would be easy enough to find someone who would shatter a kneecap for a few pounds; she hadn't given up all of her old contacts when she'd married Robinson. She hadn't told Locke about her plan, of course. He wouldn't have been pleased, even if it allowed him to escape conscription.

That is, she didn't *think* he'd take such a plan well, but you never knew. He might have had a plan of his own, like shooting himself in the foot. That one not only got you out of being conscripted, it got many a man out of the trenches and home.

Robbie Christopher, his "hired man," had gotten off by virtue of the fact that he could dislocate both shoulders at will. The trick had not only come in handy for escaping conscription, but for escaping police custody in the past.

Robbie was extremely useful to Locke, and not just as a driver and lifter of heavy objects. Robbie liked fires. Locke sometimes arranged them. Robbie liked hearing other peoples' bones break. Locke went places where his slight frame would attract unwelcome attention without someone like Robbie around. And it would not have surprised Alison at all to learn that Locke also arranged for Robbie to break other peoples' bones for a consideration. Locke was clever enough to fix things so that Robbie could enjoy his favorite pastimes without being caught. It was a profitable partnership, no doubt.

"No, I wanted to tell you in person that I've found a loophole in the law regarding your inheritance problem, and I cannot believe that I didn't think of it sooner," Locke told her, with an air of triumph. "All we have to do is to arrange for the girl to be rendered incapable of taking care of herself in some permanent way, and when she's twenty-one the entire estate will be assigned to whoever is her guardian and caretaker. Since *you* have been her guardian all this time, that will be you, and that wretched solicitor who is the trustee of her fortune will have no more to say about it."

Alison smiled, slowly. "What would you suggest?" she asked.

Locke laughed, and leaned back, one arm cast carelessly along the back of his side of the booth they shared. "My first thought was to drive her mad, of course," he replied. "Since we wouldn't want the unwelcome inquiries that an accident might cause, and you certainly wouldn't want to leave her still capable of speaking for herself, so that lets out breaking her back. You're an Earth Master; you ought to have enough nasty beasties at your beck and call to do that. The fact that she's got powers herself means she'll see them, doesn't it?"

Alison frowned slightly. "There are a great many hobgoblins and wraiths that would do," she admitted, "But I don't like to use them. They're expensive in terms of power. Perhaps some other way—"

He shrugged. "We have a year to plan it out. We should be able to think of something. Aren't there poisons that make one mad? I seem to recall something about hatters—"

"Hmm. Mercury, I think." Alison tapped her cheek with one perfectly manicured nail. "Finding a dose that wouldn't kill her could be a problem."

A very nasty smile crept over Locke's face. "You know," he said, leaning over the table and lowering his voice to almost a whisper, "There *are*—the illnesses that one doesn't talk about in polite society—that do the same thing." He raised an eyebrow. "I could arrange for *that*—if you could arrange for the disease to act rather more swiftly than it usually does."

Alison stared at him for a moment, then suppressed smile of her own. "Now that is an interesting thought. Especially if I were to lodge a complaint with the police that she had run away, perhaps with a soldier, and she was to be brought back home by you very publicly, and in a—less than pristine state."

Locke spread his hands wide. "Sad thing, but an old story these days," he said. "Sheltered little country-girl, handsome fellow, and 'I'll marry you when I come home, but why should we wait?' Men are *such* cads."

"And she needn't even actually leave the house," Alison said thoughtfully. "Carolyn bundled in a cloak could stand in for her when you 'return' her. No one would think twice about her not wanting to show her face after such a disgrace."

"The only thing I can think of that would cause a problem is—she still *is* showing signs of coming into her power as a Fire Mage, isn't she?" Locke asked. "And the nearer she gets to twenty-one, the harder it will be to keep her suppressed."

"Distressingly true; mind you, I've seen no signs, no signs at all, that she's coming into any significant power, only that she isn't ever burned, no matter what she does around fire," Alison replied, and pursed her lips. "Still, all the more reason *not* to use magic to drive her mad. *Much* better to use something purely physical."

Locke shrugged. "It's all one to me; one will be expensive in magical coin, the other in real money. I'll have to find the proper man—and it will have to be someone who wouldn't be missed, because when the job is over, if we want to *keep* things quiet, Robbie will have to take care of him."

"Well, Robbie would enjoy that, wouldn't he?" She smiled silkily.

"And we always like to give Robbie his little pleasures." Locke returned her smile. "He is such a loyal employee, and he asks so little in return for so much."

Deciding to proceed with caution, Alison elected to have Robbie drop her at Victoria Station, and took a taxi back to the Savoy. She was glad that she had; there was a messenger waiting for her in the lobby, and the packet he handed to her in return for her signature was sealed with Lord Alderscroft's signet.

Although she was impatient to see what was inside, she gave no outward sign; she tucked it under her arm and took it upstairs.

This was not just simple caution; the moment she touched the seal, she had known it was not just a physical protection against prying. So whatever lay within would be rendered unreadable if the seal was broken without the magical component being properly released. Not the wisest thing to do in a public place.

The girls were at the window of the sitting-room, putting charms on passers-by in the street below. They had moved on from simple lust-charms; she noted with approval that they were also distributing anger, depression, and quarrelsomeness with an even hand. Not all the charms "took," of course, but every failure was a lesson in what not to do—or who not to do it to. There were those who had mere touches of magic about them who were never touched by such things. It was best to learn to recognize such people so that if one *had* to curse them, one would know to use a stronger spell.

Seeing that they were gainfully occupied, Alison moved to the little writing-desk and opened the envelope, first tracing the counter-sigil on the seal so that the contents would remain intact. She never failed to feel amused at how those foolish men, with their silly White Lodge, refused to let her past the public rooms of their little club because she was female. They were like schoolboys, with their "No Girls Allowed" signs—or cavemen, superstitiously afraid of the "unclean" woman!

As she had hoped, the letter contained the dossier of the woman she was to impersonate. Alison Stanley, of the Northumberland branch of the Stanleys, had died when the hospital ship *Britannia*, on which she was a nurse, had been torpedoed, but because no one had printed a new edition of Burke's since the war began, she would still be listed as living. Early in the war, the casualty lists had been suppressed, so only Alison Stanley's immediate circle would be aware she was dead. Alison nodded with satisfaction. The northern Stanleys were as poor as church mice for all their pedigree, what little income they got went straight into trying to keep the roof on their ancient barn of a manor house patched, and no one from Longacre would ever have met any of them.

Lord Alderscroft gave her the particulars of her "family;" it was numerous, and she was going to have to memorize it all later.

And he enclosed a letter of introduction to Reggie's mother that made her smile widen. *I have written her ladyship myself,* he said in his cover-note. *Telling her about my "cousin" who was supposed to have married a fellow called Robinson down there in or around Broom, and asking if she'd heard of you, and if she had, would she look you up to see that you were all right. The rest is up to you. Reginald isn't likely to be discharged until May at the earliest, so you should have time to establish yourself before he's brought to Longacre.*

She laughed silently. If Alderscroft only knew how he was setting a fox to guard the hens!

However—

She rested her chin on her hand for a moment, as a complication occurred to her. *Whatever* she did to Eleanor, it would have to wait. She could not afford a scandal before she got one of the girls safely married to Reggie. Afterwards—well, these things happened to the best of families these days, and at any rate, Eleanor was not, strictly speaking, *related* in any way to her or her girls. The Fenyx family would move heaven and earth to keep things hushed up. It was the way these things worked, after all.

So—plans for wretched Ellie must go to simmer. It wouldn't matter; Alison would get what she wanted in the end.

She always had, no matter who was in her way.

At night, once all the visitors were gone, but before most of the men fell asleep, was the easiest time of Reggie's day. That was when, freed, perhaps, by the dim light, and the first fuzziness of opiates, freed by being just one more whisper in the dark, the men talked openly among themselves of what they would not tell anyone else.

There was a new patient in the bed to Reggie's right; a cavalry officer, with an empty sleeve pinned against the breast of his pajamas. He had stared at the ceiling all day, saying nothing, not even whimpering when his dressings were changed. Now, suddenly, he spoke.

"Don't you think it's a relief?" he said, with surprising clarity, still staring at the ceiling.

Reggie thought, *Do I think* what *is a relief?* but the man continued before he could ask the question.

"Finally—no more ruddy show for the folks back home. No pretending it's all beer and skittles and no one ever gets hurt. Not that they don't *know,* of course, because they do, but you have to pretend anyway. No reckoning how much life you're going to pack into a ninety-six hour leave 'cause it might be the last one you get, while pretending it's nothing much. No more careful letters that don't let on. No more wondering if you're going to do a funk. It's over, the worst has happened." He *did* sound relieved. Reggie swallowed, his mouth gone dry. Maybe for his neighbor, the worst *had* happened.

"That part's a relief," someone else agreed, out there in the dimness.

"No more guns," someone else moaned. "All day and all night—pounding, pounding, pounding—"

"Ah," said Reggie's neighbor in an undertone. "PBI. I'd've done a funk six weeks ago if I'd been PBI."

Reggie turned his head, took in the neat moustache and what he could see of the other man's remaining hand, and made a guess.

"Cavalry?" he suggested.

The other finally turned *his* head and looked at Reggie. "Most useless waste of man and horseflesh on God's own earth," the other agreed, and though the voice was cheerful, the bleak expression on the man's face gave it the lie. "Should have put my horse on a gun-carriage and me in a trench. All we existed for was to be shot to pieces. All they could think to do with us was send us across the wire again and again and let the machine guns have us."

Reggie winced. The cavalry had not fared well in the war. And the face on the pillow of the bed next to his was, behind its brave moustache, disturbingly young.

"My brother's PBI; told me enough about it before he caught it that I knew I wouldn't last a day," the youngster continued. "Thought, since I was a neck-and-nothing rider, I'd try the cavalry. I," he concluded bitterly, "was an idiot. All a man on a horse is out there is a grand target."

"But the worst is over," Reggie suggested, echoing the young man's own words.

"Oh, yes, the worst is over." The young man sighed, with a suggestion of a groan in it. "If I keep telling myself that, I should start believing it soon."

He blinked owlishly at Reggie, then looked back up at

the ceiling; another moment, and his eyelids drooped, and he fell asleep.

Out in the ward, the whispering went on.

"—watched that gas coming closer and closer; couldn't move, didn't dare, had a machine gun above us to get anybody that bolted that took out two of my men that tried—"

"—one minute, passing me a smoke, the next, head gone—"

"—arm sticking out of the trench wall. Men used to give it a handshake as they went past—"

"—sweet Jesus, the *smell!* If I can just get it out of my nose for a minute—"

"The smell—" Reggie repeated, with complete understanding. No one who had not been *in* the trenches understood what that meant. He hadn't not really, until he'd been buried in a bunker. One part, the stink of aged mustard gas. One part, stagnant water. One part, rat urine, for the rats were everywhere and only a gas attack got rid of them. One part, unwashed human body, for what was the point of washing when you were standing knee-deep in stagnant water? And one part dead and rotting human flesh. When somebody died, you gathered up as much as you could of him to bury—but sometimes your trenches were dug across an old burial-field, or sometimes, when a bomb or a barrage had hit the trench directly, there were so many bits scattered about that you just cleaned up what you could and dumped what might remain after the stretcher-bearers left into a hole. It wasn't the first time that Reggie had heard a story like the hand and arm sticking out of a trench-wall. Soon enough, you got numb to seeing things like that. Especially if you were in the PBI.

But that stink never left you. It got in your nose, in your hair, lodged in your memory until you couldn't draw a free breath anymore.

Yet his exposure it had been so brief—many of the officers in this ward had lived with it for weeks, months. Maybe they got used to it.

Maybe they just got numb to it.

"Know what the real relief is? Not having to bloody lie to the boys anymore."

That was another new voice, a tired, tired voice from the other side of his new neighbor. Reggie got himself up on his elbow and peered through the gloom.

It was, indeed, a new man—older than Reggie, old enough to have been Reggie's father, in fact. *Oh, God,* he thought in sudden recollection. *They've raised the conscription age to fifty, haven't they?* One eye was bandaged; in fact, half his head was bandaged on that side, and his shoulder as well.

"I mean," the man continued, doggedly, "They're just kids, and they believe you when you tell them that bunk about 'one more push,' 'over the top and on to Berlin.' *They* tell you to tell it to these kids, and you do, and you *know* you're lying to them, that you're all going over the top and nothing is going to change except that half of them aren't going to be in the trench when you scramble back. *God* how I hate the lying—"

There were uncomfortable murmurs, but no one disagreed with him. What was treason to say on the front was of little matter in the ward. What was the War Department going to do, anyway? Line up a lot of men with empty sleeves and empty pant-legs and shoot them? Especially when they were only telling the truth?

Insanity. Pure insanity—the generals at the rear giving the same orders, over and over and over again, regardless of the fact that all those orders did was to kill a few thousand men and maim a few thousand more without winning back an inch of ground. Reggie lay back down and stared at the ceiling himself, seeing the future stretching on, bleak and full of death. He had the sudden notion that this was *never* going to end, not until the generals found there was no one to put in the trenches but toddlers and senile old men. Or until one side or another found some weapon so vile, so destructive, that it would sweep from the Western Front to the Eastern Front in a path of lunatic carnage, leaving nothing alive on the entire continent . . . and he no longer had the illusion that such a weapon, if found, would not be used. Give a man who saw his fellow men as markers on a board such a weapon, and he *would* use it, and damn the consequences, and there were plenty such men on both sides of this conflict.

"I'm tired," said the man who had said he hated lying. "I want—"

But neither Reggie, nor anyone else, was ever to find out what he wanted, for he suddenly shivered all over so that the bed rattled, and then lay terribly still.

A deathly quiet settled over the ward, a quiet in which Reggie heard a steady thumping as of distant thunder. The sound of the guns across the Channel, carried on the wind.

Someone cleared his throat. "Poor bastard," said someone else, in a voice of detached pity. "He's out of it now."

"Maybe—" Reggie began, then kept the rest of what he would have said behind his teeth, and listened to the barrage falling, somewhere—somewhere—out in the darkness.

Eventually the nurse made her rounds, discovered the death, and an orderly brought screens to put up around the bed. That had never made sense to Reggie; what difference did screens make? Everyone knew the poor blighter was dead. The presence of the screens only confirmed that. A metal frame and a bit of cloth was not going to create the illusion that he was still alive.

A VAD girl put out all of the lamps but the one at her duty-station; and Reggie steeled himself for the night. Night was the worst. Night, when the ward closed in around him, when the men drifted off into drugged slumber, and there was no one conscious to talk. He wasn't supposed to get morphia to sleep, but it was the only way he *could* sleep, because those horrible things that had tormented him had come in the dark, and even though he didn't have magic to attract them anymore, he lay in fear that they would come for him, anyway, that they would know him without magic and come for him. They'd come out of the shadows and surround him, and take him back under the ground, under the stifling ground, and the torture would begin again. The long, thin, fingers, dry and rustling, that had clutched at his throat—the heavy, leaden weight pressing down on his chest—the lidless, glowing eyes in the darkness—the fetid ooze that had dripped into his face from mouths with swollen tongues protruding from between stained brown teeth—

He clutched the blanket with both hands and stared at the ceiling, willing his eyes to stay open, unable to move, as he had been unable to move then, completely paralyzed. His heart pounded like the distant guns, shaking him. The VAD girl passed and looked at him; he tried to open his mouth to ask for help, for water, for anything to keep her there for a precious few moments, but his body no longer answered to him. He couldn't scream, couldn't speak, couldn't even whisper. Fear flooded him. There was nothing in his world but fear and the darkness, the darkness that was slowly eroding that last circle of light at the end of the ward, and when it was gone, they would come, and they would take him as they had always wanted to do.

Or worse, the nurse would think he was dead, she would tell the orderlies and they would come and take him away and put him, still living and unable to show it, in the ground, and then—

—then, with a sudden spasm, he could breathe again, and move. The fear receded—not much, but enough for relief.

With an effort, he threw the memories off, and stared fixedly at a wavering spot on the ceiling, cast by the dim lamp. They weren't here. The wights, the wraiths, the goblins of the Earth, they weren't here. They could never find him. He had nothing about himself to tell them where he was.

He wasn't an Elemental Mage anymore. They couldn't touch him, they couldn't see him, they couldn't find him. It was magic that called them, and he had given his up, burned it out, walled it away. He had no magic, nothing for them to find, and without that to call them, they wouldn't find him. No matter what those lipless mouths had whispered into his ear in the dark of that buried bunker.

So he kept telling himself, shivering under his blanket, long past the time when the orderlies came and took away the body on a stretcher and carried off the screens, long past the time when a new, groaning body was placed in the newly changed bed, right into the moment when gray dawn began to creep across the windows. And then, only then, could he let go his hold, and fall, senseless, into exhausted slumber.

7

March 18, 1917
Broom, Warwickshire

EYES NARROWED IN CONCENTRATION, ELEANOR knelt in front of the kitchen fire and stared at the hearthstone directly before her, willing the symbol that she knew was magically embedded there to appear. As she did so, she felt a thin trickle of power flowing from her to it, a sensation that was unsettlingly like blood flowing from a wound.

This was the first time she had dared try anything with the spell binding her to the house. Every time she meddled with one of Alison's spells in order to bend it even a little and change the conditions by which it held, she got this sensation. Sarah said it was because she wasn't yet able to get power from outside herself.

The spells guarding the pantry were weak, easy to bend enough that she could walk through them just by sheer willpower, because Alison had not troubled herself about them very much. Because this particular piece of magic had been laid using *her* flesh, blood, and bone, it was one of the strongest spells in the house, and if she actually *broke* it, no matter how far away her stepmother was, Alison would feel the backlash and know what had happened.

She had asked Sarah why they couldn't simply dig up the

stone and destroy the finger (or what was left of it), but Sarah had blanched. "Don't even think of trying that," the witch had said earnestly. "It would kill both of us. The layers of protection she has on that stone would fell a charging elephant. It's not like in a fairy tale, child, where all you need do is find the thing and be rid of it. No magician worth his salt would put his major spells in place without protections."

That left the difficult task of insinuating around the protections and the spell itself, of twisting and distorting the original spell to give Eleanor more freedom, until the spell snapped back to its original form. Sarah could show Eleanor how to work the magic that would lengthen Eleanor's invisible chain for a few hours, but Eleanor was going to have to learn how to actually perform the magic for herself.

Her shielding circle of protection was small, just big enough to hold her and the stone. It was a good thing she wasn't claustrophobic; she could actually feel the boundaries of the circle pressing in on her.

There must be something missing here. Why can't I finish this thing? She stared down at the stone, and tried to remember what had let her get into the pantry—

I was angry. Would that help? She let some of her anger and impatience trickle down into it along with the power. And that turned the trick; the first hints of a sullen glow appeared on the dull, grainy surface of the rock, then the glyph came slowly to life, as if painted in lines that burned with malevolence.

She knew now it would make her ill merely to touch it with a finger. Fortunately, she wouldn't have to.

With twigs of oak, ash and thorn bound together into a wand, she traced the lines of the glyph—and the closer she got to the end of her tracing, the harder it was, physically, to move the wand, the more the nasty thing faded back into the stone, blurring. . . .

It was as if the air had become thick and gluey, and the stone itself was trying to take hold of the end of the wand and keep it from moving any further. The last few fractions of an inch took all her strength.

The moment she finished the tracing, all resistance to her movement vanished, the glowing glyph evaporated, and she bent over her own knees, panting with exertion. Her arms trembled and ached, and she felt as if she had been trying to push Sisyphus's stone up the hill in hell.

But it was worth the effort—for a few hours, at least, she would be free to leave the house now.

She took the sprig of rosemary that she had plucked from the garden, broke it in half, and laid half of it on the stone, putting the other half inside her bodice where she could smell it. For as long as the rosemary was unwithered, she would be free of the spell. The withering of the two sprigs of herb would be her signal that she had about a quarter-hour to get back inside the boundaries set about the house. Sarah had not been able to tell her what would happen if she didn't get back in time; "I know you'll be pulled back, and all I can say," she had opined, "is that you'll regret it, for fair."

Thinking about her stepmother's temper, and her pleasure in the pain of others, Eleanor decided that she didn't want to chance it. Tucking the wand into a pocket along the seam of her skirt where it would be hidden, she dispelled her protective circle and stood up.

"Well done," said Sarah, sounding quite pleased. "Now, since you've done this for the first time, you'll be fair useless for magic today—so what would you like to be doing?"

"But how am I going to learn anything—" she began, feeling alarm.

Sarah shushed her, shaking her head. "Don't get yourself in a pother; after this, 'twill be much easier each time you free yourself. You've made the spell answer to your will now. You've put your bit of a brick in the door; it can't entirely close now. D'ye see?"

She nodded; she *did* see. "Then—Sarah, can we get help somehow?" She swallowed hard. If only someone would believe her in the village—

But Sarah shook her head. "There's no magicians in the village at all but me, and no one else is going to see past the spells she's got in place about you to keep people from recognizing you or believing you." She bit her lower lip. "Well, someone who was *completely* shielded would, but my dear—someone with that sort of shielding would be a Master. Those spells were set with your blood too, and I don't know where or how."

Eleanor closed her eyes for a moment to swallow down her bitter disappointment. "I don't remember anything," she admitted.

"You wouldn't. She probably set them outside the house, with the rags she used to clean up the kitchen after she took off your finger," Sarah said. "Otherwise people wouldn't be thinking that you're up at Oxford. Alison's set the spell to make anyone as sees you think you're some daft little servant girl she got through some charity place."

"That's what the servants we used to have thought," she said, slowly. "So even if I could make people understand what I'm saying to them, they are *still* going to think I'm mad." If she hadn't spent the last three years in complete misery, she might have been thrown into despair by this crushing of her hopes. "Well, look at me!" She laughed bitterly, because no one would ever have recognized the old Eleanor Robinson, pampered and petted, in the work-worn, shabby creature she was now. "Even without a spell, no one would know me! People don't look past clothing much, do they?"

Sarah shook her head. "I'm sorry, love, no they don't. She doesn't need a spell to make you *look* like a scullery maid, does she?"

Eleanor felt the sting of tears in her eyes, and rubbed at them angrily with the back of her hand. This was a lesson in humility she hadn't thought she needed, and yet—when she thought of all the times *she* had looked right past anyone who was dressed as a low servant, expecting only to hear, at most, a low-voiced and humble "Morning, miss," paying no attention whatsoever to anything else that might come out of that person's mouth—

Oh, she had plenty of excuses for herself! That she couldn't help how she'd been brought up, that even the old vicar had on occasion preached sermons about knowing one's place—

Yes, but— Just because you were taught something didn't make it right.

She looked down at her work-worn hands. They were a bit better now, knuckles not quite so swollen, cracks healing, but she would never lose the muscle and the callus and have dainty lady's hands again. She might as well be one of them now, because that was what she looked like, and that was what everyone who saw her would think she was. Servants. The lower classes. Inconsequential, to be silent until spoken to, never to venture an opinion, much less disagree with what their betters said. Of course, they were too ignorant to know what was good for them. That was why God had placed others in authority over them, wasn't it? And the hierarchy of master over servant didn't end there, of course, because the servants themselves had their own hierarchy of greater and lesser, each class lording it over the one beneath. And on what justification? Because you were born into a particular family!

"Gad, Sarah, why don't they all rise up in the night and slit our throats?" she cried, looking up.

Sarah didn't seem at all confused by the outburst. "I'm told," she said dryly, "That's what they're doing in Roosha. So the papers say. So Mad Ross says."

She was distracted for a moment. "Ross Ashley is still here in the village? Trying to make us all socialists?" Even before the war Ross had been notorious in Broom, with his membership in the Clarion Cycling Club, his socialist pamphlets and lectures, going about the country on his bicycle and standing up on soapboxes at church fetes and country fairs and singing "The Red Flag" at the top of his lungs at every opportunity.

Sarah nodded, half wryly, half in sympathy. "Oh, aye. Got conscripted, like everyone else, discharged last year, lost half his left hand when his rifle exploded, and lucky it didn't take all of it and his face, too. Got a quarter interest in a bicycle shop now with Alan Vocksmith. Alan's rifle blew up too; he lost an eye."

The distraction served its purpose; she lost that first, hot rush of anger. She looked up at Sarah, setting her jaw. "If I can ever break this magic, maybe I'll help him," she said. "But first, I have to break free."

"That you do." Sarah stood up and brushed off her apron. "Let's make the first start."

Her first feeling when she walked out of the garden gate was of disbelief, combined with a rush of such elation that she felt giddy. She had not been outside of those walls for so long that the commonplace street seemed as exotic as Timbuktu. She was free! At long last, she was free, free to stand on the street, free to wander where she wanted, free to—

But as she looked up and down the street—and just across the street from the garden gate, where the largest of the village pubs stood—she got the feeling that something was not right.

But what was it?

"Wait—" she said to Sarah, standing beside the garden wall, staring around her, trying to identify what it was that made the familiar street seem so unfamiliar. There were no children playing, but that was scarcely it; first of all, it was cold again, overcast and raw, and second, it was a school day. Little ones wouldn't be outside on a nasty day like this. No, it wasn't the absence of children—

Then, suddenly, as the postman came around the corner, and she saw, not trousers but a *skirt,* a post*woman,* she understood with a hideous feeling of shock what it was that was bothering her.

There were no men.

There were no men anywhere to be seen.

Not opening up the pub, not making deliveries, not making repairs, not carrying the post.

And suddenly, all those notices in the papers that she read without really understanding them became solid and real in her mind. Conscription age dropped to seventeen. Conscription age raised to fifty. No deferments for only sons, for fathers of young children, for students. No deferment for religious objections. No deferments except for what the War Department considered to be "vital work in the national interest" and severe physical impairment. Go to War or go to prison: that was your choice.

England was a nation of women now, sprinkled with old men, boys, and those whose wounds were too serious, too incapacitating to allow them back into the army.

She followed Sarah, numb, feeling a kind of cold chill creeping over her as she passed the small street of the shops and saw *women* behind the counters, *women* making the deliveries. And in the shops—the butcher shop had hardly anything on display, most of the bread in the bakery was the same, heavy, rye and oat bread that she ate, and there were more bare places in the tiny grocery than there were goods. When she contrasted those shelves with the ones in Alison's cellar and pantry, she was appalled. Where was Alison getting her treats? Not in Broom—

Everywhere there was a kind of emotional pall that had nothing to do with the weather. It was as if there was no hope anymore in Broom—

But for all of that, the little talk that she overheard was not about the war, not about the lost loved ones. That bleak December when her father had died, that was all that anyone could talk about. Who had gone, where they were, that the war would surely soon be over—hushed whispers about the slaughter at Mons and other places, with glances over the shoulder as if to talk of such things would bring disaster down upon one's own loved ones, or as if it were treasonous to even suggest that things were not going well. Teas and entertainments were being planned for boys in training at nearby camps, there was talk of volunteer work, of parties to knit scarves and roll bandages—

There was none of that now. Just sharp-voiced complaints about the price of butter and the impossibility of getting sugar—of having to make do on thin rations, and the talk of further privations. Of the impossibility of getting servants, of the only help at the farm being Land Girls. Of longing for spring "when at least we'll have our veg garden and won't feel the pinch so—"

Ordinary talk, unless you heard the barely repressed hysteria or depression under the words, the attempt to cover up hopelessness with chatter about nothing. She ghosted along in Sarah's wake, and now saw the signs of actual, physical privation in some places, of sunken cheek and waistbands too large, and realized she wasn't just seeing the effect of lack of luxuries, she was seeing real hunger.

And if that were so, in the country, where people were likely enough skirting the rationing by hiding pigs in the forest, geese and ducks on the farm-ponds, chickens, pigeons, and rabbits in the garden, reporting less milk than their cows actually gave—what was it like in the city?

She felt battered, actually battered, by revelation after cruel revelation. She couldn't have managed to speak to any of these familiar strangers, even if she hadn't been walled off from them by appearance and spell. She didn't *know* them. These were not her people. They were some odd breed of changeling that looked superficially like her old neighbors, but who were mere shells, filled with despair, over which a cracking veneer of commonplace was held in place by a fading will to pretend that everything was all right.

Sarah glanced soberly at her from time to time, but said nothing. She only led the way to her little cottage, propped up on either side by larger Tudor buildings, and opened the door to let them both inside, hanging up her plain brown wool shawl on the peg beside the door.

Once inside, Eleanor put her back to the wall and stared at Sarah incredulously. "Why didn't you tell me?" she blurted, wanting nothing more than to bolt back to the safety of her kitchen where the privations of the years had not penetrated, and where she could pretend that nothing outside the walls had changed.

"Would you have believed me?" Sarah countered, stirring up the fire in her tiny fireplace and putting another log on it. "Could I have told you in any way that you would have believed? You've been seeing some of the papers, now and again, I'm sure."

Eleanor collapsed into the old wooden chair that Sarah indicated, hands limply in her lap. "But—" she said, helplessly. "But that doesn't *tell* you—"

"Because no one wants the truth to be printed in the papers," Sarah said cruelly. "If they did, it'd be like Roosha all over again. Or so them fellows in the government think."

"How many?" Eleanor asked, feeling numb.

"How many what?" Sarah responded.

"I didn't see any men—" she began. Sarah nodded. "Most of them—well, we think they're still alive, though some haven't been heard from in a fair while," she said, sadly. "But then again, it's one thing to come home on leave when you live in London or you've ready in your pocket.'Tis quite another when all your pay comes home, and you haven't the money for a train ticket when they give you leave." She sighed. "I don't know but what you'll not recognize the names—Matt Brennan lost a leg. Ross Ashley you know lost his hand and Alan Vocksmith his eye. Michael Kabon—that's the butcher that came in after you were bespelled, finding we hadn't one—he's all scarred up outside and in from gas. Jack Samburs lost an arm, Eric Whitcomb his wits. Then the ones as won't be home at all—" She took a deep breath. "They're on the monument that got put up at the Church. Bruce Gulken, Thomas Golding, John McGregor, Daniel Heistand, Jock Williamson, William Williamson, Daniel Linden, Harry Brown the baker, and Sean Newton. Sean's the latest; his mum just heard last week."

Each name fell like a stone into the silence. So—it was Pamela Brown at the bakery now, not her husband. Eleanor really hadn't known most of them, but Willie Williamson had been one year older and one of the boys who had hero-worshipped Reggie Fenyx, and Sean Newton had used to ask her to dance at village fetes.

Daniel Heistand had been another of Reggie's devoted followers, and had always frowned at her so fiercely when she was the one who got to pull the wheel-chocks away. . . .

Not coming home. Or maimed so badly no one would put them back out again. Horrible. Horrible. What was that, a third of the men between the ages of eighteen and twenty-five in this village? Sean—Sean had been his widowed mother's only child.

She shook her head; it hurt, even to think about.

"It's never going to end, is it?" she asked, faintly. "It's just going to go on and on and on until there are no men left in England—"

Sarah only sighed, and closed her eyes, her shoulders hunched as if she found the weight of it all too much to bear. "I don't pretend to see the future," she replied, sadly. "But the present is nasty enough to worry about. Even Mad Ross come home all grim and quiet. No more riding about, hardly ever makes a speech, unless it's in the pub and he's had some courage in him. The ones as came home, well, they don't talk to their wives and they don't talk to their sweethearts, they just sit in pub and stare at wall. Shellshocked, they call it. I call it that they've seen too much to bear and stay entirely sane. They don't talk about tomorrows, either, and a man what won't plan for tomorrow is a man who believes he won't see it. That's what you feel on the village; that's what come home from the war with the ones that did come home. Nobody thinks about tomorrow if they can help it. Nobody. Church and chapel, they're both alike. Stopped praying for victory, they have; now they just pray for it to be over and have no faith it ever will. I s'pose it's easier to whinge about not having beef and the cost of butter than it is to have hope."

Eleanor shuddered. "What is going *on* over there?" she whispered. "What is it?"

"I don't know," Sarah said, staring deeply into the fire on her hearth, as if searching there for answers. "But I'll tell you this much. Whatever it is, it eats a man's soul. They talk to each other, them as came home, but never to the rest of us."

She had thought to walk about the village; now she couldn't bear the idea. "I'm going to see if I can get as far as the aeroplane field at Longacre," she said, standing up. "I'll do it now, while the spell's still fresh."

Sarah just nodded. "Mind the wind," was all she said. "You can borrow that shawl by the door, if you'd like."

Eleanor hadn't thought to bring a shawl when they left the kitchen, and for a moment, she looked at the plain, shabby garment with the disfavor the old Eleanor might have—

Oh, who and what am I to be so picky? she asked herself. "Thank you, Sarah, if it's no inconvenience—"

"I won't be going out before you're back," Sarah said with certainty. Eleanor paused with one hand on the door.

"Sarah—what is it you *do?*" she asked, bewildered. "For a living?" She couldn't bear it if Sarah was teetering on the edge of poverty.

Sarah laughed. "What, no one ever told you? I'm the district nurse and licensed midwife! Never a doctor between here and Stratford almost, especially now, so I do for all of those that need simple tending." She nodded at Eleanor's silent "oh" of understanding. "It's what my sort does now. Hide in plain sight. People call me 'witch,' they're joking—and I've license to cure as much of their ills as I'm able. I do well enough. Better than some—most of my patients are farm folk, and barter is better for them than money, so I get some of that butter and beef no one else can find. And it's a help to have enough of the magic that I have a good sense of when I'll be needed, and often as not, where. So shoo—off with you, find out how far you can go. Nobody'll call me out until after dark, when *you* had best be back in your kitchen."

"Thank you," Eleanor told her, then wrapped the heavy shawl around herself, pulling it up over her head, and went back out onto the street. It smelled pleasantly of lavender, and was softer than it looked. No one gave her a second look; she had the feeling this was part of the magic her stepmother had put on her. People wouldn't look at her, probably, unless they actually bumped into her.

Well, that was one thing working like a slavey all these years had done for her—a walk she would have quailed at four years ago was nothing. She set off up the road, heading for Longacre, to see how far she could get before she was stopped.

The village was tiny; five minutes, and she was off cobbles and onto hard-packed earth, rutted by farm carts and marked by hooves, passing between farm fields she had known all her life. Hedgerows showed a lack of tending that would have been shocking three years ago. It was too early for planting, but the meadows were full of cattle and sheep, the only creatures that looked to be prospering at prewar levels. As she passed the Gulkens' dairy-farm—Theresa's now, alone—she heard Louis Blue's shrill whistle, and saw the cattle raise their heads and begin to amble in the direction of the milking-barn. So Louis, probably around about sixty now, was old enough to escape conscription; though she didn't know Theresa except as the supplier of butter and milk, she still felt an absent sort of relief. Hard enough to find yourself a widow, but how could one woman keep up a busy dairy farm by herself? Louis, however, she knew from her rambles about as a child; always with a kitten in his pocket, for cats and dairy farms went together like clotted cream and jam. He could never bear to drown the kittens, and was always looking for homes for them. The thought of him going off to the horror that this war must be was an obscenity, he, who couldn't bear to kill a kitten. At least he'd been spared that.

Beyond the dairy-farm was the Scroggins' orchard, and again, with relief, she saw another bit of normality. Brian Scroggins was out, checking the apple trees, with his wife Tracy in the next row, and Brianna and Zach picking up every twig of fallen applewood they could carry. Everyone liked a bit of applewood on their fire, and applewood-smoked bacon and ham were a treat; no wasting in Brian Scroggins' orchard. But he couldn't be fifty. How had he escaped being called up?

Oh— as Brian plodded like a donkey along the row of trees, head down, she remembered. He was so short-sighted as to be almost blind; Tracy did anything that required reading and writing. Just as well. If anyone dared to call up the maker of the best scrumpy in the county, she didn't doubt there'd be an uprising. . . .

She trudged along the road, pulling the shawl out of the grip of the wind. The lovely weather a few days ago had been a lie, it had. There might even be snow tonight. Or if rain, it would be ice-edged.

Across from the Scroggins was the farm of Joanne and Michael Van, and here it was painfully clear that all was *not* as normal. There was no sign of Michael, who surely must be in France now, and all of the figures picking stones in the field were female. One was probably Joanne, but no Broom native had red hair of the sort that flamed under one of the scarves, nor the midnight-black bob of another of the girls. Were these Land Girls, young women who volunteered to work on farms and take the place of the absent farmers? If so, they were Eleanor's first sight of the breed, and for all the complaints of how they were lazy or vamps out to tease the country boys, they seemed to know their job well enough, and they were sensibly clothed in heavy coats, boots, and long, warm skirts.

Finally, the last farm before the fields belonging to Longacre began, was the Samburs' sheep farm. And as she trudged up the road, she saw Sarah hurrying after a male figure with one sleeve pinned up to his chest, supporting himself with a stick, following two sheepdogs with more determination than steadiness. But she didn't call after him, did Sarah, nor did she take over the direction of the sheepdogs. She seemed more like one of the dogs herself, waiting to see what her husband wanted, then doing it, without a word, just as silent, just as faithful. *You do for yourself,* she seemed to say, *until you can't do no more. I know you have to.*

It made tears spring into Eleanor's eyes, and she had to turn away and hide her face in the shawl. The last thing she wanted to do was let either of them catch this sign of her pity. They likely got more than enough of it as it was.

But neither of them looked in her direction as she hurried past, the cold, raw wind plastering her skirts to her legs. All of his attention was on the dogs and the sheep, and all of hers was on him.

Eleanor passed their farmhouse, and more of their fields, dotted with sheep, who raised their heads and looked at her with their foolish faces when she passed.

And then—the hedgerows became fences, marking the beginning of the fields of Longacre.

She paused for a moment at the side of the road; these were grazing fields too, but for horses, not cattle or sheep, the hunters of Longacre Park. The grass was thick and rank here, for the horses were gone, gone to the war, to pull gun-carriages, not leap fences in the hunt. Only off in the distance were three old, gray-nosed fellows, too old to be of use across the Channel.

She had gotten this far. Could she possibly get so far as the field where Reggie had kept his aeroplane?

She trudged on, past the horse field, past one of the woods kept stocked with pheasant for the shooting season. Was there still a shooting season? Did anyone come out to hunt, or were they all hunting men now in the trenches? And then, the second field; she climbed over the stile and down into it. The grass was up to her knees, but this was it; this was Reggie's field.

She could walk here, just.

Trembling a little, and feeling the pull start, she paused beside the old shed, empty and falling to pieces, where the aeroplane had lived. No sign of it now, beyond a discarded and broken propeller, some bits and bobs of wing-struts and a half-rotten roll of canvas inside. She lingered as long as she could, but the pull homewards became more insistent with each passing minute, and when she pulled out the rosemary sprig, it was clearly beginning to wither.

But she turned her back on the place and headed back in the growing gloom with no real sense of disappointment. She had gotten this far—and this place held nothing but melancholy, as sad and abandoned as the places in the village where the men used to gather and socialize.

Enough despair for one day. Time to go back to Sarah, and try to scrape up enough hope to carry on her own fight.

8

April 3, 1917
Broom, Warwickshire

"NOW WE MUST PLAY THESE cards slowly and carefully, girls," Alison said, as the three of them sat over a light luncheon of potted-shrimp sandwiches and teacakes. The girls had taken up smoking while in London, and were indulging in malicious enjoyment as they ruined their left-overs with ash and stubs. So much for the stepsister grazing on what was left. Oat-bread and bean soup was more than good enough for her.

Alison reflected for a moment on the quiet occupant of the kitchen. That wretched girl Eleanor didn't seem any the worse for having been left on her own for longer than usual, and in fact, the absence seemed to have made her more subdued. This was a pleasant development. More than that, it now seemed more likely that Alison would find a way to render her into a helpless object without having to resort to any of Locke's complicated schemes.

While she had initially been in favor of the idea, Alison dislike complication intensely. The simpler the plan, the better, for the less there was that was likely to go wrong. She didn't like the idea of bringing in a stranger, who certainly would be a criminal, and thus, unreliable. Criminals often thought they would be clever and turn on the one who had hired them.

The more she thought about it, the more she began to believe that in dealing with the girl Eleanor, it was probably better not to bring Locke or any of his friends into it at all. After all, she *was* an Earth Master. There ought to be some way for an Earth Master to damage someone's mind irreparably. And much as she would enjoy Eleanor's pain, there were other ways to extract the same pleasure.

She took a reflective sip of her tea, and returned her attention to the subject at hand.

"By now, the first letter will have been received up at Longacre Park," she continued, "But we must not give an appearance of being too eager to make this connection. The opposite, in fact; the last thing we wish is to make it seem as if we are pursuing the Fenyx family. Remember, I allegedly married far below me, and I might find that fact uncomfortable. In fact, we must appear to be—"

"Diffident?" suggested Carolyn. "Shamefaced?" was Lauralee's choice.

"Diffident," Alison replied decidedly, which made Carolyn smirk and Lauralee pout a trifle. "These days there is nothing shameful about repairing a great line's fortunes by marrying into trade. The only shame comes about when one tries to push in before one is invited, or to use one's name and connections as a kind of commodity." She pursed her lips; frowning only made the brow wrinkle. "You see, Lauralee, we must appear to be *modest* above all. We must appear to be reticent about taking advantage of this tentative connection. *You* two should look hopeful and eager but say nothing until we are actually established and accepting invitations. And when the invitations arrive, you must be—"

"Retiring and modest," Carolyn supplied, with a glance at Lauralee. "No flirtations. Friendly wallflowers, so to speak."

"Exactly right." Alison bestowed a smile of favor on her elder-born. "You must appear to be grateful without fawning, and without any hint that you intend to take advantage of the new situation."

"New situation?" Lauralee laughed, and flicked her cigarette ash into the remains of her buttered toast. "Any parties we're invited to will be rather thin on male company! Unless you want us to cozy up to grandfathers and schoolboys."

Alison stared at her in astonishment. " 'Cozy up!' Where did you get that expression? You've been going to too many American cinema shows, young lady—"

"Well—" Lauralee flushed, and looked at her in defiance. Alison quelled the defiance with another look.

"No 'well' about it." Alison sketched a sign in the air, and Lauralee squealed in pained surprise as her mother administered a mild correction. "Let that be a lesson to you: no slang, no impudence. You will maintain impeccable manners from this point on. No, you will not be courting old men or schoolboys. You will be comforting Reginald Fenyx, who is returning to Longacre in extremely fragile condition on medical leave. You will be compassionate, understanding, and willing to listen to or do anything he asks, which likely won't be much. You will become indispensible to him. And I don't care which of you does it, either, so long as one of you gets him to the point where he cannot do without you, at which point we will ensure he asks for your hand. I will be assisting considerably, of course," she added. "Let's just say he'll be plagued by things he would rather not see, and the only time he will be free of them will be in your presence."

Lauralee understood immediately; Carolyn took a moment or two of thought, and the hint, from her older sister, of "he's *shellshocked.*"

It was Alison's considered opinion at that point, that regardless of Carolyn's superior looks and predilection for flirtation, Lauralee was probably going to win this particular contest. "That will be up to the two of you," she said serenly. "I will supply the structure."

"Which is all any good daughter could ask, Mama," said Carolyn sweetly. Lauralee leveled a withering glance at her, but said nothing. Alison was pleased. With a contest of rivalry set up between the two, things should proceed apace, as soon as Reggie made his appearance back home.

"Now, I have something important that I must tend to," she said, and got to her feet. "A small matter on behalf of the Lodge and the Department combined. I will take the auto, and I should be back by dark. Has that odd butcher sent anything of my order? Or the tavern?"

Carolyn shook her head. "Just notes that there is no meat to be had today, so no roast and no ham."

"Have the girl do something with potted pheasant then," Alison said, absently. "Get it out of the pantry for her."

"Certainly, Mama." Carolyn always enjoyed the opportunity to humiliate Eleanor, even when it meant having to set foot in the kitchen. Eleanor still wasn't much of a cook. Fortunately, there wasn't much that the girl could do to ruin a potted pheasant

"I will see you at dinner, then," she repeated, and went out, jingling her keys.

It was a distinct inconvenience to be required to drive herself, but there wasn't a man to chauffeur to be had, and Alison had learned to cope. The auto was less than comfortable on the country roads around Broom, but a carriage would have been just as bad, and at least the weather hadn't left the roads nothing but muck or kicking up choking clouds of dust. She needed her duster and her hat and goggles though. This time it was going to be a considerable drive—into Stratford.

Even now, three years into the war, Stratford-on-Avon was an attraction for visitors, who came to see Anne Hathaway's cottage and other Shakespearian landmarks. That most of them were elderly or female was of no matter. Strangers, even strangers with accents, occasioned no undue attention. There was an industry—no longer thriving, but still in place—of people renting out their cottages to visitors.

The Lodge had been good enough to give Alison not only a name, but directions to the quarry, who had established himself in a cottage on the outskirts of Stratford, one that had once been a farm cottage for a tenant, until the land was given over to grazing.

Rose Cottage was exceptionally remote, tucked off by itself down a little by-lane; the owners had probably been pathetically grateful that anyone was willing to take it these days. Grateful enough to look the other way when the man claiming to be a refugee from Belgium had turned up wanting to take it.

Alison stopped the car at the head of the lane in the partial concealment of some overgrown hedges, and cautiously cast a shield of protection about herself. She had no intention of going into this unprotected. Then, without taking off the enveloping duster and goggles that hid her identity, she walked cautiously down the lane. That few people came this way was given mute testimony to by the grass growing rank over the road. That fit with what Alison had been told.

As she approached the cottage, it was clear that it was several hundred years old, and "improvements" to it had been minimal. No gas, probably no water pipes, certainly no electricity or telephone, and what heat there was would be supplied by one or two fireplaces. There was a single chimney, and the roof was of thatch.

The aura of magic was muted and subdued; probably no one would have noticed, if not for the tell-tale traces of Elementals that were strangers to this part of the world. What was it about Germans that so attracted them to Tibetan magic? That was something that had always puzzled Alison. Weren't their native creatures powerful enough for them?

Well, the little air-demons of the Everest were not going to be able to deal with the Earth Elementals of England on their own ground.

Particularly not as Alison had surprise on her side.

She stopped just long enough at the gate to invoke a gnome, a twisted and ugly little manikin the color of old stone.

"Where is the master of this place?" she asked quietly, as

it emerged out of the rock of the garden wall and stood there, rock-silent itself, looking at her.

"Gone," the gnome croaked, and waved in the direction of meadows.

Good. She dismissed the creature, which melted back into the stone. She entered the garden gate and sauntered up the path to the cottage—it had been gravel once, but was now as overgrown as the road, and as she took in the rather picturesque little dwelling, she could not help but smile broadly. A *vine-covered* cottage—and beneath the vines was stone. Good Cotswold stone. Thatched roof. Earth and earth and earth. What had he been thinking?

Probably not that an Earth Master would come hunting him.

She laid one hand on wall beside the thick oaken door, and allowed the stone to speak to her. Her duster blended nicely with the gray of the stone, and even if anyone came along here and saw her, she could claim to be looking for the tenant. Not that anyone would. The spell of avoidance she had laid across the lane would keep even cattle from wandering down this way.

Needless to say, the German agent did not work his spells within the confines of the cottage; the spells he had laid here were all of protection, a dome of mixed shielding that melded with the walls of the cottage. His purpose here was twofold: to gather information by means of his Air Elementals, and, whenever possible, to disrupt the training of the Royal Flying Corps. Now, from the little that Alison had learned about the RFC, it took very little to disrupt that training. Fog, rain, contrary winds—things that were all easy to direct and create would render it difficult and dangerous to go up, and they were all things that occurred frequently and naturally. Impossible to say how many casualties, if any, were due to his interference. Possibly none whatsoever; the Flying Corps was quite efficient at killing off its young recruits all by itself. One recruit a day died at each of the two training fields, so Alison had been told, and there could be upwards of two dozen crashes a day, and that was without any magical interference whatsoever.

Insane. But no more insane, presumably, than the generals whose only strategy seemed to be that of amassing men in trenches, then sending them in charges against machine-gun nests across open land littered with shell-holes, razor-wire, and bits of the *last* lot to make the charge.

Absolutely insane. If Alison had been in charge of the war, the slaughter would certainly have been as great, but it would have been to more purpose. There were other ways of killing men than flinging them straight to their deaths. And she would not have pursued a policy that spent so much to gain nothing.

She didn't know this man's real name, and she didn't care to learn it. She didn't want to know precisely what he was doing, outside of what he was doing magically. She did not care to know who he was reporting to, or how. The War Office, of course, did want to know these things.

The War Office would have to go on wanting.

If the War Office was interested discovering these things, the War Office could send its own men.

Of course . . . they had *tried* doing just that. They had sent conventional agents against Elemental Masters before, but like the generals, it seemed that they never learned what not to do. They had gotten less than satisfactory results in their investigations of this man, for instance. Those two agents that had been sent to find out what this man was up to, at least according to what the Lodge had told Alison, had been found wandering around the countryside, scorched and witless.

Lightning, of course. Well known as the weapon of choice for Far Eastern Air Elementals, especially the ones associated with Tibetan shamanism.

Alison might have started life as an ignorant working-class girl, but knowledge was power, and she intended to be as powerful as knowledge could make her. It was astonishing, the amount of information that she had accumulated about traditions other than her own. Thus far, the magic of choice for Germans seemed equally split between Nordic and Tibetan; agents of the Irish in league with the Germans stuck to their dark Celtic ways. The walls of this cottage spoke to her of foreign creatures with multiple limbs and eyes, and boar-like tushes. Definitely Tibetan.

So, her quarry was out in a field somewhere, communing with his slant-eyed demons, interfering with the lives of the young bucks at the two Schools of Military Aeronautics, one at Reading, one at Oxford. And all without going more than a half mile from this house.

So why choose Stratford as a base? That Alison couldn't guess, and didn't really care. Perhaps it was simply that there was nothing much of military significance around her, and so there was less chance of his being found out. It didn't matter where an Air Master was in relation to what he wanted to investigate. The only question was how long he was willing to wait to find out the information, and how sure his control over his Elementals was. He could operate at a distance of a couple hundred miles if he had firm control of his creatures. It was certainly less than that from Stratford to Oxford or Reading. He would have no difficulty at all in controlling weather from here, and depending on how fast his Elementals flew, he could have his information within an hour or two. Of all of the Elemental Masters, it was the Air Masters who made the best spies, for precisely that reason. Earth and Water Masters tended to have more control over their creatures, but needed to be in close proximity to what they were investigating, because their Elementals could not travel nearly so fast. And Fire Masters could work at a distance, but their control tended to be problematical. If Fire Elementals did not *like* you, they didn't have a great deal of difficulty in slipping their bonds. And when they did, even the friendliest ones could prove deadly. So Fire Masters, in general, were very poor intelligence agents.

Well, the one thing that this Air Master had neglected to do was to leave one of his little servants here to guard his dwelling in person. That had certainly been a mistake. Even an Elemental with no power could have run to alert his Master that there was another Elemental Mage in his territory, and she probably would not have been able to catch or stop it.

Well, perhaps he had made the mistake that so many in the past had. He had looked for a *male* Master, assuming that a female would be inconsequential. The Germans seemed to have that habit of dismissing female Masters out of hand. Or, like many Masters of a "superior" Element, he could have assumed that an Earth Master was in control of an inferior power.

If that was the case, he should have known better. There was a reason why opposite pairings were considered inimical to each other. It might be a bit more difficult for an Earth Master to get an Air Master in a position where he was under her control, but when it happened—the results were unfortunate for the Air Master.

Or it might be because he had never seen an Earth Master who had dominion over the hostile creatures of the Element. Earth Masters tended to be healing, nurturing types. Alison curled her lip in contempt. If that was the case, if he hadn't bothered to do his research, he deserved what he was about to get.

She placed both hands on the wall, and summoned her own creatures. They would bypass the protections on this place—one great fault Air Masters often had was that they forgot that things could come up from below as well as down from above. Their protections tended to be domes rather than spheres. Water Masters and Fire Masters rarely made that mistake.

Up they came, slow and cold, investing the walls and the floor with their presence, swimming through the stone as an undine would swim through water. Kobolds and tommyknockers, mostly, those creatures that invested rock rather than earth, and who hated mankind with an enduring passion as the invader and despoiler of their secret underground fastnesses. They had the power to bring down mines when angered, and the only reason that they weren't more dangerous than trolls and giants was that they were slow to work on their own, and solitary, and found it difficult to work with one another.

She bound them with spell and command; it wasn't difficult, given what she intended them to do. They hated mankind in general, and Air Magicians worst of all. Ah, the benefit of working against a Master of the inimical Elemental; it was seldom that she commanded any of her creatures under these circumstances that was not pleased to do her will.

The spell was set, the trap laid, and there was no point in remaining. The Air Master would be returning soon. He would check his boundaries and find them untouched, because her invaders had not forced, had not even crossed them. Only when the clock crossed into the dark side of the night, at just past midnight, would her minions—"strike" was not the correct word, for they would approach by stealth. "Envelop" was more accurate. As he slept, they would creep upon him, imprison him, paralyze him. And then, they would slowly, so slowly, squeeze the breath out of him, sitting on his chest while he struggled for air, until the lungs collapsed and the laboring heart gave out. There would be no sign that he had died of anything other than natural causes.

This was far superior to invoking a were-creature and tearing her victim apart, which is what she had been forced to do the last time. Stealth was always preferable to direct conflict. Whenever she could avoid a mage-battle, she felt that she had won two victories in one.

She sauntered back to the waiting automobile, feeling altogether pleased with herself. The amount of terror and pain that this particular murder would produce would be remarkable, and that in turn, would enrich the power given up at the death. The victim might well last most of the night. The kobolds would absorb that power—retain some for themselves—but deliver the lion's share to her.

Which would, in turn, give her more power for the conquest of Reginald Fenyx. She would need extra power; Earth Elementals had already feasted on his fear and pain, and would hunger for more. If she had meant to destroy him, that would have been fine, but she would need all her magic and cunning to keep them restrained and held in check.

She drove back home in the sunset; the auto was constructed of enough of the materials of Earth—though it was powered by Fire and Air—that it did not dare misbehave under her hand. Which was more than could be said of horses, or, for that matter, any other living beast that she hadn't specifically bred, altered, and trained. That was the drawback to being a Dark Master; animals didn't much care for you.

Well, the antipathy was mutual.

She brought it to a halt inside what had been the stable, and turned it off as the last light of the day slowly faded. Through the garden door she came, walking briskly up the path as light shown warmly through the kitchen windows.

Of course, she did not have to go through the kitchen, for there were two doors into the garden—the kitchen door and this one. It would never do for *her* to take a servant's entrance, not even when there was no one there to see; the passage from the garden led directly to the sitting and dining rooms. However, the savory aroma coming from the kitchen told her that the girl had concocted something tasty with the potted pheasant.

She went upstairs to clean herself from the drive, and smiled at herself in the mirror. It had been a most satisfactory day.

Orders to use potted pheasant for dinner had made Eleanor seethe with repressed anger, and this time, it was not only on her own behalf. Outside these walls, people were getting by on a few ounces of meat in a day, stretching it by stewing, putting it in soup, concocting pie—using parts of the cow, pig, sheep, and chicken that no one would have dreamed of using before this. Here within the walls of The Arrows, the announcement that there would be no ham or roast had been met with an order to make a meal with a potted pheasant, as if this was a great hardship. While the trio had been gone, Eleanor had learned a great deal about life in the village in this third year of the war, and she knew that the steady submarine attacks on convoys coming from the United States were taking a significant toll on what was getting to the island. It wasn't only munitions. Far more than she had ever dreamed came into Britain from across the oceans.

Taking a greater toll on people's everyday lives was the rationing and simple scarcity, for there was no need to formally ration what simply was not available. The greater share of meat, white flour, fat, dairy, and sugar was simply taken to go to those who were fighting, or who, like the medical services overseas, were serving those fighting. The result had an impact everywhere. She wasn't sure if people were actually hungry, but it wouldn't surprise her.

There were no sweets in the village store for children, for instance, and when sugar was available, everyone rushed to get what they could. The butcher, Michael Kabon—to Eleanor's initial shock, he was a black man, from somewhere in Africa—made the most of every bit of meat and bone that fell beneath his cleaver.

Mr. Kabon was well-regarded in normally insular Broom, but then, when his personal sacrifice was so visible in his own flesh, Broom would have found it difficult to turn away from him, even had he not been as good-natured as he was. Whatever had moved him to volunteer, she could not say, but he was never going to go back to the lines again—not the way he fought for each breath after the dose of mustard gas that had also scarred his face and body.

And he had proved to be very useful for the village. Of course, here in the country, no one ever complained about eating organ-meat, so he had no trouble finding buyers for kidneys and livers, lungs and brains. But he knew of other options. People were poor where he came from; he had some interesting suggestions about how unlikely things could be cooked, and by this time, the women of Broom were getting desperate enough to try them.

Chicken feet, it turned out, *did* make a tasty soup when cooked long enough . . . and cow hooves were not all that far from pig-trotters and could be used to make more than jelly. So long as housewives disguised the origin of their culinary adventures, no one seemed to mind where the taste of meat came from. Any bone could be used to make a stock, and stock meant soup. It was amazing how much meat could be gotten when you scraped bones, too.

So, outside these four walls, families were dining tonight on chicken-foot soup and oat-bread, while within, the ladies of The Arrows thought it hard that they were reduced to a casserole of potted pheasant. If there was a sweet course on the tables of the village, it would probably be a jam tart—with the jam spread as thin as might be. Alison and her daughters feasted on sugar-frosted cake.

Eleanor wondered just what the reaction would be in the village if anyone knew this. Or knew that the innocuous parcels that came on a regular basis to The Arrows contained foodstuffs no one in Broom had seen for days or weeks, or even months.

Certainly Alison's reputation in the village would suffer the loss of some of its shine.

Eleanor had planned to go to visit Sarah tonight, but as she had gotten ready to add Sarah's herbs to the tea, something had hissed out of the fire.

She had turned to see a Salamander writhing on the hearth, watching her with agitation. When it knew it had caught her eye, it beckoned her nearer.

"Not tonight," it had hissed. *"She walks and wakes tonight. Tomorrow."*

For a moment she had hesitated, but then had put the herbs away. The Salamanders didn't often speak to her, or even appear in the fire during the hours in which they might be seen by someone else. If this one felt it needful to deliver a warning, why take chances?

So she resigned herself to a night of hard work alone. If Alison was going to be awake, there was no point in fighting the compulsions and arousing her suspicion.

She stared at her own reflection in the window as she washed up the dinner dishes. In some ways, none of this made any sense at all. At this point, there were days when if Alison had simply come to her and said, "If you sign over your inheritance, I will let you go" that she would have agreed in a flash. It wasn't as if, given all she had learned perforce, she couldn't earn a living *as* a servant.

Of course, that would have meant giving up a great deal of what made life tolerable. Servants didn't have a lot of time nor leisure to read. And once she did that, the life of an Oxford scholar would have been quite out of reach.

But why *should* she give up what was hers? Especially when Alison had essentially stolen it in the first place?

Because freedom was worth more than things. If she had learned one lesson in all of this, it was that. Freedom was worth far more than things.

She finished the dishes, and sighed. Alison would never let her go, not even for that. She knew too much. Ordinary people might not believe in magic, but there were more like Alison out there, and if she was ever able to leave these four walls, she would be in a position to tell them herself what Alison was up to, how she had bewitched Eleanor's father, and all the rest. Those people might not pay attention, but then again, they might. Alison would never let her go as long as there was a chance that her scheme would be exposed.

Because even if those people did nothing about what had happened to Eleanor and her father, they would be warned for the future, and any new scheme Alison had in mind could be thwarted.

She reached for a towel to dry off her hands, and made a face as she looked at the left. Well, there was another reason for Alison not to let her go. She wouldn't even have to say anything about *magic,* just that her stepmother had kept her prisoner and abused her all these years, and here was her little finger buried beneath the hearthstone to prove it. She certainly wouldn't have chopped her own finger off and buried it, now would she?

With the dishes finished, she took some mending and sat beside the hearth to do it. The Salamander was still there, coiling restlessly around the flames, sometimes flickering out and around her ankles before diving back in again. She had expected the house to settle, and indeed, she heard the two girls going to their rooms, but Alison kept walking back and forth restlessly.

Or was she walking back and forth?

Eleanor cocked her head and listened intently. No, this wasn't a simple to-and-fro. Alison was walking in a circle. The house was too well-built for her to hear if her stepmother was saying anything, but—

The Salamander looked up. *"It is near midnight,"* it observed. *"She walks."*

"You mean, she's doing magic?" Eleanor whispered.

The Salamander nodded.

So that was what the creature had meant!

Eleanor looked up and shivered. Whatever was going on, it couldn't mean anything good. Who, or what else, did Alison have in her power now?

And what was she doing to them?

9

April 20, 1917
Longacre Park, Warwickshire

REGGIE GOT OUT OF THE car stiffly, gazing up at the imposing front of Longacre feeling not that he was coming home, but that he was a stranger in a foreign land. He wasn't comfortable standing on the steps of a place like this anymore; he kept wondering when the next barrage would come in and knock it all to pieces. This was not reality, this quiet, peaceful country, this grand house with its velvety lawns. This was not where he lived. His home was a tent or a hastily-thrown-up wood hut, the earth churned by bombs, with the echoing *thud* of cannon that never stopped. This was no longer his world. Beautiful, yes, it was. With its stone columns rising to support a Grecian-inspired portico, it looked more like a government monument than a place where people lived. The Georgians built to impress, rather than to house.

He took the first few steps, knee crying agony at him, and looked up at the portico again. *What am I doing here?* he thought. The uniformed staff was lined up beside the door to greet him. Uniformed staff? Neat suits, proper little gowns and aprons?

His world contained slovenly orderlies that stole your

whiskey and tobacco, piles of dirty uniforms pitched in the corner of the tent, clutter that was never cleaned, only re-arranged.

He took another three steps upwards, feeling as if he was a supplicant climbing to the throne of God. The scene had that same feeling of unreality. Pristine white steps going up to a colonnaded portico, cloudless blue sky, larks overhead, a line of solemn, priest-like people waiting to greet him—

He realized as he was halfway up the stairs that once he had thought he loved Longacre, but he was not the same person who had given that love to this place.

In fact, he was only just coming to the realization that what he loved was not this great stone pile, this display in marble, it was the land around it.

What had he remembered, after all, in those days when he waited to be sent up, in those nights when he listened to the guns? As he climbed all those stairs, what occurred to him was that it had not been the memories set in those rooms with their twenty-foot ceilings, but the ones spent in woods and fields, in the stables and the sheds, that had kept him alive and sane.

There were 6,500 acres of field and farm, meadow and woods belonging to this place; he felt more at home in any of them than in the building itself. If it had not been too much effort to go back down all those steps, he might just have gone down to the car and ordered it away, far away, anywhere but here, this strange place that should have been home and wasn't.

His mother had the entire staff lined up out front to greet him, as if he was some sort of medieval monarch re-turning. *Bloody hell,* he thought, with weary resignation. *Don't they have things to do?* Of course they did. But this was traditional. This was where the staff of Longacre got their largesse—

So why don't I just pay them decently instead, and we can do without this mummery?

But no, no, he must follow the tradition. Noblesse oblige. Can't disappoint the staff.

So he hobbled forward, as one of the men detached himself from the line and moved to his elbow, and pressed several coins into his hand.

Surely they would prefer this in their proper pay-packet?

First and foremost in line were Mrs. Dick, the housekeeper, and James Boatwright, the butler. They had held those positions on the estate for as long as Reggie could recall, and in all that time they had not apparently changed; no one knew if Mrs. Dick had ever actually had a "Mister" Dick; one just referred to the housekeeper by the title of "Mrs." because that was how things were done. He vividly recalled the day he had learned her given name of Catriona—all his life until then he had thought "Mrs." was her first name.

They, at least, seemed genuinely moved to see him. "Boatwright," he said, shaking the upright old man's hand. "Mrs. Dick." They didn't even acknowledge the largesse, simply slipped it into a pocket and went on shaking his hand, and somewhat to his shock, there were tears in their eyes.

Why? What should they care? Even if they remembered him as a child, they could not have done so all that vividly. The people he had spent the most amount of time with had been his nurse, his governess, and then his tutors and his father. All of *them* were gone, and of all of them, only the nurse remained anywhere nearby—in the pensioners' cottages, if she hadn't died of old age yet.

And he felt so unmoved . . . as if it wasn't *he* who was standing here, greeting old family retainers who, with so many going off and being slaughtered, hadn't expected to see him alive. As if he actually *was* dead, a ghost come back to observe, but not feel.

Next in the hierarchy, he greeted with somber gravity the cook. Mrs. Murphy was not quite as intimidating as Mrs. Dick, being all Irish and beaming. "Mrs. Murphy," he said, shaking her hand—every time he did this, of course, he left that money in their hands: gold sovereigns for the upper servants, smaller coins for the lesser, the tips that servants in great houses were accustomed to get from visitors and on occasions like this, from the family. Or at least, the head of the family, which he now was. His father had simply dropped where he stood, on the first of June, 1915, after Reggie was already in the RFC.

It should have been his father standing here. For God's sake, why couldn't this have been done with less fanfare? It was humiliating, surely, for them, and no great joy for him.

And his knee hurt abominably.

He could remember his father doing this, on occasions like the King's birthday, or Boxing Day, or the day he, Reggie, had taken his Oxford degree, just before the war began. Devlin Fenyx had never seemed to find this the ordeal that his son was now experiencing.

Beside him was Michael Turner, his valet, unobtrusively handing him the gold sovereigns. Turner had been his father's valet, and knew the secret that father and son kept from his mother, that both of them were Elemental Masters. Only with Turner did he feel something like normal, and he wished that, if this had to be done, it could have been Turner who attended to it.

I don't belong here. I don't belong to this world anymore, these piles of showy stone, these devoted family retainers. My world is not this place. My world is a world of blood and ruin, of bombs and cannon and the stink of gas.

Still he moved on, smiling, pleasant, while pain lanced through his knee and more and more he wanted only to go lie down somewhere. Next to Mrs. Murphy was Thelma Hawkins; Thelma cooked for the servants. Quiet word, shake hand, slip in the coin, move on. What were these folk to him, or him to them? Just "milord," or something more? And was that something nothing more than a chimera, a fata morgana, an illusion? He was a ghost, a ghost of the past, and no more real than the dreams of a poet.

Then there were the cook's helpers, four of them: Cheryl Case, Marla Bracken, Amanda Hart, and Mary Holman the tweenie. He wasn't supposed to know them, but he did, all but Mary Holman; Turner murmured their names as they curtsied, and this time it was Turner who gave them their largesse, not Reggie, because these were under-servants, the bottom of the hierarchy. And little Matthew Case, who ran errands, was hardly even in the hierarchy at all.

And just why should that be? Reggie knew the helpers better than he knew many blood relations. Reggie had spent many hours in the kitchens as a boy, running away from lessons. The little Holman girl looked up at him in awe, as if he had been the king. It was embarrassing. In the end, he was no better than she. She might one day come to produce something good and useful—all he had produced was death.

Next, the housekeeping staff, women first. Upstairs maids in their crisp black dresses with white collars and cuffs and starched white aprons with lace caps—all of which must have been wretched to keep clean when your job *was* to clean. Downstairs maids, in gray-striped gowns of the same cut. One of them, Mary, had been the one who had taught him how to slide down the banister. Turner gave them their little gift. They didn't say a word, other than a murmur of thanks directed to him and not to Turner.

They curtseyed, too, like stiff little puppets, their faces without expression. Even Mary. Didn't she remember? Or was this one of the things she wasn't supposed to remember, lest she embarrass the master?

Men next, the footmen, George Woodward, James Jennings (Reggie remembered this old fellow was a talented hobbyist cabinetmaker), and Steven Druce. All three of them were from his father's staff, and definitely too old to be conscripted. Poor old men! They should have gone to a pensioners' cottage long ago. He couldn't help but think of the prewar descriptions in the newspaper for those seeking footmen—tall, of particular hair-color, and with a handsome leg—well, George and James probably looked like that when his father was a youngster, but they were very much past their prime now.

In contrast to their years was the hall boy, Jason Long, who couldn't have been more than fifteen. The hall boy had that name because his position required that he sleep in the hall to answer the door after hours, but Lord Devlin had found that distasteful. *"That might do for some medieval blockhead,"* he had said with a grimace, *"but I am neither, and we do have some modern conveniences these days."* So instead of sleeping in the hall on a cot behind a screen, the hall boy had a room just off the kitchen, with a bell connected up to the door. And if anyone was foolish enough to come calling after everyone had gone to bed, Lord Devlin had felt that they deserved to have to wait in the cold and dark until the hall boy made his way to the door.

Reggie was glad the change had been made.

The head stableman was in the same age-bracket as the two footmen. And the stable boys were both *boys,* perhaps fourteen or fifteen, and looking stricken and anxious as he greeted them.

There was a pattern building here. No men between the ages of seventeen and fifty. He had known that in the abstract, but seeing it on the staff—babies and grandfathers. How many hundreds of thousands of men were dead in the killing fields of Flanders and France? No way of telling, not when a barrage came in and blew everyone to bits, and you just estimated who had been there. But it was bad—bad—if you could look at people here at home and see a gap where there just were no men of a certain age. Of course, it cut across all nations, and surely the French had suffered the worst of all, but—but this was home—

He moved on, looked down at a face, and got a shock that almost made him stagger. The head gardener—who was responsible for Longacre's famous rose garden—was not the man he recalled, but a woman. "Mrs. Green" was murmured into his ear, and he recalled with a start that her husband had been killed in the first year of the war. "A sad loss," he said, with as much sincerity as he could. The next face was another shock, for another mere boy was the second gardener.

Now the staff that did not get largesse, the business staff. Gray old Paul McMahon, the estate accountant, and the estate manager, which should have been Owen McGregor, but Reggie found another female face looking at him where a man's should have been. "Lee McGregor, sir," she said to him, without waiting for Michael. "Owen was conscripted in June of '16 and we heard we'd lost him in January."

"Good Lord," he said, feeling knocked a-kilter. He took her hand and shook it. "I'm so sorry—"

She managed a wan smile. "I'm hoping you'll keep me on in his place, sir."

He glanced over at McMahon, who lifted his brow and gave a slight nod of approval. "If Paul thinks you're handling the job, then certainly," he replied, still feeling off-balance.

So now women were taking men's jobs, because there were no men to fill them. What else? When he went down into Broom, what would he find there? Female shopkeepers, surely—female postmen? Female constables?

Female farmers—how many of the tenant farmers are gone? Are their wives managing? Do we need Land Girls to help them? He hadn't been home half an hour, he was supposed to be here to recover, but already he felt burdens settling onto his shoulders—

Until he looked down at Lee McGregor again, and realized that his concerns were misplaced. Old Paul approved. She probably already had everything in hand. He would just be meddling.

But then he moved to old friends; he was so happy to see Peter Budd, despite his new chauffeur's hook-hand, that he nearly shook the hook off. Budd had been the one responsible for helping to dig him out of that wretched bunker—Budd had heard him screaming his lungs hoarse, insisted there was someone still alive in there, and had begun the digging with only a bit of board to help him. And that, ironically, had led to the loss of his hand; he'd gotten a splinter of all damned things, the wound had gone septic immediately as happened all too often in the trenches, and before anyone could do anything about it, it had gotten so black it had to come off. When Reggie had gotten wind of *that,* he had sent to his fellow-sufferer to offer him a job. Peter had been a chauffeur before the war; Reggie assumed that anyone with the gumption to dig a man out with a board had the gumption to learn to drive again with a hook.

"How are you doing, old man?" he asked.

Budd grinned. "Ready to race, milord," he said saluting with his hook. "Took the liberty, milord, of lookin' up me mate, Bruce Kenny, and turned out he was already working here." He jerked his head to the side at another new face. "Good mechanic, milord, and made bold to conscript 'im. Wasted on horses."

It was obvious why Kenny was working at Longacre, given Reggie's standing order to replace staff that were not going to return with unemployed veterans of the war. Kenny had a wooden leg. A wooden leg was unlikely to impede his abilities as a mechanic.

"Excellent," Reggie replied, feeling much more heartened than he had been a few moments ago. And feeling relieved that the review of the staff was apparently over. There might be some groundskeeping staff, and eventually Gaffer Norman, the gameskeeper, would present himself, probably with his pretty daughter Eva in tow (Gaffer had read too many romantic novels in which the gameskeeper's daughter marries the lord of the manor). He would be expected to make the rounds and meet all of the tenant farmers. And he should inspect the woodlands. Not that he intended to hunt, but there was a sawmill on the property, and it might not be such a bad idea to think about producing lumber for fine cabinetry . . . the woodlands were old, and properly managed, could remain woodlands *and* provide timber.

No, he wouldn't hunt. He had had enough of hunting. He never wanted to shoot anything again. Not ever.

But he should also look over the accounts of all the rental properties in Stratford and elsewhere; reliable sources of income needed to be cared for.

The welcome being over, the staff filing away to their various duties, he could now enter his house—

How can anyone call this monster a "house"?

The first room was the Great Hall, and it was guaranteed to make virtually anyone feel utterly insignificant. Here, the ceiling was thirty feet above the floor, and the magnificence of the room matched the size. It might be beautiful but it had never been built for humans—

But that was the moment of epiphany when Reggie realized that it *had* been built for Air Masters.

He stepped inside, and between the height of the ceiling and the windows up high as well as low, he realized that he felt—comfortable. He could draw a breath as easy as if he had been outside. For the first time since he had come back, he was in a room that didn't feel as if it was pressing in on him.

Of *course;* this wasn't just a monument to display, it was the retreat and stronghold of someone who needed the sky above him to feel truly happy. The public rooms on the ground floor, all with twenty-foot ceilings with the exception of the Great Hall, virtually guaranteed that no Air Master would ever feel claustrophobic. And the private rooms on the next floor were nearly as spacious. He mentally apologized to his ancestor. What he had thought had been built to intimidate had actually been constructed to comfort. . . .

He'd suffered from gnawing claustrophobia, he suddenly realized, ever since his return from France. The proportions made sense when you thought of it as a house built for those most comfortable under the open sky. Even the ceiling murals with their clouds and birds made sense.

His mother was waiting for him, posed in the exact center of the Great Hall, with her hands outstretched. He limped toward her, and took both her hands in his.

She studied his face anxiously, and he produced a surface smile for her. His poor mother! She was not very clever, being one of those fluttery, helpless creatures, but she had loved her husband dearly, and he, her. She just hadn't known what to do with the two Fenyx males in her life, who had bonded more closely than mother and child right from the first. "Oh, my dear boy," she said, "You look so pale—"

"I'm tired, mother," he replied, with partial honesty. "It was a brutal trip down. Not good on the knee." That was nothing less than the truth. Every little bump had sent a lance of pain through it. And he hadn't had a decent night of sleep without being drugged for months.

"Well, go along to your old room then, dear, and have a lie-down. You don't mind that you're still in your old room, do you?" her voice sharpened with anxiety.

As if I'd want father's room. Not a chance. "It will suit me just fine," he told her, and followed one of the footmen up the stairs and down the corridor, though he hardly needed to be shown the way.

His room had not been touched since he left, except to clean and tidy it. He paused just over the threshold, feeling, with another sense of shock, that it had been preserved as a sort of shrine. Perhaps to his safety—perhaps to his memory.

And because of that, it was now a shrine to something that didn't exist anymore.

He'd known this when he had come home on leave, in a vague way. But now—now the contrast between what he had been and what he had become could not have been greater.

Here was his room—it was, thank goodness, not the room of the cricket-playing boy-in-a-man's-body that had gone off to Oxford. He had made some changes since that time. But it was the room of an enthusiast, for everywhere you looked were items having to do with flight. Books, models, pictures of 'planes, a stack of the blueprints for his own 'bus, framed pictures of himself in her. Bits of a carburetor were still lovingly arranged on the desk from the last time he'd taken it to bits. Whoever had been doing the arrangement had lined up the parts by order of size, and had polished them until they gleamed. How long had *that* taken?

He could not help but contrast this room with the aerodrome on the Western Front he'd last been posted to. More of a cubbyhole in a tent, really, his sleeping-quarters had been cluttered with binoculars, maps, bits of aeroplanes—some souvenirs, some just picked up out of idle curiosity. He generally shared his quarters with at least two cats on account of the rats and mice being everywhere, but in general, an aerodrome was overrun with dogs.

It was mad, really, there were always dogs everywhere, puppies peeking their heads out from under cots, adult dogs fighting or fornicating in the runways. Dogs in the club, dogs in the enlisted men's tent barracks, dogs of every shape and size but with no pedigree whatsoever. Why all the dogs? It had finally occurred to him that the aerodromes were probably where every pet in Belgium and France that had been bombed out of its home had come—in the cities that were still intact, they had their own pets, and there was no safety nor comfort in the trenches for any animal. So the aerodromes were where the homeless hounds of France had come, following their noses to where there might be food and friends.

He hadn't much cared for the fleas that the dogs brought, and liked the quiet company of cats, so there were usually a couple lounging about his bunk. He, like so many others, decorated the canvas of his tent or hut with enemy insignia cut from downed planes, and illustrations cut from magazines—

Then there had been the photos. Every flier had them, layered onto the wall. He'd never indulged in the gruesome hobby of snapping dead enemies and posting them on the walls of his quarters, though plenty of the others did, but in a way, his collection was quite as bad, for so many of those in the snaps were dead. Ghost arms circled the shoulders of the living, dead eyes shone at the camera with the same enthusiasm as those who had survived.

Usually there wasn't room for more in his sleeping quarters than bed, kit-bag, a little table and a chair—with perhaps an ammunition crate serving as a bedside stand. The bed would be covered in cats and clothing, the stand would have something to give light, the chair would be draped with two or three jackets or waistcoats.

And on his table, more bits of motors, bills, brandy bottles half-full, whiskey bottles either full or empty, letters, tobacco for his friends, light novels borrowed from those who had finished them, boxes of stomach pills, for every flyer he knew ate them like candy, himself not excepted. How not, when every time you went up you stood a good chance of coming down in pieces? The RFC pitied the PBI, but the PBI called the RFC the "suicide corps" or the "sixty-minute men" because a total of sixty minutes in the air was allegedly the average lifespan of a pilot.

Dirty clothes on the floor, a floor of rough wood full of splinters—the sound of a gramophone bawling somewhere down the row, Harry Tate or sentimental music-hall songs. In the last bivouac, it had been "The Rose of Tralee," over and over; the chap with the gramophone never shut it off. The smell—as distinct as in the trenches but thank God not so—unbearable. Oil, hot metal, glue, paraffin, the French cook conjuring up something—tobacco—brandy.

His unit had a French cook and kept hold of him grimly. Having a Frenchie to do for you meant you could actually eat the food—the sad substitutes for cooks supplied by the British Army took whatever they got, boiled it for three hours, then served it with a white sauce with the look and taste of flour-paste. The Frenchies did you right; a good soup, a little salad, and making the most of whatever they could get from the quartermaster and by scrounging. He suspected horse, many times, but that was preferable to the slimy "bully-beef" which he also suspected to be horse.

He'd always been in places where the commanding officer took as firm a hand as one could over such a collection of misfits as pilots tended to be, so there had always been some semblance of order, at least on the surface. The monkeys were kept on leads, the goats in pens, the trash policed, the meals on time. But even in the English aerodromes, no two pilots were alike. Take an inventory, and you could come up with anything. He'd served with fellows who'd left the seminary to fly, and fellows who he suspected had been (and might still be) whoremongers. With country lads and cockneys. With fellow Oxford and

Cambridge men, and men who could barely read. With Canadians and Americans, raised on Wild West shows and inclined to die rather quickly from an overabundance of enthusiasm combined with a lack of skill and an absolute certainty that instinct was better than training. . . .

He propped his cane on the bureau and laid himself down on the bed, staring up at the ceiling. Another mural of sky and clouds.

And I'm up above the ground floor. Too far up for them to find me. They won't come up here—

Relief washed over him. He had thought that coming home to convalesce was the worst thing he could have done. Now he was prepared to admit he might have been wrong.

And for the first time in far too long, he felt his eyelids grow heavy, and he let them close, and drifted into sleep.

Not a true sleep; it was too light for that. A kind of half-conscious doze, for he heard the servants moving about in this wing, going about their duties. Mrs. Dick was very strict with her girls; unless some task was so heavy it needed two, they were to keep to the schedule and stay strictly apart to avoid wasting time on gossip. But evidently, she wasn't so hard on them that they were unhappy; as a counterpart to his dozing he could hear the one working across the hall humming to herself.

Heavier footsteps in the hall; the girl said, "Right there, please," and there was a thud of logs, the rattle of a scuttle. One of the boys must have brought up coal and wood for the fire.

More humming; it was so unlike the sounds in the hospitals or the camps that it felt as if he was in another world entirely.

Well, he was, really. Though it wasn't the world he had left behind.

Mind, he hadn't been *home* on leave for more than a year; instead, he had come over to London, roughly ever other time meeting his mother there instead of coming down to Longacre. It was easier that way; making a round of theater prevented any need to talk. She didn't want to hear about the war, and he didn't want to hear about the nice young ladies she wanted him to meet.

When he'd come over on his own, there had been other entertainment than theater. And his mother, no doubt, would have been shocked to learn that some of those same "nice young ladies" were dispensing their favors with freedom and enthusiasm at the parties given by William Waldorf, Viscount Astor, Lady Anson. Always it was the war, the war, the war, giving a feverish cast to these parties, with everyone grimly determined to have—if not enjoyment, then pure physical pleasure.

Here it seemed as if his mother had dedicated her life and all of her strength to trying to preserve life here at Longacre as it had been before the war. He had noted the last time he was on leave that she assiduously avoided any mention of the war and anything connected to it, and there had been a kind of brittleness about her.

He wondered what would have happened to her if he had died. Would she have dedicated the rest of her life to keeping things absolutely the same, frozen in time, like an Edwardian iteration of Miss Havisham?

He could easily see that. Poor mother.

It was a lost cause, of course. The juggernaut that this war had become had its own momentum. It was devouring everything in its path, and everything it could possibly touch. She didn't have a chance against it.

In the end, nothing and no one did.

He came down to dinner, to discover, to his horror, that he and his mother were not alone in the house. His grandfather on his mother's side was in residence. Unfortunately, the old man considered himself a military expert, having served in a tame regiment in India, that saw no more exciting action than polo games.

He kept a civil tongue in his head all through the rather strained dinner, while the old man held forth on the wisdom of the war Office, the grand strategies of Kitchener, and the superiority of "real army tactics" to the new weaponry of tanks and machine guns and, especially, aeroplanes.

"Damned useless, said it before, and I'll say it again," the old man fulminated, as Reggie shoved bits of rabbit cassoulet around on his plate. "Damned cowards are what's holdin' the victory up! Too damned cowardly to *make* the charges. One good push, over the top, that'd be all it'd take!"

Reggie closed his eyes, counted to ten, feeling a vein throbbing in his temple. He thought of all the times he'd looked down on the PBI in their "big pushes," how often he had watched them slaughtered by the machine guns. Thought of the men who had become his friends back on the ward, men who had been thrown into a meat-chopper by old fools who could not and *would* not understand that war had changed, changed in unrecognizable ways, and that the old tactics that had worked once did not work anymore.

He held his temper and his words all through dinner, and after, when what should have been a nice, quiet moment for a smoke in the sunset turned into another occasion for a rant from the old man, who seemed determined to confront him, for some reason. Finally, it was only when his mother retired, that her father came to the real point.

"Now that we're alone, boy," Grandfather said, with a particularly vicious look out of the corner of his eye at Reggie, "I want you to know I don't hold with this 'shell-shock' nonsense. A bust-up leg, that's fair. But the other, that's just malingering." The old man gave him a particularly malicious glance. "I've got my eye on you."

Suddenly, a fury that Reggie had not realized he possessed welled up in him, and he actually began to shake. He clenched his fist around the handle of his cane to stop it from trembling, a bitter bile rose up in his throat.

To keep from giving the old man the answer he deserved, he bit down hard and clenched his teeth together. Life was difficult enough for his mother; he was not going to make it harder by having a row with her evil-minded old father.

"You can believe what you like, sir," he got out between his clenched teeth, staring at the old bastard who stood a silhouette, black against the fire in the study. "I cannot hope to change your mind."

"Huh," Grandfather snorted, and turned away. Reggie, still full of fury, limped off out of the study, not really knowing where to go, but only knowing that if he didn't get away from that house and that horrible old man he was going to say or do something that would make his mother unhappy.

He forced himself into a walk around the garden; it might be night, but the layout of the rose garden hadn't changed in two hundred years, and he didn't need light to know his way around.

But after limping around the turfed paths for a half an hour, his temper still hadn't cooled, and he knew he wanted something he could not get in that house.

He limped down to the stables, where horses were sharing their accommodations with his motor cars. There were three of them now, an enclosed model for his mother, his own fast Allard, and a Bentley that he could either drive himself or be chauffeured in. Or rather, he could when the knee healed up. The condition of the knee made shifting problematic for a while.

But down there in the stable were two men with whom he had something in common. A million times more than he shared with that vicious old man who had driven him out of his own house, though they were neither officers nor gentlemen.

The stables had been neatly divided into horse and auto sides, with the autos being housed in the part that had once held the carriages. There was one farm cart there now, one pony trap (perhaps his mother liked to drive herself around) and one small, open carriage. The rest of the space was made into a proper garage, and the glow of a cigarette in the shadows told him that someone was out for a smoke.

"Care for a gasper, milord?" asked Peter Budd.

"Thanks," Reggie replied, taking the metaphorical strides that crossed all the boundaries of rank, class, wealth, and education, to arrive at the side of someone who deserved a hundred times more respect than that horrible old man. "I would."

10

April 24, 1917
Broom, Warwickshire

THE BROOM HALL INN WAS where the autumn hunts began, the hounds and horses assembling in the courtyard for the traditional stirrup cup, marking it as a distinctly upper-class establishment. It was certainly of the proper standard for Lady Devlin to meet Alison Robinson and her daughters for tea.

It was a safe way for Lady Devlin to examine these curious women for herself, without incurring any obligations beyond a single meeting. Tea in an inn didn't require a response other than a "thank you, I enjoyed your company," and it didn't imply that invitations to one's house should or could be forthcoming.

Alison knew all of this, and also knew that she had passed the first test by agreeing to this meeting. It was a public place, and while that was an initial advantage, socially, it could prove to be a disaster if the single meeting was all that there was, and the rest of Broom could read the snub for themselves.

This was all part of the social game that the gentry played among themselves, to ferret out the unworthy, the unmannered, the ill-bred.

Alison knew all of the moves of the game by heart, and there was only one question in her mind as she listened to her girls snap waspishly at each other while Howse attended to their hair.

To drive, or not to drive?

The big Crosley auto could fit four, which the Hispano-Suiza would not and the inn was just far enough away that driving would not be terribly gauche. On the other hand, it was within easy walking distance, and these were times in which some self-sacrifice was expected. Decisions, decisions. . . .

It was the shoes that finally decided her; the frocks she had picked out for all three of them required town shoes, not country shoes, and in their high-heeled town shoes the girls were at risk of spraining an ankle. So off they went, rattling and chugging up the street, and when she arrived at the Inn, Alison was glad she had made that decision. Lady Devlin's auto, a magnificent Rolls-Royce Silver Ghost, and her chauffeur were already there.

And Lady Devlin waited in a private parlor.

It was not, by any means, the first time that Alison had dined here, and this place and the Broom Pub with the White Swan alternated in supplying some of their meals. But this was not the usual private parlor she took; it was clear from the outset, that this room was not available for just anyone.

Lady Devlin had already ordered tea; it was waiting when they arrived, and she served as the hostess, pouring for all four of them. She was of the kind that Alison thought of as "wispy"—soft, blond hair going to gray, styled in a fashionable chignon, soft, gray-blue linen walking suit, slight figure, doll-pretty face with soft blue eyes.

"Mrs. Robinson," she said, as she poured the tea as a good hostess did, "I understand that you have lived in Broom since just before the war began."

"That is quite true, Lady Devlin," Alison replied, taking the cup and saucer from her hostess, and making sure that their fingers touched as she did so—

Because, while Alderscroft would never have dreamed

she would use magic to ensure that she became Lady Devlin's bosom friend, Alison had no scruples whatsoever on the subject. But it would have to be subtle, and work with more mundane methods of influencing Reggie's mother. So what passed between them in that moment, was a spell as wispy, as fragile, as Lady Devlin herself. And, unless you were very, very good, it was exceedingly difficult to detect.

Affinity—we are the same, you and I—

"Then I wonder why I heard nothing of you until now?" Lady Devlin continued, pouring tea now for Carolyn, who accepted her cup with a diffident murmur of thanks.

"Oh, Lady Devlin, I would never have dreamed of pushing myself into your notice!" Alison replied, putting down her teacup and looking at Lady Devlin in consternation. "Truth to tell, I do not know why my cousin Alderscroft elected to do so for me. But Alderscroft is a kind man, and perhaps. . . ." She looked away and let the words trail off. The letter to Lady Devlin had stressed how lonely, how hungry for refined company Alison was. But that was not what one would say for one's own self. "One wishes for compatible company, now and again. One does one's best," she murmured, dropping her eyes. "But sometimes, I worry about my daughters. I should think that Broom would feel very confining for a young person."

"Oh, no, Mama, not at all!" Carolyn, looking very pretty in soft lilac, exclaimed. "Why, our days are very full here! We have the parish work, the Red Cross, the Ladies' Friendly Society—now that spring is come, there will be tennis at the country club—we scarcely have time to ourselves, some days!"

Now Alison exchanged a significant look with Lady Devlin. *These are all productive things, no doubt, but hardly entertaining for a pretty young girl! And they do not put her into company appropriate to her breeding.*

"And of course—the war—" Lauralee's hands fluttered over her cup, the sleeves of her pink gown fluttering gently as well. "There are so many things one can do for the war—"

"Well, when we were your age," Lady Devlin said, with

a friendly glance at Alison, "I'm sure we didn't think half as much about parish work and the like. It seems a pity this war has reached so far into our lives."

Alison let the corners of her mouth droop. "All of England seems so sad," she agreed. "And yet, one feels guilty if one does anything the least frivolous, when so many are suffering."

A slight movement of her hands drew subtle attention to her lapel, where she wore her widow's ribbon.

"And your dear husband was one of the first of our sacrifices," said Lady Devlin, with an air of sympathy.

"Mr. Robinson and I were only just married, too," she replied, now putting on a faint look of patient suffering, one she had practiced long in the mirror. "My first husband—the father of my girls—was a fine, fine man, but Robinson was my true love, late though he came to my life, and brief though his stay in it was."

Calculated, slyly calculated, to appeal to the romantic in her. And it worked, sublimely well. Lady Devlin passed her the plate of potted-salmon sandwiches with a sigh of commiseration.

"You poor dear!" she said, with an air of having made up her mind after careful consideration, which Alison did not in the least doubt. "You must come up to tea at Longacre next week, you and your charming daughters. Will Tuesday be reasonable for you?"

"My lady, any day you choose to honor us will be convenient," Alison replied, with eager humility. "We would never wish to be a burden on you, no matter what our cousin has told you."

"Oh, pish-tush," Lady Devlin said, waving her hand. "How could three more ladies be a burden at tea? The vicar and his wife will be there, and Roberta Cygnet and her daughter Leva, and Gina Towner, Miss Elizabeth Tansy—the Devon Tansys, you know, she's visiting with Leva, and Mr. Hartwell—"

Alison placed her fingers over her lips and allowed a smile to appear. "You don't mean William Hartwell, surely? The one who keeps exploding his sheds with his inventions?"

Lady Devlin laughed. "He does seem convinced that he will win the war, does he not? Well, he's a dear, and the worst that will come along with him is a faint aroma of gunpowder—"

There was a light tap at the doorframe, the stocky form of the innkeeper hunched diffidently there. "Is all to your liking, my lady? Is there anything else I can serve you with?"

"No, Mr. Caffrey, thank you," Lady Devlin sighed. "You've done a remarkable job under the trying circumstances that surround us. Thank you."

"Very well, my lady." The innkeeper bowed himself out, leaving them alone once more.

"Will your son come to tea, Lady Devlin?" Carolyn asked, ingenuously. "I had heard that he was home at last. I have always wanted to meet an aeroplane pilot! It must be so thrilling to be able to fly!"

But to both girls' vast disappointment, she shook her head. "I'm afraid not, dear," she said, in a kindly tone. "Company is a trial for him right now. But that's all right; sometime soon you'll be sure to meet him."

I hope to hell I don't meet Mother or any of her kittenish friends, Reggie thought, as he drove the auto at a snail's pace down into the village. Every bounce and rut made his knee sing with pain. This was not a bad thing, in some ways; when he was in physical pain, he could ignore the emotional turmoil within him. Grandfather had been up to his old tricks this morning, hovering just on the edge of his vision and glowering, every so often mouthing the word, "Malingerer." He'd taken refuge in the garage to overhaul the Vauxhall Prince Henry he'd bought just before the war.

That was when Budd had made the current suggestion, and he couldn't have leapt upon it faster if he'd had both good legs back.

He had Budd along with him, just in case his knee gave

out and he couldn't wrestle the old bus any further along, but he was looking forward to the day when he could go out on his own. On his own—because then, he could open her up and let tear, and if he went smash, he'd hurt no one but himself.

And if I go smash, no one's to know how much of an accident it is . . . or isn't. Once he had fought death off like a tiger. That had been before every day was a battle, and every night a little war, and he could feel his sanity slipping through his fingers like water. Maybe death was just the door into another life. At the moment, he didn't believe it. He didn't believe in a higher power, either. What higher power would *ever* let the slaughter across the Channel go on and on and on as it had? Unless that higher power were stark raving mad.

So the big thing would be to do yourself in a way that was fast, and hopefully painless. A good smash into a solid oak tree at the Prince Henry's top end would do that.

But that wouldn't be today. Today, Budd had tendered that rather awkward and shy invitation to—a pub.

"Not just any pub, milord," he'd hastily said. "Used to be the workingman's pub, afore the war, so they say. Now—" He'd shrugged. "Not many workingmen in Broom. Them of us got mustered out, took it over, more or less."

He'd captured Reggie's dull attention with that. The only men that were "mustered out" these days were those who were too maimed to go back into the lines.

"Really?" he'd said, looking up at Budd over the Prince Henry's bonnet. "Tell me more."

"Not much to tell," Budd had replied. "Just—we didn't feel none too comfortable around—people who weren't there, d'ye see?"

"I do see, believe me, I do." He had tried to give Budd that *look.* "So, no one else ever comes in?"

"Mostly not, and they mostly goes back out again pretty quick." Budd had sighed, and stared glumly down at the carburetor. "Not a cheery lot, are we. Don't go in for darts, much. Skittles, right out. Tend to swap stories as make th' old reg'lars get the collie-wobbles and look for the door.

Now, we're a rough lot. And old Mad Ross the socialist is one of us. But I wondered, milord, if you might find a pint there go down a bit easier than a brandy—" and he had jerked his head up at the house.

"I have no doubt of that," he'd said savagely, giving his wrench a hard crank. "And I'd be obliged if you'd be my introduction."

So that was how he found himself now on dusty High Street holding his fast auto to a chugging crawl she did not in the least like, while curious urchins came out to watch him pass.

Now, he had not, as a rule, held himself aloof from Broom in the old days. He wasn't at all averse to a pint or a meal at Broom Hall Inn. He tried to make some sort of a point of knowing a bit about his villagers, and he'd had a good memory for names and faces. And it was a shock, a real shock, to see what was going on now.

There was a woman delivering the mail. He thought it might be Aurora Cook. The postman *had* been Howard Sydneyson—the postmaster had been Thomas Price—

Who were both something like thirty. . . . Gone, of course, by now. Conscripted. Neither job came under the heading of "vital to the needs of the nation."

David Toback had been the constable—another shock came when Reggie saw poor old sixty-year-old Thomas Lamont making the rounds in his stead. What would *he* do to a miscreant? Talk them to death? It was a good thing that most of the troublemakers were gone too—also conscripted, or else told by the judge it was the infantry or jail.

Carlton McKenney's blacksmith shop was closed; there were no sons to take his place at the forge, and blacksmithing was no job for a daughter. . . .

Thank heaven for a moment of normality—Stephen Kirby's apothecary shop was still open with Kirby in it—but then, the poor man was the next thing to blind, and his wife Morgan had to read out all of the doctor's prescriptions to him. Not good on the front line.

The saddlery was closed. Reggie bit his lip, remembering that one of the last things he had done before going off to the RFC Flying College at Oxford was to take his hunting saddle down there for repairs.

He finally stopped glancing to the side; there always seemed to be more bad news than there was good. Finally Budd directed him to park next to a whitewashed, two-story building he wouldn't have known was a pub except for the sign "The Broom" over the door.

"Here we are, milord," Budd said, getting out. "Now, don't you mind Mad Ross. He'll probably be on you the minute you're inside."

Reggie raised an eyebrow. "If I can't manage Ross Ashley, I'm in worse condition than I thought," he said wryly.

Budd held open the door for him, and the two of them entered, Reggie going first, his cane thudding on the dark wooden floor like a third foot.

It was dark inside, with a low, beamed ceiling, and plastered walls that hadn't been painted in some time and had turned the color of perfect toast. The usual pub furniture. Big inglenook fireplace at one end. Nothing roasting on it though; whole pigs were hard to come by these days. Just a little bit of a fire to keep the chill off.

All eyes were on them as they stepped up to the bar.

"This'll be—" Budd began

"Reggie Fenyx," Reggie said gently. He held out his hand to the barman, who took it gingerly.

"Thomas Brennan, sir," the man said. "What'll it be, gents?"

"Bitter," said Reggie, and "Stout," said Budd. They took their drinks, both in good pint glasses, solid and substantial.

"That'll be my round, then," said Reggie, loud enough for the rest of the pub to hear, and cast a look around to make sure that everyone *did* hear him. Then he left a pound note casually on the bar. "And one for yourself," he added to Brennan. "Let me know when that runs out."

"Thenkee, sir." The barman made the pound note vanish.

There wasn't a rush for the bar, more of an orderly shuffle. Everyone seemed to know his place in the pecking order, and no one was in such a tearing hurry as to care to dare to jump the queue. Budd and Reggie took a little table at the back of the place to wait for people to come to them.

And predictably, the first was Ross Ashley, stumping over to them with determination on his face and a pint in one hand.

And before he could say a word, Reggie beat him to it. "Take a chair, Ross," he said mildly. "Don't stand there and sing *The Red Flag* at me, you couldn't carry a tune to save your soul, and I already know all the words."

Budd kicked a chair over to Ashley, who, all the wind knocked out of his sails, took it.

"Now, old man, if you're more of the 'share the wealth' sort of socialist and not the 'murder the oppressors in their beds,' sort, I think we can talk," said Reggie, as the rest of the pub denizens pretended to be very interested in their beers, while their ears were stretched to the furthest extent. "If you persuade me of a few things, you're a good enough speaker, and you aren't too mad, I might be persuaded to help you stand for Parliament. But you'd better be able to make a good speech and prepared to live up to what you promise in it."

Now Ross's mouth was opening and closing like a stranded fish's. Reggie was quite enjoying himself at this point—a sardonic sort of enjoyment, but more amusement than he'd had since the day Emily Welsh, his nurse in the hospital, had tipped a matchbox with a live spider in it into a particularly abusive doctor's pocket, and when the man had gone to light his cigar—

Served him right, too; acting as if the VADs were his personal slaveys.

Now, he wasn't going to do anything malicious to Ross, who he recalled as being passionate, but not particularly obnoxious. The man probably resented having one of the gentry, the oppressive ruling class invading his pub, and Reggie didn't blame him.

But he was tired of class separation. He was tired of officer and enlisted. He was tired of RFC and PBI. And he was tired to death of the boundaries between men that the war should have broken down and smashed to bits by now. He would have to take his father's seat in the House of Lords eventually—if he didn't do himself first—but he damned well would like to see a man in Commons for this district that had some ideas that weren't spawned in the seventeenth century.

Finally Ross managed to say something. "You'll not be bribing me, Reginald Fenyx," he growled. "You'll not be paying me off with the promise of a seat!"

"Of course I won't; I don't intend to." Reggie took a pull on his pint and sighed. He was very glad that Budd had brought him here. If nothing else, Brennan could brew. "And it's not a promise of a seat, it's a promise of support. You'll have to win the seat yourself; if you can't persuade people to vote for you, too bad. I want a fellow from here who'll argue for the people, even if it's against me. Better butting heads in Parliament than storming the walls of Longacre."

Ashley regarded him with a remnant of suspicion for a moment. "And I can say what I like?"

"I wouldn't begin to try to stop you," Reggie said sincerely. "Just remember you aren't recruiting for the socialists if you do go out there for a seat. You'll be stumping for votes. That's two different things. About as different as PBI and the sixty-minute men."

Once again, Ross sat there opening and closing his mouth a few times before stopping it by taking a pull of his pint.

"You are the damndest fellow I ever did see," he said, coming up out of the glass at last.

Reggie looked around, at the scarred faces, the missing limbs, the haunted looks. "I think we're all damned, Ross," he said quietly. "I think this is hell's own waiting-room. And I think we might as well make good company for each other while we're still here."

With Alison and the girls out of the house for a little, Eleanor hastily painted the glyph on the hearthstone with her sprig of rosemary (which worked better than the wand, actually), cracked it in half, and slipped out the back door and the back gate.

What she wanted was a newspaper and gossip, in that order.

It never failed to amaze her, every time that she slipped out, how no one ever recognized her, not even the people she knew well. Their eyes just slipped past her, almost as if they actually could not see her. If something happened, such as physically bumping into someone, the person in question would look down at her in puzzlement or irritation, as if they could not imagine where she had sprung from, and depending on their natures, pass on with a vague smile or an annoyed frown without saying a word.

Then again, as a scullery maid, she didn't warrant a second glance, much less an apology.

I swear, if this is ever over, I will hunt down Ross Ashley and become a socialist. . . .

The newspaper could be found on the top of Morgan Kirby's dustbin, neatly folded. An old one, of course, but *old* was better than *none.*

The gossip could be heard by creeping under the window of Nancy Barber's hairdressing establishment and listening there. Her husband had been the eponymous barber of the village, but he was gone, and Nancy had children to feed, so the barber-shop became a ladies' hairdressing salon where esoteric creations like marcel waves were produced, the very daring (or very young) had their hair bobbed, and the gossip flowed. . . .

Eleanor crept into place beneath the window just in time to catch the tail end of a sentence.

"—oh definitely back! Colonel Davies, the stationmaster, saw him when he got off the train, and his people sent a car down for him from Longacre."

Longacre! Well either they were talking about a guest or Reggie Fenyx was back from the war.

"Well, how did he look?" someone asked.

"The Colonel said none too healthy," replied the first speaker, sounding uncertain. "Though what he meant by that, I can't say."

"It could be anything," a third woman said, with resignation. "Men have no notion."

"Well, he *was* wounded. I should think he has every right to look unhealthy," said the first. "What's more interesting to me is that his mother, Lady Devlin, is having tea right this minute with Alison Robinson and her two girls."

"No!" "What?" "Really?" The replies came quickly, too quickly for the speaker to answer.

And now I understand why she was in such a pother over going to tea. It's not just that it's Lady Devlin and nobby society. It's Reggie. Unmarried Reggie.

"And her with two pretty daughters too. Hmm," said the owner of the third voice thoughtfully. "Well, we know where the wind blows *there.*"

"Social climber," said the second with contempt. "So Broom society isn't good enough for milady Robinson—"

"Be fair! She never said anything about being gentry!" said the first. "Some nob relative of hers sent Lady Devlin a letter about her."

"At least *now* she'll stop her girls angling for every lad with a bit in his pocket here," said the second. "Not that they're so many on the ground anymore, but still."

"With your Tamara about?" giggled the third. "Those chits didn't have a chance. Oh, I wish you'd seen them at the Christmas party, swanning about in their fashionable London frocks, and in comes Tamara in her two-year-old velvet from Glennis White, and there go all the officers! Oh, their faces were a sight!"

"Fine feathers aren't everything," the mother of the village beauty, Tamara Budd, said complacently. "Nor, when it comes to it, is a pretty face, if there's a mean, nasty heart behind it."

Eleanor didn't have to hide a smirk, since there was no one to see her. If there was a single soul in all of the village that her stepsisters hated, truly hated, it was Tamara Budd. She had been pretty when Eleanor had been locked within the walls of the house. Now, evidently, she had blossomed into true beauty, for any time some entertainment was on offer, be it a tea-dance for soldiers or a gathering at some house or at the Broom Hall Inn, according to the girls, it was Tamara who was the center of male attention.

There was no doubt that the stepsisters would have killed or disfigured her if they could. Eleanor could tell that from the vicious things they said, the way they stabbed their cigarettes in the air, the mere tone that their voices took when they spoke about her.

For her part, she might have been alarmed that they would succeed in doing Tamara harm, except that she also heard them complaining that something protected their rival from any charms or cantrips they attempted to cast. She had a good idea that it might be Sarah who was responsible, but you never knew.

She listened a while longer, but it was clear enough that there was nothing more to hear, and it would not be long before Alison and girls returned from their tea with Lady Devlin.

She crept out of hiding, and hurried back to the kitchen with her purloined newspaper hidden in the folds of her skirt. From there it went underneath the pile of logs for the stove and the kitchen fire; there wasn't a chance that either of the girls nor Alison would move a single one of those logs. Now that she had gotten outside—and discovered what shocking changes had happened to the world that she had known—she was afire to find out how much more had been happening.

Not that any of it had been good. She had read with horror of ships being torpedoed by German submarines and sent to the bottom with most of their human cargo—even hospital ships! Bombs had actually been dropped on parts of London and the eastern coast by both zeppelins and huge aeroplanes and several hundred perfectly innocent people had been blown to bits. As for the war itself, her head reeled to think about it, and she knew she was getting no more than the barest, most sanitized idea of what was going on from the papers. How could something be a "glorious victory" when all it got you was possession of a long trench a hundred yards east of where you had been when an assault started—a trench you had occupied several times already, only to have been driven out of it by the Germans—who doubtless also crowed about their "glorious victory."

She couldn't help but wonder, was *this* how her father had died? No one had ever told her the details. All that she had ever known was that he was dead. She had nightmares about it sometimes; that he was blown to pieces by a shell, that he was killed in a charge, that he was shot by a sniper. That he died instantly, or that he had lain in agony for hours, while his fellow soldiers watched, unable to help him. It was horrible; she woke from those dreams sobbing, and only seeking solace from the little Salamanders in her fire helped.

She sighed, and went to work on dinner preparations. The girls were going to get chicken stew and dumplings, and like it, for it was the only way to stretch the poor, thin chicken that had come by way of the butcher shop today.

So, Reggie Fenyx was home again—and looking ill, and had been wounded. She could not imagine the energetic young man, boiling over with enthusiasm that she had known, as being ill or hurt. Such a thing never seemed possible.

But she couldn't imagine him in a uniform, either.

She couldn't think of him as shooting people, and killing them; he had always seemed so gentle in his way.

As she chopped vegetables, she reflected that now she knew why Alison was so afire over the invitation to tea with Lady Devlin—so much so, that the girls had left frocks spread all over their rooms for her to pick up, trying on this one and that one until Alison was satisfied with their appearance. It all made perfect sense. Alison wanted to get invitations up to Longacre Park so that the girls would have an unrestricted chance to snare Reggie.

She chopped savagely at the old, withered carrots. Miserable creatures! They would do nothing other than make poor Reggie unhappy! Here he was coming home in a weakened state, and they were going to descend on him like vultures to nibble on the carcass—

But wait a moment; hadn't Sarah said that the Fenyx family were Elemental Masters?

She had!

Eleanor felt her shoulders unknot. Of course. Reggie was an Air Master; Alison's girls would have no more chance of bewitching him than of taking one of his aeroplanes up by themselves.

But that opened up another thought. If Reggie was an Air Master, wouldn't he be able to *see* the magic spells on her? And even if he couldn't do anything about them himself, couldn't he tell someone who could?

Her heart fluttered in her throat at the very idea—

Don't get your hopes up, she scolded herself severely. *First you have to get out of here. Then you have to be somewhere that he is. And last, he has to be willing to help you.*

Still, the mere *chance* of a hope was more than she'd had in a long time.

I can at least make plans.

11

April 23, 1917
Broom, Warwickshire

"SO THE BLOODY YANKS FINALLY decided to give us a hand, then." That was Matt Brennan, the barman's brother. Poor Matt had lost a leg and his arm had been terribly mangled, and half the time seemed to have lost his speech as well. Brother Thomas kept him on as potman, collecting the glasses, doing a bit of sweeping up, and let him sleep somewhere on the premises once the place was closed. It wasn't much, but it was work.

The news had finally percolated to Broom that the United States had actually joined the war that the rest of the world had been fighting for the past three years, and it was likely to be the sole topic of conversation here in this pub for the rest of the week. Everyone who came in started it over again.

"What d'ye think of them Yanks, captain?" Ross Ashley asked. "Never caught sight of one myself."

"Well," Reggie said, measuring his words carefully. "We got quite a few Yanks in the RFC, boys that wouldn't sit still and watch while someone else was having a fight. I heard the French picked up a few, especially in the Foreign Legion."

"So they got the gumption to stick it, ye think?" asked Will Stevens, who had been a good yeoman farmer before the war began, and was again, just without three fingers on his right hand.

Reggie shrugged. "Hard to tell, really. The ones I saw all seemed to think of themselves as being in some sort of Wild West show. Talked about 'flying by the seat of the pants,' didn't pay a lot of attention to instruction, and tended to be 'thirty-minute men' if that. Though when they were good enough to survive, they were *quite* good. I don't know what their infantry will be like."

Young Albert Norman (chest wound, lost a lung) coughed and cleared his throat. Mind, he coughed a great deal, but this was the sort of cough he used when about to say something.

"There are a great many of them," he said carefully. "It's a bigger country than Canada. And I shouldn't think it would be too terribly difficult for them to turn all those factories to making armaments."

Reggie nodded. Albert was well read; Reggie didn't doubt in the least that he had the right of it.

"So," Doug Baird (shrapnel to the legs) said bitterly. "We'll have fought the Kaiser to a standstill for three bloody years, and the Yanks will just come in with convoys of fresh troops and all the damned supplies you could ask for, roll over the trenches, and take credit for the whole thing, then?"

Reggie sighed. To be brutally honest, he didn't see it turning out any other way. But he decided not to say anything. These men were bitter enough without his adding to their discontent—or despair.

"At least it will be over," Richard Bowen said, with resignation. "That's all I care about. Just let it be over."

Thomas Brennan cleared his throat. "Last call, gentlemen."

"My round again," Reggie said decisively.

He did a lot of round-buying—not so much as to make it seem as if he was patronizing them, but because he knew very well that there was not a lot of money to spare in their households, and it seemed a hard thing to him to have a man leave bits of himself in France in the service of his country only to find he couldn't afford his pint when he came home again. A hard thing, and a wicked, cruel thing; there wasn't a lot of pleasure left in the world for these men.

Those that had gone back to their work—farmers, mostly—were finding it difficult. Those who hadn't lost limbs outright still had injuries bad enough to muster them out. Legs didn't work right anymore, arms didn't have the same strength. They found themselves depending on their wives or children to help them with difficult physical jobs, and that was humiliating. Often the young horses they'd depended on to help with plowing had been taken for the war, leaving only the old fellows who should have been taking up pasture-space. They found themselves with a house full of Land Girls, who might or might not be of any use. Nothing was the same, everything was more difficult, and what had they gotten out of it all? Nothing to speak of. The best, the very best that they could say was that because they were at the production end of the food supply it was easier for them to hide a bit from the government and circumvent some of the shortages. If you were a farmer, you could still have your sweets, if you made do with honey instead of sugar, and though sugar was rationed for tea, it was, oddly enough, *not* rationed for jam-making—you could hide a pig in your wood-lot, or raise rabbits openly, since rabbit-meat wasn't in short supply. When you brought your wheat to David Miller, he'd generally "forget" about a few of the bags of white flour he loaded back on your cart. And if you had a cow of your own, your kiddies weren't forced to drink that thin, blue skimmed milk that made the city children so thin and pale-looking.

But that was the best you could say. For the rest, between rationing and scarcity, the prices were up, and what you got for your produce was the same as it had been before the war, just about. Someone was making a profit, but it wasn't you.

And if you didn't own or lease a farm—well, things were very hard indeed. Sometimes you couldn't do your old job, and it was hard to find a new one. Especially around here.

So if Reggie could help out a little by buying more than his share of rounds, it seemed a small thing.

Mater wouldn't like it by half if she knew where I was going of a night. Hanging about with socialists. . . . But what she doesn't know, she can't object to. I'm more welcome here than there. Her father had gotten so poisonously aggressive in his accusations of malingering of late that even *she* had started to protest weakly. Never mind that there were days Reggie couldn't leave his room, days when he locked the door and spent half the day crouched in a corner like a terrified mouse, too afraid to so much as move. "Acting" was what Grandfather Sutton would have called it. Oh, yes, acting. As if he enjoyed spending his time huddled behind the furniture too afraid to make a sound, and completely unable to say what it was he was afraid of, only knowing that the bottom was out of the universe and doom was upon him.

But there was a letter in Reggie's pocket right now that might well prove to be the old man's undoing.

The address on the envelope said it all: *Brigadier Eric Mann (Ret.) The Elms, Dorcester.*

The Brigadier had been a great friend of Reggie's father—he had more experience in a single month with actual combat than Grandfather Sutton had in his entire career. His letter had been phrased with great delicacy, but Reggie had no difficulty whatsoever in interpreting it. The Brigadier had heard about Reggie's injuries, he actually *knew* what life was like on the front, and he wanted to come visit and offer whatever support he could.

And although in general the very last thing that Reggie wanted at the moment was a parade of visitors through Longacre, this was one letter he had answered as soon as he had read it, in the affirmative. The Brigadier *did* know what life was like on the front. He had been there. How? Reggie had no idea how he had managed to get out there—but the little he'd read in the letter told him that

Eric Mann knew what conditions were really like. The Brigadier would not tolerate any nonsense from Grandfather Sutton. With any luck, once they butted heads a time or two, Sutton would elect to clear out and go back to his club in London and leave Reggie in peace. At the very least, he would keep his mouth shut as long as the Brigadier was there.

Reggie could hardly wait.

"Time, gentlemen!" Thomas called, recalling him to his present surroundings.

There was little more than a half inch of bitter in his glass; he swallowed it down with appreciation, left a little something under the glass for Matt to find, stood up, and pulled on his driving coat. That was one good thing about having an auto over a horse; he didn't have to worry about leaving a horse standing tied up for hours.

On the other hand, the auto won't get you home by itself if you're drunk. . . .

He made his farewells and went out into the night; he really couldn't bear watching the others make their way home. It was just too heartbreaking. If a man staggered away from his favorite pub of an evening, it should be because he'd had just a wee bit too much, not because his legs were too painful to hold him.

Nor because one leg was gone, and he wasn't used to walking on the wooden one.

Instead, he paid excruciatingly careful attention to getting the auto started; by the time he'd done, they were all gone. He climbed stiffly into the driver's seat, and chugged away.

"Well! There goes that Reggie Fenyx again," Sarah said, as the unfamiliar sound of an automobile engine chugged past the front of her cottage.

Eleanor looked up from the runes of warding that she had been learning. "How do you know?"

Sarah snorted. "And who else is it that would be leaving Thomas Brennan's pub after last call in a motorcar?" she asked rhetorically. "Doctor Sutherland's choice is the public bar at the Broom Hall Inn when he goes anywhere, Steven Zachary hasn't *got* a motor of his own yet, the vicar doesn't drink in public, so there you are! Besides, I happen to know the lads that have all been mustered out have taken the place over since Matt came home, and I expect he feels more at ease there among them than anywhere else."

Eleanor looked down at the little firepot she was using. "It's horrible, isn't it." It was a statement, not a question. "It's horrible, and they can't talk to anyone else about it."

"Well, they *could,*" Sarah replied, somewhat to Eleanor's surprise. "They *could* talk to their wives, their sweethearts, their mothers. We're stronger than they think. They keep thinking they have to protect us from whatever it is that they went through, so there they are, suffering behind closed mouths, building walls to protect us, they say, but it's all so we won't see they're weak." She shook her head. "As if we don't. But there it is. Silly, isn't it? That they daren't let us see them as less than strong?"

Eleanor looked up and lifted an eyebrow. "I think I see why you never married, Sarah," she replied, with irony.

Sarah laughed. "Well, and I reckoned if I wanted something that'd come and go as he pleased, take me for granted, and ignore me when he chose, I'd get a cat. And if I wanted something I'd always have to be picking up after, getting into trouble, but slavishly devoted, I'd get a dog."

Eleanor shook her head and went back to her firepot, which was a little cast-iron pot on three legs, full of coals over which flames danced bluely. She was learning to write runes in the fire, which was the first step to making it answer her. A Salamander was coiled in the bottom of the pot just above the coals; it watched her with interest, and hissed a warning when she was just starting to go wrong.

Her moment of inattention made it hiss again, and Sarah paused to look down at it. "They're not supposed to do that, you know," she said, in surprise. "Warn you, that is. It's almost like it's trying to help you."

"I think it is," Eleanor said, canceling the rune with a wave of her wand, and holding out her hand to the pot. The salamander uncoiled itself and leapt out of the pot, circled her wrists like ferret three or four times, then leapt back into the pot.

Sarah shook her head. "They're not supposed to do that. I'd not have believed it if I'd been told. There's summat about you they like."

"I hope so," she replied.

"Aye, well, they're not so changeable as air and water, though be wary you don't go angering them," Sarah warned. "They're quick to anger, and they ne'er forget, nor forgive."

Eleanor nodded, and bent back to her work. But part of her mind was on Reggie, wondering if Carolyn and Lauralee had been introduced to him, yet, if they'd started trying to charm him yet. It made her angry, that thought, and—yes—jealous. Which made no sense at all. He probably didn't even remember her, and if he did, it was as nothing more than a hoydenish tomboy, a silly little girl with a wild notion of becoming a scholar. He probably wouldn't remember her even if someone reminded him of her.

And as for now, he wouldn't look at her twice. She certainly was so far beneath his notice that if they passed on the same side of the street he wouldn't even see her, not really.

Stop thinking about Reggie! she scolded herself. *Get your mind on your work. Because if you can't learn this soon, Alison and her girls will have him, and then where will you be?*

"Don't bother fixing anything for tea, Ellie," Alison called through the open kitchen door. "We're having it at Longacre. In fact—" Eleanor could not help but hear the gloating sound in her voice "we'll be having our tea at Longacre for the foreseeable future."

"Yes, ma'am," Eleanor said dutifully, but her heard leapt. Tea at Longacre Park? And for the foreseeable future? That would mean she would be able to get away for the whole afternoon.

Of course, Alison would see it as another privation—if she wasn't permitted to get out tea-things for her stepmother and the girls, she wouldn't be able to make any tea for herself. Which meant that she would have to wait until suppertime for a meal.

Or so Alison thought. *Well, that's what I want her to think.* So Eleanor contrived to look disappointed and hungry, though she was neither. She could hardly contain her excitement as Alison and her girls bundled up into the motor and chugged off in the direction of Longacre Park. And the moment she was sure they weren't going to return, she wrote her runes on the hearthstone and was off like a shot.

The sky was bright and blue, the wind high, and she only had a few hours—but she knew where *she* wanted to be. Down at the opposite end of the six thousand or so acres of Longacre, in the round meadow in a little copse of trees at the end of what she still thought of as the Aeroplane Field. No one would see her there, no one ever went there; she was half mad to get out of the house for some sun and air. And this was the farthest Alison's spell would let her go.

She wrapped up a couple of slices of bread and jam for her own tea, broke her sprig of rosemary and left half on the hearthstone, flung on a coat and ran out the door.

She wasn't even entirely sure what she was running *from.* Maybe it was—well—everything. Her own imprisonment. The war news. Alison's glee and the girls' gloating. And fear, fear, so much fear—now she knew she had a chance to set herself free, and she was afraid. Afraid she would never learn all she needed to, afraid that she would never be able to command her Element as skillfully as Alison could and would lose, and her imprisonment would be even harsher than it was now. Afraid that ever if she did escape, no one would believe what she had to tell them, and she would accomplish nothing, or worse than nothing—that she'd be locked up as mad, or given back over to Alison, or else would have to turn drudge for someone else in order to put food in her stomach and a roof over her head. In a way, things were worse than before; before she'd had no hope and so nothing to lose. Now—now she had hope and all to lose.

So she ran, hoping to outrun her own fear and uncertainty. Hoping to outrun the bleak air of depression that hung over the entire town. Hoping to get to one place where none of this mattered, where she could just *be* for a few hours, and pretend that there was no war, there was no Alison, that the days of peace and plenty were still upon them all, and that when she came back to the house her father would still be alive and waiting to share supper with her.

She pushed herself so hard, trying to outrun her very thoughts, that she arrived at the meadow winded and out of breath, and flung herself down in the middle of the clear space among the trees to lie on her back in the old, dry grass and look up at the clouds and pant.

And it was glorious, because she could just empty her mind and not think, not about anything or anyone, and just stare up into the blue and watch nothing.

She could, in fact, have lain there forever, with the warm sun shining down on her. At that moment, cutting free of Alison and just *going,* finding someone else to work for, didn't seem so bad an idea—

Except—

If she did this to me, and to Papa, what would she do to Reggie?

The question struck her like a thunderbolt out of the blue sky, but at that moment she knew that if either Carolyn or Lauralee married Reggie Fenyx, no matter how strong his Air Magic was, he would remain alive no longer than her father had.

She sat bolt upright at the thought—

—and a yelp of strangled fear met her sudden appearance out of the grass.

She twisted around onto her knees to face the sound, and found herself staring into the white face of Reggie Fenyx.

He was sitting on a fallen tree-trunk at the edge of the tiny meadow, quite alone, and clearly her sudden appearance had frightened the wits out of him. As he stared at her with wild, wide eyes, all she could think of to do was to hold out her hand and say, soothingly, "I'm sorry—I beg your pardon—I'm really very sorry—"

He trembled as he stared at her, as if he didn't quite recognize her for what she was. And then, quite suddenly, she saw sense come into his gaze, and of course, he *did* recognize her, and passed a hand over his pale face. "No—no—" he said, finally. "No, it's quite all right. It's just my nerves. I wasn't expecting anyone—that is, I thought I was alone; no one ever used to come down to this part of Longacre but me."

"Well," she said, slowly getting to her feet, brushing down her threadbare skirt with one hand, and wondering hesitantly if she should leave. "That isn't quite true. But most of the people who used to come here are gone."

"Gone. That would be—the boys, wouldn't it?" His hand was still over his eyes, and still trembling. "Yes. Not boys any longer, though, and they *would* be gone, wouldn't they? Even the youngest." With an effort, he took his hand away from his eyes and looked at her again. She was horribly ashamed of how shabby she was, but he didn't notice, or at least, if he did, he wasn't letting on. He squinted at her, and then managed a tremulous smile. "You're that little tomboy, Eleanor Robinson from the village, aren't you? Only not such a little tomboy anymore." The smile faded. "I heard about your father. I'm dreadfully sorry."

She looked down at her hands, clasped together in front of her. "Thank you," she said quietly. Then she looked back up again. She kept her frown to herself, but—

But wasn't he supposed to be an Air Master? Yet there were none of the energies, none of the Elementals of Air anywhere about him! Why, he showed no more of magic than—than the schoolmaster, Michael Stone! Less!

Surely that wasn't right.

"So, do you come and invade my private property often?" he was asking, trying to sound normal, trying to make an ordinary conversation of the sort he could so easily back before the war began.

And now she found herself fighting against the prohibitions of Alison's other spells. She would have *liked* to say, "When I can escape my stepmother's spell—" or "When no one is going to catch me and make my life a purgatory—"

But all she could say was, "When I can." Then she sighed. "It's so peaceful here, and sometimes I can't bear how things are now. Here, nothing's changed. It's all the way it was—before. The meadow probably hasn't changed in a hundred years."

"That's a good answer, Eleanor Robinson," he replied. "That's a very good answer, and I give you leave to come here whenever you want. It's the reason I came down here—well, I tell a lie, it's *one* of the reasons." He smiled wanly. "My teatime has been unconscionably invaded, and I came to escape the enemy."

She furrowed her brow in puzzlement, and stepped forward a pace or two. "Enemy?" she asked uncertainly.

"Women," he elaborated. "A gaggle of women. Invited by my mother, with malice and intent. Those that weren't there on their own to simper and flirt at me, were mothers eyeing the goods before they set their own daughters on the scent." He shuddered. "I felt like the only fox in the county with three hunts in the field at once."

She couldn't help it; she had to laugh at that. Especially considering that Alison and the girls must have been in that group he so openly despised.

And they thought they were the only ones with an invitation to tea! That was more than enough to make her smile. Oh, they would be so angry when they came home! They hadn't reckoned on there being competition. They should have, though. Reggie would have been quite a prize before the war, and now, with so many young men dead in France and Flanders, he was an even greater prize.

And the best part was that they would be blaming one another. Alison would be blaming the girls for not being sufficiently charming to keep Reggie there, and the girls would be blaming their mother for not knowing this was going to be a competition staged by Reggie's mother, inadvertently or on purpose. There was not a single thing that any of them could blame on *her,* so they would make poisonous jibes at each other, or stare sullenly, all through dinner.

And meanwhile, here he was, the object of their hunt, hiding from them.

"I'll go if you want to be alone," she offered. It only seemed fair. He'd come here to *be* alone, hadn't he? "I just—I just wanted to go somewhere today where I could pretend that—all that—hadn't happened. At least for a while."

"I wanted the same thing," he said, and somehow, the wistful, yet completely hopeless way in which he said it, made her heart ache for him. "And—no, Miss Robison—"

"Eleanor," she said, instantly.

He smiled a little. "Then if I am to call you Eleanor, you must promise to call me Reggie. No, please don't go. I'm not much company, but I don't want to think I've driven you away from the only peaceful place you can find."

He patted the tree-trunk beside him in a kind of half-hearted invitation to sit; instead, she sat down in the grass at his feet.

He looked a great deal different from the last time she had seen him, and it wasn't just the little moustache or the close-cropped military haircut. He was very pale, and every movement had a nervous quality to it, like one of those high-bred miniature greyhounds that never seems entirely sure something isn't going to step on it or snatch it up and bite it in two. He was also very thin, much thinner than she remembered him being.

And his eyes, his gray-blue eyes, were the saddest things about him. "Haunted" was the very expression she would have used, had anyone asked her. These were eyes that had seen too much, too much loss, too much horror.

She felt tongue-tied, at a loss for anything to say to him, and it was clear that he felt the same. Finally, she said, in desperation, knowing that the topic of an automobile was at least safe, "I heard your motorcar go past the other night. Is it a very fast one?"

With relief, he seized the neutral subject as a drowning man seizes a plank, and went into exacting, excruciating detail about the auto. She had to admit, although she didn't care a jot about the insides of the thing, the other things he could tell her about the auto itself were fascinating. Evidently its type had won many races, and there was no doubt that he was as proud of it as he had been of his aeroplane.

And something instinctively warned her about not talking about flying, though she couldn't have told what. Perhaps it was the vague recollection of hearing his wounds had come when he had crashed. Perhaps it was because he himself didn't bring the subject up, and before he had gone off to the war, that had been the one thing in his life he had been the most passionate about.

When he ran out of things to tell her about his motorcar, she asked about what he had read for at Oxford, and what his friends had been like. He relaxed, more and more, as he spoke of these things, and she thought she just might be doing him some good. Finally, when he looked as if he was searching a little too hard for another good story, she smiled, and asked, "I have some bread and jam. Would you like to share *my* tea?"

And at that, he laughed weakly, and quoted, " 'Better a dinner of herbs where love is?' Yes, thank you, I should very much like to share your tea. And—" He reached down behind the trunk of the tree and brought up an old rucksack, rummaging around in it for a moment. "Well, yes, good, my old instincts have not failed me; as I fled the harpies, I carried off provender. I can provide drink. I have two bottles of ginger-beer."

With great solemnity he opened the bottles and handed her one; she passed over half of her slightly squashed jam sandwiches.

"I think it was very rude of your mother not to have

warned you that guests were coming," she said bluntly, after they clinked bottles. "Especially so many. That was not at all fair."

"Yes, well, if she'd *told* me I'd have done the bunk beforehand, now, wouldn't I?" he replied logically. "I suppose now I'll have to find some excuse to avoid teatime every day from now on—"

"Oh, don't do that—she'll just invite them to supper or something equally inconvenient!" Eleanor exclaimed. "No, the thing to do—" she screwed up her face as she thought hard. "The thing to do is to sit through it once in a while. Every other day, or every third day, or the like. Only have something, some appointment or task later in the afternoon that you *have* to do so you can excuse yourself after an hour or two. That way your mother won't ever know when, exactly, you're going to take tea with her, and *you* will have a good escape ready."

"By Jove, Eleanor, I think that will work! And I know my estate manager will be only too ruddy pleased to have me in the office as often as possible, so I can make that my excuse." He actually looked—happy. Wanly happy, but definitely for one moment, happy. "You should be a tactician, old girl!"

And just at that most pleasant moment, she felt the first faint tugging of Alison's hearth-spell, and looked down to see the sprig of rosemary pinned to the breast of her shirtwaist starting to wilt. She could have cursed. "I have to go!" she exclaimed, jumping to her feet. "I'm really sorry, but I must—"

"What's the hurry?" he asked in bewilderment, as she shoved the empty ginger-beer bottle into his hands. "I say, I haven't said anything to offend you, have I?"

"No, no, no, I just have to get back, I don't have a choice," she shook her head and felt the sting of disappointed tears in her eyes. "It's nothing to do with you; I enjoyed talking with you. I have to or—or—or I'll be in trouble—" she shook her head, and turned away.

"Well, at least say you'll be here tomorrow!" he called after her, as she began to run across the grass.

"I can't—" she called back over her shoulder, then at the sight of his stricken face, she made a reckless promise. "I'll come—I'll come whenever I can! At teatime! Whenever I can!"

And with that, she had to turn to race back to the house, back to captivity, an imprisonment that was now more onerous than it ever had seemed before.

12

April 28, 1917
Broom, Warwickshire

DINNER WAS NOT PLEASANT TONIGHT. Animosity and suspicion hung over the table like the cloud of cigarette smoke rising above the heads of all three of the Robinsons at the table. "I don't understand it," Alison said, glaring at her daughters. "He hasn't shown the least bit of interest in either of you. That is just—unnatural."

"It wasn't my spells, Mama," Carolyn said petulantly, tossing her head. "You checked them yourself. You *watched* me work them." She looked sideways at her sister. "Unless *you* interfered—"

But Alison wasn't accepting that excuse. "She didn't interfere; don't you think I would be able to tell?" Alison snarled. "No, it's not that. I've never seen anyone who was so unaffected by spells, and that's not natural. Even men with no magic at all respond to sex-charms."

Eleanor was unashamedly eavesdropping, and by a means that her stepmother would never guess. If Alison came to look, she would find Eleanor stoically peeling potatoes at the hearth, staring into the fire. Little did she guess that what Eleanor was staring at was not the flames. She had learned a new spell, or to be more precise, she had improvised it out of a scrying spell in Sarah's grimoire, that was supposed to use mirrors, linking the mirrors together, like a transmitter and a wireless radio, so that whatever was reflected in the target mirror was reflected in the one that the scryer held.

Only instead of mirrors, Eleanor was using the flames on the hearth in the kitchen and the one in the dining-room. It had been very odd, actually—Sarah had been struck dumb when she first tried it. And she could not imagine where she had gotten the idea that such a thing would work, either; it just—came to her, as she was reading the grimoire, as if someone had told it to her.

Now it was as if she was looking out from the fireplace there, and what was more, she was able to *hear* everything that went on as clearly as if she was sitting right there.

"It isn't only sex-charms he doesn't respond to," Lauralee said, stabbing her cigarette down into the center of her plate. "I tried to make him loathe that Leva Cygnet girl, and instead, he sat next to her at tea!"

"And I thought you said he was an Air Master, Mama," interrupted Carolyn. "But I haven't seen a single Sylph anywhere about him, nor any hint of magic. Are you *sure* he's an Air Master?"

And when Carolyn said *that,* Eleanor watched Alison go through the most curious pantomime she had ever seen in her life. Alison opened her mouth to say something—then a puzzled look came over her—then she closed her mouth, opened it again, closed it, and frowned.

The girls stared at her, as if they had never seen their mother so nonplussed either.

Eleanor wondered what it meant.

"No Sylphs about," Alison said, consideringly. "As if the Sylphs do not recognize him as having Air Mastery either. No Zephyrs. They can't see him—I'm sure that's what that means. And yet, no shields, either. As if . . . as if he is a magical cipher, a null. . . ."

"Actually, Mama," Lauralee said reflectively. "It's more as if the spells we cast on him are just swallowed up."

"Drained away," Carolyn echoed. "Or reflected, but not back at us."

"How . . . odd. Then I believe we are going to have to rethink our strategy," Alison brooded. "I wanted him to be attracted to you before I went to work more directly. I am going to need to make new plans."

"What new plans, Mama?" Lauralee asked leaning forward over the table eagerly. "Are you going to teach us new magic?"

Eleanor watched as Alison rubbed her hands along her arms uneasily. "Well, the magic that you two can cast is clearly not going to work. In fact, I would say he is probably resistant to all but the most powerful magic."

Both of them gazed at their mother with hunger now. Eleanor had wondered, ever since Sarah had come to the door, if Alison had been purposefully holding back teaching her daughters, or if her daughters were just not capable of greater magic. It was hard to tell—though it was true that none of the Earth Elementals were attracted to the girls.

Now she heard the answer, or at least, the answer that Alison was going to give them. "I'm afraid, my dears, you have no more inborn ability with magic than Warrick Locke. And I don't think at this point it would be wise to use my greater magics for more than I already have planned. So instead of using magic, use your wiles; show no jealousy of the other girls, but be the most pleasant and charming creatures in the room. Pay attention to everything he does and says. Work out what pleases him and what he would prefer not to deal with. Be sympathetic, and find things to get his mind off the war. That will do for now. Meanwhile, I will need to do some research of my own."

Eleanor had wondered about that. Her own feeling, once she had begun learning about magic herself, had been that neither girl would ever be a Master—because if that were possible for them, they would have surely shown some sign of it by now.

"Yes, Mama," the two chorused as one. They left the table to go up to their rooms, as Alison rang for Eleanor to clean up.

Is that *why Reggie recognized me, when no one else in the village does?* she wondered, as she carried plates back to the kitchen. *Because Alison's spells just don't work on him?*

It hadn't been until she had gotten back to the kitchen after first meeting him that she had realized Reggie had *recognized* her, had known who she was, almost from the first moment he had seen her. Other than Sarah, he was, apparently, the only other person who did. And she hadn't been able to get away to ask Sarah why that could be since the meeting.

Events in the household had conspired against her. First, despite Alison's assertion that she and the girls would be having tea up at Longacre for the foreseeable future, that hadn't exactly come to pass. The next day had been Alison's "at home," and although Alison certainly wanted to claw her way into the social circles of Longacre, she knew better than to abandon her post as leading light of Broom. For one thing, there were quite a number of things that the ladies of Broom could do to undermine Alison's progress if they chose. And for another, as she explained to her daughters, there was no point in prematurely burning bridges. The social set of Broom was still useful—particularly that centered around the vicarage, for the vicar, Donald Hinshaw, and his wife Theresa were the one couple who traveled socially freely between village and the big house.

Then the next day had been a meeting of the Ladies' Friendly Society, and it had been held at The Arrows, though under the auspices of its president, Amy Hammer. It had been yet another bandage-rolling meeting, and as a consequence, the house had been filled with women, all of whom required tea and refreshments. Now, those meetings were ones at which Eleanor had to be particularly careful of what was served; it wouldn't do at all to make it look as if this household was immune from the current privations—but at the same time, Alison was adamant that the tea be something that would elevate her status as a hostess. It all came down on Eleanor's shoulders, of course. It meant a great deal of cutting up heavy brown bread into thin, thin slices, toasting it delicately, and removing the crusts, spreading it with layers of jam and potted shrimp. It meant cutting more wafer-thin slices of brown bread and adding wafer-thin slices of smoked Scottish salmon atop. It meant baking whatever sort of cake could be managed with what was available in the village shops.

So that pretty well put paid to getting away that day. And the next, Warrick Locke had come for the afternoon. It had been all about business and legal papers; there was a good clue now to which sort of "business" was going on when Locke showed up. If it was mundane business, he brought with him his personal secretary, a curiously opaque lady named Jennifer Summers, as well as his "man," Robbie Christopher. Eleanor was not around Miss Summers enough to make a judgment of her, but Robbie made her flesh crawl. There was just something not right about him. As a consequence, she kept well out of their way. Locke spent the entire afternoon closeted with Alison, going over any number of matters concerning the manufactories.

He might be a horrible man, but he did know his business.

So, that meant no leaving the house on that day.

Finally, though, today had sent Alison and the girls out into the village on a series of meetings and whatnot concerning the annual May Day fete for the church, which brought them home exhausted, and made them perfect targets for Sarah's herb-spell. They were in bed by nine and fast asleep by ten, all three of them, and Eleanor was free to cast her spell and run to Sarah's cottage.

Sarah wasn't alone—Annette Monstead, the village midwife-in-training, and sister to Eric, the village sexton, was with her, discussing a possibly difficult case. Rather than intrude, Eleanor didn't even knock; she just waited outside until Annette left. It was scarcely a hardship; it was a beautiful evening, the kind on which—before the war—courting couples would go out walking.

Though that "walking" sometimes resulted in cases for Annette. . . .

Proper young ladies weren't supposed to know about

that sort of thing, but Eleanor had never been proper as such—and since the war, there was, if not actually condoning of such matters, certainly more understanding of them, and of the acts of desperation that led to an unexpected pregnancy. A fellow could get emergency leave, at least to get as far as London for a day or two to "put things right." There was not so much counting of months between the wedding-day and the day of the baby's arrival.

Eric turned up to escort his sister home—he, too, was above the conscription age, though his sister was at least twenty years younger. He was the eldest, and she the youngest, of a truly enormous family. Not so much a family as a tribe, in fact. Small wonder Annette had turned out to have a talent for midwifery!

Only after they were gone out of sight did Eleanor knock on Sarah's door and let herself in.

"I've met Reggie!" she burst out, unable to hold herself back. "And Sarah—he *recognized* me!"

"Well, and he would, wouldn't he, being an Air Master—" she began, but this time Eleanor interrupted her.

"Yes, but there's no Sylphs around him, and no Air energy," she continued, and went on to describe what she had learned watching the fire night after night.

When she was finished, Sarah stood next to her own hearth, arms folded over her chest, tapping her foot. "Hmm. That's a different kettle of fish altogether. It almost sounds like—" But then she frowned, and shook her head. "No, I don't know. And it's not right to speculate. I don't know nearly as much as your mother did, and sending you off in the wrong direction wouldn't do either of you any good."

"Sarah!" Eleanor cried indignantly. "At least give me a hint!"

Sarah pursed her lips, and ran her hand through her hair. "Well, if I were to guess, and not being a Master, I have no business in guessing, I would say that something happened to him to make him afraid of using any magic. Now, when a Master decides not to use any magic, none at all, sometimes they stop thinking straight, and their heart—not their heads, the thinking parts, put the heart, the feeling part—is so frightened that the heart decides that means no magic by anyone else is going to get used around them either. So magic around them gets kind of—swallowed up. Things that the heart decides usually happen unless the head is well in charge." Sarah shrugged. "But that's just a guess. People like me don't have enough magic to do that sort of thing."

"But if that's the case, then why couldn't I tell him about Alison?" she asked, feeling desperate now. "Why didn't *that* spell stop working?"

Sarah grimaced, but with an air as if it should have been obvious to Eleanor that she had no idea why these things had happened or not. "Don't know. Maybe because that spell is stronger. Maybe because the spell to keep people from recognizing you is set to work on *them* and the one to keep you from telling people the truth is set to work on *you.*" She shook her head. "I don't know, I'm just guessing. I'm not the Master Alison is, nor the Master your mother was. I know I've had my own counter-charms set that let *me* see you and talk to you freely, but then, I already knew what and who you were and I had a bit of your baby-hair I could use to work them. I don't *know* the complicated spells; I never bothered to learn them. I'm only strong enough to work cantrips and charms. In the case of countering what's on you, I can make them work for me, but not other people, unless I were to set the charm on each one of them. And maybe all of this guessing is going wide of the mark. I've no way to know."

It was terribly frustrating. To know that she had someone within reach who *probably* could help her break the spells that were on her, if only he knew what was going on, was agonizing.

"What do I do?" she wailed. Sarah gazed at her sternly.

"You stop whingeing for one," the witch replied. "It isn't going to help. For another, if you can find out what it is he's so afraid of, maybe you can do somewhat about it. Do that, and he may come out of that shell he's built around himself. If you can crack that, he should see you're set about with spells yourself, and wonder why, and try untangling them himself. But you can't do any of that if you're wasting your time feeling sorry for yourself."

Eleanor felt herself flush with anger, but kept a curb on her tongue. Sarah was right—but the witch's tongue got oversharp when she'd had a long day. And it wasn't as if Eleanor's day had been any shorter.

"Now, in the meantime," Sarah was already continuing, "While you're here, you might as well learn something. If Alison ever decides to challenge you Master to Master in a Sorcerer's Duel, your little Salamanders aren't going to be causing her more than a minute of amusement. So you might as well start learning how to call the Greater Fire Elementals, and the best time is now. We'll start with the Phoenyx."

Eleanor was quite ready to fall asleep on Sarah's floor when the wilting of her rosemary sprig told her it was time to go. When she got back, she made up her bed on the kitchen floor again, rather than take the chance of stumbling on the stairs and waking the household. She thought she saw eyes in the embers as she drowsed off—not the golden eyes of the Salamanders, but a hot, burning blue. . . .

Reggie showed up faithfully in the meadow at teatime, every day—though after the second day that the girl failed to materialize, he had brought the 'bus with him, so he could go on down to the pub if she didn't show up. After the third day, as he sat in the sun and listened to the wind in the grass watched the branches overhead with their haze of new green buds, he wondered why he kept coming here—there was nothing very special about her—

—well, other than her quick wit and agile mind.

It wasn't as if she were especially pretty; certainly not compared with all the elegant, doe-like creatures his mother kept trotting past him. She was as raw as a young filly and just as awkward. She seemed to be as poor as a church-mouse, too, from the state of her clothing. That was odd; as he recalled, old Robinson had been something in the way of a manufacturing fellow, and when he'd known her last the girl had certainly dressed well enough. But maybe the money was all gone, thanks to the war. There were a lot of places that had failed; couldn't get the raw goods they needed to keep making whatever it was they were making.

She looked as if she worked for a living. Maybe she was a maid now, or a kitchen-girl. Or maybe she worked in one of the other pubs or something. Maybe that was what she meant when she said she'd be there "if she could."

What was it about her that made him desert his mother's carefully gathered bouquet of well-bred beauties and come down here to sit on a log for an hour on the chance that she might appear?

She can talk, for one thing. She knows how to listen, for another. And when she talks, she doesn't talk nonsense.

That was half of the reason why he hated those afternoon teas, the inane chatter. What was wrong with those girls, anyway? Half of them acted as if the war didn't exist, and the other half as if it existed only to inconvenience them!

She didn't talk about the war—but it wasn't because she was trying to play as if it wasn't going on. It was as if she was avoiding the subject so as not to trouble me.

It occurred to him that if she was working, working hard somewhere now—well, she wasn't going to be all that sheltered anymore. Maybe he could talk to her, about some of the things you just didn't talk about among men. All right to be bitter, angry, depressed; all right even to admit to being white-knuckle terrified in the night, and ready to do a bunk. All right even to admitting to want to take your faithful old Wembley and stick the barrel in your mouth and—

But you didn't talk to another man about losing your sense of wonder and beauty. You didn't tell him how your ideals were lying dead beside your comrades. Oh, maybe you could with the rare fellow like one or two of his former Oxford chums, the ones that had written damn good poetry, for instance. Not Steven Stewart, for instance—someone who'd call you "Reg" and talk about how he was going to start an air mail service when it was all over. Not Walter Boyes, either; plain as toast and solid as a rock, but who was reading history, and liked facts, plain and simple. Maybe William Howe—he was sensitive enough, just think about the stuff he pulled up for the regimental band to play, not just marches and bombast but Bach and Handel. But Howe was still at the Front.

Daniel Heistand— One of the ghosts, the men in the photos probably still on the canvas wall of his quarters, a dead man with his arms around the shoulders of the living. *He* was someone Reggie could have talked to about this. He hadn't written poetry; he was a musician, and not one of your ukulele players nor your accordion men. He was a violinist, and composed as well as played; Reggie remembered listening to him play during the pauses in the shelling, on the long, long, nights when nobody could sleep, playing some wistful haunting thing, too melancholy to be a lullaby—

Well, he hadn't lasted six months; a "sixty-minute man"—that was about how much time he'd had in the seat before a Hun in a Fokker shot him down.

Chris Whitmore? Maybe. Hard to tell. . . . That mania he'd had for photography might have been the stirrings of an artist's nature or just that of a tinkerer. He was supposed to be taking recon photos now, last Reggie'd heard, in the Sudan.

No bloody mud in the Sudan.

Not Geoffrey Cockburn, that was certain. The boy who put his motorcar into the ornamental pond next to the cricket-grounds because he was roaring drunk the night before vivas was not the sort to have a sensitive soul. And no Lyman Evans, either, who'd been pouring the bubbly in the first place.

Maybe Rene Comeau; he was one of the better-educated French infantrymen attached to the air wing as local guards, and the French—well, they were French. They understood that sort of thing. But Rene was still over there too—unless he was dead.

Melancholy was certainly on him this afternoon. And he desperately wanted someone to talk to about it.

Oh, not Allan McBain either, that hard-headed Scots engineer who cursed them all whenever one of "his" runways got a shell-crater or a bomb-crater in it. As if it was *their fault!*

Though in a sense it was—if there hadn't been 'planes and pilots there, no one would bother to shell or bomb McBain's runways.

Vincent Mills... Another sensitive ghost out of the past, but this time a ghost that hadn't even made it to the Front. He'd trained with Reggie at the Oxford-based branch of the Flying School—and he'd been one of too-frequent fatalities. They'd found him upside-down in a tree, neck broken, a strange and puzzled look on his face as if he couldn't quite fathom what had gone wrong. His demise had been a shock; he was a *good* flyer. Perhaps the machine had done him wrong. Reggie still had one of his poems, or at least, it was folded into one of his books of sonnets back at the Front, an articulate yearning for higher skies—

No, there wasn't anyone *here* and *now.* And the girl was. Perhaps it was no bad thing that she wasn't pretty, wasn't his class, was, in fact, poor from all appearances. She didn't look like the sort to read trashy romantic novels and dream of marrying the duke. She looked like the sort who could be sensible. She'd certainly been more sensible than some of those boys who'd flocked around him.

He nodded to himself, as the golden-green light flooded around him. Maybe that was why he kept coming here. Someone sensitive, and sensible at the same time. Someone he could talk to that wouldn't go carrying tales. Who'd believe a kitchen-girl who told tales about meeting up with Reggie Fenyx in a meadow on odd afternoons to talk, anyway? No one. Without witnesses—and really, no one ever did come here—she'd never be believed.

So, content with his reasoning, he dozed a little in the sun until his watch told him the pub would be open. Who would ever have thought that a working-man's pub would become his refuge?

The Brigadier would be arriving in a few days, though. Perhaps then he wouldn't need a refuge as much.

Reggie came in through the garden entrance; it was just as easy to get to from the stable, and a great deal quieter. He took the entrance beneath the grand marble staircase, rather than the one on the terrace; this passage was generally used more by the staff but as a child he had scampered in and out of all possible entrances. The place was dark, as it should be; his mother and grandfather retired early when there was no entertaining going on, and she hadn't entertained since his father had died. None of the staff was down here now at this time of night, and it felt almost as if he was alone in the huge old house. He walked carefully, his path brightened only by a few gaslights, turned low.

He remembered how his father had brought in the gas. It hadn't been that long ago, it seemed. And now—

Electricity. We need to bring in electricity. And the telephone. He shook his head, and made his way up to the first floor. It was easier to get to the family staircase from this part of the house.

Stone floors below, polished wood above, and all of it too noisy, for all he was walking as quietly as he could. Tonight he was feeling more than a bit tipsy; it had been one of *those* nights. Something had set off Matt Brennan, and he'd gone down on a chair in the corner and just sat and rocked and wouldn't talk to anyone.

Shell shock. They all knew the signs of it, and Brennan—well, Brennan had more than a few reasons to suffer from it. It was the first time he'd gone into a fit of it in public though (and Reggie could only be grateful that he himself had managed to keep his own fits behind the closed doors of his rooms).

Well, they weren't doctors, but the only doctor that Reggie knew that had any success with shellshock was Doctor Maya, and she wasn't there. They had their own rough-and-ready remedy; maybe not the best, but a damn sight better than doing nothing, or telling a fellow he was malingering. They physically hauled him out to the middle table, put a glass in his hand, and poured drink into him until he came out of it—and of course in order to keep him drinking they had to match him drink for drink. They'd all gotten bawling sentimental, even Kevin Eaches, one of Reggie's tenant farmers, who'd wandered in by accident and somehow never made it out again.

When Brennan was well in hand, Reggie took his leave. It wasn't quite closing time, but this might be one of those nights when Tom locked the doors on a few of the oldest friends, and moved the "cure" into the private part of the building. He wasn't in that select group yet, and he was not inclined to intrude. So out he went, into the spring-scented night.

It had taken some careful navigating to get the 'bus up to the house without incident. Fortunately, there'd been a moon. Unfortunately, there had been cows. He'd had to stop and shoo them off the road.

Not the easiest thing to do, when you were staggering a bit. Cows didn't seem to be impressed with a man who wasn't able to stand without weaving back and forth.

He left the auto in the middle of the round stableyard; the men would park it in the carriage house. He knew that tonight he was in no condition to try and put her away himself.

With the hour so late, and the house so dark and still, he assumed that everyone, including all of the staff, had gone to bed. He expected to get quietly up to his rooms without anyone the wiser.

The last thing he anticipated was to find his mother waiting for him in the settle at the top of the family staircase.

She had an oil-lamp burning on the table beside her, and was pretending to work on some of that infernal knitting every woman seemed to be doing these days, making stockings for soldiers. He staggered back a pace or two on seeing her. "Ah. Evening, Mater," he said carefully. "I've been out."

"So I see." She put the knitting down in her lap. She was still dressed for dinner, in a navy-blue gown. Her tone could have frozen the flowers in the vase beside her. "I presume it was the same place you have been going to every night. The working-man's pub. The—Broom."

She acted as if she had never heard the name before. As if she had been completely unaware that there was a working-man's pub. He drew himself up. "Yes, I have. I've been to The Broom. I went last night, I went tonight, and I intend to go tomorrow night. In fact, I will continue to go to The Broom for as long as I am on medical leave."

Her face crumpled. "Reggie—how *could* you? Everyone in the village certainly knows—it won't be long before the whole county knows, you're down there every night, consorting with *socialists* and riff-raff—"

"Who give me a better and warmer welcome than I have in my own home," Reggie retorted, anger burning out some of the whiskey fumes and clearing his head. "Where I'm not called coward to my face, and told I'm malingering! Why, I'd rather spend four hours in Mad Ross's company than five minutes in your father's!"

Even as he said the words, he was glad they were out, that it was all out in the open, at last. He didn't need the Brigadier for this. Not to lay the truth plain to his mother. He should have stood on his own two feet a long time ago.

His mother cried out, and her hands flew to her mouth. Tears started up in his eyes.

He felt coldly, curiously unmoved.

"If you want to know why I go there, why don't you watch how your father drives me out of my own home every night?" he asked, angrily. "And you had better get used to my new friends, Mater, because they *are* my friends, and I have far more in common with them than you could ever understand! We're—" he could find no words to tell her. "We're *soldiers,*" he said at last. "Real soldiers. Not tin-toys like your father, who strutted his way around cowing poor little Hindu heathen until he was old enough to claim a pension, and now wants to lord it over me the same way."

He stared at her, stared her down, stared at her until she shrank back in her seat and dropped her eyes. He took a deep breath, and walked past her, all the stagger gone from his step. He walked straight to his rooms, feeling full of a cold dignity he hadn't known he possessed.

And then, once the door was shut, he sat down abruptly on the side of the bed, and blinked.

"What did I just do?" he asked aloud.

But of course, there was no one there to answer him.

13

April 30, 1917
Broom, Warwickshirte

THE ARROWS WAS EMPTY; ALISON was gone. So were Carolyn and Lauralee, and it wasn't off to tea at Longacre again. It was a two-day excursion somewhere that they did not talk about even amongst themselves. But it was going to involve Warrick Locke.

And it was going to involve the contents of three brass-bound cases that Alison had taken with her.

Magic. That was Eleanor's guess, anyway. They were going somewhere to work magic, somewhere that was special. There were a lot of special places of power around, or so Sarah said; Stonehenge was only the most obvious. There had been enough blood spilled on English soil to make plenty of spots where Alison and her nasty Earth Elementals would feel right at home. Eleanor only hoped that they hadn't gotten hold of anything personal of Reggie's. With luck, this wouldn't have anything at all to do with Reggie, or this new magic would just break itself on the walls of his unbelief.

But that meant that at long last, she was going to be able to run down to the meadow at teatime—and hope against hope that Reggie Fenyx was the sort of fellow who kept his word.

The lot of them were finally packed up and gone by luncheon, a meal that stretched on interminably so far as she was concerned. She had to keep her mouth shut and her eyes cast down meekly the whole time, as the foursome pretended she didn't even exist while she waited on them.

Finally they packed up the big motorcar and all four of them drove away, with no more clue as to where they were going than Alison's careless, "Keep the house neat and clean, Ellie, and don't expect us back before Saturday."

When she was utterly certain they were gone, she could scarcely believe her luck. And the first place she went—since, of course, *she* had not had time or opportunity to snatch more than a bite of bread for luncheon—was the pantry.

This time she packed a basket with a real tea, recklessly plundering the stores she wasn't supposed to be able to get into for the making of a meal that even Reggie Fenyx would find appealing. Sarah walked in on her in the midst of her preparations.

"Well, what's all this, then?" she asked, hands on hips, surveying the state of the kitchen. "I thought we might do some work, with Alison gone—"

"I—" Eleanor found herself flushing. "I was going to take a picnic to Round Meadow."

Sarah blinked her deceptively mild eyes once or twice, then a slight smile curved her lips. "So that's the way the wind blows. No wonder young Reggie's been there every afternoon."

"He has?" she gasped. "But—how do you know?"

"He leaves his auto parked below it," Sarah said dismissively. "It's *his* meadow, after all, and it's part of the field his aeroplane used to be in, I doubt anyone thinks anything at all about it. *I* just wondered, why does he always come at teatime?"

"Because that's when I met him there the first time." She looked around distractedly for something to take with her to drink. "Does wine go with tea?" she asked, rather desperately.

"No, wine does *not,* and moreover, you're not used to it,

you'll be tipsy in no time," Sarah scolded. "There's the stream running through there; drink water. But go, go now, before he gets tired of waiting and goes off to his cronies at The Broom."

She caught up the basket, and ran.

The few people on the street did not seem to notice her as she ran; that was something that seemed to happen a great deal. Unless she was actually in the way, no one in Broom paid the least bit of attention to her no matter what she did. Today that was all to the good.

Her heart lifted as she saw in the distance that there was an automobile—presumably Reggie's—tucked off the road down near Round Meadow.

Her feet felt lighter at that moment too, but she was struck with a sudden feeling of shyness, and instead of speeding up, she slowed down to a walk. And then the doubts began.

After all, why should Reggie care if *she* turned up? He was probably just down here to enjoy the solitude of his own meadow. She'd be an invader, as she had been the first day. Oh, he'd be polite, but he wouldn't want her there, surely—

She almost turned back at the stile; almost didn't climb it to get into the wooded end of the field. But she'd come this far—and she had a lovely tea with her. He'd surely appreciate that. And she wouldn't chatter like the girls his mother was inviting for tea.

I don't have to stay very long, she told herself, as she clambered over the stile. *The minute it seems as if he wants to be alone, I can go.*

After all, what did they have in common? She hadn't been to university, she didn't drive a motorcar or fly, she knew nothing about the war except what she read in the papers, and besides, he wouldn't want to talk about that. She was years his junior. She couldn't even talk to him about magic, which was probably the *only* thing they had in common. He probably was only being polite the last time—

And what happened last time? A voice like cool flame in the back of her mind said, in a reasoned town. *You didn't talk about anything. You* listened. *He did the talking. Just go. See what happens.*

By that point, she was among the trees, with the meadow just beyond her, golden sunlight pouring down before her at the end of the corridor of trees. *I might as well go as not,* she thought, and tossed her head. *He did ask me to come back, and if he didn't mean it, he shouldn't have asked me.*

When she came through the trees, at first she didn't see him. He wasn't sitting on the tree trunk where he had been the last time she had seen him. Then she saw he had spread a blanket out on the new grass, and was lying on his back—she thought he was looking up at the sky, but as she got closer, she saw that he was asleep.

She sat down carefully, just on the edge of the blanket, to avoid waking him. There were dark circles under his eyes and it seemed to her that he looked more tired and worn than the last time she had seen him. *Isn't he getting enough sleep?* That seemed strange to her; wasn't that why he was here in the first place, to rest and recover from his injuries? Why shouldn't he be sleeping enough?

He looked so sad; there were so many lines in his brow that only unhappiness and pain could have put there.

In fact, he looked so very vulnerable that she began to feel uncomfortable about watching him like this; it seemed a violation of his privacy.

She began to look around, feeling more and more uncomfortable. And that was when she saw—*Them.*

Horrible, ugly, deformed little gnomes.

She could tell, just by the sickly yellow-brown shimmer around them, that they were not something that most people would see. So they must be Elementals. They ignored her completely, concentrating avidly on Reggie, as if he was something tasty, and they were ravenous.

They had mouths full of nasty, yellowed, pointed teeth, tiny eyes like black beads, and they drooled. No two of them were alike, but they all looked misshapen, and all were colors that just seemed unhealthy.

They stood on the edge of the meadow, just under the trees, skulking in the underbrush, and as she stood up, slowly, she saw that they had formed into a rough circle, completely surrounding the place where Reggie was sleeping.

The sight of them absolutely infuriated her, for no reason that she could name, except perhaps that these evil little creatures were clearly ganging up on a sleeping, helpless man.

She stood up, and quick as a thought, cast a Fire shield around both of them.

That certainly got their attention. The expressions on their faces changed abruptly from the sort you might see on the face of a schoolyard bully, to startled alarm and shock.

Now they looked at her—and she glared back. *Can I call a Salamander here? Now? Without a physical fire around?* She didn't think she dared try anything larger and more powerful, but she didn't know if the Salamanders would answer her here, either—

Nothing ventured, nothing gained. She sketched the proper signs in the air, and concentrated, not commanding, but entreating. The last thing she wanted to do now was to anger an Elemental by commanding it. Not when she was so new to this sort of thing.

To her amazement and delight, she was answered immediately, and not by one, but by a bevy of the fiery little creatures, who appeared within the shield as she had specified, and swarmed all over her, twining around her ankles, her arms, around her head and neck like so many fiery ferrets. And then, suddenly, they all stopped moving. And their heads moved as one, as they stared at the evil gnomes ringing the meadow.

They hissed; it sounded like a hundred steam-kettles, and there was absolutely no doubt that whatever those things were, the Salamanders hated them on sight.

"Go!" she whispered. "Get them!" And the Salamanders flowed off her, surging across the perimeter of the shield, and heading for the gnomes at a speed that made her blink.

The gnomes apparently did not intend to wait around to see what the Salamanders could do to them. They made no sound, or at least, no sound that Eleanor could hear, but they turned with looks of frantic fear and began *swimming* into the turf.

It wasn't digging, because the ground remained physically undisturbed, without so much as a blade of grass being displaced, and the motions they made reminded her far more of swimming than of digging. But there was no doubt that they were trying to escape the Salamanders, and when one of her Elementals caught up with one of the gnomes that was a little too slow, she saw exactly why.

The Salamander writhed around the gnome with blinding speed; there was a "pop" like a champagne cork, and a puff of muddy brown smoke, and the gnome was gone.

No more than a couple of the gnomes were too tardy to escape, however. The rest were under the turf by the time the Salamanders reached them.

The Salamanders surged around the periphery of the meadow like terriers hunting for rats, but the vast majority of the gnomes had escaped, and the Salamanders didn't seem able to follow them underground. Finally they gave up, and flowed back to her, winding around her again until she giggled under her breath, clearly wanting to be told how clever and brave they had been. She obliged them, though keeping to whispers, not wanting to awaken poor Reggie. Finally they seemed content with the praise, and she sensed they were ready to be dismissed. With a wave of her hand and the proper glyph she obliged them, and they dispersed, fading into the sunlight, leaving nothing of themselves behind but the faintest of warmth around her ankles and wrists.

Which left her still with the unanswered question of what to do about Reggie. Finally she dispersed the shield, picked up her basket and walked to edge of the meadow. Once there, she did the only thing she could think of. She began to whistle, and saunter along as if she had only just arrived.

As she had hoped, his head popped up immediately; eyes a little startled, but she ignored that. "Hullo!" she called, waving her hand. "I've brought some nice things for tea, if you want some!"

"And I've brought ginger-beer," was his reply, as he sat up, shaking his head, and rubbing at his eyes. "Hang if I didn't doze off—must've been the sun, makes a chap sleepy."

She paced up to him as he stood up and took the basket from her. "I say," he said, a little shyly. "I'm awfully glad you came. I've been here nearly every day, hoping you would."

It was her turn to blush and feel shy. "It's hard for me to—to get away—I have to work, you see—" she managed, around her stepmother's prohibitions. "Perhaps you shouldn't waste your time."

"It's my time to waste, isn't it?" he retorted, and softened the words with a smile. "Besides, this is probably exactly what the medical johnnies have in mind for me, dozing out in meadows and what-all. They'd probably be perfectly happy about it. In fact, if it will make you feel any better, I'll write one of 'em and ask her to write out a prescription for just that. Before I came out here she was threatening to descend on Longacre to make sure I rested; I'm sure she'd be pleased to find out I had a reason to want to."

Her smile faltered a little. "She?" she replied. "A lady-doctor?"

Of course, and a lady-doctor would be just the sort of woman he'd be fascinated by; able to stand up for herself and clever, and able to talk to him about all manner of things—

"Oh, yes, the only one I really know personally, Doctor Maya Scott," he said happily, completely oblivious to the fact that she had gone quiet. "Married to a friend of mine; capital wench, and does she know her business! If there were any justice, she'd be head of surgery at least, maybe head of an entire hospital." He shook his head, as she belatedly reacted to the words "married to a friend of mine" and brightened again. "Well, maybe she doesn't want that, come to think of it. Can't say I would."

"If she is a really good doctor, she probably doesn't want to be made head of anything, so long as she's left to do what she feels is right, and that she needs to do," Eleanor replied, thinking as she spoke. "It seems to me that taking a good doctor and making her into a—a glorified clerk—isn't the sort of thing that a good doctor would want."

"You probably have something there," Reggie said, with a nod. He patted the blanket. "Well, you're here *now* and I'm glad you could get away. Come sit down and we'll have our tea. What have you been doing with yourself all this time?"

"Work," she replied truthfully. "Not at all glamorous. Servant's work, to tell the truth." That last was pulled out of her, almost unwillingly, but she felt she owed it to him.

He reached into the basket and handed her a sandwich without faltering. "Our good vicar would tell you that there's no shame in an honest day's labor," he replied. "And I'd second him. We got all sorts in our air-wing. Not just the mechanics and the orderlies, either—truth is, I never saw where being a cockney guttersnipe or a Yankee cowboy made a fellow a worse pilot, or being a duke's son made him a better one. Opposite, more often than not, in fact." He bit hungrily into his sandwich, cutting anything else he was going to say short, and she nibbled on hers to keep from having to respond. It was a rather astonishing thing for him to have said; he certainly wouldn't have felt that way before he went off to war.

Yes, and he's been spending all his time down at The Broom, and not at the Broom Hall Inn, hasn't he? she answered herself.

"Did you meet a lot of Americans?" she asked, seizing on his last statement as a way to draw him out a little more.

"More Canadians, which aren't quite the same thing." He ate the last few bites of his sandwich neatly, then uncorked a bottle of ginger beer and handed it to her, before taking one from his rucksack for himself. "The Canadians were—quieter. Didn't seem so intent on making a rowdy reputation for themselves. Mind you, the Australians are at least as loud as the Yanks. Only ever met a few of the Yanks, and they were all cut of the same cloth—right out of a Wild West show, tall, loud, rough. Good lads, but seemed determined that they were going to show all of us that they were larger than life."

She laughed a little at his quizzical expression. "Maybe they only thought they had to live up to what's written in their novels?" she suggested. "And the only novels I've ever heard of that had Canadians in them were all about the mounted police, not about cowboys and outlaws."

"Which came first, the novel or the stereotype?" He grinned and shook his head. "Well, if I could answer that, I'd be a wiser man than I am. All I can tell you is that the Yanks fly like they're trying to ride a wild horse, all seat and no science. It makes them either brilliant, or cracks them up, and nothing in between. The Huns are all science and no seat—"

"And the French?" she prompted.

"Ah, the French. Science with style, and a great deal of attitude." He nodded wisely. "They fly like their women dress. They take a little bit of nothing and make everything out of it, throw themselves at impossible targets and often as not, pull the trick off on the basis of sheer *savoir faire.* Then when you try and congratulate or commiserate with them, you get the same answer. *'C'est la vie, c'est la guerre,'* and then they beg a cigarette off you and make off with the whole pack, and you end up feeling privileged they took your last fag-end." He shook his head again, chuckling.

She smiled. He seemed easier talking about the war and flying today than he had been the last time she'd seen him. But she didn't want to press things too hard, so she asked him what he had been doing since they'd last met.

He sighed. "Oh, being horribly lord-of-the-manor. Meeting my tenant farmers. Looking at alternatives to some of what we've been raising—things that won't need as much labor. Going over the books with my estate manager. Mater didn't bother; mention the accounts to her and she flaps her hands and looks a bit faint."

"Poor thing," Eleanor said, feelingly. "I hate accounting. I keep thinking I've put numbers in all the wrong columns, even when I haven't."

"Well, she *would* do just that and never know it, and that's a fact." He set his empty ginger-beer bottle down, and rummaged in the basket inquisitively. "I say! Tea-cakes!"

"They're from a tin," she warned.

"That's the only kind we could get, over there," he replied. "Wouldn't remember what a proper one tasted like. We were always starved for sweets, on account of it being so plaguey cold and never really able to get properly warm except during summer. All tents do is keep off the rain—and sometimes not even that."

"Well, have my share," she told him generously.

The rest of the afternoon went by much as the first had; in inconsequential chatter. Any time he started to run dry of inconsequentials, she prompted him with something else light. Somehow she *knew* that this was what he needed. When he talked about the war, he shouldn't be talking about the *war,* itself, but about things on the periphery. And above all, she was not going to ask him about fighting.

Books, though—that was a safe enough topic. And he had read an astonishing variety. It seemed that once someone was done with whatever volume had been sent him by friends, lover, or relatives, if it didn't have sentimental value, it became common property. A surprising amount of poetry ended up making the rounds of the barracks—somehow he had ended up memorizing a great deal of it, and without too much coaxing she got him to recite quite a bit of it. It wasn't too much of a surprise that he found Kipling to his taste; when he recited "The Bridge-Guard at Karoo" she could almost see the scene played out in front of her, the sound and lights of the train coming out of the hot, dark silence of the desert night, the men on their solitary, isolated duty grasping desperately for the few moments of civilization they were allowed, and then the train moving on again, leaving them—"few, forgotten, and lonely"—to their thankless post.

She thought that he could see it, too. Perhaps that was why he recited it so feelingly.

Then he had her in stitches as he related the rather improbable tales found in some of the American dime novels that had been left with his air-wing.

"How can anyone take *any* of that seriously?" she gasped, after a particularly funny confrontation between the hero and an entire tribe of Red Indians, complicated by a buffalo stampede and a raid by the James Gang. It probably hadn't been intended to be funny, at least not by the original author, but it was so utterly impossible that it ended up being a parody of itself.

"I have had men swear solemnly to me that such things, if they hadn't happened to *them,* personally, had certainly happened to a friend of a friend, or a distant cousin, or some such connection," Reggie replied, as she held her aching side. "Great tellers of tall tales, are the Yanks. Even the ones who never got farther west than New York City in their lives seemed to think they should be cowboys."

She looked down at her rosemary sprig, and saw with disappointment that it was starting to wilt. "Oh, bother," she said aloud. "Reggie, I would so like to stay here until suppertime—"

"No, no—I quite understand. Stolen hours, and all that." He said it with surface lightness, but she saw the quickly veiled disappointment, and it gave her a little thrill to realize that he had *enjoyed* being with her, and he wanted her to stay.

"I have to go," she said, honestly. "I don't have a choice. I can be here tomorrow, but after that—I can't tell you when the next time I'll be able to get away will be."

She was packing up the basket as she spoke. They both reached for the same item as she finished the sentence; she flushed, and pulled back her hand. He placed the saucer in the basket, and said, "If I had my way, you'd be a lady of leisure—but I haven't been getting my way very often lately."

"I don't think any of us have been," she replied, again truthfully. "So we muddle through however we can. Tomorrow?"

"Tomorrow," he pledged.

She couldn't help herself; she looked back twice as she

trudged away, and each time he was watching her, and when he saw her looking, he lifted his hand to wave.

She carried that image with her all the way home.

Reggie decided not to go down to the pub tonight; he returned to Longacre feeling more alive than he had in a long time, even though his nap on the cold ground had made his knee ache abominably. He left the motor at the stables and limped his way up to the main house, entering by the terrace-door as the sun began to set, only to find his mother waiting for him in the sitting-room with a letter in her hand, and her father beside her with a scowl on his face.

"Reggie, did you invite Brigadier Mann here to visit?" she asked abruptly, before he could even so much as greet her.

Ah. That's what this is all about. I did not ask the king her father for permission to bring a guest here.

"As a matter of fact, yes, I did," he replied, "I am the head of this household; he wrote to ask if he could come for a visit and see how I am doing, and I of course was delighted to invite him."

His grandfather bristled all over at that. "Now you see here, you young pup—"

"No, Grandfather, *you* see here," he interrupted, throttling down an irrational fury that was all the worse because his good mood of the afternoon had been spoiled entirely. "It was all very well for you to play at being the head of this house while I was away, but I'm back now, and I'm perfectly entitled to invite one of father's oldest friends for a visit if I choose."

"And put more work on your mother!" the old man snarled.

Well, that was the feeblest of feeble excuses. "Oh, please," he snorted. "There is a house full of servants here for the three of us, and what is more, I can distinctly recall mother entertaining forty guests for the better part of three weeks during the hunting season with hardly more staff. Are you suggesting she has suddenly become such a ninny-hammer that she can't arrange for an extra plate at meals or bear the conversation of one more old man?"

"Please," his mother said in distress, putting the letter down as if it had burned her, "don't argue."

"I'm not arguing, Mater, I'm standing up for you. Your father seems to be under the mistaken impression that you've regressed to the mental capabilities of a child. I'm correcting that impression." He looked down his nose at the old man, who was going red in the face. "Besides, it isn't as if the Brigadier needs *entertaining.* He'll probably want to use the library for his researches, he'll be looking forward to the odd game of billiards, and I might persuade him to go riding. I think we can manage that."

"That—so-called friend of your father's can't even be bothered to speak a civil word to me!" his grandfather got out from between clenched teeth.

Yes, and that is the real reason you object, isn't it? Because he doesn't treat you like royalty. He outranks you, old man, in or out of the service.

"Perhaps that was because you sneered at him and his military record the moment he walked in the door," Reggie said, with dangerous calm. "But if you find his company so intolerable, why don't you go back to your own home? We are perfectly capable of managing without your advice, you know."

The old man lurched to his feet. "I ought to horsewhip you for that!" he roared.

"Don't try it, unless you want the favor returned," Reggie replied contemptuously. Even though his stomach was turning at the confrontation, and he wanted badly to retreat to his room, *this* time he was, by heaven, going to stand his ground. And his grandfather might as well hear the unvarnished truth for once in his life. "I'm weary of your muttered insults, of your accusations of malingering, and your insufferable arrogance. I'm tired of you turning mother into a spineless shrinking violet with no will of her own. Go home, Grandfather. Go and learn some manners. Come back when you're fit to be company for good men like the Brigadier; until then, go roar at your poor valet and threaten your housekeeper like the petty tyrant you are."

He turned to his mother. "Mater, you've always liked the Brigadier's company in the past, and I see no reason why that should have changed. You might see your way clear to inviting a few more people down as well; it would do you good to have some company here. My Aunt April, perhaps; that would give us enough for a good round of bridge of an evening."

His grandfather was still spluttering; his mother was distracted by the thought of inviting someone whose company *she* enjoyed.

"Lady Williams?" his mother faltered. "But I thought her chattering—"

"I should welcome her chattering, Mater," he replied, gently. "It is good-natured and good-hearted. It would be very pleasant to hear *good-natured* conversation around here. Perhaps if there were more of such pleasant conversation, I would find the pub less congenial."

By now his grandfather was nearly purple with rage, and driven into incoherence.

"If you were to choose to stay, Grandfather, I'll thank you to remember that," he continued. "And don't bother trying to think of a retort. I'm going to dress for dinner. You, of course, are free to stay or go, as you choose—but if you choose to stay, you know what you can expect. The gloves are off, Grandfather, and they are remaining off."

And with that, he turned on his heel and stalked all the way to his rooms.

Once there, however, he turned the key in the lock and locked himself into his darkened bedroom, and sank nervelessly down onto the neatly made bed, shaking in every limb.

I cannot believe I just did that.

All his life, his mother's father had been the one person

that no one dared to defy. Even Reggie's own father had never openly flouted the old man's edicts.

But tonight Reggie had challenged him. Whether or not he'd won remained to be seen. But the challenge had been uttered and had not been answered.

It should have felt like a triumph, but all that Reggie felt was a kind of sick fear that made him curl up on the counterpane and shake. Maybe precisely because he had overturned the old order—it had to be done, but it was one more bit of stability gone.

And he hadn't even done a *good* job of defying the old man. There had been nothing measured or politic about the way he'd laid into his grandfather; in fact he'd probably made an enemy of the old man. He hadn't planned any of it, hadn't chosen his subject, time, or grounds, and just might have made things worse. It was only that he had been pushed once too often and now he felt he had to push back or die.

He felt too sick to go down to dinner now, stomach a wreck, head pounding and aching like someone had taken a poker to it.

Well, after what he'd just done, the old man probably wouldn't be down to dinner either. Still, he couldn't leave his mother to sit at that long, empty table alone.

So after he got his shaking under control, he dressed, and waited for the gong, and went down, down to a mostly-empty table, the silently rebuking presence of his mother, and food he scarcely tasted and ate very little of.

It should have been a triumph, but it tasted of ashes and gall. And in the end, it led to yet another sleepless night, during which he stared at the ceiling, rigid with fear, and was completely unable to muster a single coherent thought until dawn.

14

April 30, 1917
Chipping Norton, Oxfordshire

"I WISH THAT THESE PLACES were somewhere more convenient. Or at least, had decent hotels nearby." Lauralee sighed dramatically, and pouted at the old four-poster bed she was going to have to share with her sister. Carolyn was already sprawled across the expanse of it, and had voiced complaints about the quality of the mattress and the size of the room.

There really was no reason to complain; the room was big enough by coaching-inn standards. It was certainly solid and well-kept. The furnishings might date back to the previous century, but they, too were solid and well-kept. Their early dinner had been palatable, and neither under nor-over-cooked. The real cause for discontent probably lay in the fact that it was *not* a posh hotel and *not* in London, nor Bath, nor any other metropolis.

Alison frowned at her offspring; it was occurring to her just now that they were mightily spoilt. The Crown and Cushion in Chipping Norton was the nearest inn to her goal, just outside the village of Enstone, and as such things went, was superior to a great many places where she'd been forced to stay in the course of her occult career. "You ought to be grateful you have a bed, much less a room, much less a *decent* room in a good, solid inn," she told them, tartly. "I've stayed in hovels, or camped on the ground with gypsies before this. You're just fortunate that there actually *is* an inn within walking distance of the Hoar Stones."

"And that's another thing, Mother—" Carolyn began.

"Shut your mouth," Warrick Locke said, unexpectedly. "We're not here for your amusement. We're here to *work,* and if that requires a little walking on your part, so be it. *You* are the ones ultimately benefiting from this, after all; you ought to be pleased, not whingeing about it."

Carolyn, caught in mid-complaint by Locke's surprising display, gaped at him for a moment before closing her mouth. She still looked sullen, but at least she had shut up.

Not that Alison was particularly happy to be a mile and a half from the hoar stones, but at least it *was* walking distance, and the stones were secluded in an ancient grove of trees, which would give them privacy and security over the course of the next three days. To her mind that privacy was worth any amount of moderate discomfort.

Fortunately, the Hoar Stones were *not* associated with any May Eve celebrations on the part of the locals. If anything, they were shunned. Another indication that this site was exactly what Alison needed.

"You had better have packed for the walk, as I instructed you," Alison said, with a hint of threat in her voice. "Or you'll find yourself tottering down the road on whatever shoes you *did* bring. I have need of you; four is the minimum of participants for these ceremonies. We aren't trifling with Beltane rituals of fertility or lovemaking you know. The things I plan to awaken need coercing and confining. And to that end, thank you, Warrick. I appreciate you being willing to participate."

Her solicitor looked both surprised and gratified. Well, she didn't often thank him, or anyone, for that matter. Not that she intended to start handing out thanks any more frequently; being sparing with them made them that much more valuable.

"I don't often get to see a Master performing a major

ritual," he replied, with a nod of thanks. "I'll certainly learn a lot."

He might at that. Not that it would be anything he could actually use. He wasn't strong enough for that.

She had set the first batch of minor Earth Elementals on Reginald's trail some time ago—but they had been consistently thwarted by the protections Devlin Fenyx had set about the manor house itself, powerful protections that had kept them completely out. Alison had intended them to attack him only when he was asleep, or in that twilight state between waking and sleeping, when they would be best able to terrify him, and they had been unable to catch him sleeping outside the walls of Longacre.

Until today.

Apparently he had drowsed off in the sun somewhere outside this afternoon; her minor goblins had caught wind of this, and had surrounded him.

Then something went wrong.

They weren't even as bright as pigeons, and she could get nothing out of them of any real substance, only that Reggie had a protector that had destroyed several of them and sent the rest fleeing for their lives. She thought it might be the village witch; the old woman wasn't really powerful but she was strong enough to destroy a few minor goblins, and Reggie had been spending a lot of time down at the Broom pub. And while it wasn't likely that the witch would concern herself with something happening up at Longacre, even Alison could not entirely blame her for interfering with something that happened in her own personal sphere.

But that only meant that stronger measures were called for here. As it happened, the timing could not have been much better. Beltane was an ancient night of magic; it would be much easier for her to pull through what she needed on May Eve. There was no light without shadow, and though the traditional magics of Beltane were those of growth and life, it would be no great strain to bend some of the solstice power to other paths.

And in fact, the tradition, though not a British or Celtic one, was already in place in other parts of the world.

For every joyous Beltane, there was a terrifying Walpurgisnacht.

Samhain would have been better, of course—the time of waning light, and of death, rather than rebirth—but any of the greater pagan festivals would do for her purposes, for every one that celebrated light had the counterpart that celebrated the shadow.

The sun was going down now; soon enough it would be time to slip out of the inn—probably the best time would be while people were coming and going from the bar—and begin the walk to the hoar stones.

"Time to change and gather our things," she declared, leveling a look at the girls that warned them that tonight she would tolerate no nonsense. She and Warrick left the two to follow her orders, while they went to their own rooms.

Any other time she would not have allowed herself to be caught dead in trousers; this, however, was an occasion for the deliberate perversion of society's norms, and she clothed herself in sturdy walking shoes, men's pants, and a warm jumper, with a long coat to go over it all. She stuffed her hair up into a working-man's cap, and picked up the rucksack that she had already packed. Besides being warm and practical, the outfit had another purpose. Anyone who saw them on the road would see two men and two women, and assume he was seeing two courting pairs. He would also think twice about accosting them.

The girls were not wearing trousers, but they *were* clothed all in black, with sturdy walking-shoes, plain woolen skirts, equally plain shirtwaists and their oldest coats. Warrick Locke followed their example in being clothed plainly and in black. He had the other rucksack.

They slipped out of the inn to discover that night had already fallen. Well, that was all to the good; they were able to move at a brisk walk to the south and east, heading for their goal a mile and a half away.

The moon gave enough light to walk by, and though there were one or two May Eve bonfires in the distance, these were a fraction of the number that used to blossom before the war. Another thing the war was good for—with most, if not all, of the young men across the Channel, the kind of May Eve celebrations that ended in couples and unattached young girls scattered across the landscape to see the sun rise on May Day were probably not taking place this year at all.

Why bother to wash your face in May dew to make yourself beautiful? For whom? The septuagenarian shepherd? The Land Girls?

The boy you'd once giggled over who'd come home without arms or legs or wits? If your lover was still alive and whole, he was probably in the trenches tonight, and would not be home for months, if he ever came home at all. And if he did—

It might have been better for him if he had died.

Alison could taste some of that anguish in the air this night, but it did not come from the area of the few bonfires. It came from the cottages, where lights were going out; May Eve was just another night, and May Day would bring nothing good except, perhaps, a few early strawberries, a few flowers.

Alison kept her ears open for the sounds of other footsteps in the fields, but heard nothing but owls and sleepy sheep, and the unhappy mutterings of her own footsore offspring.

And as for the few couples left, the men either home on leave, or spared having to go to the war by infirmity, like Broom's own Scott Kelsey, with his collapsed lung—well, they were already coupling in conjugal beds, without needing to find May Eve bowers for clandestine trysts. Marriages had been and were being made that would never have been countenanced before the war, some with babies already in the offing, though by no means most. She'd been the avid eavesdropper on the end of one of those little cottage dramas, sitting behind the parents of the prospective groom as pretty Tamara Budd and her handsome young officer-fiancé stood to have the banns read in church last Sunday. The groom's mother was sniveling—overdressed for a village church-service, and in lamentable taste, the couple was clearly prosperous enough to have assumed their boy would marry above his class, not below it. "Quiet, woman!" the husband had hissed. "She's not what *you* want, but she's what *he* wants, and do you want a grandchild to have his name before he's killed or don't you?"

Oh, those words, and that delicious, delicious despair! People were *saying* now what they had not even dreamed of *thinking* before—not "if" he's killed, but "when." Women sent off their men with that despair in their hearts, open and acknowledged. And if any of their men came home at all, no matter how damaged, they thanked God and thought themselves lucky. Every time the telegraph-girl came riding into Broom on her bicycle, that despair followed her like the wake of a boat, spreading through all the village until she brought her anticipated, but dreaded burden of bad news to her destined door. There was no other reason for a telegraph to be sent to anyone in Broom except for the most dreaded of reasons. "Killed in action." "Missing in action" (which was the other way of saying "blown to bits and we can't find enough of him to identify"). "Wounded and dying."

And every time the telegraph-girl entered Broom, Alison knew it, and reveled in that wash of fear and anguish. She'd even sent a telegraph or two to herself, when deaths were few, just to trigger it, and the power it unleashed. For all the inconveniences that the war had brought, *this* was worth it, and if only it could go on for three, four, five more years—

She made a mental note to strengthen those demons of illness she had sent to America. Not tonight, but soon. The longer the war lasted, the greater her power would be.

There was no traffic tonight; none at all, not even when they passed through Enstone itself. Not a foot-traveler, not a cart, certainly not an auto. There was some small activity around the pub, two men going in as they passed the first houses in the village, but no one came out during the time they were on the Enstone to Ditchely road. Not that she had expected any fellow travelers, but she was pleased that things were so quiet.

Alison had an electric torch, but she didn't use it; she was navigating by the "feel" of things, rather than looking for landmarks. After a bit less than an hour of the four of them plodding down the uneven road between the high hedgerows, she began to sense what she was watching for, southwards, off to the side of the road, a sluggish, stagnant pool of power that had not been tapped in a very long time.

"Watch for a gap in the hedge to the right," she ordered. "It will probably be a stile going over, but there might actually be a path."

But it was the crossing road that they saw first, and only after looking closely for it, found not only a stile but a path, off to the right.

Both hedge and stile were in poor repair, as reported by Warrick Locke, who went over first. Now Alison used her torch; the last thing any of them needed was to be lamed by a sprained ankle at this point!

The path lay along the line and under the shelter of another hedge, but now it was clear to Alison where their goal was, and a tingle of anticipation made her want to hurry the others towards that wooded enclosure whose trees shielded imperfectly the glow of power that roused sullenly at her presence.

The enclosure was little more than a couple of wooden railings; they went over and pushed through the holly and other undergrowth to arrive at her goal.

It stood upon a small mound, an arrangement of six stones forming the remains of what had once been a large, chambered structure. A tomb, perhaps; at least, that was what the old men she had questioned in Enstone had said it was, the tomb of an ancient tribal chieftain long dead before the Romans came. She didn't much care; two powerful ley lines ran through it, and it had been made other use of for some time after its former occupant had been looted away by Romans searching for British gold. The largest of the stones was a good nine feet tall.

She wedged her torch where it could best illuminate the interior of the tomb, and set Warrick and the girls to making the place ready, while she slipped out of sight long enough to don her robe. She usually didn't bother with ritual robes, but this was too important and dangerous a ceremony to leave anything to chance. Besides, the things she intended to call might not recognize her authority without her robes. When she re-entered the tomb, Warrick had already gotten the altar-cloth laid out on the ground, and had lit candles and stuck them wherever he could, to save the batteries on the torch. The others' modern clothing would have looked very out-of-place if they had not worn simple black. Instead of being glaring anachronisms, they looked like minor acolytes of no particular order.

The candles, stuck in places sheltered from the breeze, flickered very little. Alison was struck by how timeless the scene seemed. There was nothing to tell that this was 1917—or 1017—or even the first century Anno Domini.

"Take your places," she said, and took her short-sword from the rucksack. It was a genuine Celtic relic, of bronze, and had been the means that ended more than a dozen lives before it had been left in a tomb very like this one. Locke took a candle and stood in the east, Carolyn in the south, and Lauralee in the west. Alison reserved the north, the most important in this ceremony, for herself. When the others were in place, she took the bronze blade in her hands and cut a circle of protection and power around all of them, moving widdershins as she did so. It was a little crowded in the tomb, for the space inside it could not have been more than eight feet across, but when she was done, the light from the candles faded into insignificance as the interior sprang to life, the stones themselves glowing a dull ochre with pent-up power. She took her place in the north, and nodded at Locke to begin.

Locke looked excited; the girls, wide-eyed.

"I guard the East in the name of Loki, the malicious, the betrayer," Locke said, raising his candle to the level of his eyes. "In his name do I call the power of Air."

The candle flared, its flame turning blue, to confirm that Locke had made all the right occult connections. He grinned at Alison, but she was already turning and nodding to Carolyn, who was raising her candle.

"I guard the South in the name of Hecate, the Queen of Witches, the bringer of burning plague, of drought and despair," Carolyn said carefully, her voice sounding higher than usual and a bit strained, her eyes glinting at her mother over the flame of the candle. "In her name do I call the power of Fire."

As Carolyn's candle-flame burned the crimson of blood, Alison was already turning to Lauralee. Other than her own part, this would be the trickiest.

"I guard the West in the name of Tezcatlipoca, the Smoking Mirror, Mist on the Lake, the eater of hearts," Lauralee said, very carefully, without tripping even a little on the difficult name. "In his name do I call the power of Water."

Alison's triumph tasted sweet as the candle-flame flared green; it had been a risk, using that foreign deity—but she had wanted something uniquely *western,* and could think of no god more bloodthirsty than one of the ancient Aztecs.

But now it was her turn. "I guard the North and close the circle in the name of the Morrigan, Death and Despair, the Storm-Crow, the Blood-Raven, the goddess of battles and harvester of souls," she said, holding aloft her own candle. "In her name do I call the power Earth!"

The flame of her candle was already yellow—but it flared up like a pitch-soaked torch, until for a moment it licked the stone above their heads before subsiding. She didn't need that sign to know that she had tapped into the power sleeping uneasily here in the stones, however; to her senses the place practically hummed, and as the stones increased their glow, you could have read by the light that they shed.

The four of them bent as one to secure their candles in saucers at the four edges of the altar-cloth, then rose again.

And Alison began her chant.

It predated Christianity, this chant; the stones here recognized it, as did the power within those stones. The stones vibrated in sympathy with it, and the power leapt to serve. It was an old chant designed to serve, protect, and avenge those who were great in power but few in numbers. With this magic, they did not have to muster an army. With this magic, the army would come of its own.

An army of the dead.

Not ghosts or spirits called from some afterlife, but *revenants,* the emotionally charged remnants of the unquiet dead still bound to earth by their own will, the executed, defeated in battle, murdered. Any whose remains were interred in the earth, whose deaths had not brought peace, but anger and pain, who were not at all ready to *move on—*

On this night when the doors to the spirit-world were cast open, they came, from every direction they came, from hallowed and unhallowed ground, from unmarked grave, from crossroad-burial, from forgotten forest mound they came. Ancient, merely old, and new, they came, singly, then by dozens. They came on the wings of hate, of anger, and of despair. They pressed in upon the shield of power as the air outside it grew thick with their restless spirits, until the pressure outside the shield threatened to crack it. There were so many that they merged into a circling miasma from which only an occasional glimpse of ghostly-glowing face emerged—here a hairy tribesman, there a close-cropped Roman, here an arrogant Cavalier, there an equally arrogant Roundhead, here a robed Druid, there a tonsured monk—faces old as this island, and as new as yesterday.

And Alison's chant bound them to the torment of her chosen target, and painted that target with words that made him the enemy of each of them.

To the flint-wielding tribesman, he was the effete and sophisticated embodiment of the end of the *old ways,* a man who no longer hunted his food with spear and knife, but who spent his nights in *housen,* and tilled the soil. To the Cavalier, he was the upholder of the way of Parliament. To the monk he was that horror of horrors, a Protestant—to the Roundhead, he was a man who paid no more than lip-service to God, who blasphemed and gambled and sinned the sins of the flesh. To the poor peasant, he was the noble, the oppressor—to the noble, he was a man who shunned his proper class for the company of the base-born. To the Roman he was a Saxon, to the Saxon he was a Norman. To the Druid, he was the servant of the White Christ who put paid to pagans with fire and sword; to the highwayman, he was the embodiment of the law that had hung him and the hand that had done the deed. And to the shattered wreck of the just-buried war-victim, he was the man who had escaped alive, because he was wealthy, privileged or just plain lucky, when *he* had not. To the betrayer, to the betrayed, to the killer and the victim, to each of them, Reggie Fenyx became that which he hated the most. They swirled widdershins around the shield of protection, faster and faster, pulling in more and more of the power of this place, the power that would enable *them* to go forth and torment.

So that in the end, when she uttered the word that freed them and bound them at the same time (all but those few spirits that still had the ability to *think* as well as *feel,* and had slipped away before she could ensnare them), no matter what hate had brought them here, the focus for that hate became *Reginald Fenyx.* She gave them the look, the sense of him; told them without words where to find him.

This was why she had chosen so carefully her gods of East, South, West, and North. Each of them embodied, in his or her own way, the spirit of deception.

She bound the whirling circle of spirits with a word, and set them free with that same word, a single syllable that exploded outward, sending them, the deadly spiritual shrapnel, flying.

The circle of mist burst apart; the light of the stones went out like a snuffed candle. And all of it in a strange and echoing silence in which nothing could be heard but four people breathing as one.

And with that word, she dropped to her knees, exhausted.

But the deed was complete. The tomb was empty, the power within it and beneath it drained. The only glow now came from the guttering candles.

Carolyn and Lauralee stared at their mother, mouths agape, and shaking. In spite of her weariness, Alison could not help smiling. She'd never done a Great Work in their presence. Now perhaps they'd think twice before challenging her.

Warrick Locke was clearly impressed, but not nearly so cowed. And it was he who—following her instructions, true—recovered first, and began the dismissal ceremony, speaking his words and snuffing his candle. Blinking and uncertain, the two girls followed his lead as Alison got back to her feet again.

She snuffed her own candle, then cut the circle rather than going through the tedious business of uncasting it. With the circle cut, the shield dispersed, leaving them all standing in the rock-walled tomb, looking—a little silly. Especially her, in her black velvet, hooded ritual robe.

She wished now that she had given in to the girls and driven here in the auto. But—

But what if someone had seen it here?

On the other hand, Warrick was looking decidedly chipper. . . .

"Warrick, could please I prevail upon you to get the motor from the inn and come bring us back?" she asked, and offered him a smile that promised a great deal more than she was prepared to give. The Morrigan, the deceiver, was still with her, it seemed.

Well, she would let the Morrigan continue to have her way. If he demanded, she would let him take her to his room, then cast a spell of sleep and self-deception on him, and let him dream that he had what he wanted. She had strength enough for that, and even tired, he was no match for her.

Weak-willed man that he was, Locke saw the promise and leapt for it. Then again, perhaps Loki was still with him, and thought to trick his way to what he'd never gotten before. "Of course!" he replied, with a sly smile. "After all that, I'm not surprised that you're tired."

Before she could say anything else, he was off, leaving her to drag off her robe and change back into her masculine garb, then join her daughters in waiting for him

She looked up into the night sky at that waning moon. And smiled. Well, let him think he had the upper hand. A contest between the Morrigan and Loki for craft and trickery was no contest.

No contest at all. . . .

"Mother?" Carolyn said, timidly. "Were those ghosts?"

"Of a sort," she replied. "They are properly called *revenants,* and they fall under the power of the Earth Master, since they are bound to earth for—well, for whatever reason. They are the unquiet dead, who never took the step through the door of the afterlife. Some Earth Masters spend their entire lives going about freeing such things and sending them on their way through the door they have been avoiding."

"Why?" Lauralee asked.

"Because some Earth Masters are idiots," she said, surprising a giggle out of both of the girls. "It makes about as much sense to me as going out to be a missionary. Both careers are fraught with hardship and difficulty, and ultimately in both cases you are dealing with creatures who have little or no interest in what you are trying to tell them."

"But you—you told them what they wanted to hear?" Lauralee hazarded.

Alison smiled. Well, it looked as if at least one of the girls had inherited *some* of her intelligence. "That is how you bind them to *your* target instead of their own," she explained. "After all, most of the time the target of their hatred is as dead as they are, and generally has more sense than to linger. You tell them how *your* target represents everything they hate. Then you give them enough power to do what they want, and turn them loose."

"Can they break through the protections on Longacre?" Carolyn wanted to know.

"Some might. But even if they don't they are powerful enough to force Reggie to see them, awake or asleep." She sighed with content. This had truly been a job well done. "We'll let them torment him for a while, and use up all that extra power I gave them. Then you'll move in."

"But how will we banish *ghosts?"* Carolyn cried. "We can't even make a simple love-charm work on him!"

"Ah—" Alison laid a finger aside her nose and nodded. "There's the beauty of it. Once they use up that extra power I gave them, the geas I put on them will start to fade, and they'll lose the ability to make him see them. And as the geas fades, they'll forget why they're haunting Reggie and start to drift back to their old homes. You won't have to do anything, yet Reggie will *think* that it's you."

They both stared at her, looking awestruck. They hadn't given her that particular look since they were tiny children, and she had amused them by catching a faun and making it dance.

And as she heard the chattering of the motor in the far distance and chivvied the girls into cleaning up the site and heading back down the path to the road, it occurred to her that this evening might represent a triumph in more ways than one.

Not only had she gained supremacy over an army of the dead, she had once more gained the upper hand, most decisively, over her own children. They would be long in forgetting this.

And that was—a good thing.

15

April 30–May 1, 1917
Longacre Park, Warwickshire

REGGIE HAD COMPLETELY FORGOTTEN—UNTIL his mother reminded him of it over dinner—that the next day was May Day, the day of the school treat at Longacre and the school prize day. Well, why *should* he remember? The day of the school treat and prize day had always been June first, not May Day when *he* had been growing up.

But the war had changed this, as it had so many other things. School ended early now, so that children could help with the farm work their fathers and brothers were not here to attend to. The country, and more importantly, the army, needed to be fed; farm work came before schoolwork. And the traditional May Day festivities were not nearly so festive as they had been. There would be no church fair, or at least, not the sort that delighted children—the half-gypsy traveling fair folk with their swinging chairs and carousels, their booths of cheap gimcrackery and games like coconut shy and pitch-toss were not traveling any more. In fact, most of them were off in the trenches themselves, and the old men, children, and women that were left simply could not cope by themselves. With sugar and other things being rationed now, there would be no stalls featuring the forbidden foods that one was only allowed to eat at a fair. The church fair would be a very sad and much diminished version of its former self. Someone would probably set up a hoop-la game and a coconut shy, but the prizes would not be the glittery fairy dolls and wildly colored crockery of the past—no, they would be home-made rag-babies and whatever someone had found in the attic that hadn't made it onto the white elephant table. There would not be a greased-pig race, not with pigs being war resources. There would be no egg-and-spoon race for the same reason. Oh, there could have been a race using rocks or plaster eggs, or potatoes, but it wouldn't have been as much fun without the hazard of breaking the egg. No one left in Broom was nimble enough to climb the greased pole, so that had been canceled as well. There would be no Morris dancers, who by tradition were all men. No procession through the town of the hobby-horse, green man, Robin and Maid Marian—once again, tradition decreed these May Day heroes must be men. There would be a maypole, but only girls really took pleasure in the dance around it.

With all these childhood pleasures revoked, it only made sense—and of course Reggie was in complete agreement on this—to combine the school treat with the May Day fair and have it all on the lawn of Longacre. The children might not be able to have rides on the great swing, but they could play in the maze, be driven around the grounds in the ancient pony-cart or Reggie's own auto, and hunt for early strawberries among the fallen leaves of the woods. Through means Reggie could not quite fathom, his mother had managed to connive, beg, or blackmail the authorities into releasing enough sugar to bake cakes and make ice cream for the treat, so if the children could not eat themselves sick, they would at least have some sweeties.

And of course, Reggie himself would have to present the prizes to the winning scholars, to put the final fillip of glory on the whole day.

No, he quite agreed with the whole notion, and the only

thing that made him wish the school and the children to the steppes of Mongolia was that because he had forgotten, he had not been able to tell poor Eleanor that he would *not* be at the meadow at teatime.

And he did not know how to find her to send her a message to that effect, either.

The thought of her arriving at the meadow only to find it deserted made him feel sick—she would be so disappointed, and he found the idea of disappointing her made him feel like a right cad.

Well, maybe someone would remind her what day it was. Yes, hopefully, wherever she was working, she'd be told, and wouldn't turn up only to be disappointed.

Meanwhile, he listened with some surprise and growing pleasure to his mother go on about *her* preparations for the great day. It was the liveliest he'd seen her since he had arrived. Of course, her father was still sulking, taking his meals in his rooms, so that particular pall was not being flung over the dinner-table.

And perhaps he will *leave. Or at least, go off to bully his own servants until—*

No. He would not think of going back to the Front, to the war. Not now. He turned his mind resolutely to the plans for the morrow.

"It seems like an awful lot of work for you, Mater," he said doubtfully.

She laughed—really laughed. "Don't you remember? You did most of the planning work, when the date was first changed last year. It was all in your letters. Everything was a great success, especially the prizes."

Good gad—I do remember—telling her that the vicar could give out Bibles and prayer books all he liked, but that we ought to be giving things the kiddies would enjoy reading. Picture books for the littlest. Good ripping yarns for the boys—

"You told me to patronize the local shops, so I did. Really, all I had to do was to consult with Pearl Shapland at the bookstore about what was popular—she's been a great help. She's picked out truly delightful books this year—

and for the older girls, lovely writing paper and pen sets instead of books. Well, I *did* make one little change." She blushed. "When I found out that Lisa Satterfield, the head girl, had won the first prize for essay, I thought, a pretty girl like that, and *no* money to spare in her family—well, I went to Annie Hagan the milliner, and I got her a hat. I thought she would like it so much better than writing paper."

"I think you're entirely right, Mater," he said, hiding his amusement. School prizes were supposed to reward scholarship—trust his mother to think of giving a hat instead! Then again, he'd seen perfectly sensible girls go all foolish with inchoate longing over a milliner's window display. "That was a capital idea, and terribly kind of you."

It really did seem as if he had been very clever in his suggestions—it was just too bad he didn't remember them very clearly. Those letters seemed to have been written a century ago, by someone he couldn't even recognize. Swings hung from the trees in the park—a treasure-hunt among the paths for tokens to be exchanged for little bags of nuts and other small prizes—crackers at tea to ensure that every child went home with at least some trinket—it amazed him. How had he thought about such things in the middle of death and gunfire?

"So you see, I really had very little to do—other than this year, finding ways of getting the sugar for the cakes and ice creams," she concluded. "The rest of it, I just left orders for."

"I don't believe you for a minute, and you are an angel, Mater," he said warmly.

She smiled at him, then sighed. "It's so little, really, when there isn't a family in the village that hasn't got someone at the front—or has lost someone," she said, pensively. "If I can just help those poor little ones to forget that for part of one day—"

He went up to bed now feeling guilty that he had put his *own* pleasure ahead of those poor kiddies. As if they had anything much to look forward to anymore. They weren't the only ones who were trying to forget, for just one day, what was going on outside the walls and fences of Longacre Park.

Knowing he would have to look presentable for the children, he took the precaution of using a strong sleeping draught to insure he got a decent night of slumber. He'd avoided them in hospital—preferring to doze during the day when *they* were less inclined to try and attack him—and since coming home, he'd generally found his drinks at the Broom to be soporific enough. *But we don't want to frighten the little ones,* he told himself, as he felt the narcotic take hold. *You don't want to look the way you feel.*

He still felt a bit groggy when his valet woke him, but a couple of cups of good, strong "gunpowder" tea chased most of the mist from his brain. He thought about wearing his uniform to make the presentations, then decided against it. The children saw too many uniforms as it was; he didn't want to remind them of fathers and brothers who were gone, fighting, missing, or dead.

By the time he finished breakfast, his valet Turner came to tell him that the old pony had been harnessed to the cart, and it and the auto were waiting on the driveway.

"What else is done?" he asked.

"The gardener and her helpers have finished seeding the garden with the buttons that will serve as prize-tokens, sir," Turner said, "And the tent has been set up for the refreshments. Her ladyship is already out there, overseeing everything."

He might have known; he finished breakfast and strolled out to be, as he expected, "made useful."

Within the hour, the vicar, his wife, and the entire contingents of the Ladies' Friendly Society and the Women's Institute had made the pilgrimage up the drive with farm carts full of tents and stalls and the bric-a-brac to fill them. And by ten, the fair was set up and waiting for the children. There were already adults moving among the stalls in summer frocks or tea-gowns and tennis-dresses, and cricket-flannels or summer suits suitable for a day at Brighton Pier, or at the very least, their Sunday best.

It all looked so normal until you noticed that frocks outnumbered suits by a factor of four or five to one. It was at that point that Reggie elected to go and stand by his auto and wait for the children to arrive.

Fortunately, they did turn up very shortly after that—being hauled up from the village in two old hay-wains pulled by four ancient workhorses that were spared being sent to pull guns because they couldn't have gotten out of a plodding walk if their lives had depended on it.

Having had the experience of last year, Lady Devlin had very sensibly decided that the first thing to do was to allow the children to run off as much of the energy of excitement as possible. To that end, it was the button-hunt that took place first; well *away* from the flower-beds, with the buttons seeded all over the artificial "wilderness" and the follies that some Georgian Fenyx had erected. He thought to improve the landscape by dotting it with completely manufactured ruins. With happy disregard for the state of their best clothing, the younger children swarmed the wilderness while the older ones sauntered along, pretending that they were too sophisticated for such a childish pastime, but just as excited as the little ones when they found a button.

It took a good hour before the last button was found and handed in for a prize; by then, the smaller ones were lining up for rides in the pony-cart while the older boys were doing the same for a ride in Reggie's motor. The swings in the trees were all fully occupied, the maze had its own set of explorers, and the games at the booths were doing a surprisingly brisk business.

At one, there was a break for luncheon in the refreshment tent, a break that Reggie was pleased to see. He had forgotten, when he had volunteered to take children for rides up and down the long driveway, that this would mean hours of *driving*. His leg was telling him that it would be some time before it forgave him.

After luncheon, to his relief, came the official proceedings of the day, beginning with the Maypole dance. Reggie's gramophone was pulled into service, with Jimmy Grimsley, the head boy, dragooned into service to keep it cranked up. It had to be the first time in the history of Broom that Maypole dances were held to the tune of melodies by Bach instead of the pennywhistle and fiddle. The adults dutifully gathered around to watch, first the little ones blunder through an attempt at a simple in-and-out weave, then progressively more complicated weaves as the teams of dancers increased in age—the girls with enthusiasm, the boys with reluctance. The eldest—all girls, since not even the headmaster could convince teenaged boys to dance around a Maypole—did a quite credible job, leaving the pole with its crown of flowers covered in a tightly woven, patterned set of ribbons. Then it was time for everyone to assemble for the academic prizes.

A low platform had been erected for the purpose, and the audience sat on blankets and tablecloths usually used for picnics. Reggie and the teachers all stood on the platform, while the children waited, squirming, on the blankets in the very front "rows."

First, Miss Kathleen Davis, the teacher for the youngest children (who were not segregated by sex at their age), announced the winners of Best Penmanship, Most Books Read, Best Speller, and Best Recitation. The children solemnly and shyly, and with maternal encouragement, paraded up to the platform, and Reggie gave them their picture-books, wrapped in beautiful paper and ribbons, with just as much solemnity as if he had been distributing medals.

They all sat through a repetition of the prize-winning recitation—predictably, "How Doth the Little Busy Bee"—which at least the child in question managed to get through without needing to be prompted, without mumbling, or without bursting into tears, all of which Reggie could recall happening on previous prize days.

Then it was Miss Judith Lasker's turn to announce the prize-winners for the older girls. Best Penmanship, Best Recitation, Spelling Prize, Literature Prize, and Best Essay on the subject of (Reggie tried not to groan) "My Country." The winner of the Best Essay looked very surprised when Reggie presented her with a hatbox instead of a stationery set or a book, and when she and her friends gathered around to discover what could be *in* the intriguing box, the winner was so delighted to discover that it really *was* a hat she almost forgot to return to the platform to read her winning essay aloud.

Next time it'll be two hats, Reggie thought, ungraciously. *That ought to keep them busy enough they'll completely forget to read the blasted thing.*

The Literature Prize winner, Maria Holmes, did not get a stationery set; that seemed wrong to Reggie, who had instead culled several unread volumes from his own stores—things given to him in the hospital that he had not had the heart to read. *Poems of a V.A.D.* seemed appropriate enough, and the complete Kipling verse as well as *Kim* and *The Light That Failed,* and a book of Shaw's plays. They weren't the sort of thing that a girl would ordinarily be given, but he had the feeling that a "bookish" girl was more than ready for something stronger.

The Best Recitation was from a girl improbably called Marina Landman, and was, to Reggie's complete shock, "The Last Meeting," written only the year before by Siegfried Sassoon. She recited it beautifully, clearly—he had to wonder if she really understood what the words she was speaking from memory actually *meant*—

Or to her was it all Romeo-and-Juliet, doomed, romantic young love? Certainly the poem was written that way. Where had she found it? *Dear God, if she had seen any of his other poems, she surely would have tossed the book away, weeping.* Sassoon might have begun writing his poetry about the nobility of sacrifice in war, and the glory of a grand death, but he was not writing of that now. . . .

Well, it might make *him* uncomfortable, but evidently no one else was bothered. Or else they had no idea who had written this piece; well, truly, there was nothing in it to mark it as the work of a man in the trenches.

Probably someone saw it in The Strand *or some other magazine or newspaper, and thought it appropriate for a young girl to recite,* he decided. *She can't possibly have seen any of Sassoon's other poetry.*

He presented her with her prize of stationery and a silver pen-set. She seemed pleased. "I want to be a teacher," she told him, when he'd asked her the usual question of what she wanted to do. "Like Miss Lasker."

Miss Lasker colored up and looked pleased. "I'm sure you'll be a fine teacher," Reggie told her, and signaled the headmaster with his eyes that it was time for the boys to receive their prizes. *One more lot, and then I can sit down....*

Michael Stone stepped forward and announced the winners. Mathematics Prize, History Prize, Geography Prize—why weren't the girls given challenges like that?—Latin Prize, Best Recitation, and Best Essay on the subject of Patriotism.

The recitation, unmercifully, was "The Charge of the Light Brigade." Reggie tried not to listen. It called up too many memories of similar idiotic charges he had seen from the relative safety of his aeroplane—yet another suicidal dash "over the top" straight into the machine guns. He kept his face fixed in what—he hoped—was a vaguely pleasant expression and wondered what idiot had encouraged the boy to memorize this particular piece at this particular time.

He expected much the same out of the Grimsley boy's essay—

But got a shock. It read like the poetry of Wilfrid Owens, or at least, a very, very young Wilfred Owens, one who hadn't yet seen the slaughtering grounds with his own eyes, but knew very well they were there, and knew that their leaders were idiots, and while questioning the sanity of it all, did not question that doing one's duty was the right and proper thing to do.

Oh, it wasn't laid out so skillfully as all that, and there was still more than a veneer of the youthful idealism that sent those first boys to their deaths in 1914, thinking it was a glorious thing to fall in battle. But still, the bones of intelligent questioning were there—and it astonished him.

So much so that the headmaster caught sight of his startled expression and leaned over to whisper, "Jimmy is the only boy left in his family. Father, both brothers, three uncles and all his male cousins. He'd like to go to university in two years, but—" Stone shrugged. "Whether he can get a place, I don't know."

"You just get him ready for the entrance examinations," Reggie said, fiercely. "I'll see that he gets there." He hadn't even known that he was going to say such a thing until after the words were out of his mouth, but he was glad that he had done so a moment later as he caught the look of astonishment, followed by gratitude, on Michael Stone's face.

He nodded to confirm the pledge, then returned his attention to the boy feeling a kind of proprietary determination. Too many of the bright intellectual lights of his generation had been put out already. He would, by heaven, save this one, at least.

After the prizes came the highlight of the day—what one little fellow joyfully called "A *proper* tea at last!" with jam buns, currant scones, and iced biscuits, ice creams, honey and more jam for the proper sandwiches, all the sweet things that children craved. And if they could not, as they had in days gone by, eat sweet things until they were sick, well perhaps that wasn't so bad a thing. There was just enough of the rationed sugar to make sure every child got enough to feel properly rewarded—to fill them up, they had to make do with slightly more wholesome fare. The adults did have to make do with what they could purchase at the church fair stalls; this was, after all, the school treat. Every child also got one of the finest crackers obtainable, with little prizes inside like pennywhistles, so that they all went home with at least a bag of nuts from the button hunt and a cracker prize in their pock…s with the memory of a day stuffed full of fun witho… …hadow of war on it. After tea, the wagons arrived to… them back down to the village again; the adults lin… …until the church fair officially closed.

Reggie kept himself mostly out of the way. By …s time, his leg was a torment, but the last thing he wanted …as for anyone to notice.

Between the Longacre staff and the men from the village who came up to help with the dismantling, the tents came down and were stowed in the hay-wains. The stalls and booths did not come down quite as quickly as they had gone up, but by sunset, the only vestiges of the May Day festivities were the trampled grass, a few bare places where little girls had been unable to resist picking flowers in the gardens, and the swings still hanging in the trees.

Reggie got up onto the terrace without drawing any attention to himself, and paused there ostensibly to admire the setting sun, but in reality to give his knee a rest. Lady Devlin came up from the gardens when he had been standing there for a few moments to stand beside him. She surveyed the empty lawn and sighed happily. “Well, we’ll be scraping our jam a bit thin for the next several weeks, and the gardens will look a little motheaten for a week or two, but it was worth it,” she said with content. “Did you see their little faces?”

“And their not-so-little faces,” Reggie told her, putting his arm around her shoulders to give her a squeeze. “Well done, Mater; you put on a ripping treat for them. Oh, that Grimsley boy—”

“If you’re going to say we’re finding him a place at Oxford, good,” she interrupted. “That was an amazingly mature essay. Your father always meant to have a fund for the village, and never got around to taking care of it.” She stopped for a moment, closed her eyes, then went on, bravely, “Since he never got the chance, we should do it for him. We’ll make that boy the first to have it, shall we?”

He blinked at her, then grinned. “Mater, you are trumps!” he exclaimed warmly. “I’ll get it set up with Mrs.

MacGregor [illegible]drew Dennis tomorrow. I'll have Andrew set up [illegible], and Lee can tell me what we should use to fund it [illegible]

“That [illegible]ld be the wisest, I think.” She nodded decisively. “[illegible]u know, I'm glad you invited the Brigadier. You were r[illegible]t; we need more people about. I *will* invite your aunt—[illegible]erhaps Lady Virginia too. We'll have some small summer weekends—”

So long as you don't plan to have 'em with the sole intention of trotting potential brides in front of me, he thought, though in truth, he knew that any such hope was probably in vain. What he said aloud was, “It'll be good to have people around. But at the moment—if you'll forgive me, dearest, I am going to go to my room, put my leg up, and have someone bring me a tray with the sad remains of the feasting. My leg is not at all pleased with me.”

Truth to be told, his leg was telling him that if he didn't get weight off it soon, he might not like what it was going to do. He'd been able to ignore the pain for most of the day, but it was coming on with a vengeance now.

“You do look pale, dear,” she said, casting a worried glance at him. “And do you know, that sounds like a capital idea to me, too. A hot bath, a book, and whatever the cook can throw together on a tray. The staff have worked their hearts out for this, too.” She smiled. “However, I am *very* glad it is only once a year! Now I'll go and let the housekeeper know we'll be making an early evening of it. I'm sure the staff will be pleased.”

She kissed his cheek and wandered back into the house; he waited, though his leg was really beginning to throb, until she was unlikely to see the difficulty he was in. Only then did he limp towards the door, and seize, with wordless gratitude, the cane that was in a stand beside it. His valet had silently, and without being asked, installed stands with canes in them in practically every room he was likely to be in, and at every outside door. Now he rested his weight on the handle and reminded himself to make sure Turner was properly thanked.

As the dusk began to descend, shrouding the rooms he

passed through in shadow, he wondered how difficult it would be to get electricity and the telephone up to the place. Mad Ross's wife, Sarah Ashley, a Yorkshire woman, was the local telephone operator, although there could not be more than three or four telephones in Broom itself—so it would certainly be possible to at least get the telephone installed up here. Yes, he would see to that, no matter what. It would be another way to get his mother connected back to the wider world. With the telephone would come invitations to go and do things from her old friends, and he knew from personal experience that it was a great deal easier to refuse invitations that came by mail than it was to refuse the ones that came in person.

Yes. I'll get the telephone in at the very least, and electricity if I can manage it. That should help the staff out a bit, too. Electric lights took less tending, or so he was told.

He paused at the foot of the stairs, looking up to the next floor with a feeling as if he was about to try to scale the Matterhorn. He gritted his teeth, braced himself, and with the cane in one hand and a death-grip on the balustrade, he began the long climb. His knee now felt as if someone was putting a bullet into it with every step he had to climb.

Halfway up he had to stop. *I really did overdo. I should have had one of the lads take the kids out after the first hour.* He'd thought the leg was in better shape than that. Clearly, it wasn't.

He made it to the top of the stairs on will alone, and stood there for a moment with sweat trickling down his back. He wanted to sit down, and knew he didn't dare; he'd never be able to get to his feet again. At least now he wasn't going to have to climb any more stairs.

But it's a long way to my room.

When he had just finished that thought, his valet appeared as if summoned by magic.

And as he looked into Turner's concerned face, he decided that pride was a great deal less important than pain.

"Milord, may I—" Turner began, diffidently.

"Oh yes, you certainly may," Reggie sighed, and allowed

Turner to help him back to his rooms. The valet was a lot more help than a mere cane.

"Milord, if you don't mind my saying so, you've over-done." Turner regarded him sternly. "Now, it's not my place, and I'm no doctor, but—"

"Please, old man, if you don't mind playing nurse, I've no objection to behaving like a patient," he replied.

"Then, I believe that hot water is in order." Turner nodded briskly, and took him straight into the bathroom, almost carrying him—which Reggie was not at all averse to. "Have you actually eaten anything today, milord? Since breaking your fast, I mean."

"Ah—" he blinked, and thought. "A sausage and toast at luncheon. A jam-bun and lots and lots of tea."

"I thought so. The pain takes the appetite, doesn't it?" Turner helped him out of his clothing and into the hot bath; he sank into it with a hiss for the heat, and a sigh of relief as the heat took the edge off the pain of his leg. "You stay there for a bit, and let me deal with this, milord."

Reggie was only too happy to do just that. Once he was in the hot water, he realized that it wasn't just his knee that hurt—the rest of his wounds and broken bones were aching; the knee was just so bad it had overwhelmed the rest.

He remained in the steaming water until it had started to cool, when Turner appeared and helped him out again, and then into bed with a hot compress wrapped around the knee. There was already a tray with hot soup and some assorted sandwich quarters waiting.

And when he saw the familiar bottle on the tray along with his food he did not object. Instead, he looked at Turner with a raised eyebrow. "Was it your idea or Mater's to get this refilled?"

"Mine, milord. I thought you were likely to need it, and I also thought you would not wish to worry your mother." Turner's face was a study in the unreadable.

"I don't pay you enough. We'll have to attend to that in the morning," he replied.

Turner smiled faintly. "I believe, milord, you won't need me any more tonight. Goodnight, milord."

"Good night, Turner."

He took his dose first, then dutifully ate everything on the tray. It meant that his reading was cut drastically short once the narcotic set in.

But considering how he had felt before he took the stuff, that was a very small price to pay.

I hope someone warned Eleanor, was his last thought as he drifted off to sleep. *I don't want her to think she was abandoned. . . .*

16

May 1, 1917
Chipping Norton, Oxfordshire

ALISON WOKE LATE, WITH THE sun streaming in the window of her room in the Crown and Cushion, feeling entirely contented with her life. As it had happened, she had *not* had to do anything about Locke at all. The Old Gods didn't like machinery; by the time he had arrived at the Hoar Stones with the motor, the last vestige of Loki had long since departed his erstwhile host, and Warrick Locke was back to being his old obsequious self.

Nevertheless, she felt as if he ought to be rewarded in some small way. So on the drive back last night, she had said, quite casually, "Warrick, don't you think it would be useful for us to have something at our disposal that is a bit *faster* than this? More powerful? It probably isn't going to be the last time we'll have to traipse out into the countryside. It might be a good thing to have something fast enough to take us to our destination and back to Broom in the same night."

"It would be useful," he had replied, doubtfully, "But really powerful autos take a great deal of practice to handle, Mrs. Robinson, and to be honest, I understand they need a certain amount of strength too. Are you certain you want to take something like that on?"

She had laughed. "Oh, *I* don't mean to handle it; a fine Guy I would look, got up like some demon racer! No, why don't *you* draw what you need out of the accounts and purchase something appropriate in your own name. Then if we need to make a fast run into the country, I can ring you."

She didn't have to be able to see him—not that she'd have been able to in the dark, even if he wasn't wearing driving-goggles—to sense his rush of elation. She had settled back into her seat feeling amused and content; men were such simple creatures! Give them a new mechanical toy, and suddenly they felt like gods!

As to whether a fast automobile would be useful or not, she had no idea, and didn't really care. It provided an excuse to permit him to draw out a great deal of money and reward himself without actually *giving* him the money, which would set a bad precedent. And he would be ever so grateful; although he was not doing badly by himself as her solicitor, he would never be able on his own to afford the sort of fast, powerful auto that *she* could purchase.

It was a bit of an extravagance, but then, once one of the girls was safely wedded to the Fenyx boy, such things would be mere bagatelles.

She had gone to bed feeling supremely satisfied with the night's work. She woke feeling, if anything, even more contented.

Too contented to go back to Broom.

It was, after all, May Day. She particularly did not want to return today, since May Day meant she would have to attend that tedious church fair and school treat nonsense.

She had decided months ago that she was *not* going to help out with this function, even though it was to be held at Longacre Park. The only way she would be able to attract the attention of Lady Devlin would be to volunteer for literally everything, and she would be only one person among the horde of common housewives from the Women's Institute and Ladies' Friendly Society doing the same thing. And she really didn't want to attend, either.

Merely attending, no matter how much she and the girls spent at the church stalls on things they didn't want and had no use for, would still call up the question of why she wasn't participating. On the other hand if business had called her unexpectedly out of town, she would have the perfect excuse not to even go to the wretched thing. The mere idea of being surrounded by a pack of sticky children, forced to listen to recitations and to buy handmade garbage she would not even dare to throw away, made her nauseated. The only bright spot in the whole day would be in watching the virginal little maidens of Broom trotting around the phallic Maypole in the recreation of a fertility rite, without anyone else having the *least* notion of what they were doing. And that was not amusing enough to have to tolerate the rest of it.

London, she thought with longing. Yes, and why not? She deserved it. The girls had been very good; they could do with a treat. She could renew her assault on Lady Devlin once her ladyship had recovered from hosting all those wretched children.

A night or two in London would be just the thing. Some theater, there were things she had forgotten in the spring shopping trip. And above all, it would give her a chance to recover her powers before she returned home.

When she went down to the dining room, the girls were already there, pensively eating toast and tea with Warrick Locke; they brightened up considerably when she suggested the trip.

"Mother!" Lauralee said, her face alight with pleasure. "Oh, grand! There are ever so many things I forgot last March—that wretched laundress manages to ruin my stockings with appalling regularity—"

"We were a bit rushed," Alison admitted indulgently. "And Warrick, you can get that automobile I was talking about; with me there, I can simply write a cheque for it and there will be no tedious nonsense with drawing money on account or answering to the trust about it."

The usually dour expression on the solicitor's face brightened to that of a boy on Christmas morning. "That would be more convenient, Mrs. Robinson," was all he said, but she held back her own smile. Men were so transparent!

"Then let's gather up our traps and make for the railway station," was all she said. "I suspect we can purchase a few more new things to eke out the clothing we have with us sufficiently. You know," she added thoughtfully. "The one thing we did not plan on is that we have no *common* clothing, and if we are going to be making excursions to—special sites—this summer, we really should not be wearing things that will draw attention to ourselves."

"You can get some quite nice frocks ready-to-wear, Mother," Carolyn observed. "Nothing that I would wear to Longacre Park, but good enough for—excursions."

"Then it's settled. Away you go, girls; be so good as to pack up my things as well, while I settle with the innkeeper."

The girls scrambled to obey, leaving her to enjoy her own breakfast in peace, and in the certainty that what had begun so well last night was only going to get better.

May 1, 1917
Broom, Warwickshire

Eleanor had had a restless and uncomfortable night, and was mortally glad that Alison and the girls were away. She had been reduced eventually to sleeping on the kitchen floor, near the fire, inside a circle of protection before she could actually get to sleep. Only when her circle was around her and a couple of her Salamanders were frisking about with her would the unsettled feeling that there was something horrible outside the walls of The Arrows leave her.

Then, of course, she overslept—although, for her, oversleeping meant rising around seven. It didn't matter though, since the compulsions that Alison had put on her had weakened to the point that if she was merely *in* the kitchen at dawn, she would be left alone. So once she slept, she slept long and deeply, and only awoke at the insistent tugging of a Salamander on her finger. The moment she awoke, she knew by the chill even here next to the hearth what it wanted; the fire had burned down to the barest of coals, and before she did anything else, she rubbed the sleep out of her eyes and got it rekindled. Then she returned to the pallet—which, now that she was able to take pretty much what she wanted or needed within the walls of the house, was now as comfortable, if not more comfortable, than her bed in the attic room. It *looked* as it always had, but she had carefully hand-stitched a tattered rag of a coverlet over the top of a very nice woolen blanket, had more blankets in hiding if she needed them, and had made up a decent mattress out of one of the featherbeds left in the upstairs maid's room. Anyone looking in on her as she slept would only see her wrapped in something that looked as if she had rescued it from the bin, and once she was awake, the sham was carefully hidden away in a cupboard that had once held enormous pudding-basins. Eleanor could not have boiled a pudding to save her soul, so the basins, now stowed in the cellar, were not required. In all the time she had been here, Alison had never once opened the cupboards, and Eleanor was fairly certain she wasn't going to begin now.

So when she lay back down to wake up properly, it was with no sense of hardship. She did, however, want to think very hard about the dreams she'd had.

Unlike the ones that had driven her downstairs, these had been quite interesting. Not pleasant precisely—she was left with the impression this morning that whatever else had been going on, she had been *working* very hard—but certainly not disturbing.

"Am I supposed to remember them, or not?" she asked aloud. And that seemed to trigger something—a memory of—voices.

She closed her eyes, and relaxed as Sarah had taught

her, because she knew if she strained after those dream-memories, they would vanish.

Voices. The first thing that came into her mind was the hollow, ringing quality of them. Then words. *"She's not ready! I care not if she can* wield *the power, she is not yet ready to do so!"*

That was a female voice, more annoyed than angry. But there was something not—quite—human about it. As if it belonged to one of those fiery creatures that she had called "fire fairies" that had appeared to play with her in her dreams as a child. There was a resonance to it that she had never heard in a human voice.

"When are they ever? But the knowledge must be *there when she needs it."* That was a male, gruff, with the impression of immense age. Now, if a volcano could have a personality, this would have been it. Immense power was in this one, held barely in check; a slow power, slower than that of the first voice, but somehow the impression was that the speaker's strength at need was exponentially greater than anything the first speaker could command.

And a third voice—also male, and by contrast, quite human-sounding. *"Very well. But see to it that she forgets when waking."*

After that—nothing. No matter how much she blanked her mind, she could remember nothing else, except that she had been working as if she were studying for the examinations to enter Oxford.

Ah, now that was another clue. Whatever she had been "doing," it hadn't been physical labor, it had been entirely mental.

Assuming it was anything other than a dream. Which was a rather major assumption. Yes, she knew very well that magic was real, and very much a factor in her life, but it didn't follow that things she dreamed about were also real. Whatever, that was all she had of it. With a sigh of frustration, she stretched, opened her eyes, and started the day.

Which, once she was clean and dressed, was interrupted

again almost immediately, by the sound of a great many people and wagons coming up the street.

This was hardly usual for Broom, and even less so this early in the morning. What on earth could be happening out there?

She left by the kitchen door and went to the garden gate to peer out, and saw, to her puzzlement, a veritable procession of wagons and carts carrying canvas and parcels and no few of the village women, all of it heading up towards the road leading out of the village. Where on earth could they be going?

Across the road, watching with the greatest of interest as he leaned on his stick, was one of the oldest men in Broom, Gaffer Clark. Under the thick thatch of white hair and the equally white beard, it was hard to tell exactly *how* old he was, and he himself wasn't entirely sure, because there weren't too many other people in Broom old enough to say that they knew they were older than Gaffer.

Well, if anyone would know what this was all about, it would be Gaffer. But—asking Gaffer was like breaking down a dam holding back a lake of words. The moment you asked him the simplest of questions, a veritable torrent of words came out—as Gaffer would say, "Words bein' so cheap an' all, why not make a great tidy heap of 'em?" He was never one to keep his thoughts to himself, and one of those was always that there was no reason to use one word when a dozen would do.

Oh well, she crossed the street and approached him.

He gave her that puzzled look that always came over the villagers, because of her stepmother's spells—the look that said, "I think I ought to know you, and I can't imagine why I don't." She just nodded to him in a friendly but subservient fashion; Alison wanted her to appear to be a very, very low-ranking servant who was not a native of Broom, and so she would try and fit in with that. Besides, that very guise would give her the excuse to ask questions.

"Please sir, could you tell me what's going on? Why are all those carts out here this morning?" she asked, looking up at him with feigned timidity.

"Oh, now, well, it's May Day and all, do ye ken?" the Gaffer said, opening his bag of words and beginning to strew them about with a great smile on his face. "And when it's May Day, it's only right and proper that there be something to celebrate! Only that's being a bit hard these days, seeing that the Nine-Man-Morris is down to two men—two and a half, if you counted that poor lad i' there—" he nodded his head at the Broom pub—"what's on'y got half of what he left here with. And there's none of the lads what does the hobby-horse, nor Robin Hood, nor Maid Marian neither, nor not even a decent fiddler, so what's to do? *And* none of the travelers, nor the peddler-men that does the May church fair, or at least, not many and they ain't men. *And* school be closing short, so as the little 'uns can be helping with the farming. So, says good milady Devlin, may God himself bless her kindly heart, let's make the May Day fair and the school treat all in one, and have it all up at Longacre! Well, no sooner she says that, than everyone thinks, Hoi! A grand idea, that! And bein' as she's her ladyship and all, she's got—*means,* d'ye ken?" He stopped just long enough to give Eleanor a huge wink. "She's a-got hold of stuff to make sweeties for the kiddies, so it'll be a real school treat and all, and may God bless their innocent hearts, they can be eating sweets till they be sick, just as is proper for a school treat. And Master Reggie, who's Lord Fenyx now and all, he'll be a-handing out the prizes, as it's prize day along of being school treat. None of your Bibles and prayer books, neither, not that *I* hold with your prayer books, being chapel, and beggin' your pardon if I've offended ye, miss, but that's the bare truth, for a true man don't need a book to tell him what to pray, and I reckon God Himself gets tired of hearin' the same words bein' prattled every Sunday with no more understanding than a babe. Still! Prizes a youngster'd be happy to have, not that they shouldn't be happy to have a Bible, but 'tisn't as if they don't get Bibles every time yon vicar has an excuse to hand 'em around. No, none of your Bibles and prayer books for Lord Fenyx, no—he'll be handin' out picture books and grand stories with plenty of pirates and bandits and happy endings and what all! So 'tis to be a grand day, all around. I'll be hauling me old bones up there myself, see if I don't! Gaffer, he's old, but not too old to know what a good time is."

Gaffer paused for breath, and Eleanor took that opportunity to thank him and scuttle back across the road and in through the garden gate—because she greatly feared that once Gaffer got his breath back, she'd be given a detailed account of every good time that the Gaffer had ever enjoyed.

Once inside the safety of the yard, she paused to consider what she had been told. And now that she recalled—there had been the same sort of to-do last May Day, but Alison had not given her the leisure to think about it, much less ask.

And of course, Reggie hadn't been up at Longacre either—

Reggie! If he was to be handing out the school prizes, then of course he wouldn't be able to get down to Round Meadow by teatime. He'd be lucky to get away before sunset, if at all. If she knew Reggie at all, she knew he wouldn't just be a figurehead, he'd be doing something to help.

And she wouldn't be seeing Sarah, either; Sarah herself had said as much. Well, May Day . . . there was undoubtedly something witchy to be done on May Day. Sarah had been quite reticent about her plans, and Eleanor knew better than to pry.

There was no way that she could get the bond to stretch all the way to Longacre Park. She was lucky to get as far as Round Meadow—which was far enough from the manor that Reggie drove his automobile to get there.

It was hard not to feel disappointed and deserted, as she walked back into the kitchen and stood staring at the fire on the hearth. Everyone, it seemed, was going to be having some sort of celebration but Eleanor.

As the last of the carts rattled out of the village, a strange quiet settled over the place. It was, quite literally, as still out there as if it was two or three in the morning, except for bird-calls and the occasional distant crow of a rooster. She hadn't until that moment realized how much sound there was, even in such a small village as Broom, until the moment when it was gone.

She was all alone. There was no one to talk to, no one to be with. One of the few days she would be able to get away to see Reggie, and he wouldn't even be there, because he was up there at that enormous manor, playing His Lordship. Tomorrow Alison and the girls would probably be back, and her imprisonment would begin again. *It's not fair—* She sat down on the kitchen stool and stared out the window. *It's not—* And she felt tears of self-pity start to well up.

And then, she blinked, and firmed her chin, and sat straight up. What had she to feel sorry about? Good heavens, it was *May Day,* and Alison and the girls were somewhere far, far away, and *she* could go out to Round Meadow or anywhere else she could reach and go and gather the first May Day flowers she'd have been able to pick since before the war! And there were at least four old ladies on Cottager's Row that *no one* would be bringing May bouquets to, and who were too old to get up the hill to the fair! Four poor old ladies who had given all their best years to the service of someone else, and who were now sitting in their little cottages with no one for company except each other. Now there were people who had a right to feel sorry for themselves.

I might as well find out if I can manage two *excursions outside The Arrows in a day.* With resolution, she got her sprig of rosemary, broke it, and made the proper incantation, then got a basket and went a-Maying.

She wandered through pastures deserted by all but the sheep and cows, finding flowers she hadn't seen in three years. She visited little copses where she recalled the shyer flowers blooming, and there they were, untouched by anyone else.

Of course, that only made sense. The children who *would* have picked this May Day bounty had been too excited by the coming treat to go make May baskets for their mothers and little sweethearts. And the older girls—

The older girls have no sweethearts to make May garlands for, either. Suddenly, she stopped feeling quite so sorry for herself. In fact, the last wedding in the village had been her old schoolmate Cynthia Kerns—who'd had one day with her husband before he went back to the Front. One day—

No, it was no wonder that the flowers were still blooming here. There was no one to pick them. All the young men were gone, and the young ladies didn't have much heart for picking flowers.

She returned long before the sprig had withered with a basket full of cowslips and primroses, lilies-of-the-valley and other early flowers. With a skill she had thought she had forgotten, she wove grasses into little May-baskets, then raided the tea-cakes for a couple of sweet treats, laying them in the baskets with her own bouquets.

She surveyed her handiwork with pardonable pride. *There! Now that's right and proper!* She had made up four lovely little May-baskets of the sort she remembered from much happier days. The baskets wouldn't last a day, the flowers would linger only for two or three more, but it was the thought that counted, wasn't it? She cast the spell a second time, and with a larger basket laden with her offerings, went down to Cottager's Row.

The proper May Day protocol was to lay one's offering on the stoop, knock at the door, and run away. The problem was, Eleanor very much doubted that any of these old ladies would be able to bend down to pick up her offerings, and even if they could, they might not be able to get back up again. So she went to each in turn, knocked on the door, and presented very surprised and touched old women with her gift and a simple, "First of May, ma'am," with the little curtsey you would expect from a lower servant girl. And then, with eyes cast down, before any of them could ask who she was or who had sent her, she hurried away. She went around the corner and waited until her recipient went back into her house before going on to the next one. They would probably get together over tea and compare notes, but there was no harm in that. The point was that each should have a pleasant surprise, from someone unknown.

Not that any of these old women would know who she was even if she gave them her real name. The likelihood that any of them would even be aware of a Robinson family living at The Arrows was pretty remote. As servants up at the manor, they knew less than a quarter of the very small population of Broom, only those with whom they had family ties. Servants at a great house had very little time to themselves, no more than a half day or so off every couple of weeks, and even less to spare to go visiting even their own families. From the time they had entered service to the time when they were pensioned off, their social circle had been among their fellow servants, not down here—and any old friends they'd once had might well themselves be dead at this point.

And once again, she realized that she had very little reason to feel sorry for herself. Even if her stepmother's spell kept people from recognizing her, people still knew who she was—and at least one remembered her *and* recognized her.

As for those four old ladies, at least they knew that *someone* had remembered them today, and Eleanor found a little smile of pleasure playing about her lips as she hurried back to The Arrows.

She indulged herself with a slightly extravagant luncheon, but as she finished it, a spirit of restlessness overcame her, and she felt far too unsettled to spend the day reading.

So instead, she went all over the house, flung open all of the windows to the spring breezes and—after a moment of thought—began to clean.

Oh, not the spring cleaning that Alison would, without a doubt, set her to the moment she and the girls got home. No, this time she would clean what *she* wanted to clean. In the years since the war began, she'd not been able to air out her own bedding or clean her own room more than twice, and only after she was exhausted from her daily work. So it was *her* tiny room that got turned out and swept and dusted until there wasn't a speck of dirt anywhere in it, the mattress put out in the garden to air, the blankets and coverlet left to hang over the line, the threadbare carpet beaten within an inch of its life. It was every stitch of her *own* clothing that got washed and hung to dry, then put away with rosemary sprigs to scent it. It was the pallet-bed from the kitchen that got the same treatment as her bedding from her bedroom. And with time still on her hands in the late afternoon, she decided to go upstairs into the attic and see what was there.

She honestly didn't expect much. After all, she and her father weren't the family that had owned The Arrows for the last however-many generations, and she fully expected that the original family would have cleaned out every bit of their ancestral goods.

Except that once she climbed the stairs and unlocked the door to the long-ignored room—she discovered that they hadn't.

She had never been here before; not even once Alison had turned her into a servant. Perhaps everyone had assumed that the attic was empty, and since the war, there had been such a shortage of things that no one actually had anything to *go* up in an attic to stow things away. Not even clothing; once Alison or the girls deemed a frock too worn or too out-of-date to wear, it went to the church for distribution to the deserving poor in an ostentatious display of false piety. So the piled up furnishings and dust-covered trunks came as a startling surprise as she blinked at them in the musty gloom.

The air was full of dust, and light shone only dimly through the single grimy window. But there must have been enough in the way of furnishings here to fill two or three rooms, and a great deal more in the way of trunks, boxes, and crates.

To the windowless back of the attic, she could dimly make out the shapes of exceedingly old-fashioned furniture piled up to the ceiling; heavy stuff, ornately carved. At least one very old-fashioned four-post bed with a wooden canopy, straight-back chairs, a table so heavy she wondered how anyone had gotten it up here. In front of the furniture, were the trunks and boxes, piled upon one another. No books, which seemed odd—but then, perhaps most of the former owners hadn't been readers to speak of.

Surely there isn't anything usable up here, she thought doubtfully. But something of the child who cannot help but see a trunk and think "treasure" must still have been in her, for she went to the nearest, and flung open the lid to look. And then the next—and the next—and the next—

Soon enough, she had been half right—and half wrong.

The trunks were full of all manner of things. Children's books, battered and torn, and broken toys. Trunk after trunk full of threadbare linens, moth-eaten blankets, and ancient curtains. More trunks full of antique clothing. All of the clothing dated to the last century at least, from the era of the bustle and the hoop-skirt, and had been thriftily packed away, with springs of lavender so old it crumbled when she touched it. The silks were so old that they practically fell apart when she picked them up; merely lifting them made them tear. The furs had evidently been raising entire hoards of little mothlets, and so had the woolens. And yet, not everything was a complete loss. Most of the trimmings, the laces, the beads, and the embroideries, were still sound. And there were gowns that somehow had escaped the moth and the mildew and dry-rot. Anything linen or cotton was perfectly good, for instance, and there were a couple of Victorian ball-gowns that were, if terribly creased, also wonderfully evocative of the by-gone belles who must have worn them. Of course the ball-gowns were absolutely useless to her, but she gathered up the linen skirts, well aware that each of the voluminous things, made to wear over the huge hoops formerly fashionable, would make two or three modern walking skirts for her. She would have to be very careful, and do all her sewing at night, but she wouldn't have to look quite as shabby as she had been doing. Shirtwaists and blouses, plain ones at least, hadn't changed much in all that time, either. Perhaps a little altering of collars would be needed, but not much more than that.

Then she came upon the trunk that had been tucked

away under the dust-covered window, well away from the rest. It was a very small trunk, hardly more than a box, and as she brushed the dust from the top of it, she froze.

For there, carefully written on a paper label stuck to the top of it was her own name.

Eleanor Robinson.

17

May 1, 1917
Broom, Warwickshire

ELEANOR STARED AT THE FADED words on the old paper label, transfixed. This wasn't a hand that she recognized; certainly not her own writing, and not her father's. Whose, then?

Could it possibly be?

She hardly dared think of it.

She finally took a deep breath, and opened the box. Her hands were trembling as she did so.

It contained two things: an envelope and what looked like a copybook. She lifted both out, carefully, as if they might disintegrate like the shattered silks of the ancient gowns in the other trunks.

She peered at them, and tried to make out what was written on them, only to realize that the light was too dim in here to read the fading words.

I need proper light.

She bundled up her linen skirts and shirtwaists under one arm, put the envelope with great care inside the front cover of the copybook, and took everything downstairs, trembling inside, knees feeling weak, both excited and afraid to discover what it was she had found.

She left the clothing in the wash-house where it was unlikely to be discovered, then, realizing that the sun was setting, she took her two finds into the parlor and lit the oil lamps—

And then, of course, she realized just how grimy she was, so she delayed the moment of discovery still further by going to wash her hands and face. Somehow she didn't want to touch her discoveries with filthy hands. It didn't feel right.

And somehow, she wanted to delay that moment of discovery; she was not sure why, but she both longed for and feared the moment when she would open that envelope and learn what lay inside.

Only then, with clean hands and face, did she sit down at the table, remove the envelope from inside the copybook with hands that shook with excitement, and opened the flap.

There was a note inside, a very short note, in the same hand that had written her name on the box. The paper had yellowed, the ink had browned, but the writing was clear enough. The words hit her like blows, burned into her mind as if they had been branded there.

My dear daughter, it began, and she bit back a cry to realize that the writer, as she had not dared to hope, was her own long-dead mother. *My friend Sarah would laugh at me if she knew I was doing this. She would say that I am anticipating the worst. I would only say that since neither of us have the gift of scrying into the future, one cannot anticipate anything, and I am taking precautions. If you have found this, you have found my most important legacy to you, my daughter, whom I knew would one day wield the power of a Master of Fire. Sarah is neither a Master nor of your Element, and cannot teach you most of what you need to know. It was hard for me to find a teacher; it may be that by the time you find this, you already have determined you, too, will not be able to find a Fire Master willing to teach a mere girl. In this book you will find all that I know. If you have not already done so, go to Sarah, the midwife some call our village witch, and ask her to help you, since I am not there to do so myself. Be fearless and strong, and seize your birthright with all the strength that is in you.*

And that was all. Eleanor felt—

Disappointed. Horribly, dreadfully disappointed. Where were the tender sentiments, the assurances that she had been loved and cherished, and that wherever her mother was, she *still* loved her daughter? Where were the gentle words of encouragement from beyond the grave? This might just as well have been a note from one of the tutors at Oxford, for all the warmth that was in it.

She held the note in hands that shook, and felt like a little girl on what she dreamed was Christmas morning who awakens to find that it is not the glorious holiday, but just another day. She had always thought, always *assumed,* that if she ever, ever found something for her from her long-lost mother, it would be full of messages of love and devotion. This—this was more like the old Roman matron's cry to her son departing for the wars: "Return with your shield, or on it." Where was the love in that?

Maybe she didn't care about me after all. Maybe all she thought of me was that I was someone to follow in her footsteps.

She felt bereft, as if something had been taken from her. And as she sat there, the copybook still unopened, two huge tears gathered in her stinging eyes, overflowed, and burned their way down her cheeks.

"Ah, *here* you are!" Sarah exclaimed from the parlor door. "What on earth are you doing in here?"

She turned, and Sarah started a little. "And why on earth are you *crying?"* the witch exclaimed, looking astonished. "What's happened?"

Eleanor sniffed back more tears, and held out the note and the unopened book. "I—went up to the attic," she said, around the enormous and painful lump in her throat that threatened to choke her. "And I found these."

Sarah made quick work of the note, her eyes widening and her face taking on an expression of astonished pleasure. "Good *heavens,* girl, don't you realize what this is? It's what I *can't* teach you! This is wonderful! Why are you weeping like that?"

"She didn't—she didn't—" Eleanor began to sob; she couldn't help it. The tears just started and wouldn't stop. "She never says she loved me—"

"Oh, my dear—" Suddenly Sarah softened all over, in a way that Eleanor had never seen her do before. She sat down on the chair next to Eleanor, and took Eleanor into her arms. Unresisting, Eleanor sagged against her. "You silly little goose," she said fondly, holding Eleanor against her shoulder, and wiping away Eleanor's tears with the corner of her apron. "Of course she didn't. Why should she? She never expected you to read that note! She always thought she would be there, teaching you herself! Can't you read how self-conscious her words are? How stiff?"

"Yes, but—" Eleanor began.

"Well, there you are, she was just being what *I* would have called silly-cautious, and she knew I would have made fun of her if I'd known she was writing that." Sarah stroked her hair, her voice full of such unshakeable conviction that Eleanor could not disbelieve. "She told you every single day, several times a day, how much she loved you, first thing on waking and last thing at night. I *heard* her. She showed you hundreds of times more in a day. Why should she tell you in a note, when she thought she would always be here to keep telling and showing you?"

Eleanor managed to control her sobbing, and Sarah's words penetrated her grief somewhat. "But—why didn't she think—"

"Now, silly child, *look* at that note, why don't you?" Sarah said, half fondly, half scolding, giving Eleanor's shoulders a little shake. "In her best copper-plate handwriting, and phrased as formally and stiff as an invitation to Lady Devlin to tea! Your mother was a simple village girl, child! She loved to read, but *writing* things? For her, when you wrote something, it was formal, stiff, and important! Well, except when you were writing down recipes. I don't think she ever wrote a letter in her life, not even to me, her best friend! Your father might have written *her* a love-letter or two, but she certainly didn't write any back! Do you understand what I'm saying? She could no more have written anything sentimental than—than commanded an Undine!"

The words penetrated the fog of her distress—and more than that, they made sense, perfect sense. Slowly the grief faded. "So she—"

"Yes, you green-goose, she loved you more than her own life," Sarah scolded. "She loved you enough to spend *hours* writing down everything she knew about Fire Mastery! And this from a woman who, I *know* for a certain fact, would rather have scrubbed out the wash-house on hands and knees than pick up a pen."

Put like that—

Eleanor freed herself from Sarah's motherly embrace, smiled wanly at her, and wiped her eyes with her own apron-corner. "I suppose I am being silly."

Sarah shook her head, fondly. "No, you *were* being perfectly natural. If you go on weeping, though, you *will* be acting in a very silly and selfish manner. Have you looked at the book yet?"

Eleanor shook her head.

"Then it can wait until you've had some supper." As practical as ever, Sarah drew her out into the kitchen where they put together mushrooms and eggs and wild herbs that Sarah had brought with her, along with careful gleanings from Alison's stores. Only when both of them were finished, the dishes and pans washed and put up, and everything tidy again, did Sarah go out to the parlor and return with the book and the lamp.

"Let's have a good look at this, shall we?" she said, conversationally.

An hour later, and Sarah was sitting there shaking her head, while Eleanor's head ached from trying to understand what was written in the pages of that copybook.

"Now I *know* I never want to be a Master," Sarah said decisively. "I like things plain! Plain as plain! I like earth to *be* Earth and not—" she waved her hand helplessly, "Not Erda and Epona and gnomes and fertility and not wrapped up in symbols and fables!" She frowned. "I like things to be *one* thing and not like one of those silly dolls you open up and find another, and another, and another."

Eleanor blinked, her eyes sore, and rubbed both temples with the tips of her fingers. "It's going to take me a long time," she admitted. "I can—it's like reaching for something on the top shelf that I can't see. I can barely touch it, make out the edge of it, but I know it's there, and if I can just reach a little further, I know I can grasp it—"

"Well, if *that's* what your mother mastered, all I can say is that I had no idea." Sarah looked forlorn. "She seemed so—ordinary."

"It was all inside her," Eleanor mused, shutting the book with a feeling that if she looked too much longer at those words they would start dancing about in her mind. "I wonder where she learned it all? She doesn't say. She must have found *some* great Master to learn from, but who?"

Sarah sat back in her chair and reached for her teacup. "Now that is a good question. *I* don't know who the Masters are, for the most part. They like to keep it that way, so people don't have a chance to let things slip. Other Masters know, of course, but that's all within their own circle." She frowned. "And another thing; the Masters *in* that circle are almost always men. Hmm. . . ."

"You think she must have found a lady Master of Fire? A secret one?" Eleanor asked eagerly.

"Or one found her. There is that old saying that when the student is ready, a teacher will find her." Sarah nodded. "And there's no telling who it would have been; she was from Stratford-on-Avon, so it wouldn't be anyone I could point a finger at. Stratford's always produced its share of odd ones and wizards, and it's not so much of a city that a Master would feel uncomfortable there. Not like London or Glasgow or Manchester." She licked her lips. "The more I think on it, the more that makes sense. I remember her telling me that the magic ran in her family, but deep; her grandsire was a Master, but not her father. Huh. Maybe 'twas her grandsire found her the Fire Master."

"Well, who*ever* it was, he or she was like a university don," Eleanor replied ruefully. "This—this is—oh!"

An idea had suddenly occurred to her, and she sat up straight.

"What? What?" Sarah asked sharply.

"I just realized that I recognize this!" she said "From the medieval history I was studying for the examinations to get into Oxford. This is *alchemy*—alchemy and medieval mysticism! The 'how many angels can dance on the head of a pin' sort of thing! Maybe it was some sort of don she was studying with—"

"Well, it's like no way that *I* was taught or even heard of, but if it works well enough for you, that is what counts." Sarah stood up to go, and hesitated. "Do you think that book should stay here?"

"No," Eleanor told her instantly. "I want to take no chances that *she* might find it. I was going to ask you to take it with you and keep it. Besides, if what mother learned *is* based on alchemy and that sort of thing, there are books in the library here that can help me, that have been here all along. If Alison sees me studying one of those, she'll just assume I'm in desperate want of something to read."

Sarah gathered up the old book and tucked it under her shawl. "I think that's wise, very wise. Well, *my* day began before dawn, so if Alison doesn't come back, I will see you on the morrow."

"Thank you, Sarah," Eleanor said, getting to her feet and letting her mentor out the kitchen door. "Thank you *very* much."

She should have been tired, but somehow she wasn't, and she decided to go to the library with the lamp and see if she couldn't find the books she thought that she remembered.

There were a lot of odd books in this room, things that certainly hadn't matched with any of her father's interests, and that up until now, she hadn't associated with her mother, either. Old things, that didn't even have titles imprinted on the spines, much less an author's name. But sure enough, when she took them down, she found that there were several on *Natural Philosophy and Alchemie, Ye Historie and Practice of Alchemie,* and that when she looked inside the front cover, there was a name in crabbed and faded handwriting utterly unlike her mother's, and a date—the earliest she found was 1845, and the oldest, 1880. The first name was clear enough—"Valeria," which did sound like a woman—but the second was indecipherable.

So I'll probably never know if these were Mother's books given to her by her teacher, or things picked up at a jumble sale. Still, they might prove useful, if her mother's teaching *was* based on creaky old mysticism, and not the practical approach that Sarah preferred.

She rearranged the rest of the books to keep it from looking as if she had taken anything. No use in alerting Alison or the girls to the fact that she was reading *all* of the books on alchemy. If they found her reading one, they'd assume it was a fluke.

You know, in all of the time they've been here, and the things they've let slip about their own magic, I don't think they've ever said anything that sounded like the things in mother's workbook. I don't think they were *taught the same sort of way she was.*

Well, that was all to the good.

She took the books up to her room and after some thought, distributed them around the room in ways that made it look as if she was doing anything *but* reading them. One went under the too-short leg of a wobbly dresser, one could be placed to hold open the shutter—the rest she placed here and there, anywhere that looked as if she didn't care what happened to them, as if a brick or a stone could have served the same function. That way, if anyone noticed that they were all about alchemy she could say that she had taken the books she thought no one would ever want to read.

She lit a bedside candle, changed into her night-dress, climbed into bed, and settled in for a read.

Within a few paragraphs, she knew that her hunch was right. Her mother's workbook had paragraphs that were very like a condensed form of what she found here.

Mind, these books were altogether too wordy. But she was used to that; the great classic writers tended to be just about as wordy; they were just better at it. The study of alchemy, according to this philosopher, had *never* been about finding ways to change base metal into gold. That particular transmutation itself was merely a philosophical expression for the evolution and maturation of a human spirit. . . .

To change one's own self from the heavy, leaden soul who could scarcely lift his eyes to the heavens, much less soar among them, to the winged, pure, and precious intellect that could neither tarnish nor be debased.

The Philosopher's Stone was not a *thing,* but a *process*—as, so the book said, a spell was not really a *thing* but a *process.* Spells were the processes by which a magician imposed his or her will on the surrounding universe. The Philosopher's Stone was the process by which the magician transmuted his or herself into a state in which he or she could understand the universe. Maybe even become one with it.

And if her mother's workbook had been dense with symbolic meanings, this book was overflowing with them. Nothing, it seemed, existed without having double and triple meanings. Not even the most commonplace items. A broom was a broom, and a means of cleansing, the symbol for cleansing, and a symbol of the cleansing power of Air. Even the old gods were merely symbols for other things, powers, emotions, stages on the life-journey.

But here were the old, familiar friends—Earth, Air, Fire, and Water . . . if you knew what to look for, you quickly realized that the man who wrote this book understood Mastery. The book was written in such a way that those who were not magicians could take it as pure philosophy—but for those who were, this book, and probably some of the others, were a guide beyond the practical application of magic into the theory behind it.

And when you knew the theory and the philosophy, you could create your own pathways and applications.

Slowly, with much reading and rereading of the same paragraphs, things began to fit into place.

She had originally intended to concentrate only on her own Element, but it soon became clear that this was a bad idea. Not only were the powers and meanings of all four Elements incestuously intertwined, but after all, Alison was an Earth Master and Reggie an Air Master. To defeat the one and help the other, she had to learn about *their* Elements, and at that point it made little sense to skip learning about the Antagonistic Element to her own, Water.

She finally felt her eyelids growing too heavy, and set the book aside, blowing out the candle, phrases from the book still echoing in her mind as she drifted into sleep. She didn't understand them yet—but soon—soon—

. . . the first step must be into the first Sphere, the Sphere of Imagination, for Intellect must be the servant of Imagination, and not the master. . . .

Eleanor woke slowly, with the strangest feeling—as if, once she had put the book down last night, she had gone into dreams only to find that in her dreams she was still trying to come to grips with what she had read. Except that in the dream, there was something or someone helping her grasp it.

And the moment she woke, she realized that she *did* grasp some of what she'd been reading, and had put it together with what had been in the workbook.

In fact, that was exactly what she needed to do—start putting things together, since all things were connected, and each had aspects of the rest. The only actual starting place was the intellect, which led into the imagination. After that, the imagination led everywhere.

She'd been trying to think of all of the Planes of her mother's book—or "Spheres," as the Alchemy book called them—as being separate, and that things somehow passed from one to another. But it wasn't like that at all; *everything* was layered on top of everything else, and everything coexisted at once. The physical world that everyone saw and lived in was overlaid with all of the magic worlds. The difference between a regular person and a magician was whether or not you could see each layer.

Which was why those nasty little gnomish things in the meadow had seemed to dig their way into the ground without actually disturbing it; they weren't really digging into the *ground,* they were moving themselves out of the Plane of the "real world"—which the alchemy book called "Middle Earth," and into one of the lower Planes, probably the Dark Earth Plane, where she couldn't see them anymore. And the Salamanders couldn't follow, both because they weren't creatures of Earth and because they weren't creatures of the Dark Ways. Every Sphere had a corresponding Dark Side, and as a Light Path magician, you didn't want to go there, unless you absolutely had to. Not because you could get hurt, but because you could get seduced and corrupted unless you were very, very careful. You *couldn't* go there, if you were a Light Path Elemental.

She could have, if she had known how to get her imagination to move her awareness into the Plane of Earth, because humans were uniquely able to move among all the Planes. But she wouldn't have been comfortable there, because it wasn't her Element, either.

Imagination. That was the key. Whatever she could imagine, if she could do it well enough, and believe in it, she could see.

Intellect ruled the Middle Earth, which lay between the Spheres of the Light Path and the Spheres of the Dark. It reflected both, though the balance shifted as affairs in the Middle Earth itself shifted, and as the balance of power between the Light Path Spheres and the Dark Path Spheres shifted.

Those who subscribed only to Intellect could never

move beyond the Middle Earth. But those who explored Imagination and Intuition found the way into the other Spheres open to them.

And once you learned the symbolic logic of those other Spheres, you knew how to manipulate *your* magic, and how to counter the magic of other Elements than your own. Now, that meant that Eleanor would have a fighting chance of undoing what Alison had done to her, even if she wasn't as strong a magician as Alison. It didn't take a hammer to crack a nut; a little pressure applied at the right place would split it open. What was more, Eleanor had a shrewd hunch that Alison's spells only worked against her on *this* Plane. Once she learned how to move among the Planes, she could travel them relatively unhindered.

Once I learn to move among the Planes, once I really understand the Plane of Earth magic, I will find the key to break her spells! She knew that; it made perfect sense. Knowledge and understanding, not force, were going to be the keys to her shackles.

But to do that, to be able to step beyond this Middle Earth and into the rest, she would have to do a lot of work. She had once thought that preparing for the examinations to get into Oxford was hard work. This would be ten times harder. She was going to have to go completely beyond what she had always taken as "the truth" into a whole new set of truths—and then believe in them. *Well, no one said it was going to be easy.*

She got up and ran through her usual chores in an absentminded fashion; her hands and body did the work, while her mind repeated some of what she thought she was beginning to understand from the books.

It might have seemed odd, but amid all those philosophical musing, she did not forget to wash all those cotton shirtwaists and linen skirts she had brought down from the attic, nor to put them up—well out of sight of the bedroom windows—on lines in the garden to dry. It seemed very strange to be doing all these intensely common and practical things while her head was buzzing with alchemical esoterica.

And as she worked, she kept remembering links to the symbology of even the most ordinary things—as she scrubbed, she was also thinking. *Water, is the Sphere of Emotion; although there are emotions associated with all the Elements, they all have more strength here in Water. Especially the nurturing ones—that's the Light Path, though, the Dark Path is the emotions that destroy, like a flood washing everything away in its path. And Water is mutable—solid to liquid to gas and back again, so it represents change, while unchanging Water, the Dark Path, is stagnation. And nothing can grow without it, so it also has an aspect of growth, but too much water can kill, so there's death. It can purify and pollute. It can fill or drown. The alchemical creature is the Hippocampus, showing the links among Water, Air, and Earth. Water is hard to control because it's hard to contain, not as hard as Air, though.*

And then that, and a whiff of flowers, sent her into *Air, the Sphere of Mercury, the Sphere of Memory. The strongest memory-trigger there is, is scent. More of a Sphere of Intellect than Emotion, though Mercury is changable and volatile, more so than water. The Zephyr refreshes, the Tempest sweeps away. Too much Air can intoxicate, too little and you die. It can cleanse, too, or destroy. Mostly, it's too thin to support emotion, or at least, intense emotion. Memories generally come at a distance; you can forget how you felt when you went through those incidents originally. Pride, though; there's pride there. And that's why Mercury is the god of liars, because people lie to bolster their pride and maintain their pride. And thieves, because thieves are proud of their skill. That's the Dark Path; there's no reason why you shouldn't take pride in your work, and there's nothing wrong with change. Hardest of the Elements to contain, but not so hard to control, since Fire devours it, Water ignores it, Earth deflects it—the Alchemical creature is the Phoenyx, even though the Phoenyx is also a Fire Elemental, showing the links among Air, Water, and Fire.*

Scrubbing the floor led to—*Earth. Alison's Element. The Sphere of Passion—Love, on the Path of Light, Lust on the Dark Path. Seduction, which sits on the line between the two*

Paths. Not changeable, no—it takes a lot to force the Earth to change. Passion is a really useful thing; you can't really create something that will live without it. Passion is an implacable force, like an avalanche—once you start it, it takes a long time to stop it. Maybe that's why she had to wait until I was in an emotional breakdown before she could bind me. The Dark Path isn't stagnation though—it's rot or sterility. Creator and Devourer; Earth is, among others, the Goddesses Erda and Hera, who are both prone to creation and destruction. There may be a key to defeating Alison in that, but what is it? The Alchemical creature is the Gryphon, showing the links among Earth, Air, and Water, even though the Gryphon is also an Elemental of Air.

She mused over that while she cooked, then lingered over her breakfast, having come around to her own Element at last. *Fire—Sphere of Anger. Mars. The Alchemical Creature is the Dragon, showing the links among Air, Earth, and Fire. The Dragon of the Light is wise and ancient, the Dragon of the Dark is almost mindless and constantly in a rage. Fire cleanses and destroys. The Dark Path is the Fire that only devours, I suppose, since there is no Fire that is not in a state of constant change. The Light Path would be the Fire that cleanses? Or maybe the Fire that serves, instead of the uncontrolled fire that eats everything in its path. I suppose Anger can be productive; righteous anger, but what a narrow divide between Light and Dark! Righteous anger should lead you to Justice, which is why Justice is also here, but . . . but Justice is blind, and there is no Mercy in the Sphere of Fire. Justice? Judgment is more like it. And Anger, like Fire, is hard to control and the most apt to turn and destroy the person trying to control it. Hate—channeled anger. How do I control my anger? Because if I don't, it will control me. . . .*

Intellect and imagination; that was what it had to be. That was what it seemed to come down to. Somehow she had to use both. No wonder Fire was supposed to be the most dangerous of the Elements! And the most seductive; anger was intoxicating, she knew that already. And when anger ran out—

Another branch on the Dark Path—Despair. Oh, I know the taste of that. Despair, because it's Self Hate; yes, that belongs here in Fire, too. Like Fire, Despair devours what sustains it . . . and Despair can coil you right back to Anger again, unthinking Anger, the kind that just lashes out.

She almost wished she had never picked up that book; never read what was in those pages. Sarah's way had been so much simpler!

Sarah's way would never have gotten me where I need to go.

She had to become a Master if she was going to break Alison's hold on her. She was beginning to think that there were masters and there were Masters—those who used their magic, and those who really, truly understood it. And maybe Alison hadn't gotten to her Mastery by following this course, but—

But if she hasn't, then that *may be her weakness. If she's gone the simpler, most direct route to power, it means she's left all those other paths that are still there unwatched, unguarded. It's like having a fortress and leaving all the windows open while you carefully lock the only door.*

Eleanor finished her breakfast and tidied up, her mind still turning over all the things she had studied. *Fire is Swords, in the Tarot deck; there's Mars again. So that's* my *weakness, the one she'll try to exploit, because if there's one thing she really does understand, it's how to use someone's weaknesses against him, and how to turn a strength into a weakness to exploit. Anger, hate, and despair—*

She stopped dead in the middle of the kitchen and clapped her hand to her mouth as a sudden revelation hit.

She already has! She already has! The night we got the news about Father being killed! I was in despair, and she pounced on it!

And the more she thought about it, the more it seemed to her that Alison's spells *always* got stronger the more depressed that Eleanor was. The question was, did Alison know about the alchemical philosophy, or was this a case of something else—the simple siphoning of dark power from someone who was generating a lot of it?

The sooner she knew the answer to that question, the better off she would be.

And—Imagination and Intellect—the answer just might be right under my nose. . . .

18

May 2, 1917
Longacre Park, Warwickshire

REGGIE HALF-WOKE SEVERAL TIMES DURING the night, responding to a vague feeling of *presences* in his room with him. Most narcotics and soporifics actually had the effect of taking down the mental barriers between even ordinary folk and the Unseen, but Doctor Maya had seen to it that Reggie's prescriptions had added components to them that had the opposite effect. Or so he assumed, anyway, since after he had started taking the drugs that *she* had prescribed, his sleep was no longer troubled by unwanted visitors.

So the feeling of *presence* was never enough to trouble his dreams or fully wake him out of slumber. The painkillers did their job, and he woke late in the morning of the second of May feeling stiff and sore, but not half-crippled. He dressed without assistance, and made his way down to breakfast with only the aid of a cane.

There was an odd addition to the usually spartan breakfast menu. Tea-cakes, split and lightly toasted, in place of actual toast, scones, or crumpets. He eyed them with amusement; it seemed that there were still leftovers from the School Treat.

"Waste not, want not," he said aloud, and treated them like toasted crumpets or scones. His mother, always an early riser, had long since had her breakfast, and was probably out with the gardener, dealing with the inevitable damage done to the gardens by the children. There were always accidents, and little ones too small to know any better who would tear up flower beds making bouquets. Fortunately the famous roses were perfectly capable of defending themselves, the herb garden was in a walled and hedged space of its own that was off-limits during the school treat, and the current gardener was not likely to threaten suicide over some torn-up plants.

After a quite satisfactory breakfast, he went to the windows of the terrace and spotted her, as he had expected, pointing to places in the flower beds and presumably talking over repairs with the gardener. It was too far for him to hear what they were saying, but when he went outside to the balustrade, she saw him watching and waved, and shortly thereafter joined him upon the terrace.

"The little terrors!" she said fondly. "The primroses are quite decimated, and the tulips and daffodils as well. *Luckily* they did not actually tear up any bulbs this year, and we planned for this, at any rate. There are more than enough plants coming along in the greenhouse to cover the damage. In two days no one will know they were here."

"Hmm," he replied, giving her a sideways glance. "I seem to recall a certain little boy who presented his mother with a May Day bouquet of all of the *exceedingly* rare double-ruffled tulips that the gardener had been cosseting over the winter in hopes of finally getting a good show out of them."

"And very lovely they looked in a vase on my desk, too," she chuckled. "Furthermore, despite all predictions to the contrary, they gave just as good a show the next spring. And the times being what they are, I would rather have happy children than a perfect garden."

"You're a trump, Mater," he said warmly, bending down to kiss her cheek.

"I have my moments," she agreed. "Oh! Your aunt is definitely coming, and I must say, I am glad of it. The Brigadier offered to bring her in his motorcar, so they'll be arriving together."

"Good! And we ought to start having small parties with some of our neighbors, too," he said, even though that was really the last thing he wanted. He was going to enjoy having the Brigadier here, and his aunt would be good company for his mother, but—

But the truth was, he would have been a great deal happier with no more than that. *Aunt has an instinct for when I want to be left alone, and the Brigadier does a good job of keeping himself to himself. But some of the neighbors. . . .*

Nevertheless, he could see for himself how much more animated his mother was. *She* needed the company, even if he didn't want it. It was about time she started to live again.

"Well, we'll see what your aunt suggests," was all his mother said—but he knew there would at least be some dinners, and some card-parties, and very probably things would start simmering and break out in tea dances and garden parties, and tennis parties, and possibly even—

He resolved not to think about it until it happened, but he knew what his mother was thinking when she said, altogether too casually, "I must say I was pleasantly surprised by the strength of your gramophone. It quite takes the place of musicians, doesn't it?"

May 2, 1917
Broom, Warwickshire

It was the second of May, and Eleanor was still alone in the house. She could hardly believe her good fortune. Whatever was keeping her stepmother and stepsisters away,

Eleanor hoped it was vastly entertaining. The longer they stayed away, the better.

Now, since the entire party had gone off by motorcar, Eleanor knew that she would not be seeing them until evening at the earliest if they even returned today at all. Alison preferred to rise as late as possible and travel in a leisurely manner. So this meant that today, at least, she should have the whole of the day in freedom.

Or at least, relative freedom. More freedom than she'd had for three years. . . .

In that moment, she felt a shadow of depression fall over her. Freedom! She wasn't free. To use that word, even to herself, was to mock her own condition. She could only leave the house for an hour or two at most. She couldn't talk to anyone and be believed. What food she ate that wasn't stolen was scant and poor. Her clothing was the rags of what she'd owned three years ago. She labored as a menial from dawn to dusk, unpaid, no better than a slave. Any tiny crumb of pleasure she got could be snatched away at any time. Such freedom! When her stepmother was in the house, she couldn't leave it. Only one person besides the village witch recognized who she really was, and she couldn't tell him the truth, because her very words were hedged about and compelled by spells.

Freedom . . . scullery maids had more freedom than she did.

She felt her eyes stinging, and stifled a sob.

What's the use? I'm a prisoner no matter what happens.

But she felt rebellion against that despair stirring inside her after a moment. And she scrubbed the incipient tears away with the back of her hand, fiercely. All right. She was a prisoner now—but less of one than she had been a few months ago. Alison was no longer the only one with magic at her command; her compulsions and spells were weakening under the steady pressure of what Eleanor was learning to master. And there was the promise of freedom in her mother's workbook. One day, Eleanor would be a Master of Fire.

She would hold to that hope, and that promise. Hope—so much could be endured so long as there was hope.

I will work! she pledged herself, fiercely. *I* will *become a Master of Fire! And then I will take back my freedom. Nothing else matters. Even if I have to make my way as a servant because no one will believe what happened, I will have that!*

And meanwhile—meanwhile life would go on. She would steal what pleasure she could. She would win whatever scraps she could. She would learn by day and hide her growing power under the mask of the meek and frightened girl that Alison expected to see.

And she might as well use Alison's absence to remake some of those skirts and shirtwaists, for instance. Or one set, at any rate. A simple, unadorned skirt and an altered blouse should not be beyond her sewing ability.

In its way, that was rebellion too. Maybe no one would notice, but she would be less ragged, less beggarly, and have regained just a little more dignity, if only in her own mind. It was hard to feel anything but a victim when all you had was patched and threadbare clothing not even a street urchin would want. She would gain back a little of her own pride, in spite of Alison.

The thought was the parent to the deed; after as little cleaning of the house as she could get away with to satisfy Alison's spells, she attacked the now dry and clean skirts and blouses with scissors and needle. She did all her cutting-out at once, because she might not get another chance, took the scraps and put them in the rag-bag to hide them, then laid the pieces away under her bed—all but the makings for one new skirt and shirtwaist.

She had been an indifferent seamstress before Alison arrived; why should she be any good at it, when she'd never had to so much as turn up a hem in her life? But she'd been forced to learn, mostly by observing the maids, for Alison had no intention of parting with a single penny to keep Eleanor clothed—and of course, once all of the maids were gone, Eleanor added the task of mending her stepsisters' clothing to the rest of her chores.

By then, she had learned on her own garments, as they grew shabbier with each day. Hems came down, seams ripped, and when one did all the rough work of the house, sooner or later things got torn. All of her current clothing dated from 1914 and before. Most of it was looking like something even a gypsy would be ashamed of, and the best of it was shabby.

Well, there's one blessing, she thought, as she sat out in the garden, sewing as quickly as she could. *There's not a lot of material in a modern skirt, compared to the ones I just cut up. If I'd been living fifty years ago, this would take days.*

The old linen was soft and heavy, like a damask tablecloth, and if the color had faded from its original indigo to a softer blue, at least it had faded evenly and the color was still pretty. And she could use the time while her fingers worked to continue to puzzle out the cryptic things she had read in the alchemy books last night.

She began by trying to puzzle them out, rationally and logically, but as the needle wove through the heavy linen, it became more of a meditation. Fire . . . flame . . . heat. The heat of passion . . . of love and anger. Righteous anger, carefully controlled. Anger as a weapon. Could love be a weapon?

A weapon—well, perhaps not, but armor, certainly armor! And as a shield. . . .

It was hard to get past her own education, in a way. Young ladies weren't supposed to think about anger, or passion. Young ladies—

Young ladies weren't supposed to think about a great many things, but she had never let that stop her before.

It was long past the time when what young ladies were "supposed" to think about was changed.

Passion. Passion was dangerous; passion overcame reason. Yes, it could, but only if you surrendered your own will to it. That was in the alchemy books, too. If your will was strong, and your heart listened to your head, passion could be a great force for good. Passion could drive a person to do more, far more, than she thought she could. Passion became strength. . . .

She thought about the book that had held drawings of some strange cards, cards unlike the playing cards she was used to. The card called "Strength" was a picture of a beautiful maiden gently holding the jaws of a lion shut with a single hand. That was passion in control of will, the heart obeying the head. Fire yearned to blaze without control, and yet, under the gentle guidance of will, it was a willing servant. Not tame, but tempered. . . .

The needle flashed in the sunlight, the seams grew of themselves. It was a pleasure to sew out here in the sun, and by just luncheon, she was finished. As she surveyed her handiwork with pleasure and a little pride in her accomplishment—three years ago she would haven't even have been able to sew up the hem!—she couldn't help but wonder that if she wore these up to the meadow, would Reggie notice?

Ah, what am I thinking? Why should he notice what I wear or don't wear?

She shook off those thoughts, changed into her new outfit with a sense of making another little step back toward that world she had been evicted from, and ate her luncheon with her nose firmly in her alchemy books. One of the authors was very taken with a magical discipline called the Kabala, but the moment she tried to puzzle *that* out, she felt her eyes practically watering. If her mother had ever mastered that school, there was no sign of it in the notes she had left, and all of the numbers and letters and strange words just made Eleanor's head ache. She went back to her medievalists. The book with the drawings of the cards attracted her profoundly; she couldn't have said why, because she wasn't interested in the so-called fortune-telling abilities of the cards. No, it was more as if they could tell her something about the powers of the Elements in a more understandable way than that Kabala book.

It was not exactly pleasure-reading. She had to reread most paragraphs several times, and then pause and think about what she had just read before she went on. She didn't manage to get through more than a couple of pages at that speed. So when teatime approached, she packed up her basket with a sense of reprieve.

Even if he's not there, she thought, as she walked bare-headed in the beautiful May sunshine, *I'm staying out for a while, as long as I can. Who knows when I'll get outside the garden again once Alison returns?*

No one paid any more attention to her today than they did any other day, but as she made mental comparisons between her new clothing and that of the other girls she passed, she was pleased to see that it held up in the comparison. Of course, this was nothing like the nice frocks she used to have—and as for the wardrobes of Alison and the girls—you might as well compare a head of cabbage to a hothouse rose.

Reggie would not be impressed, she suspected. Not unless he was seeing her in anything like the kind of clothing the girls of *his* set wore, and that was about as likely as being able to fly. But at least she wouldn't be looking like a beggar or a gypsy.

More like a poor governess, she thought, as she reached the outskirts of the village, and sighed. *But then, it isn't as if I have any hope of—* She resolutely turned her thoughts away from hopes of any kind. She was spending time in the company of someone who was intelligent and friendly and *knew who she was.* That was enough. It had to be enough. It was all she was going to get.

And I might not get that today, she reminded herself, as she reached the border of the manor lands, and made her way through the trees, and through grass that seemed longer today than yesterday. *After all, what am I to him? Nothing more than someone his mother* isn't *trying to get him to marry!*

And, maybe, a friend.

I want to be his friend, she realized, with an ache of longing. *Surely that much isn't too much to ask for. . . .*

And how much of a friend could someone be, who probably hadn't said more than a few hundred words to him over the course of a decade? Oh, she could be *his* friend, readily enough, but why should he be hers?

No, he probably wasn't there. He had no reason to be. She was someone pleasant and intelligent to talk to, but he could find that in any of his old friends from the University.

If any of them are still alive. . . .

But to her undisguised delight, he was waiting for her at the usual spot, reading something, as she came up through the last of the trees.

He looked up with a start as a twig broke under her foot, his head jerking wildly as he scanned the trees for the source of the sound. He recovered quickly, and waved at her, but that first reaction made her furrow her brow as she approached him. What on earth had caused *that?*

Was he seeing some of those wretched goblins?

But—no, if there were any here to see, *she* would be seeing them.

But his expression was affable enough as she approached, and as she got near to him, wading through the calf-high grass, he flung himself down on his knees, and looked up at her in imploring mockery.

She bit her tongue. *Oh dear. Now what is he about?* She was afraid he was making fun of her. But on the other hand, it made her smile to see him doing something silly. How long had it been since he'd felt easy enough to be silly?

"Oh, gentle maid, forgive, forgive!" he cried out melodramatically, holding out a bouquet of cowslips and primroses that he must have picked while waiting for her..

"Forgive *what?"* she demanded with a giggle, taking the bouquet. "Don't be so ridiculous, you'll get grass-stains on the knees of your trousers!"

He clambered to his feet. "Forgive that I wasn't here yesterday," he said in a more normal tone of voice. "I completely forgot that I had obligations to deal with yesterday. I should have remembered, and I should have told you."

She felt a thrill of delight, at his words—he *had* thought about her!—but shrugged. "Oh, that! I wasn't here either. I heard you were giving the prizes at the school treat and I know how these things go—it isn't just prizes, it's speeches and the Maypole and all of that, so I knew you'd be busy all day, and I didn't bother to come."

"Sensible girl!" he said, relieved. "And so I was. I've brought things to make it up. Real bottles of lemonade, the fizzy kind, and some only *slightly* squashed tea-cakes, and jam. *And—*" he paused significantly. "Chicken sandwiches. That's the great benefit of being the lord of the manor, you see; no pesky officials coming around to count how many chickens you've got, and whether one's gone missing." He shook his head. "And if you think I am going to feel guilty about depriving some poor PBI of a tin of chicken paste with my scandalous and unpatriotic behavior—"

"Actually," she said, "I doubt very much if you're depriving anyone of anything. Most of the villagers have rabbit hutches and unreported hens, and I know for a *fact* there are unregulated pigs in the woods. No one is feeding any of the contraband animals any rationed grain; they're living off what they can scavenge, and I suspect that's true for what went into your sandwiches."

He regarded her thoughtfully. "I expect that's probably true. My cook has an odd pen on wheels full of birds that she moves over the vegetable garden, and I've never seen her throw any grain to them."

"Exactly." She smiled at him. "The chickens are eating bugs, seeds, and weeds, which is saving manpower in the garden, too. They're probably roosters, or at least, capons, which would have been culled anyway as chicks. So no one is being deprived of anything."

"You salve my conscience as well as my easing my mind." He sat down on the old blanket he had brought and patted it. "Come feast with me, then."

Perfectly happy to, she sat down across from him. Truth to tell, she was rather glad that he had brought most of the tea this time. Without Alison around, there wasn't much bread left, and she had given the old women the last of the cakes yesterday. Her offerings were a bit scanty.

"So how was the school treat?" she asked, conversationally. "Were the children absolute demons?"

"They were rather decent, actually," he replied. "That might have been because we thought of a few more things to keep them out of trouble this year. Swings in the trees, rides in my motor, that sort of thing."

"That was rather kind of you!" she exclaimed, a bit

surprised that he had done any such thing with his fast motorcar.

He shrugged, but looked pleased. "Oh, it was just to the gates and back. But they seemed to like it. Played the very devil with my bad leg though. I forgot how much work there would be, what with all the gearing changes and braking. By the end of the day—"

He broke off, a little flushed. Embarrassed? It could be. There were those who would think that, because he wasn't lacking an arm or an eye, he was malingering. "What?" she supplied, trying to sound casual. "You could hardly walk?"

He looked shamefaced. "Something like . . ."

"Then I suspect it's a good thing you found that out driving the children up and down to the gates, and not some other way," she said, trying not to be too specific. "It does seem to me at least that your doctors are right about taking a long time to heal."

"Well, I think you'll be happy about one thing, anyway," he said, sounding as if he was changing the subject. "Listening to the speeches, one of them was—well, rather better than I had any expectation. So Mater and I decided that we're going to put up a scholarship for the village boys to go to Oxford. Father always intended to, so now we shall."

At first, she was irrationally pleased. How many clever boys had *she* known who could have done very well at university if only they'd been able to go? But then, she thought, *All very well for the boys, certainly,* but felt a twinge of resentment thinking about the number of equally clever girls who ended up just like their mothers, birthing lambs and babies at nearly equal intervals. "What about girls?" she asked aloud.

"What?" He stared at her as if she had said something startling.

"I said, what about girls?" she repeated, firming her chin stubbornly and daring him to look away. "Why only boys? Don't you think girls from the village ought to be able to go if they're clever enough?"

"But—but—" Now he *was* really staring at her. "But what are they going to *do* with a university education? A boy can teach—become an engineer, a scientist, a doctor, a scholar—"

"And a girl can't?" she retorted, now feeling *quite* angry with him. "What about that lady doctor you were always talking about? Why can't a girl become an engineer or a scientist?"

He looked at her as if she had suddenly begun speaking in Urdu. "But—but—"

"I was going to go to Oxford," she reminded him. "What's more, you told me I should, and that I shouldn't let anyone dissuade me!"

"Yes, but these are just village girls, farmer's daughters, with no expectations!" he said, then continued to make his situation worse with every word. "It's not as if—I mean, you're not the same class as they are—I mean—"

His mouth snapped shut as she flushed, as he realized he had just said something horribly rude. She looked down for a moment at her handmade skirt, then looked defiantly up into his eyes, *daring* him to make the comparison between the class she was supposed to be in, and the one she was apparently in now. "Maybe they have no expectations because no one ever let them think that they *could,"* she said bitterly. "Maybe, if someone *bothered* to show them that they could *have* dreams, they might be able to dream them. Mightn't they? Just because they're shopkeepers' girls and farmers' daughters doesn't mean they don't have minds. Some of them have very *good* minds. And I think it's a shame and a sin that all they're thought good for is tending babies and putting up jam."

His eyes looked miserable. But she was very angry now. And she wasn't going to let him off the hook.

"Besides," she pointed out, with coldly, poisonously perfect logic. "*Someone* had better start helping ordinary girls to do things like becoming doctors and teachers. Because thanks to that *bloody* war, there aren't going to *be* any doctors and teachers otherwise. And I don't see the pretty young ladies of *the proper class* rushing off to university to fill the void! Do you? Of course not. It wouldn't be *ladylike.* It wouldn't be *proper."*

He made a strangled little sound in the back of his throat, and looked away.

I shouldn't have said that, she thought. And then thought, rebelliously, *But I'm right. And I'm not going to apologize.*

"You are a truly horrible young woman, you know," he said, very slowly, as if he was weighing and measuring each word, still looking away from her. "Only the truly horrible and the young would dare to tell that much truth."

"Only someone who doesn't have any room for illusions anymore would dare to tell that much truth," she corrected, as the anger slowly faded and cooled to an emotion that was darker and bleaker than that flare of temper. "I can't afford illusions; they are altogether too expensive to maintain. There are a great many of us in that position now."

"Yes," he replied, turning back, slowly. "There are."

They stared at one another, and he finally heaved a great sigh. "That was a very stupid thing to say, wasn't it?"

"It's that whole *game,"* she said, the bitterness back, redoubled. "That whole game of class. It's not going to work, you know! If this wretched war is ever over, it's just not going to work anymore, the whole construction is just going to go smash!"

"Like it did in Russia?" he replied. And managed a wan smile. "You've been listening to Mad Ross Ashley."

"I've been reading," she retorted. She didn't say anything more, but she was thinking a great deal. *I don't know what's going to happen, but—well, just look! Even fifty years ago, you had rich American girls with piles of new money coming over to marry a lord with a name but no prospects, and rich tradesmen's boys getting themselves blue-blooded wives out of the Royal Enclosure that were desperate to get themselves out of tumbledown Tudor manors and into a nice London townhouse in the West End! It can't go on, can't you see that? You can't go on playing that silly game of* we *and* they *and by now you should know it!*

But she didn't say anything. She'd already said more than enough, actually. If he couldn't see this for himself—

But he passed his hand over his eyes, as if his head hurt him. "It's—" He shook his head. "I don't know. I don't even know if we're going to see an end to this, not even with the Americans coming in. Sometimes—" He took his hand away, and looked past her, into the distance, his voice flat. "I don't know if anything matters anymore, because all we are ever going to see is that Juggernaut grinding on and on until there isn't anyone left to fight . . . so what's the point of anything anymore? Why bother trying to change anything, when there isn't going to be anything left to change?"

She bit her lip. She hadn't meant to throw him into this slough of despair, and the worst of it was, she couldn't disagree with him.

And there didn't seem to be anything she could say to make any difference. Or at least, nothing that wasn't at least partly a lie.

"I'm sorry, Reggie," she said, finally. "I didn't mean to—to remind you."

He looked up, and at least he didn't try to smile. "I don't know how any of us can get through the course of a day without being reminded," he said, quietly. "You have to be lying to yourself, I suppose, or purposefully blinding yourself. Like the people who can't seem to find anything to talk about except how hard it is to find a good servant or the impossibility of getting a good chop. Anything except about what's across the Channel."

"But there are good things left, still," she replied, forcing herself to rally, and trying harder now to give him some sense of hope. "I can't see that it's wrong to remember *that.* Pretending the bleak things don't exist is wrong, and not trying to do something about them is worse yet, but it can't be wrong to also remember that there is still joy, still a little peace, still things to laugh about, and still love." She felt her voice faltering, but forced herself to carry on, hoping that she didn't sound too maudlin. "If we forget *that,* we'll lose hope, too."

"Ah, hope," he said, his voice growing a little lighter. And he did manage a smile. "Hope, the last spirit left in

Pandora's jar, after she let all the troubles and plagues of the world out."

"And she let hope fly free, too," Eleanor said softly. "Because when all is said and done, hope is sometimes all that keeps us from surrendering to despair."

He heaved a great sigh, and nodded. "That is as true a thing as I think you have ever said," he told her. "You're quite right, and right to remind me. No, we mustn't lose hope; if we do that—"

He looked off into the distance again, but this time as if he was actually looking *for* something, and not to avoid her gaze.

Perhaps—hope?

"If we do that," he repeated, quietly, as if he was telling *himself* a great truth "We really shall be utterly lost, and there will be no turning back for any of us."

She shivered. Because that had sounded altogether less like an aphorism, and far more like a prophecy.

19

May 2, 1917
Broom, Warwickshire

LITTLE ELEANOR DID HER DISAPPEARING act not long after the quarrel had foundered and crashed, leaving Reggie alone in the meadow, staring glumly after her. The stupid words he'd said, the bitter ones she had responded with, still hung in the air. Nothing was resolved, except, perhaps, she seemed genuinely sorry she had thrown him into a mental funk, and he was genuinely sorry he hadn't thought before he'd spoken.

In fact, in retrospect, he hadn't been at all observant. He'd been so preoccupied with his own thoughts—well, that was a kind way of saying he'd been paying no attention to anything outside of himself. It should have been obvious that her circumstances were changed, drastically, from the last time he had seen her, before the war—her clothing alone should have told him that.

He gulped, as something else occurred to him. *Oh, hell. I've put my foot in it, well and truly.* She had every intention, the last time he saw her, of going to Oxford, and her father had clearly had the means to send her. Her clothing had been good, she had mentioned tutors and special studies in order to pass the entrance qualifications, so although all Reggie knew about her father was that he was a well-off manufacturer, there was certainly money to spare in their household. But her father had been an early casualty of the war, and where had that left her? Had his businesses gone to pieces? So many businesses had—either wrecked without a supervisory hand on the tiller, or collapsed because the war effort siphoned off more and more in the way of manpower and resources until there was no way to keep going.

So—now she was poor. Having to work for a living—that much was obvious from her clothing and her hands. Probably she was a maid somewhere in the village or the surrounding farms—the *servant* of one of those shopkeepers' or farmers' daughters whose intelligence and expectations he had so maligned.

And he had babbled on about scholarships for the boys, when she, so quick, so intelligent, with all of her dreams and expectations blighted, had sat there and let him blather fatuously about what he was going to do for boys he didn't even know—

And he had thought that he was being her friend. She assuredly was his—and look how he had treated her! *Oh, very clever, Reg. Take a juicy chop and dangle it in front of someone who's been dining on crusts, then tell her she can't have it.* He felt sick, absolutely sick as a cat. No wonder she'd blown up at him. He could not possibly have managed anything more cruel if he'd set out to torture her on purpose.

And now, of course, he had set things up so that if he offered her a scholarship, he would look as if he was humoring her, patronizing her. Throwing her crumbs out of misplaced pity, even though he didn't think she had any future other than as the wife of a menial laborer and that any education given her would be wasted. Or worse, as if it didn't matter if he offered her a scholarship because he didn't expect her to last out the first term.

You really are a prize idiot.

She would probably never come back here again after this. And he wouldn't blame her. Why would she care to continue to befriend someone who treated her so shabbily?

But then, guilt turned to irritation. Hang it all, this was at least her fault in part! Why hadn't she simply said something about her current straitened circumstances? She didn't have to *ask* for help, but if she had just *said* something about not having the money to go to Oxford, well, of course he would have jumped in with an offer to help her out! Why did females have to be so confounded complicated! He was in hearty sympathy with Bernard Shaw's Henry Higgins. . . .

Except that he was also in hearty sympathy with Bernard Shaw's Eliza Doolittle. Actually, more so than with Higgins, if it came down to cases. Guilt resurfaced. Why *should* she say anything about her current state? It wasn't as if he had any right to know—and it must be profoundly shaming to her.

Torn between guilt and exasperation, he did the only thing a man of sense would do at such a time. He went in search of his motorcar and a drink.

The first was easy enough to find, as it was parked just off the road where he had left it. The second lay no further away than Broom, and his haven of the Broom Pub.

By now, he was one of the regulars; he was well aware that three years ago, he would never have been accepted as a regular in here if he had been coming for ten years straight. The class differences between himself and the men who made this their refuge would have been too much of a chasm to bridge. But the war made more than strange bedfellows, it made comrades of strangers sharing the same suffering, and moreover, he had, from the beginning, tried to leave the lord of the manor at the door. So he was welcomed for himself, as well as for the fact he could be counted on to buy more than his share of rounds, and in that haven of resolute masculinity, he felt his spirit soothed and his guilt eased the moment he crossed the threshold.

Good beer was balm for the soul, and a good barman has, by convivial nature and training in his trade, as great a fund of wisdom as any counselor and often quite a bit more than most clerics. Tom Brennan was such a barman, and his "gents" felt completely at ease in unloading their woes within his walls.

It is as probable as the sun rising that when fellow sufferers meet together over drinks, before the evening is out, one of them will say "Women!" in that particular suffering tone that makes his fellow creatures shake their heads and murmur sympathetically until the particular grievance emerges.

Reggie had every intention of being the sufferer that evening, but one of the others beat him to it.

Joseph Atherton's hour of discontent was made evident by his heavy footsteps as he pushed open the door. He ordered his pint, took a long draught of it, and as the rest waited and listened in expectation, the cause of his unhappiness was revealed.

"Women!" said Farmer Joe, with unusual vehemence.

Murmurs of sympathy all around, intended to encourage more revelation.

"I mean!" he continued, aggrieved, "A fellow's got enough to do in his day, don't he? And when she *says* that May Day is all stuff and nonsense, and that she don't hold with sech childish farradiddle, a fellow's got a right to take her at her word, don't he? I mean! Cows need milkin', stock needs feedin', and there's enough to do without muckin' about gettin' a lot of silly flowers, *and* on the day of fair and school treat, no less, and all them tents and kiddies to be hauled up t'manor!"

With those words, it all came clear to every man in the pub. Clearly, Mrs. Tina had been expecting to get her May Day tribute, no matter what she had said to the contrary. Clearly, what with young Adam being the sort to "volunteer" his father's services—Joseph having one of the few farm horses old enough to have escaped being "conscripted," but young enough to do his work—Joseph had found himself dragooned unwilling into helping out on top of an already heavy workload.

And clearly, when the aforementioned May Day tribute did not materialize, Mrs. Tina had made her displeasure known. Which was probably why Joe was here, and not sitting down to his dinner.

"Unfair, that's what it is," replied another farmer, Albert Norman. "How's a man to guess, when they say one thing, and mean the opposite?"

"Or when they don't say anything at all," Reggie put in, with feeling. "And they expect you to somehow *understand* what's going on in their heads without any clue! And *then* when you blunder into some hideous mistake, they turn on you!"

"That's a fact," Joseph sighed. Albert nodded glumly.

"Dunno why they can't just say straight out what they want." A new country heard from: Michael Van, off in the corner with Mad Ross. "I mean! Tha's *logical,* ain't it? Do *we* go around sayin' one thing and meanin' the contrariwise?"

Reggie nodded along with the others, and signaled for another pint.

"You say to a girl," said young Albert, to no one in particular, "You say, 'a feller I know was wonderin' if you're seein' anyone in particaler,' an' *she* says, 'no, not in particaler,' and you get all set to—to see if she'd *like* to be seein' anyone in particaler, and then you turns around, and whup, there she is, *at* fair, *with* another feller, with all the parish t'see! So if she ain't *with* 'im, then why's she actin' like she's *with* 'im, is what I want to know!"

More shaking of heads. "Can't account for it," said Michael Van. "And you'd think, wouldn't you, if you'd offended some 'un, they'd tell you, wouldn't you?" He appealed to Ross. "If I said something that made you mad, you'd say!"

"I'd say," Mad Ross replied, with a glint in his eye. "Or I'd punch your nose. Either way, you'd know."

"So there's no call to be mad at a body if he's said summat you didn't like, and you didn't *tell* him, is there?" Michael continued, sounded aggrieved. "And 'specially if it was months and months ago, and you never said, till it's too late for him to remember what he *did* say, much less why you should be mad about it!"

"That's a fact," replied Albert.

"My round, I think," Reggie said.

Reggie would have liked to air his own grievance—but with his nerves rawly sensitive, he didn't want to put his standing in jeopardy with the other Broom regulars. He ran it over in his mind. *No matter what I say, it's going to offend someone. If I tell them what I told her, surely they'll think I was being patronizing too. It's that lord of the manor business—and it wouldn't matter that not one of them has* ever *given thought to his daughter doing anything other than marrying another farmer or laborer—the moment* I *say anything about it, they're going to think the worse of me.*

So instead, he just shook his head and murmured, "Women! There's no pleasing them."

The others nodded sagely.

The barmaid, Jessamine Heggins, glanced sideways at young Albert with compressed lips as she passed him, collecting glasses, delivering fresh pints. Reggie wondered if she was the one that Albert was referring to, and felt a distinct touch of annoyance at her. That was a cruel thing, stringing the poor fellow along!

"Well," he said looking into his glass, "Seems to me pretty unfair of them to expect us to know things without being told them. Seems to me it's pretty unfair to expect us to figure things out from a couple of hints not even King Solomon could guess at."

"Aye," Michael grumbled, tossing back his pint.

That was about as close as he dared come to his own grievance, and eventually someone ventured an oblique guess as to the likelihood of rabbitting come fall.

Now Reggie felt a bit more comfortable. "You know," he said, thoughtfully, and with an artfully casual manner, "My manager says that the rabbits are multiplying something awful this year. Three years now, no one's been thinning them out with shooting. *I* think a few snares wouldn't come amiss." He looked around the pub, as if he didn't know very well that every one of these men had been poaching "his" rabbits for generations. "Any of you fellows know someone that might be willing to put out some snares in the Longacre woods? Proper rabbit snares now, not something to catch a pheasant by accident."

Slight smiles. "Might," Ross offered.

After all, everyone poached. Especially now. But no one wanted to admit he knew how to.

"Now mind," Reggie went on, carefully not meeting anyone's eye, "He'd have to be careful of the season. We wouldn't want any orphaned bunnies. Not unless there were youngsters who knew how to catch them and raise them on goat's milk or something of the sort."

"Orphaned beasties is a sad thing," Michael Van agreed. "But the kiddies do like to make pets of 'em. Wouldn't hurt for 'em to go looking, now and again, just to make sure. No one'd set a snare this early, or at least, I misdoubt, but there's other things that make orphan bunnies. Dogs."

"Cats," put in Albert.

"Stoats," offered Ross, who Reggie knew for a fact kept ferrets. "Even badgers, can they catch 'em."

Reggie had a long pull on his beer, hiding his smile. That was settled, then. *They* knew that he would tell his gamekeeper not to pull up proper rabbit snares, and *he* knew that anyone that caught a doe out-of-season would send his children, or a neighbor's to look for the nest. And he'd probably lose a pheasant or two; some temptations were too strong to resist.

But he'd have lost a pheasant or two anyway, probably more than one or two. When you worked vigilantly to keep someone from doing something he felt he had a right to do, he often felt justified in taking a little revenge.

Giving tacit permission, on the other hand, was likely to make them more honest.

He'd never felt very comfortable about telling people they couldn't snare rabbits on Longacre property, anyway. After all, what did *he* ever do with them except in that they kept foxes fed for the autumn hunts? And smart foxes would steal the caught rabbits from the snares anyway. Oh, there was some rabbit shooting in the fall, or there had been before the war, but most gentlemen felt that rabbits were poor sport compared to birds. When meat was getting hard to come by, and hideously expensive, even with the illicit pigs in the woods, a rabbit was a welcome addition to the table.

Besides, you have to wonder how many of my generation are going to be particularly interested in shooting things for sport, when all this is over. . . .

He sighed, and signalled another round, while the talk drifted amiably to other shifts for keeping food on the table. Pigeons were being considered, though with some doubt. As Ross said, "Once you get the feathers off, hardly seems worth the time." With the river so near, and plenty of free grazing at the road's edge, geese were popular, but the problem was sorting out whose belonged to whom. Goats were not highly regarded. Having eaten goat on occasion in France, Reggie fully understood why.

Tonight there had been no bad news from across the Channel to stir up melancholy, good spring weather here and summer coming, and the school treat and fair so fresh in everyone's mind, the conversation stayed relatively light. "Relatively," since no one really had the heart for games of darts or shove-ha'penny in this pub. When Reggie left, it was in an even temper, and not the same unsettled state he'd arrived in.

So when, just past the last house in the village, a black mood descended on him—it made no sense.

It came down on him like a palpable weight, and it wasn't grief. It was bleak, despairing anger. It made him shift gears with a harsh disregard for the complaining clatter his motorcar made in protest. It made him want to strangle his grandfather—or hang himself, just to show the old man. Or both. It made him want to find that baggage of a girl and—

And that was where his good sense finally overpowered his mood, because the images that began to form in his mind at the thought of Eleanor were so vicious that they shook him, shook him right *out* of his mood. He looked sharply around, having even lost track of where he was, only to find that he was on the driveway of the manor and didn't recall actually turning in through the gates.

What is wrong with me? he thought, aghast. And, now with a frisson of fear, *Am I going mad?*

Because he could not imagine a sane man thinking those things that had just come into his head.

Now feeling both depressed and afraid, he parked the motor and went straight up to his room, not wanting to encounter either his mother or his grandfather.

His valet wasn't about, and he didn't ring for him; in this mood, he wanted to be completely alone—was this some new phase to his shellshock? Or was this something else altogether, the sign that he was truly coming to pieces in a way that would make him dangerous to those around him as well as himself?

If that were the case—

Then, he thought, grimly, as he got himself ready to sleep without the aid of his valet *I had better keep away from Eleanor. For her sake. At least until I know—*

And that was his last thought as he drifted off into a fully drugged sleep. *—at least until I know. One way or another. And if I am—I am going to have to make sure that there is nothing I can do to harm her.*

Alison and the girls did not put in an appearance that evening, and Eleanor took herself to Sarah's cottage in a mood of prickly determination. As she had hoped, Sarah had anticipated her coming, and had laid out her mother's workbook and the few bits of paraphernalia that a Fire magician deemed necessary.

But her mind wouldn't settle, and even the Salamanders that now always appeared whenever she was around an open fire and either alone or with Sarah, could not be calmed. Reflecting her restlessness, they wreathed around her like agitated ferrets, never pausing long, twining around wrists, arms and neck. They were a distraction, and she welcomed it.

Sarah was not in much better case. She couldn't keep her mind on business either. Finally, after the third attempt at scrying by flame, she threw up her hands.

"It's not going to happen," she said, with a snort of disgust. "Your mind isn't on it, and neither is mine. What's got *you* all of a pother, anyway?"

"Reggie," Eleanor said, wrinkling her nose, and described the quarrel. Even though they had made it up, she was still annoyed with him. It was difficult not to be.

I'll try to settle my mind so I don't go to sleep on it—but how could *he have been so obtuse?*

"Men!" Sarah said, with a dismissive contempt. "A dog's more protective, and a cat will catch mice, but a man causes more problems than he cures, I swear it. I'd have been angry too, in your place."

Reluctantly, Eleanor felt moved to defend him. "He did apologize," she admitted. "Eventually."

"And then he ran right back to his pack at the pub, where they are all maligning the female race even as we speak," said Sarah, with just a touch of a sneer. "I know; I heard his motorcar go by and stop at the Broom. By the time he motors home, he'll be feeling perfectly justified in speaking every word he said."

Eleanor felt her temper flare again, and throttled it down. "Well, then I hope he has a hangover for his pains," she replied. "Why are *you* so out-of-sorts?"

"Something nasty is out there tonight," Sarah said abruptly, and uneasily, casting a glance at the windows, where the curtains were drawn tight against the dark. "It can't pass the bounds I put on the village, but I can feel it pressing against them. Whatever it is—or *they* are, since I can't tell if it's one thing, or several—they're angry."

Eleanor felt her annoyance with Reggie melting away. "What is it?" she asked, urgently. "More of those Earth-goblins?"

But Sarah shook her head. "No. I'd recognize those. This is very different. More of this world than the goblins are. No, it's something else. If I didn't know better—and come to think of it, maybe I don't—I'd say it was spirits. Ghosts."

Eleanor blinked. "Ghosts?" Somehow it had never occurred to her that, along with Elemental Magic and everything else, ghosts might be real, too. "But why would ghosts be trying to get into the village?"

"Now, that's where you have me," Sarah admitted candidly. "I don't know. Ghosts usually don't leave the spot where they're rooted. Sometimes it's a place they loved, sometimes it's one where they had something terrible or wonderful happen to them, but mostly it's where they died or their bodies are buried. It takes a lot to uproot them, and a great deal more to set them to some new task of haunting. That's why I can't imagine why or how it could be spirits."

Eleanor shivered, and cast a glance towards the windows herself. "What else could it be?"

"I don't know," Sarah replied, and shook her head. "Whatever it is, it won't disturb anyone inside the bounds, and outside, well, you'd have to be able to see them, and most people can't." She pulled on her lower lip with her teeth for a moment. "I'm inclined to think at the moment that it's just a blow-up left over from May Eve. That's one of the four Great Holy Days when the boundaries between the spirit world and the real world are thinned. Witches—well, we tend those doorways on those days—let the ones that want just to look in on their loved-ones out, and keep the doors open so they can all go back at daybreak. You know the old song, where the lady's three sons come back to her? She called them on May Eve—'I wish the wind would never cease, nor flashes in the flood, till my three sons return to me in earthly flesh and blood.' "

"But—" Eleanor began.

Sarah shook her head. "Can't tell you more than that; it's witch's business. But like every other job, witches have been lost to the war, and if one of those doors wasn't tended—or if it was opened by someone inexperienced who let it slip closed too early—" She shrugged. "If that's all it is, then they might be angry because they know a witch is in this village, and they want me to let them through."

"Well, why don't you?" Eleanor asked, reasonably.

"Because I don't know what door it is." She sighed. "If

things don't improve, I'll have to arrange something, but otherwise, we're probably better off leaving well enough alone. There's always the chance they'll find their own way over. There's help on the Other Side if they truly want back."

Eleanor wanted to ask more, but the look on Sarah's face told her that she wasn't going to get anything more, so she changed the subject. "One of the books I found in the library talked about fortune-telling cards," she said instead. "And the one they talked about seemed—well, it seemed to make more sense than some of the other things I was reading."

Sarah's tense expression eased. "Ah. The Tarot. I can see where that'd be useful, and fit right in with your mum's notes. Wait a moment."

She turned and went to a cupboard, bringing out something rectangular wrapped in silk. She set the package down on the table and unwrapped it. It was an oversized deck of cards.

"These are the Tarot cards," Sarah said, picking up the well-worn pasteboards, and separating out one smaller stack from the rest. "The ones that'll be the most use to you right now, for giving you things to think on, are these—"

She fanned out the cards in her hand; Eleanor could see that they didn't look anything like playing cards. They were pictures, like the one she'd seen in the book, called Strength.

"These are the cards called the Major Arcana, the most powerful in that there's the most meaning packed into them, and the most symbolism. There's twenty-two of them, and this," she pulled one out of the deck "is the first, the last, or the card that travels through the whole deck. And in this case, since you're the Seeker right now, this card represents you, on your journey through the Powers as you try to master them."

Eleanor looked down at it; the card showed her what looked like a young man, dancing on the edge of a cliff. There was a little dog at his feet, the sun overhead, and he held a rose in one hand, and a stick with a bundle on the end, like a Traveler, in the other.

"The Fool," she read aloud, and looked up. "Why is that me?"

"Well, *you've* had all that study; when you look at the stories about King Arthur and the Grail, who do they call the Perfect Fool, and why?" Sarah countered.

"Percival," she replied immediately. "Because he was innocent, unschooled. He could ask questions no one else would, because he didn't know he shouldn't."

"And that's our Fool," Sarah replied, tapping the card with one finger. "The Fire in his card is his intelligence; he burns with curiosity and the need to know things. He's perfectly innocent; he breaks the rules because he doesn't know they're there and doesn't know he should abide by them. Sometimes that's for good, and sometimes it can bring disaster. He's the Seeker, who moves from card to card looking for wisdom. He's fearless, because he doesn't know he should fear. He isn't worried about being on the edge of the cliff, because he isn't thinking about the next minute when he might fall off, he's thinking about *right now,* and besides, for all he knows, he'll step out into the empty air and it'll hold him."

Eleanor studied the card closely. "So if he's concentrating on *now,* he isn't looking forward?"

Sarah nodded. "That's the negative side of him. He's not at all in the spirit, and very much in the body. He breaks rules that sometimes shouldn't be broken and will bring him grief when they are. He can fall off that cliff. He means change, but change isn't always good."

She paused, waiting. Eleanor sensed she was waiting for her pupil to come up with some answers of her own. "So, this concentration on his physical body—that's his Earth aspect? It looks to me like he's mostly Fire and Earth. Not much water symbolism here. Of course, though, there's Air—the Air he could step off into."

Sarah nodded. "Change might be the Water aspect, but mostly the Fool is Intellect and Passion, and that's Air and Fire. Which makes him even more appropriate for you."

She turned over a second card, this one showing a man in a white robe and a red cloak. He stood among roses and lilies, with a rose-vine overhead. He had a wand in his hand and was next to a table on which were a cup, a knife, another wand, and a disk. There was something like the number eight lying on its side hovering like a halo above his head. Eleanor read the card's name aloud. "The Magician."

"What else can you tell me?" Sarah asked.

She studied it, and was struck by the objects on the table, which reminded her of something in one of the Alchemy books. "That's all four Elements, there," she said, pointing to the table. "The Cup is Water, the Disk is Earth, the Wand is Air and the Knife is Fire. So he has command of all of the elements?"

"Or he hasn't yet chosen which one his Element is," Sarah countered. "That wand he's holding is a symbol of his power, not of a particular Element. He's the symbol of the mind, too, like the Fool, but in his case, it's Creativity, not Intellect. He knows what he wants out of Heaven *and* Earth, and so long as he stays focused, he'll get it."

Eleanor studied the card further. "But he can run right over the top of you to get what he wants," she said slowly. "Which is the negative side of him; selfish and self-centered. So he's like the Fool in that way, in a way, their negative side is being self-centered."

"Good!" Sarah applauded. "And what else?"

"Well, if his positive side is that he can get anything if he can stay focused, then I guess his weakness is that he's likely to lose concentration and be scattered." She pondered that for a moment. "So, where this card is all elements, I'd say that the Magician himself is mostly Air?"

"That's how I've always seen him, but remember he's a channel for all of them, more so than most other cards. So he gets being charming and attractive from Earth, he gets a streak of passion and genius from Fire, he gets independence and the willingness to break rules from Air, and the ability to handle power and make changes from Water." Sarah got up and went back to her cupboard, taking out a similar wrapped bundle. She pulled a second card out, and laid it beside the Magician. This one, too, was labeled the Magician, but it wasn't a ceremonial Magician. This one looked like a circus trickster, a charlatan, who was juggling cups and balls. "This is an older version, from a deck I don't use much. It shows you the Magician's darker side."

"A cheat, a stage-magician," Eleanor said at once. "I can see—his dark side is that charm used to gull people, the intellect used to practice deception, the willingness to break rules can make him a criminal, and Water can sweep away everything, leaving you with nothing."

"*Very* good!" Sarah replied. "And those two cards are enough to think about for one night, so the lesson is over. Did you say you had a book that talked about the Tarot in alchemical terms?"

She nodded.

"Then go home and read what it has to say about the Fool and the Magician." Sarah folded her cards back up in their silk and put them away. "We'll look at another card tomorrow. Meanwhile, you think about these tonight."

Eleanor took her leave, and made her way back to The Arrows well before her sprig of rosemary withered. She went to bed and followed Sarah's orders, reading about and thinking about those two cards until she fell asleep—

At which point she found herself in dreams, dressed in clothing of a medieval Italian page, dancing on the edge of a cliff with the sun high overhead and not a cloud in the sky. . . .

20

May 3–21, 1917
Broom, Warwickshire

MAY THIRD HAD DAWNED IN rain, and it kept raining all day long, a steady pour that made Eleanor reluctant even to venture to Sarah's cottage, much less to the meadow. Not that she ever thought that she would have met Reggie there. No, if he'd been kept away merely because he wanted to give rides to kiddies in his motorcar, the prospect of a soaking would certainly keep him inside four walls.

So Eleanor had stayed where she was, took the opportunity to further increase her wardrobe, and when she wasn't obeying Alison's spells, studied her books diligently. The dream she'd had the previous night, of being the Fool, had given her impetus. It had been vividly realistic, too; she'd felt nothing but euphoria and a curiosity about absolutely everything. No fear, none at all, when she'd stopped dancing for a moment, leaned over, and stared into the abyss below her. In the dream, the thought that she might fall had not even flitted across her mind. No fear, when she stared up into the sky, straight at the blazing sun, wondering what it was. Fortunately, it was the sun of the card, and not of reality; bright though it was, and hot, too, it didn't blind her. Of course, that had been in retrospect. At the time, all she had thought was, *What is that? Why is it so hot? Can I reach it?*

She had half-awakened, but no more than that, fallen asleep again, to find herself, still the Fool, in a garden of roses and lilies, though she had no idea of how she had gotten there. She followed a path—then she was at the end of the path suddenly, and there was an altar there. On it were a cup, a scepter, a golden disk the size of a dinner-plate, and a sword. Behind the altar was someone in a white robe and a red cloak, with a broom in her hand. A broom, because it wasn't a man, as in the card, it was Sarah.

"So, what do you see?" the Magician asked. Eleanor said the first thing that came into her mind—not an answer, but a question.

"What cup is that, and what does it hold?"

Sarah nodded. "Good. Come and find out for yourself." She leaned the broom against the altar, picked up the cup, and held it out to Eleanor, just like a priest offering the sacrament. Eleanor came and took it from her, and drank from it—

And suddenly, it was *she* who was in the white robes and red cloak and behind the altar, and Sarah and her broom were nowhere to be seen. But even as, when she had been the Fool, her mind was full of questions, *now* it was full of knowledge.

She put the cup down, dazzled by all of the things flooding through her thoughts, when a voice interrupted her from the table.

"Well, now that you have Wisdom, you ought to know what to do with the other three Gifts," the voice said, and she looked down at the Cup to see that it was much larger, nearly the size of a washtub, and there was a great salmon sticking its head out of the water and looking up at her. "Well?" said the salmon. "With all that Wisdom, what are you going to do next?"

She looked at the other three items; her hand moved towards the sword, then she stopped.

"Quite right," said the salmon, sounding like something

out of Alice's Adventures. "You aren't nearly strong enough to wield the Passion of Fire. What else is there?"

Her hand hovered between the Coin of Earth and the Wand of Air, and she had just started to reach for the latter—

When she woke up. It was dawn, and time to get to work.

It was still raining, and didn't look as if it was going to stop at any time soon. So that day was a repeat of the previous one, and at least she finished sewing all the rest of her new wardrobe, because the weather cleared off in the night, and by teatime of the fifth, there was the sound of a motorcar and Alison and the girls chugged into the old stable that now served as a garage.

There was nothing to make into what Alison would have called a "decent" tea and dinner except tinned stuff, of course. And in any event, it was too late for Eleanor to start anything, so as Eleanor hauled their baggage up to their rooms, they tidied themselves up, then pulled the motor back out again to go to the Broom Hall Inn for tea and order that a dinner be sent around. And life went right back to normal.

Neither Alison nor the girls noticed Eleanor's new clothing, nor did anyone note books missing from the library. They were all very full of chatter about London—there were Americans moving through now, and Lauralee was very taken with them. She kept exclaiming about how tall they were.

As for Alison, she acted like a cat that had gotten into cream. Whatever she had done while she'd been gone, she was very pleased with it, and herself.

So things went back to the way they had been, except that every two or three days, Eleanor would slip away after the household was in bed, and get down to Sarah's cottage, which was where Sarah would take out her cards and they would go over all of the ones that she had already seen as Eleanor tried to glean a little more meaning out of them. Then Sarah would lay out a new one.

There was no chance to get out to the meadow. But as May became June, she certainly heard enough about Reggie. The campaign to ingratiate themselves into the Longacre circle was well underway, and twice-weekly tennis-parties were the artillery pounding away at the gates. Longacre had its own courts, and Lady Devlin loved to both watch and play. Even though Reggie couldn't play because of his knee, he always came to watch his mother—and Alison and both girls were good enough to give her ladyship a good game of doubles. This, of course, was according to what Alison told her little coterie of the Broom elite over tea.

Eleanor knew the truth. Of course they were good enough—because of magic. They'd shown no aptitude before this, but one of the things that had come back from London had been a set of three tennis raquettes with a faint feeling of magic about them. Eleanor had no doubt, no doubt at all, that Alison had somehow stolen someone's tennis-prowess and put it into those raquettes.

Alison and her daughters were also up at the manor at least once a week for tea, and Eleanor expected that would change to two or even three times a week before long.

There was company due at Longacre Park in the first week of June, too—which would probably mean more entertaining. Tea-dances, card-parties, boating on the river, riding on the grounds, as well as tennis and croquet, and more chances for Lauralee and Carolyn to use whatever they could to ensnare Reggie. . . .

Well, she thought, more than once, *If he's stupid enough to let himself be ensnared, then he's not worth wasting time on.*

But she couldn't help contrasting herself with her stepsisters, whenever they sailed out of the house in their modish tennis-dresses or flirty tea-gowns. Once, perhaps, she had been the equal of her stepsisters, and might have been able to pass herself off as belonging in Reggie's social set. Money was still not the equal of breeding in the eyes of some, but it was certainly approaching that equivalency—and to Reggie's generation, perhaps it had achieved equality. At least, so long as one had the right accent, the right education, the right manners and conversation, the right outward appearance.

Now—well, he might sit with her in a meadow and be amused by her conversation, but her hands were callused and rough with manual labor, her clothing was fit only for the lowest servants, and with those two handicaps, it didn't matter how fine her mind was. If he'd been penniless but blue-blooded, perhaps—but not while he was lord of Longacre Park. With that insurmountable social gulf between them, while he might amuse himself in private, he would never acknowledge the friendship in public.

And a friend who won't treat me the same, in public as in private, isn't worth having.

She tried not to feel eaten up with envy as the girls chattered about "dear Reggie" and tormented one another over which he had paid more attention to that day. But it would have been difficult enough to watch them swanning about with their airs and their chatter about going "up the hill." It was very difficult indeed to hear them boasting about "dear Reggie" this and "dear Reggie" that.

She took what grim solace she could in her study of Elemental Magic. The sooner she mastered that, the sooner she could free herself. And then—well, then she would worry about when she was freed.

She'd had no trouble getting to sleep; now that it was June, the days were getting longer, and longer days just meant that Alison found more work for her to do. And she was not at all surprised to find herself immediately in a dream.

The dream began now in a familiar pattern; Eleanor found herself as the Fool, resolutely turned away from the cliff-edge, and passed up the path to the Magician. The Tarot cards were providing the framework for the quest for Mastery; there was no doubt in her mind about *that.* But this time, the Magician was not Sarah, but a stranger. Still, she asked the right question, became the Magician, and prepared to pass on—

The Salmon of Wisdom did not appear in the cup now

that she had the key to this card. She was able at this point to actually pick up the blade, the cup, the wand and the coin—and yet she sensed she was not able to use more than a fraction of the power in each, not even of her own Element. And she would not—she knew that now—until she had journeyed through all of the Major Arcana. But she needed to prove that she could handle the tools of the four Elements, so she picked each up in turn from the altar, sensed and identified the magical energies in each, then turned and walked up the path that appeared behind her. It led between two severely manicured flowerbeds, and she followed it until she came to a pavilion. She had been here before and knew who awaited her.

The High Priestess was an ageless woman, seated on a throne, holding a scroll in one hand. Crowned with all three phases of the moon, cloaked in blue, and poised between a black pillar and a white, she also represented Intelligence. The blue robe gave her Element away; it had been no challenge to figure out that it was Air. But not only did she represent Intelligence—more than that, she stood for Balance. The Priestess was all about balance, calm, emotional self-sufficiency. Nothing ever ruffled her feathers. She represented the mystic side of the mind in harmony with the physical side as well, and her negative aspect was to be without true emotion, sterile rather than celibate, to stagnate rather than be in balance, to be emotionally empty rather than controlled. Eleanor had been here before; it had taken some thinking to work out that she should ask "What is the key to Wisdom?" She asked that question now, and she accepted the scroll from the Priestess. As she had become the Magician, so she now became the Priestess, and this had provided her first real temptation. Because she didn't really want to go on to the next card. The Fool was full of questions, the Magician full of knowledge—but the Priestess was full of a calm, balanced, and ordered wisdom. If she had ever dreamed of being "like" anything when she attained her Mastery, it would have been to be like this.

And yet, that was a trap. She had a long, long way to go yet.

And that, too, was wisdom. She rose and descended the three shallow steps that led to her throne, and went back into the garden.

And though she should have left by the same path on which she had entered, instead, it was a path through wildly lush rose beds, intermingled with peonies and lilies, all three perfumes mingling in an intoxication of scent. And when she came to the end of the path, she found herself in another part of the garden, facing another crowned, seated woman. This was her new card.

The Empress.

Where the High Priestess was all austerity, the Empress was all abundance. She was crowned with stars, with her foot on the quarter-moon that the High Priestess wore as a crown. She carried a heart in one hand, a scepter in the other. She was stunningly beautiful, and was surrounded by roses, and from the sensuality that infused even the slightest gesture, it was clear that she was as warmly emotional as the High Priestess was austere.

Now, this was a card that Eleanor had not yet gotten past. Not that she didn't know all the meanings; her Element was Earth, she represented creativity, fertility in all things, grace and beauty. She was very aware of herself and very sure of herself. She had power, but it was the power to direct, rather than to lead or to order. Eleanor felt she had far more in common with the intellectual ascetic, the High Priestess, than this Lady of Venus.

The negative aspect was, of course, unbridled sensuality, but Eleanor felt herself very uncomfortable with sensuality of any sort.

"I don't see," she said to the Empress, in a voice that sounded rather high and nervous rather than confident, "what you have to do with me."

The three-moon headdress she wore as the High Priestess felt horribly heavy in that moment.

The Empress smiled a slow, languid smile, full of promises. "You don't deny you're a woman?" she drawled.

Eleanor tried not to squirm. "Not that it does me any good," she complained—the words jumping out of her mouth before she could think. "No one pays the least attention to me."

"That's your stepmother's doing," the Empress said, in a purr. "She doesn't want anyone to think of you as a human being, much less a woman. But until you reconcile yourself to the fact that you *are* a woman, and you can be bound by your womanhood or freed by it, you won't get past me."

"Freed?" Eleanor snorted. "Nobody is freed by womanhood! We aren't even allowed to vote! Why—"

"That has not always been so, and it will not be forever," the Empress replied, bending to sniff her roses. "That is not to the point—the point is *you.* You must embrace all sides of yourself to pass any card. Body as well as mind. What am I?"

"Umm—" Eleanor found herself blushing. "Ah—"

"Sensuality. Rejoicing in the physical. If your head is strong and full of thoughts, but your body is weak, where are you?" The Empress tilted her head to the side. "Where is the balance in that, High Priestess? Or perhaps I should say—pretty Fool." And in that moment Eleanor's robes vanished and she was back in the garb of the Fool again.

"Weak? Me?" Eleanor snorted again. "With all the work I have to do?"

"Ah, but do you take pleasure in that fine young body of yours, or merely allow it to carry your head around?" The Empress yawned.

"And just what is there to take pleasure in?" Eleanor demanded angrily. Why this card made her so angry, she could not have said, but it did, and made her terribly uncomfortable as well.

"Please. Haven't you two working eyes, two fine ears?" the Empress replied with scorn. "There are meadowlarks by day, and the scent of flowers—by night, the moon and the cool, soothing breeze. Your body is healthy and strong, and work comes easily to it. You are young, and when the song of spring sings in your veins, you feel the quickening of the earth all around you. You have more, much more, than many of those that you know possess. You are not dead or dying, maimed or ill, how can you not take pleasure in these things?"

"Um—" well, she *had* been doing just that. "I suppose—I suppose you must be right—"

"And young men," the Empress persisted, looking both wise and sly. "Haven't you felt longing for—"

"No!" she exclaimed, feeling her face flush hotly.

"Too soon, too soon, you protest too much and too soon," the Empress declared, laughing, holding up the heart she held for Eleanor's inspection. "You silly child! Do you think I do not know?"

Her face flamed so redly it was painful. No! She *hadn't* longed after Reggie! Not really. After all, he didn't think anything of her, so why should she think of him? It wasn't even remotely possible, anyway. . . .

"And who does it harm to admit that side of yourself?" the Empress murmured, hooding her eyes with heavy lids. "Who is going to tell Reggie? Not I, certainly. My dear, my dear, these things *must* be taken from your path! I cannot give you the rose to let you pass until you examine and accept what is in your own heart! Who am I going to tell, after all?"

Her face burning, Eleanor opened her mouth, shut it, opened it—then turned and fled.

The little dog yapped at her heels, sounding angry at her. She ignored him as she ignored the roses whose thorns caught at her clothing and tried to stop her, as she fled out of the garden, out of the dream, and—

—and woke up with a start.

It was still dark. It had felt as if she had been in the garden for hours, but by the moon shining in her window, she knew it couldn't have been more than an hour or two.

She was panting and winded as if she really *had* run through that garden, and her heart pounded, the loudest sound in the room.

What was I so frightened of?

Not for the first time, she wondered just who—or what—the Tarot creatures really were. At first she had thought that they were images and archetypes out of her own mind, but she had shortly realized that they knew things she didn't. And they acted in ways that seemed entirely independent of her mind. Like the Empress, for instance.

Why was I so upset with what she said?

She did not *like* the Empress, not even in her proper position. She was too knowing, too lush, too—too sensual. Too much of everything, actually. The Magician had been a wealth of knowledge, cool and aloof after that first time of being Sarah, the High Priestess was someone that Eleanor could admire, wise, controlled, and ascetic. But the Empress! She was—she was—

She's like Alison, when Alison is in one of her queen-of-everything moods. . . .

And as she lay there, staring at the ceiling, letting her thoughts settle into a pattern again, she gradually understood what was going on. The key to the Empress, that had eluded her for several nights now, finally came into her grasp.

More than ever she wished she could stop with the High Priestess. And she knew that she couldn't, that she would have to dream herself back; not tomorrow or the next night, but tonight. She had to face this and face it now, with the knowledge fresh in her mind.

She closed her eyes, moved around on her lumpy mattress until she was completely comfortable, then began taking slow, even breaths. She concentrated, not on the dream she wanted to re-enter, nor her surroundings. She concentrated on herself, on relaxing every muscle in her body, starting with her face. She felt muscles let go that she didn't even know were tensed as she worked her way from her head, to her shoulders, to her arms . . . felt herself starting to drift, as the night-sounds faded away from around her, and she felt as if she was floating, and . . .

And she found herself back on the edge of the cliff, in the person of the Fool.

She stared down at the abyss below her for a moment. The bottom was lost in haze and darkness; she'd never been able to see it. Oddly, that made it seem less dangerous, as if she could throw herself over the edge, spread her arms, and fly.

And the Fool in her would have been willing to give that a try, for the Fool had no fear and not a great deal of good judgment.

Resolutely, she turned from the cliff and took the path into the garden.

The Magician was not waiting at his altar, but the accoutrements were still there. But this time, Eleanor took the dagger with her when she went on. The dagger—the representative of her own Element. She couldn't wield that power yet, but now she knew she had to have a channel through which to use it when she did master it. And this time, she didn't change to the Magician herself when she passed the altar.

That was new.

The High Priestess smiled when she saw the dagger stuck into Eleanor's belt, and wordlessly handed her the scroll. This time, for the first time, Eleanor unrolled it, and saw, painted in brilliant colors, miniatures of the first three cards she had encountered. There were empty lozenges outlined in gilt for the remainder of the Major Arcana that she had yet to pass through.

"Wisdom," she said aloud, looking up at the High Priestess, "is knowing how much you don't know."

"That is truly the greatest wisdom," the Priestess said. "You see, you have a long way to travel now."

Eleanor hesitated a moment with one foot on the path that would lead her to the Empress, despite her earlier resolution. Did she *have* to face the card now? Couldn't it wait?

But the scroll gave her no other options. She clenched her teeth, and marched into the perfume of hundreds of flowers that always surrounded the Empress.

Surrounded? This time it seemed as if she was walking through a maze of rose-hedges! Getting to the Empress this time was no easy task, and it wasn't helped by all of the inviting nooks, the shaded seats, the tempting bowers she had to pass on the way. But Eleanor set her chin, and went on.

Finally she turned a corner, and there the Empress was, head tilted exquisitely to the side, lush lips curved in a slight smile, quite as if she left only a second ago. Well, in this dream-world, perhaps she had.

Eleanor marched straight up to the foot of her throne, stood before the embodiment of the card, hands on her hips, and scowled. "I don't like you," she announced.

Her only answer for a moment was a slow, lazy smile. "And why would that be, child?" the Empress purred.

"Because you're like *her,*" Eleanor replied, allowing her bitterness to show. "Everything is a weapon or a tool to get what she wants with her. Things that should just *be,* she has to twist and shape and *use.* Beauty, wit—" she blushed "—the—the sensual things. They're all weapons to get power! And that's what she's teaching her daughters. There's never enough power over people for her!"

"Ah, now you see," the Empress replied, with a knowing nod. "I am power, little Fool, I am a ruler. Above and before all else, I am a ruler, and everything that comes into my hand is, indeed, to be used, whether my aspect is reversed or proper. And if you are to pass, little Fool, you must acknowledge that you understand what power is, and does, not just to those around you, but to you, yourself, inside."

Gritting her teeth, Eleanor acknowledged that with a curt nod. "Power can be open or hidden, but that doesn't stop it from affecting you." Eleanor agreed angrily. "In fact, the power that is probably the strongest is the power that no one sees or realizes is there. And when you control that sort of power, you can control anything else you wish to."

"And that one day, if you master your magic, you, too, will be the Empress—" the card persisted. "And you, too, will know that all that comes into your hand will be a tool."

"But I can choose not to use the tools!" Eleanor all but shouted. "I can choose not to manipulate!"

"And that, too, is manipulation. Life is manipulation."

The Empress smiled her slow, sweet smile. "Think, pretty Fool. You must manipulate or be manipulated, and choosing not to choose is still a choice."

"Then I choose to do as little as I may!" she responded. "Only enough to keep others from manipulating *me!*"

The Empress nodded. "What else am I? Remember, that what is within me is within you." When Eleanor was not forthcoming, she laughed. "Oh come now. That beautiful man? You would have to be stone, which I know you are not."

As the Empress's words stung and dug at her, Eleanor had felt herself blushing more and more hotly, and when the woman finished her sentence, it was with fury and bitterness that she allowed her temper to burst out.

"Yes, curse you!" she cried. "I *do* fancy him, and I have as much chance of being more than a kind of pet or mascot to him as I have of flying his aeroplane!"

She waited, hot with embarrassment and anger, daring the Empress to say anything—

"I am power," the woman said, with a secret little smile. "There are many sorts of power."

"Like Lilith's?" Eleanor countered. "Using your body to get what you want?"

"Ah, now, you have your mythology mixed." The Empress laughed. "Lilith's offense was that she would not obey Adam, for she was created his equal, from the same clay and on the same day as he. For that she was banished, and God created subservient Eve from Adam's own flesh. Or so," she finished, with a chuckle, "the myth would tell us. And yes, there is power to be found in providing something that someone wants, isn't there? And if someone wants something very badly, it becomes a weapon in your hand."

"It's a weapon I'd be ashamed to us," Eleanor replied, and then wondered—*ashamed because it's underhanded, or because I'm afraid?*

"And if you could have the way of using the weapons of the senses as your stepmother does?" the Empress persisted. "If you knew by using them, you could have the young man for yourself, taking him away from your stepsisters?"

She lifted her chin and stared. "I wouldn't," she said shortly—but then, flushed again, and dropped her chin, and with a sick feeling, admitted, "Or—maybe I would. But I wouldn't do it to make him my slave the way *she* would!"

"Ah!" The Empress stood up, a beatific smile on her face taking the place of the too-knowing expression. "There you are, my dear! That is what you needed to see! That it is *how* we use the tools we are given, not the tools themselves, nor even the fact that we use them, that makes all the difference. Passion reversed is manipulation that leads to slavery. Passion proper is freedom. But both are passion—"

She took one blood-red rose from the bouquet she held, and extended it to Eleanor. "I am as much Passion—Fire—as I am the Fertility of Earth," the Empress continued. "It does not do to forget that. Pass on, little Fool, and seek the next stage of your growing."

Eleanor took the rose, and the moment she did so, the landscape around her changed.

She was no longer in a garden.

Instead, she was on a vast and empty plain. In the distance were mountains; dividing the mountains from the plain was a powerful, swiftly-moving river.

Seated before her, on a massive, square-built throne, was a man. He was dressed in archaic-looking armor, but it was very rich; gold-chased and engraved. He wore a crown and carried the traditional emblems of rule, the orb and scepter. As he looked down at Eleanor from his throne, she understood why the books called the Emperor a "difficult" card. . . .

So she began her trial of the Emperor, by showing her own temper and determination.

"Not tonight, I think!" she impudently announced to that stern face, and turning away, summoned true sleep with a wave of her heavily perfumed rose.

21

June 21, 1917
Broom, Warwickshire

"I'M NOT GOING TO BOTHER with trying to teach you anything now," Sarah said, as Eleanor finished recounting her latest dream-conquest, the Tarot card of the Lovers. She had conquered the Emperor far more easily than she had thought she would—but then, he was an easy card to understand. Not an easy card to *handle,* but easy to understand.

Secular power, intensely masculine, warlike, patriarchal . . . the embodiment, in a way, of all the traits that men found admirable. And, in the inverse—rigid, bound by tradition, unable to change, territorial—all the things that had turned the war into a disaster. His Element was Fire, a fire so fierce that nothing grew on his plain, so in his way he was as much an embodiment, even in proper position of sterility, as the Empress was of fertility . . . a curious pairing.

She hadn't had much difficulty with the Hierophant, either—who was to spirituality what the Emperor was to the secular world. Both ruled by law, by conformity, by order. Both concentrated on the obvious sources of control and power, ignoring the ones within—the male counterparts to the High Priestess and the Empress, with all that this implied. Law, infallibility (presumed or actual), an intolerance for the "heretical" and the rebellious—

It had occurred to Eleanor that the world had been run by men of that stamp for some time now, and look where it had gotten everyone. And it had also occurred to her that both the Emperor and the Hierophant would expect softness and conciliation out of a female, not confrontation. The Emperor, given his Empress, would expect manipulation; the Hierophant would expect submission.

So confrontation was what she had given them. She had stood her ground and told them both the truth about what their traits, taken to extreme, had done to the world—truly *conquering* the cards instead of merging with them—with their own weapons of order, law, and logic. Unable to face her logic, they had faded away, leaving behind the heady taste of secular and sacred power.

But the Lovers—that was another uncomfortable card. Not the least of which because Eleanor had gone through the Hierophant's rigidly designed, mathematically precise temple to find herself in the garden behind it, and there she discovered she was facing the original—and stark naked—Adam and Eve. It was quite a shock to her senses and her sensibilities. She had never seen *anyone* else naked before.

Much less a man. She had literally leapt back with a yelp, and averted her eyes from the two figures, who appeared not at all uncomfortable with their nude state. Which was odd—because hadn't the Fruit of the Tree made them ashamed? These two were not at all embarrassed.

And yet, there was nothing remotely sexual about them. The Empress had had more sensuality and erotic attraction, fully clothed, than both of the Lovers put together.

Nevertheless, Eleanor hadn't known where to look, and her face had been flaming as red the roses in the Empress's garden.

She should have *known* this was coming, after all, she had seen the card in Sarah's deck. But somehow it had come as a complete surprise and shock, and she had been so dumbstruck she hadn't known what to do.

The Archangel of the card had stepped in to save her from dying of embarrassment, shooing the two away. They had gone off to sit under the tree with the serpent in it, to immediately begin to quarrel about who had tempted whom, and whose fault it was that everything had gone wrong.

They sounded like a couple of children, and that was when Eleanor understood why they were so devoid of eroticism. They *were* children. Children without the innocence of the Fool, for they had already learned how to lay blame, to lie, and quarrel.

The Archangel sighed, and shook his head sadly. It was odd; he looked exactly like the Archangel portrayed on the card—which meant, at least to Eleanor's eyes, he didn't look all that much like an angel at all. More like an androgynous man with wings. There was none of the glow, of the majesty, that she would have thought would be the hallmarks of a real angel.

He's an image, a reflection—the symbol for something, rather than the actual thing, she decided. *And an image created by someone who hasn't ever seen the real thing, or even taken much thought of what one should look like.* It had always seemed to her that there ought to be a reason why the first thing an angel said when it appeared was "Fear not." Presumably, the mere sight of one was enough to strike fear into the hearts of those who saw him.

This angel looked as if he was more likely to say "Welcome to the garden, have a seat" than "fear not."

"It wasn't so much that they tasted the fruit," the Angel said to the empty air, carefully not looking at Eleanor. He sounded exasperated, like a teacher with two dunces for pupils. "It was that they lied about it, and then tried, and *keep* trying, to blame each other. He forgives everything, you know, so long as you admit you did it and are properly sorry for it—"

He glanced at Eleanor, and now he looked sorrowful. "They began with such promise, and yet one small thing has kept them from fulfilling that promise."

"Responsibility," Eleanor said, instantly, before the

Angel could get in another word. "They're not taking responsibility for what they did—so that's the reversed position for this card, isn't it? This card represents responsibility. And choices, and temptation, and balance between male and female—" The words kept tumbling out of her, as if she had turned on a spigot. "You're part of it too, since you—you aren't Michael, are you?"

He shook his head. "Raphael."

She nodded. "Raphael, whose sign is Mercury and whose element is Air; the positive of Air is freedom and an unbounded imagination, and the negative aspect of Air is carelessness and light-mindedness—"

It seemed as if some of the Magician's knowledge was with her now, and couldn't wait to get out. The more she babbled, the more symbols she saw here—temptation, in the form of the Tree and the Serpent, but more knowledge too. There was another tree, without a Serpent twined around it; it balanced the other. What did that tree represent?

If the first one is the Tree of Knowledge of Good and Evil, what is the other one? It seemed to be covered with little flames rather than leaves or fruit. Was it a sort of Burning Bush? That was another kind of knowledge—

"And Fire," the Archangel said, helpfully. "Don't forget that's there too." He nodded at the tree.

There was something about that Tree that should be ticking off memories and wasn't. As if the back of her mind recognized the symbolism, but wouldn't talk to the front of her mind about it.

She nodded, fixing her eyes on the Angel's face so she wouldn't have to look at the two naked people sprawled inelegantly beneath the tree. If they weren't physically upside-down, their position was close enough to make them look "reversed." "Of course—passion again, but it has to be passion in balance with everything else. And of course there's the Serpent and the Tree from the Garden—that's Earth—" But she wasn't quite grasping it.

"Ah, but what is the thing that you must take from them? The symbol of the power that's here?" the Archangel asked shrewdly. "It was the cup from the Magician, the scroll from the High Priestess, the Empress's rose, the Emperor's orb, the Hierophant's crown—"

"Knowledge, wisdom, passion, power, law—" she said aloud, thinking very hard. There was a problem here. The Lovers were both stark naked and had nothing in their hands. *Balance, responsibility—what represents that? Choices—making good ones and bad ones—* There was no symbol of any of these things anywhere about.

There were still the apples on the Tree of the Knowledge of Good and Evil, but—

But I've already had knowledge, and anyway, I don't think that's the answer.

She looked at the Archangel sharply. "It's nothing I have," he replied, with one perfect eyebrow raised at the exact angle required to convey admonition. "And don't even think about pulling out one of my feathers. Do that, and you'll find me treating you like something other than a lady."

Well, whatever these Tarot creatures were—one thing that they were *not* was to actually be what they appeared to be. This one might wear the outer semblance of an angel, but she didn't think even a minor one of the cherubim would talk like that, much less an archangel. Which, she had to admit, was something of a relief. She really didn't want to have anything to do with a real angel.

Adam and Eve were looking bored, and had even given up on their quarrel while they waited for her to come up with the symbol of what she must take from them.

What could it be?

Wait, what if it wasn't something *material?* This card was about balances, and there couldn't be anything more heavily weighted in favor of the *earthly* as a symbol than everything that stood in front of her. Except that the dominating Element of this card was Air. So—did it follow that what she was to take was the opposite, immaterial balancing earthly?

"The kiss of peace," she said, sure now of herself. "From both of them."

"Oh, well done!" the Archangel applauded, as Adam

and Even came towards them at a wave of his hand. Eleanor tried not to look, but it wasn't easy, when the two of them bracketed her and leaned forward to kiss her cheeks at the same time. She closed her eyes, but she could still *feel* them there, and as their lips brushed her cheeks, she felt her face flaming.

And that was the moment—

"That was the moment," Eleanor said, swallowing hard. "I have gotten something from every one of the cards I passed through—something that stayed with me, that is. But from the Lovers—" She shivered, and looked up at Sarah. *"Responsibility,* Sarah! It all came to me, then, just before I fell into sleep. Responsibility! The burden of making the right choices! I—I—" She couldn't put into words what she had felt at the moment; it was just very big, and very heavy, and she was only beginning to see the edges of it. But part of it was that she wasn't just responsible for herself . . . she was responsible for however she affected everyone she came into contact with.

"I'm not going to bother with trying to teach you anything now," Sarah said, gravely. "For the life of me, I cannot think what I could offer you that you aren't already getting in your dreams." And before Eleanor could protest, she held up her hand. "I am not saying not to come here anymore. But I think you have a new teacher—though I don't know who or what it could be, that can work through dreams." She shook her head. "I've heard of that, but no one I know has actually gotten *that* sort of teaching."

Eleanor went very still. "Not even Mother?" she asked softly.

Sarah shook her head. "Not even your mother."

Eleanor slipped back into the house well ahead of the return of her stepmother and the girls. They had gone to Longacre Park for a tea party—the expected company had arrived, and with it, an invitation to tea.

And while it sickened Eleanor to hear the girls try to outdo each other in their boasting about how Reggie had been attracted to them, she wanted to hear what had happened. So she sat by the hearth with mending in her hands, and waited for them to come back.

The motorcar rattled and chugged its way into the old stable, and the three came chattering up the walk and in through the door.

Or rather, the girls were chattering. Alison was silent. Rather to Eleanor's surprise, they were not chattering about Reggie; instead they were talking about his aunt.

". . . dotty!" Lauralee laughed. "Absolutely dotty! Why she couldn't even keep track of which of us was which! And if I heard one more story about her cat, I think I should have begun screaming!"

"Mother, if that's all we have to worry about, I don't believe you are in any danger of being discovered," Carolyn said, sounding complacent.

"On the whole, I am inclined to agree with you," Alison replied, her voice plummy with satisfaction. "Calling that silly old woman an Elemental Mage is beyond being charitable. She hasn't any more power than a village witch."

They moved into the sitting-room. Eleanor did not need to work magic to hear them. They spoke as if they were unaware that she was still sitting there in the kitchen.

"Aren't we doing anything tonight, Mother?" Carolyn continued. "It's Midsummer Eve—I thought you'd decline the invitation to the card party tonight."

"And *not* a time when we should be stirring anything," Alison said warningly. "No, not on the shortest night of the year. It is true that the boundaries between the seen and the unseen weaken on this night, but it is not in our favor. We will leave the work we performed on May Eve to strengthen—which it will, so long as nothing interferes with it. Our revenants will draw sustenance through the weakened boundaries on their own—and trust me, they have no wish to pass on to the unseen world."

Revenants? What does she mean by that? Eleanor heard Alison's footsteps on the floor, coming towards the kitchen, and bent studiously over her mending. It was one of Carolyn's tennis dresses; she'd caught the hem and it needed putting up again, so it was a legitimate task.

"What are you doing, Ellie?"

Eleanor looked up, and held out her hands. It was obvious that she was holding a garment that wasn't her own—she didn't own anything white. Only those with leisure, whose work was all done by servants, could have white clothing. It was a fact of poverty that Eleanor had come to learn.

"Ah." Alison nodded in satisfaction. "Yes, that will be needed tomorrow. I trust you have dinner well in hand?"

Eleanor nodded. She did—thanks to cleverly putting together things that could be made well in advance. The only things left were the new peas and new potatoes on the stove.

"We'll be eating early, then we'll be going up to Longacre Park for the evening." Alison smirked. "Put supper forward to six. I trust you can keep yourself out of mischief while we're gone."

"Yes ma'am," Eleanor mumbled, dropping her head so that Alison wouldn't see her expression.

If the girls had had their way, they'd have gone up to the Manor in ballgowns, and Eleanor would happily have let them make that *faux pas*—but their mother was watching, and chose their gowns herself. "Slightly more elegant than your fine afternoon gowns, my dears, but not evening dress. If we had been invited to dinner instead of a card-party, it would have been appropriate, but otherwise, no." They looked stunning, Lauralee in mauve silk, Carolyn in blue.

If Eleanor had dared to look up, she knew they would have seen the hatred and anger blazing in her eyes, so as she fastened hooks and tied lacings, she kept her gaze on her own hands, or on the floor. Alison shooed her back down to the kitchen so that her own maid could see to the girls' hair. Eleanor was glad enough to go.

And she could scarcely wait for them to get out of the house.

She sat next to the fire in the kitchen, trembling with anger. The anger actually surprised her a little; it had welled up the moment Alison called her "Ellie."

That name seemed to embody everything that Alison had done to her. She had never been "Ellie" to her father, or anyone else. Servants were called "Ellie" and "girl."

And I am a servant in my own house. But the moment I show any signs of rebellion, Alison is going to look for what inspired the rebellion.

So she busied her hands, waited impatiently for them to *go,* and tried to remember where she had heard or read anything about revenants.

Whatever they were, Alison was using them for something, and if Alison was using them, it couldn't be for any good purpose.

For some reason the word was making her think of ghosts—and she was sure her recollection was of something that Sarah had said, not anything that she had read.

That would make things difficult, since Sarah was out tonight, doing whatever it was that witches did on the solar and seasonal holidays.

Finally the three of them left, and once again, the house was still. Eleanor expected to hear the sound of the motorcar starting up, but instead, she heard one approaching The Arrows. And in fact, she didn't think anything at all of this, until it pulled up to the front door and stopped.

The sound of a car door opening and closing echoed over area, and Eleanor had a sudden vision of Reggie himself come to pick them up.

But no. No, she realized even as the thought crossed her mind, that it wouldn't be at all proper. Not the "done thing." No, he'd have sent his chauffeur.

But it made her angrier still that they were getting all this fuss made over them. Would it have hurt Reggie, just once, to have offered her a lift back to the village? After all, he was always coming there himself, to go to the Broom Pub—which was just across the street from The Arrows.

Of course it wouldn't have inconvenienced him in any way. But *she* was hardly in his social class, now, was she?

He would scarcely wish to be seen with the likes of her.

In the back of her mind, a small voice protested that if Reginald Fenyx were seen giving a ride in his automobile to a young serving girl, people would assume the worst—and that he wasn't being snobbish, he was protecting her reputation.

But that voice was swiftly drowned in the clamor from the rest of her mind, which bristled with envy of her stepsisters, anger at her own situation, and bitterness.

She kept her head down and her hands steady in case anyone should look in on her—but no one did. With a soft swish of silk and laughter as light as their gowns, all three of the Robinsons hurried out the door. The sound of two automobile doors slamming echoed in the street, then the chugging of the engine faded away in the distance.

Eleanor counted to fifty before she got up and went into the library.

Extravagant as ever, Alison had left a lamp burning there. In the section where Eleanor had found the alchemy books was one she had passed over as irrelevant, a book that purported to describe various supernatural creatures and how to be rid of them. Now she took it out, because she thought she remembered something about revenants in there.

What she found was a brief, and vague, reference, and she put the book back with a feeling of discontent. Ghosts, but not ghosts; at least that seemed to be the definition. Or else, some were ghosts, actual spirits unwilling or unable to move on, but others were memories, mechanically playing out whatever tragedy had created them.

She sat there, nibbling on the rough edge of her thumbnail, while she considered her options for learning anything. Sarah was unavailable; as she had been on May Eve, she was off doing something that had to do with being a witch. There was nothing in her alchemy books, and she didn't recall anything from her mother's notebook.

But what had Sarah said? That she, Eleanor, was getting direct teaching in dreams?

She was using the Tarot to guide her, after a suggestion in one of the alchemy books, and she was concentrating on the cards whenever she fell asleep, assuming that she would find her way into the Tarot realm. So if she was being taken up by some sort of teacher or teachers, perhaps they were using what she was thinking about as the structure to their lessons.

Well, what if she went to bed and concentrated on a question instead of the cards? Would she get an answer to it?

Only one way to find out.

She went up the stairs to her own room—it was unlikely the girls would come up here to wake her when they returned, since it was less work to get out of their dresses alone than it was to climb the stairs to find her and wake her—or, if Alison was feeling generous, she would send her own maid to help them. Howse would be waiting in Alison's rooms until the Robinsons returned—not that this was any hardship. There was a lounge there, and a stack of the latest magazines. Howse didn't lack for anything, truth to be told.

Though if more truth were to be told, except for the extra place at dinner, Eleanor scarcely knew Howse was in the house. She hardly spoke at all; she might have been a clockwork for all the notice she took of anything.

Then again, it was probably that Howse considered Eleanor to be so far beneath her that she would sooner turn desperado than acknowledge Eleanor's presence. If the hierarchy between lower class and upper was rigid, it was even more so among servants. Eleanor had never really understood that until she had been made into a servant herself, but it was the truth. Upper servants spoke to lower only to give orders, and would never even think of socializing with them.

So it was no great surprise that she heard nothing from Howse as she closed the door of her little garret room. Once settled into bed, she closed her eyes and concentrated. *What are revenants, and what has Alison to do with them?*

She could not have told the moment when she slipped from waking into sleeping, but she found herself—

strangely enough—walking down the road, heading to the meadow where she met Reggie. It was dark, with hardly any moonlight at all, and yet the whole landscape seemed as bright as day to her.

It was deserted, of course. Anyone in the farms along here was already in bed. Dawn came early, and with it, the demands of livestock and crops.

She wasn't so much walking, she quickly discovered, as she was *being walked.* Her body—if, indeed, this was her body and not the sort of other self she inhabited when she was in the world of the Tarot—moved along of its own volition and under the control of someone other than herself. She didn't fight it; there was no reason to. As near as she could tell, she was going to be given the answer to her question—or why else take her outside the magical protections that Sarah had placed around the village? The revenants could not pass those—therefore, to see them, she must go outside them.

Finally she came to the boundary of Longacre Park.

And there, along the fence, she saw—them. The moment she did, she felt a shock of pure terror the like of which she had never felt in all her life. The nasty little creatures that she had driven away in the meadow had frightened her, but not like this. This was pure, atavistic fear, the fear that said to the gut, *these things can do worse than kill you.*

She'd have screamed, if her instincts hadn't caught the scream in her throat before it began. They didn't know she was there yet, and there was no reason to do something that would certainly attract their attention!

Transparent, glowing, there was no mistaking them for living creatures. For one thing, they were in a variety of costumes—but for another, they weren't all whole. At least half of them were missing pieces of themselves; arms, legs, and in at least one case, a head. And most of the rest were rather gruesomely the worse for wear and time. She was very, very glad that they all had their backs to her; if they faced her, she didn't think she would be able to hold back a scream.

There were a great many of them, all pressing against

some invisible boundary at the edge of Longacre Park lands. The oldest were dressed in some sort of outlandish robes and animal skins; the newest in the uniform of the British infantry.

All of them wanted in. All of them were consumed with rage.

Why? she thought irrelevantly. *Why them? What could anyone up at Longacre Park have possibly done to anger a Druid?* That is, she assumed the ones in the robes were Druids. She couldn't think what else they could be.

Well, whatever it was, Alison had given their anger a form and a force of will, and now they were ready to press that advantage as far into the "enemy" territory as they could.

She held quite still, knowing, even if she knew nothing else, that she did not want to attract their attention.

But she also did not want those things prowling about after dark. Maybe ordinary people couldn't see them and know them to be as dangerous as an unexploded shell, but she could, and did, and she often went out at night. Maybe they couldn't get past the protections that kept the village safe—but maybe they could.

She wasn't taking any chances.

I have to get away, and tell Sarah about this as soon as I can. She has to know these things are still out here, and dangerous.

But before she could make up her mind any further, she heard, faint and muffled, the sound of another motorcar approaching. Eleanor shivered as she realized that the motor was also nearly transparent, and as for driver and passenger, they were utterly, weirdly silent. Were they some other kind of revenant? Or were they something else?

The motor chugged to a full stop alongside the fence—which, strangely enough, was *not* transparent. And as the passenger stepped down from the motorcar, she became more real, and more solid, with each step. It was like a vanishing-trick in reverse. As she became more real and solid, she also began to glow—but it was as if she had brought sunlight into the midnight world, not the sort of sickly foxfire that the revenants radiated. Just looking at her made Eleanor feel more confident, and less afraid.

But the figure that stood there, straight-backed and imperious, was no one that Eleanor recognized.

She was dressed in the most outlandish costume Eleanor had ever seen outside of a play or a fancy-dress party—quite literally, draped Grecian robes of a brilliant blue. In her graying hair, which had been braided and wrapped around her head in the style favored by Grecian matrons, was a laurel wreath. She had a staff a little taller than she was in one hand, but she didn't lean on it as if she needed its support. She surveyed the scene before her, looking down her nose at the revenants, who were only just now realizing that she was there, and frowned.

"Provide an anchor, Smith, just in case." The very feminine voice said—sounding as if she was speaking from the bottom of a well. A pale blue ray of light lanced from the man behind the wheel to the old woman.

Now the revenants were beginning to notice that they were not alone. They turned towards the woman, snarling and sneering, and one or two advanced towards her in a threatening manner.

She didn't seem to care in the least. In fact, she regarded them with the calm disapproval of someone who has found schoolboys meddling in something they should have known better than to touch. "You," she said sternly, "Have been very naughty, and whoever sent you was naughtier still."

And with that, she rapped the butt of her staff three times on the ground, and made a gesture as of one scattering a handful of grain.

And suddenly, Eleanor found herself at the heart of a tempest.

22

June 21, 1917
Broom, Warwickshire

QUICKER THAN THOUGHT, THE TEMPEST descended. Silent, invisible winds ripped through the countryside, practically picking Eleanor right up off her feet and slamming her into the trunk of a tree, to which she clung for dear life. The winds tore at her hair, sending it whipping around her, hauled at her clothing—but what they did to her was nothing to what they were doing to the revenants.

The revenants were—literally—being shredded, by the winds that spun cyclone-like in a vortex, with the old woman at their still heart. There was a clean, blue glow about the old woman and her helper now. And though the revenants huddled howling together, trying to hide themselves, nothing they did was any protection against the power that was ripping them apart, as if they were nothing but tissue-paper, and whirling the tiny pieces upwards in a reverse snowfall of glowing bits.

Eleanor looked up, involuntarily, to see that the bits were being carried up into a bottomless black hole in the sky, rimmed with glowing blue.

And yet—and there was the strangest thing of all—so far as the trees and the rest of the "real world" was concerned, there were no winds. The leaves rustled only a little; the grasses scarcely moved at all. There was no sound but the keening wail of the revenants themselves.

The hair went up on the back of Eleanor's neck, even as she clung even tighter to the tree-trunk.

Or was she clinging to the trunk? There seemed to be two trees there, a kind of faintly luminescent shadow-tree, which *was* tossing its branches in the tempest, and the "real" tree, which was undisturbed—and her arms were wrapped tightly around the former, not the latter.

A thin cry of despair arose from the revenants, and if they had been hideous before, now, with half of their substance eaten away by the terrible cyclone, they were horrible to look at. They tried to snatch at the bits of themselves being ripped off and blown away, only to see their fingers, bits of their hands, torn off too. Eleanor felt herself sickening, and couldn't help herself; she couldn't bear the sight any longer. She squeezed her eyes shut, and tried to will herself awake, for surely this was a dream. It *must* be a dream. She would make it a dream—

Oh please, let this just be a nightmare, don't let it be real. . . .

And with a start, and a jolting she felt in her heart, she *did* awaken.

She was in her own bed, crickets singing outside her window. Her heart pounded so hard she thought the bed might be shaking with the force of it, and she was terribly, terribly *cold.*

And a moment later, she began to shiver so violently that the bed did start shaking after all.

She tried to move, and couldn't, and her shivering grew worse. It was as if the cold itself held her prisoner, in bonds of ice. She had never been so cold; her teeth chattered with it, and her fingers and toes were numb with it, and she wanted a blanket desperately. But before she could make a second attempt to lurch out of bed to get one, something else came to her rescue.

Flowing out of the brickwork of the chimney came her Salamanders, three of them. They raced across the floor and slithered up into the bed, where one coiled itself against the small of her back, one wrapped itself around her shoulders, and one curled up just at the hollow of her stomach. Warmth spread from them, driving the numbing cold out of her, and after a moment, her shivering stopped and she began to relax.

As soon as she began to feel warm again, exhaustion hit her, as if she had been working beyond her strength. And when the last of remnants of her fear ebbed away, replaced by a weary lassitude, she gave in to it, and let sleep claim her again.

This time carefully *not* thinking of any questions, nor the Tarot. She'd had enough lessons for one night.

June 22, 1917
Longacre Park, Warwickshire

The card party that had begun so tediously had ended last night as a different sort of party altogether. Reggie could not have been more grateful. His aunt's good friend—and his own godmother—Lady Virginia de Marce had turned up, in her own motorcar, with her chauffeur and (though only he and his aunt knew this) arcane assistant Smith in attendance. Smith had efficiently organized the servants and gotten the formidable pile of Lady Virginia's belongings upstairs, while her ladyship tidied herself and returned to take control of the company.

Her ladyship could not help but take control of whatever company she was in. She had an air about her of absolute authority, she dressed like a queen, in her own unique style, based roughly on the enormous hats, trumpet-skirts and high-necked gowns of twenty years before, which somehow made her look timelessly fashionable rather than outdated.

While every powerful Master that Reggie had ever met

tended to exude that aura of authority, Lady Virginia had honed hers into a weapon. When she entered a room, she took charge of it and everyone in it.

With Smith's help, she had come downstairs again in less than a third of the time it would have taken any other woman, changed miraculously from her duster, goggles, veiled hat and traveling-ensemble to an exquisite gown of mauve lace. Smith, be it said, was also Lady Virginia's lady's maid—because Smith, chauffeur, arcane assistant, was a woman.

As Lady Virginia often said, "I am old enough to be able to hire whom I wish, and rich enough to be considered eccentric, rather than mad, when I do."

It was difficult to know whether one *liked* Smith; the curiously sexless servant was a past mistress of being inscrutable and virtually invisible. But there was no doubt that Smith was as efficient and formidable, in her own quiet way, as her mistress.

Reggie had more than once wondered if Smith was even human. It was possible that she was not; Lady Virginia, after all, was a formidable Master of Air, and it was just within the bounds of the possible that Smith was actually an Air Elemental of some arcane sort. Not *likely,* but possible.

As for appearances, Smith had gray eyes, curiously colorless hair kept cropped short, and invariably wore gray, either as a mannishly tailored suit, or a chauffeur's uniform (and somehow, perhaps because she looked so androgynous, no one was scandalized by a woman in trousers). She was always correct, always precise, and seldom spoke unless addressed directly.

And in fact, her name wasn't "Smith" at all. It was Melanie Lynn.

When he'd first learned this, he had been stupid enough and arrogant enough to take Lady Virginia to task for calling her servant "Smith" rather than "Lynn"—for there were people in his circle that couldn't be bothered to learn their servants' names. Instead, they had a habit of calling them whatever was convenient so that they would never have to learn a new name for the old position when one servant was replaced by another.

He should have known better. This *was* Lady Virginia, after all, who marched in the Suffragists' Parades, chained herself to the railing of Number 10 Downing Street, and helped Doctor Maya in her charity clinic.

"Are you mad, boy?" Lady Virginia had said, sternly. "It's not for my convenience! *Smith* wants me to call her Smith, and I'm not fool enough to gainsay her."

"Names are power," Smith had said, from behind him, startling him into a yelp, for he hadn't realized she had come in. "Smith is a cipher. When you are a cipher, boy, you can be anything. Standing out isn't always an advantage."

He often wondered where, exactly, Lady Virginia had found Smith, but after that day, he'd never dared to ask.

The game of bridge that had been taking place was utterly abandoned, as soon as Lady Virginia descended, tidied into elegance again. Her personality dominated the gathering without anyone other than Reggie really noticing. Within moments, she had smoothly and effortlessly redirected the conversation into a discussion of the remarkable achievements of young T. E. Lawrence in the Arabian campaign. It was a reasonably "safe" topic; an exotic enough locale that no one at the tables truly connected it with the war, and even if they had, Lawrence was leading an all-Arab army of resistance. No British lives—other than his own—were involved. He was the darling of the American as well as the British press. He was trailed about by an audacious American reporter. It was painless to find him interesting.

But there was something about the significant looks that she kept casting at Reggie that made him certain she was only biding her time until she could get him alone. Though why that should be, he couldn't guess.

Unless it had something to do with taking up magic again.

Surely not.

Nevertheless he was glad enough when his Aunt April, Lady Williams, declared that if *she* was tired, Lady Virginia must be shattered, and the local guests who had come from outside Longacre Park elected to take themselves back to their homes. He was able to slip away unobtrusively, and take to his own bed. Not that he had expected to sleep. His dreams—nightmares, really—had been so terrifying since the beginning of May that if he got three undisturbed hours in a night, it was a good night's rest. Only Doctor Maya's drugs kept the nightmares at bay, and he was beginning to feel uneasy about how much of that stuff he was taking.

He lay down in his bed, expecting to stare at the ceiling for hours, and had just begun to think about what Lady Virginia could want with him. That was when he actually fell asleep due to exhaustion.

Most nights of the last month, he had lain awake for hours, staring up at the ceiling, aware of a feeling of lurking hostility and menace, unable to determine where it came from.

So it was all the more surprising when he fell asleep immediately, and did not dream.

It was even more surprising that the next time he opened his eyes, it was morning. Real morning, not two or three past midnight, nor even predawn. The sun was coming up, filling his room with light—as with most Air Masters, he preferred to have his bedroom facing east—a cool breeze fluttered the curtains, and a lark saluted the day.

He felt better than he had—in an age. Actually rested for once, and even if his knee gave him the usual amount of trouble when he rose, it was worth it to look out his window at the sun streaming over the lawns without feeling as if he would have given his soul for a single night of undisturbed rest.

He was even whistling when he came down to breakfast to find his aunt and Lady Virginia just beginning their own meal.

"Good morning, my lady, Aunt April," he said cheerfully as he went to the sideboard to help himself—noting with a sigh that it was a dark-bread day. If there was one thing he missed more than anything else since rationing had begun, it was good white bread.

"Your dear mother is up and out as usual," his aunt told him, after presenting her cheek for him to kiss. "And where she gets that energy from at this hour of the day, I could not tell you. Certainly not from my side of the family. Positively indecent. No one should be that awake at six. Well, excepting milkmen, I suppose. And farmers. And one's maid. But they shouldn't be so cheerful about it. And your dear mother should know better. It troubles the servants when the mistress is up as early as they are."

Lady Virginia, said nothing, neatly and economically disposing of grilled tomatoes, while Aunt April talked and buttered toast without shedding a crumb.

This was Aunt April's usual sort of chatter; if there was a silence, she moved to fill it with whatever came into her head, which made for some interesting social moments, now and again. Reggie could still remember the time at a dinner party in this very house, during his first year at Oxford, when she had asked an eminent member of the the House of Lords, just as he was filling his lungs to pontificate, if there was a reason why his shirt-front popped every time he took a deep breath. Since the poor man had—up until that moment, at least—clearly been unaware that his shirt-front did any such thing, he had been left gaping at her like a stranded fish and had completely lost his train of thought. Nor was that the end of it; he had been so self-conscious for the rest of the evening that he never spoke more than a sentence or two. As this had the result (at least according to his father) of preventing at least three arguments, any one of which might have erupted into a major disagreement if not a diplomatic incident, Aunt April had earned the undying gratitude of the rest of the guests and standing invitations to more events than she could ever possibly attend. And if she had a reputation as being more than a bit dotty, every hostess worth her salt-cellar knew Aunt April could be counted on to defuse potential disasters with an unfocused laugh and a disingenuous remark at precisely the right moment. And if a stuffed-shirt or two was left embarrassed and wondering how it had happened, at least it was nothing he could take exception to.

"Mother's been an early riser for as long as I can remember, Aunt April," Reggie said, sitting down with his own plate of grilled tomatoes and eggs. "And I doubt that the servants even notice. This is the countryside; people get up earlier than they do in town."

"And I can't think *why,"* Aunt April responded, waving her knife for emphasis, her brows furrowed. "What is there to get up early *for?* It's not as if there was shooting at this time of year, and anyway, by the time it's shooting season, getting up early isn't early anymore, it's properly late."

Reggie didn't even try to wrap his mind around that statement; it made sense to Aunt April, so that was all that counted.

"You do rattle on, April," said Lady Virginia without rancor. "Reginald, I want to speak with you as soon as you have finished your breakfast. Privately."

"Oh, good," Aunt April said, looking suddenly cheerful. "We'll get *that* over with, then, and it won't be hanging over our heads like a rock of Sophocles, or was it the sword of Thucydides? Whichever it was, it was a terribly uncomfortable object to have hanging over your head, and I would hate to have it hanging over ours, spoiling the entire visit—"

"Damocles," Lady Virginia said, interrupting. "It was the Sword of Damocles, dear, as if you didn't know, since I know very well you were making better use of your brother's classics tutor than your brother did. Now, if you could take your tea to the terrace—"

"Oh, I'm finished, Virginia, and I'll run off and find nothing to do," Aunt April said, with a gay little wave of her hand as she rose in a flutter of lace flounces. "Do get him to come around to taking up his powers again, will you, dear? Of course you will, if he doesn't want to, you'll threaten him with Smith."

She trotted off, without waiting for a word from either of them, leaving him staring at Lady Virginia across the breakfast table, nervously crumbling toast and wishing he'd sent down for a tray instead of coming to the table this morning.

"Reginald," Lady Virginia said, raising her chin a little. "This nonsense of avoiding magic must stop. Now."

She couldn't have been more direct, and she left him with no graceful way out of the conversation. He clenched his teeth, and replied just as directly.

"Lady Virginia—forgive me, but you can't possibly know *why* I am—"

She did something she had never done before, in all of his acquaintance with her. She interrupted him.

"Actually," she said tartly, "I do know. I know exactly why, in excruciating detail. I have not been idle these three years. I am a VAD—a *working* VAD, though admittedly, a part-time VAD, since my old bones are hardly up to the long hours the young ones put in, and I have no intention of living in some squalid little dormitory with a pack of girls. I have been spending many long hours at the bedsides of young enlisted men, and I wasn't simply mopping their brows, as you should by now be aware. Furthermore, they talk to me, Reginald. I induce them to talk to me, because it is sometimes the only way to purge them of their horrors."

Reggie felt his eyes widen with shock. It had never occurred to him that aristocratic Lady Virginia would have volunteered to do nursing-aide work. But—she was continuing.

"And as for what happened specifically to you, not only did I get the gist of the experience from Maya, one of my working-class protégés, a clever Earth magician that I sponsored through nurse's training, was privy to some of your experience in the trenches, as you rather unambiguously shared it with whoever was Sensitive at the time."

He stared at her, appalled that he had done any such thing. Granted, he'd been out of his senses but still, "Who?"

Lady Virginia shrugged. "You weren't conscious, so you won't recognize the name. A nurse at the first field-hospital you came to, if you must know; an Earth-worker, as I told you—they can't seem to stay away from pursuing healing at the Front. You nearly gave her a breakdown and she had to come home to me for a month. Fortunately,

Maya sorted her out. Unfortunately, Maya does not seem to have been as successful with you."

He blinked at her. There didn't seem to be anything he could say. "I'm sorry about your protégée—" he began.

She waved his apology away. "She knew that she was going to encounter things like that before she volunteered, and the experience has given her better shields. And *you* could learn from her example. As soon as she could, she was back, using what power she has for the greatest good."

He flushed.

She saw the flush, correctly assumed it was embarrassment, and shook her head. "You mistake me. I am not going to act like your idiotic grandfather and call you a coward, because I know you aren't. That leg of yours can't—according to Doctor Maya—be more than half healed. And I know that *you* think that you have taken the best steps you can to protect yourself. But Reginald, walling yourself off from magic is *not* going to solve your problem. In fact, it is only going to make things worse."

Nettled, now, he narrowed his eyes. "I can't see how."

Lady Virginia sighed. "Naturally you can't see how. You haven't looked." She eyed him shrewdly. "You've forgotten that building walls instead of shields blinds you to what is going on around you. I don't suppose you'd have the effrontery to tell me you've been sleeping the sleep of the just lately, would you?"

"Last night—" he began, but she interrupted him again.

"Oh, last night, of course. But what about for the last month?" She stared at him, daring him to lie with her eyes.

And he couldn't. He gave in, feeling his fragile defenses crumple under the pressure of the knowledge she had in her eyes. He didn't know *how* she knew, but she clearly did. "No. I've gotten no more than a few hours of rest at most over the past few weeks. Most nights are as bad as they were when I was in hospital."

"I'm not surprised," Lady Virginia replied, with satisfaction. "Considering that until last night you had a small army of revenants breathing down your neck. Even walled and shielded, you would have sensed them, and had they gained in power, you would have been at their mercy. Revenants are not subject to the same laws as Elementals, as you should well know, and if they had been able to break through to you, they would have shredded your mind at the least, and possibly worse than that."

That took him completely by surprise. "Revenants? But—"

What could he possibly have done to arouse revenants? And here? There hadn't been a haunt anywhere near Longacre for generations!

But—"haunted" described exactly how he had been feeling for the last month or so.

Revenants! The mere thought made him dizzy. No, revenants were *not* subject to the same laws as Elementals. They could even make themselves seen and felt by ordinary mortals. Really powerful ones could kill.

"Smith and I encountered them clawing at the shields around the grounds last night as we came in," Lady Virginia continued ruthlessly. "We dispelled them of course. But if *you* had been properly doing your job instead of relying on your late father's defenses—which are eroding, may I add—you would have known they were there and done something about them weeks ago."

"But—" His head was whirling at this point.

"But me no buts. I will accept no excuses. Think, will you?" she demanded. "There are surely at least a handful of sensitives down in that village of yours, if not a real practitioner. What if one of *them* had been caught by the revenants instead of Smith and me?"

"I'll build better shields," he said grimly, getting his metaphorical feet under him again. "I'll put myself behind magical walls too thick for anything to sense me or find me, and I won't attract any more trouble—"

"Reginald David Alexander Tiberius Fenyx, you have *tried* that, and it *did not work!*" Lady Virginia exploded, losing her temper as she had seldom ever done in his presence. He shrank back involuntarily, as she slapped the table three times with an open palm, emphasizing her last three words. "By the Archangel Raphael, I swear, if your father was alive to hear this, he would—well, I don't know what he would *do,* but I know what he would *be,* and that is bitterly disappointed! I expect the idiots in the War Office to fail to learn from their mistakes, but I thought better of you!"

"But—" he protested feebly.

"You were behind shields—your own and your father's—and those revenants still found you! And I cannot for the life of me imagine what *you* could have done that would attract the attention of a renegade Druid, a couple of Roman-British louts in armor, an assortment of Regency highwaymen, and a spread of nasty cutthroats stretching back to hide-wearing henge-builders! Now what about that makes you suspicious?" She stared at him, demanding that he think.

And he did, though he didn't want to admit what he was thinking. "They were sent?"

She sniffed. "Better. I was beginning to wonder if you had left some of your wits back there on the Front. Yes, they were sent. I do not know by whom, or why, but they were certainly carefully called up, invoked, bound, and sent. Probably Beltane Night, which would account for your disturbed sleep since then. And with them dispelled, which their master will most certainly know, the next things that are purposed to attack you will be stronger."

He just stared at her numbly. He couldn't for the life of him imagine why anyone would set revenants on him.

"It doesn't actually matter who did this, or why," Lady Virginia continued. "The point is that renouncing magic is not going to make this person go away. I don't believe that whoever this is has any plans to leave you alone until you are dead or mad."

Her eyes glittered at him; he hadn't truly understood how *hard* she could be when she felt the need. At that moment, it came home to him that she had been an Air Master—a *combative* magician, on a Front of her own—for most of her life. She was as mentally tough as any soldier, if not more so. She might not have been a part of the Council, but he knew quite well that she was part of some other

White Lodge, and had been just as active as any of Alderscroft's Masters.

Perhaps the only difference between her and those now in the trenches was that her experience of combat had not left her disillusioned and bitter.

"Nor are you my primary concern at this moment," she said, stabbing her finger down at the tablecloth for emphasis. "You *might* be able to protect yourself behind your shields and your walls. But what about others? What about the sensitives down in your village? Can they? When whoever this is levels barrage after barrage of magical attacks against you, who do you think is going to pay the price as those attacks reflect off your defenses?"

He gulped. "I hadn't—"

But in his mind's eye, he saw the shattered remains of the villages of Belgium and France, wreckage that proved it didn't matter how innocent you were, once you were in the way.

He dropped his gaze to his own hands. They were shaking. "Did you see or sense anything that might give you an idea who was behind the attack?" he asked, instead, trying to put off the moment of decision for a little while longer.

"All that I sensed was a momentary hint of someone—a Fire magician, I thought, half-trained at best. It wasn't there for long, and I don't believe the Fire magician had anything to do with the revenants, I think it was just someone caught up accidentally. Possibly one of your sensitive villagers or someone dreaming and coming to investigate the flares of power; the aura suggested someone walking in an astral projection." He looked up at that, but she shook her head at him. "And at any rate, revenants are far more likely to be sent by an Earth magician. They don't respond well to Fire."

A Fire Magician, in an astral projection? "Could it have been one of the London Fire Masters responding to the presence of the revenants?" he hazarded.

"Possibly. More likely one of their students; the brief impression *I* got was of someone still in apprenticeship, so to speak." She frowned. "There isn't anyone in your village who would match that description, is there?"

"I never heard of any Fire Mages there." He shrugged helplessly. "Mind you, I was not *here* most of the time. If I wasn't at school, I was in London. Father never even told me who the other Masters were around here; he always said there would be plenty of time when I was finished at Oxford." He frowned as he concentrated on a fugitive memory. "I think there's a witch down there—Earth, of course—or at least, there was. I don't know if she's still alive, or if she's taken on students of her own. But Lady Virginia, if someone is strong enough to call up revenants and set them on me, shouldn't we inform Lord Alderscroft?"

Hope that he might yet evade Lady Virginia's demands sprang up in him.

"Surely this is a task for Alderscroft and the Council?" he persisted. "An attack on a Council member—"

"First, there would have to be a Council left to do something," Lady Virginia replied, caustically. "What's left, now that all the young lions are at the Front, dead, or incapacitated, has their hands full with arcane demands from the Almsley's branch of the War Office." Her lips tightened into a thin line. "But that still isn't the point, Reginald. The point is that even if *you* are safe for the moment, there are innocents around you who are not." She stared him in the face and would not let him look away. "So the question is, what are you going to do to protect *them?*"

He wanted, badly, to say that he wasn't going to do anything, that their protection was none of his business. He wanted to protest that *he* was the injured party here, that he had taken wounds to the spirit as well as the flesh in defence of his own country, and that it was past time that someone protected *him* for a change.

But he couldn't. As his father had once told him, there was an obligation that came with power. That obligation left him with a very clear code of conduct.

An officer and a gentleman. "I'll do what I must, Lady

Virginia," he said, even though his hands shook with fear and his skin crawled. "It seems I have no choice."

June 22, 1917
Broom, Warwickshire

Alison was furious, and everyone was staying out of her way.

She had every right to be furious. Bad enough that the card-party last night had been invaded and taken over by that dreadful old cow in her outmoded dresses, so that the careful work being done on Reggie by the girls was utterly disrupted as he went to dance attendance on the creature. *Worse* that she was Reggie's godmother and a particular friend of the family.

But worst of all—this Lady Virginia was an Air Master, a crony of Alderscroft's, and someone it would be very, very dangerous to cross. Any sort of covert magical work in Reggie's direction would have to stop; Alison could not take the risk of being uncovered.

Alison had been forced to sit there and smile and make polite noises, while her ladyship monopolized the conversation with tales of that fellow who'd gone native with the Arabs. As if he or a lot of unwashed camel-herders mattered! By the time she was able to make her excuses and escape, the greater part of the evening had been wasted, and Reggie wasn't even looking at the girls anymore. It had been his mother who'd sent for the chauffeur and the car to take them home.

But that wasn't the end of the evening's disasters, oh no. Because she had tried to call in her army of revenants to increase their strength—except when she tried to find them, they were gone. Vanished. Dispelled.

In fact, they had been dispelled so thoroughly that there

wasn't a trace of them left—although the signs of the magic that had destroyed them were clear enough.

And the signature of an Air Master who didn't care who knew what she had done was clear enough for anyone to read who had the eyes to see it.

It hadn't been Reggie. It *certainly* wasn't the Broom village witch. That left only the newly arrived Lady Virginia. . . .

Alison had been so angry last night that she had called up and torn to bits several of her own kobolds, just to relieve her temper. She'd have dragged Ellie out of bed and beaten her—and in fact, she was tempted to—but if she started, she had known she wouldn't be able to stop, and the complications of hurting or killing the fool began with the mere inconvenience of not having someone to cook or clean in the morning, and ended with losing the Robinson fortune.

So instead, she made an example of three of the dullest of her minions, smashed a couple of china ornaments, and still went to bed in a temper.

She had awakened feeling no less angry, but by midmorning, her temper had cooled sufficiently to allow her to think clearly.

The girls knew better than to trifle with her in her current mood; when she summoned them to her room after Howse had finished her work, they came immediately and quietly.

"We have a problem," she told them, grimly. "That woman that arrived last night is an Air Master, and Reggie's godmother."

The girls exchanged a look of apprehension. "Does that mean no magic around her?" Carolyn asked.

"Nothing directed at Reggie, at least," Alison said sourly. "Alderscroft *knows* I'm an Earth Master—after all, he was the one who sent me!"

"But mother, I thought you said your job here was to be kept secret," Lauralee protested. "Why should Lord Alderscroft have told Lady Virginia about you?"

Of all of the things that had been running through her

mind this morning, *that* hadn't been one of them. She sucked on her lower lip a moment. "In fact, he probably didn't, come to think of it. She's not on his Council as far as I know, and I can't believe he would have told an outsider War Office business."

"So it's not as bad as you thought!" Carolyn said, brightening.

"No, Carolyn, it *is* as bad as I thought," Alison corrected caustically. "It is simply not as dire as it could be. She's gotten rid of my revenants, and she will certainly be able to trace any active Earth magic used against her godson straight back to me—or to you. Which means we can do nothing directly. . . hmm."

"Mother, we can still use charms against our rivals," Lauralee pointed out shrewdly. "As long as we do so away from Longacre Park. *She* won't bother to look for magics being worked in that way."

Alison turned a surprised—and pleased—gaze on her elder. That was two good thoughts in as many minutes. "Now that is certainly a plan," she agreed. "And a good one. I approve. And as for me—you know, I do think it unlikely that Lady Virginia will even consider watching over Lady Devlin. I will redouble my efforts, and become Lady Devlin's best, most trusted friend. . . ." She felt her lips curving into a slight smile. "Yes. I could do that. It's the sort of exercise of Earth magic that an Air Master is usually blind to—slow, deliberate, and subtle, playing on the emotions. Then, I can play on her fears. Reggie will certainly have to go back to the Front. He's the only male left in the Fenyx line. He *must* marry and do his duty for the Fenyx name before he goes off again."

"And who better to wed than one of the daughters of her very good friend?" Carolyn put in coquettishly.

Lauralee laughed. "Pretty, polite, presentable . . . we're no worse than any of the other girls she's been trying to interest him in. Perhaps not as blue-blooded, but if she's growing desperate, she may overlook that." She cocked her head to one side. "Do you think we could get away with some small seductive magics, if we were careful to make them look—accidental?"

"Possibly, possibly." Alison thought hard. "It suddenly occurs to me that the reason Lady Virginia might be here is to urge Reggie back into the practice of magic. He has been walled against your charms until now—but if she succeeds, he'll be vulnerable to such things again." Her smile widened a trifle. "Now, there's a fine thought! If that is indeed the case, Lady Virginia might be doing us a favor! A delicious irony, though I doubt she would appreciate it herself."

"All I care about is that she not interfere," Lauralee countered. "Nothing else matters."

"Quite right," her mother declared, with satisfaction for her daughter's practicality. "So, we need to put together our new plans. I want you two to decide what magic you are going to use on your rivals. When you have your course of action, come to me so I can be sure it is something that won't alert Lady Virginia. I will intensify my campaign to win Lady Devlin. And the three of us will work out what sort of seductions you can use against Reggie and how to make them look like the innocent work of untrained sensitives."

"Yes, Mother," they chorused, looking maliciously cheerful as she shooed them out.

Alison went to the window of her bedroom, and looked down onto the garden below. Ellie was hanging out bedlinen, and it occurred to her that there was yet another loose end that needed tidying. She still had not made up her mind what to do about the girl. For all that her emotional self enjoyed the idea of putting Locke's plan into motion, her logical self warned that there were far too many loopholes in it—not to mention pitfalls.

The problem with adding outsiders into a plan was that you could never be sure of their loyalty—nor their discretion.

No, the more she thought of Locke's plan, the less she liked it. Still, the basic notion, of driving the girl mad—that was a good one.

She resolved to put more thought into it. Time was not on her side in this.

But there must be a better answer. And she was just the person to find it.

23

July 10, 1917
Broom, Warwickshire

ALL WAS DARKNESS, SAVE ONLY a tiny pool of yellow light from the lantern that the old man held. He looked like a monk, the sort that wore simple, hooded robes. He wasn't, of course. He was something altogether different, with no more than a nodding acquaintance with Christianity.

Eleanor had expected someone hard and ascetic, and possibly unfriendly. Instead, she looked up into the face of a man who looked down on her with kind, warm eyes. He looked like a grandfatherly wizard, and was the most real of all of the Tarot creatures she had yet met.

"And now," said the Hermit, "You come to me. Do you know me yet?"

Eleanor shook her head; oh she knew what he was, and even what he represented, but to know him, understand him as deeply as that simple question implied—no, she did not know him yet. She knew only enough to know that this was someone who had spent all his life looking for wisdom, and had learned to distill things down to their simplest, who would, unlike Gaffer Clark, use the fewest words possible to cut to the heart of something.

It was night here in the world of the Tarot cards, and the Hermit held the lantern that was the only source of light for as far as she could see. It was that lantern that had led her to him.

In fact, tonight, for the very first time since she had begun this quest through the Major Arcana, she had *not* passed through the stages she had already been tested in. That had come as something of a shock. She had gone to bed early, since Alison and the girls were at Longacre Park—again—and she was bone-weary with all the work they had put her through. They went through as many clothing-changes in a day as Lady Devlin did now, and it wasn't Howse who picked up the discarded items, laundered them, hung them to dry, starched and ironed them. Oh no—it was Eleanor, up and down the stairs three times a day, with extra demand on her because the tennis dress discarded in the afternoon would be wanted in the morning.

Alison was getting very familiar with Lady Devlin, and Eleanor didn't think it was all name-dropping. There was something going on up there at the big great house, somehow Alison had managed to worm her way into Lady Devlin's regard.

Eleanor was trying very hard not to care. After all, Alison's machinations were giving *her* the freedom to gain in knowledge and control of her magic and her Element. Her hands and body might be busy, but her mind was free to think, to reason, to analyze every tiny bit of information she got from the alchemy books and her mother's notes. And when the others weren't about, she could practice some of the smaller magics, sharpening her skills. Fire magic was quite good for keeping the iron hot, for instance. And if her hands weren't nearly as smooth and lovely as her stepsisters', the Salamanders had healed the cracked skin, shrunk the joints, made the nails stronger and neater.

Besides, as Sarah had said, more than once, "The manor's the manor and the village is the village, and the less we have to do with each other the better." There was no point in even thinking about Reginald Fenyx and his mother. The gulf between them was just too wide to bridge.

But if there was one thing that all this delving through the paths of the cards was teaching her, it was to look inside herself and be honest about what was there.

Never mind that her little passion for Reginald Fenyx hadn't the chance of a rose in midwinter. It was certainly *there.* It didn't take having her mind slip off on a daydream of what he'd looked like asleep in the meadow to tell her that. And how not, really, when you came down to it? He was handsome, he was a war hero, and he was vulnerable; put the three traits together, and how could any girl not fall a little in love with him? And he had been kind to her—carelessly kind, but kind, nevertheless. Never mind that he had most likely forgotten her entirely by now. Between his own concerns and the round of entertainments his mother was contriving, he probably hadn't given her a single thought in weeks.

Which was just as well. It allowed her to have her secret passion without embarrassing herself. There was safety in distance.

If grown women can be in love with some actor on the London stage, she told herself, helplessly, *I can be in love with Reggie Fenyx, surely. Where's the harm? So long as I don't delude myself into thinking he'd ever look twice at me in public.*

Some of that was going through her mind before she went to sleep tonight, knowing that if she dreamed, she would be facing the Hermit, the embodiment of "know thyself." She was afraid, to tell the truth, not of the card-creature himself, but of failing to pass whatever tests he set her. The more she thought about the Hermit, the less confident she was; how could she even begin to meet him mind-to-mind?

She really didn't think she was ready for this card—surely he should have come at the end of the Major Arcana, not barely halfway through! Surely the end of the journey that began with the Fool should end with the Hermit.

She had hoped to gain a bit more courage by passing through all the stages she had won through before facing the Hermit—but instead, when she "woke" in the Tarot realm, she woke to darkness, a darkness broken only by a single pinpoint of light in the distance, a light that she stumblingly made her way towards.

"I don't know you," she said, slowly, admitting her ignorance. "I mean, I know you are the Hermit, but—but that's not just some misanthropic old man in a desert. I don't know really know what you are."

"I am an eternal seeker," the Hermit said, and smiled. "I am Merlin, Taliesin, Apollonius of Tyanna, I am anyone who has ever sought for wisdom knowing that it is the search that is important and, not the end. Because—?"

"Because—there never will be an end because you never actually find wisdom?" she hazarded, feeling as if she was groping in the dark without the benefit of the Hermit's lantern. "Because if you think you've found it, you haven't? Because looking for wisdom is a process, and not something with an actual goal?"

"And?" he prompted. "Think what you have learned from the other cards thus far."

People who actually are *something don't need to make a show.* No, it was more than that. Wasn't there a quote? "To—know you know nothing—is the beginning of wisdom?" she faltered.

"And the wisest man does not claim wisdom for himself, though others may account him as wise," the Hermit said, gently, and with what she recognized with astonishment was true humility. "But that is not why you are here now. You will seek for wisdom your whole life long, little Fire-mage, and sometimes it will be through pain and trouble, and sometimes with joy and pleasure. You cannot cease from learning, especially you whose Element is Fire, for Fire changes all it touches, and everything it touches, changes. Fire is the transmuter of all. Earth becomes ash and glass, Water becomes vapor, Air is consumed. In alchemy, only through tempering and trial in the crucible, through Fire, can base become noble. Fire is a bad master, but a good servant, and for it to serve you, you must be more clever than it is."

She nodded earnestly. Not that she was entirely *comfortable* with all this business of master and servant—but some of what she had read in her mother's notes had made it clear that while there were some Elementals who were, well, *people,* the vast majority of them were no brighter than a cat or a dog. But all of them had a dangerous side. Well, look at her Salamanders, for instance. Sweet-natured with her, but she'd seen them go after those nasty little gnomes, fierce as ferrets. And the Fire Elementals were terribly dangerous when they weren't controlled.

Look what had happened in San Francisco in the United States, after that terrible earthquake.

"So you aren't to *grant* me wisdom," she said, looking up at him, for he was very tall, even stooped over as he was, bowed with the weight of his knowledge and years. "Because obviously wisdom is only earned with experience, and I haven't got much."

"But I can give you knowledge, and I have." He nodded at her, and to her astonishment, continued, "And you have shown yourself ready to proceed by admitting that you lack wisdom and knowledge both. Sometimes, little one, the answer is to give no answer. Sometimes it is better for the Fool to ask not, 'what is that cup?' but to say, with an open heart, 'I do not know, can you help me?' And now I am to take you to Justice, who marks the halfway point in your journey."

She stared at him, unable to believe that she had passed his tests, had won her way to the next card. Surely not.

But he was walking away, as if he fully expected her to follow. So follow she did, through the darkness that was illuminated only by his lantern, a thick darkness that closed in around them, until they came to another of those marble halls with classical pillars that seemed to be everywhere here. There he stood aside, and waited for her to go inside.

"I'm not ready!" she exclaimed, feeling a rising panic.

"No one ever is," he said, and—

—to her immense relief, she woke.

She realized instantly what had awakened her. It was the

sound of voices, coming up through the floor. Alison and her daughters were back, and Carolyn and Lauralee's voices were unusually shrill with excitement.

"I can't believe it!" Carolyn exclaimed. "A real weekend party and a real Society ball! Mother, *how* did you persuade her?"

Good gad, what are they up to now?

"I have my ways," Alison purred. By the sound of things, they must be in Lauralee's room, directly beneath Eleanor's. "I pointed out that Reggie certainly knew any number of officers who were on injured-leave, as well as being able to extend invitations to the pilots in training at Oxford, and suggested that a proper weekend party, the kind we all remember from before the war, could be just the thing to shake him out of his gloomy spirits. And of course, I used my influence on her." Alison laughed. "I must admit, the presence of the other guests has helped in this far past my expectations. I do believe that Lady Devlin has woken up to the fact that she's buried herself in that old place for two years, and that she misses polite society. One can hardly call her father either polite or society."

Carolyn giggled. "If he'd been my father," she said boldly, "I'd have sent him packing months ago! I'm glad he's gone. And if Reggie marries me, I'm going to see to it that he stays where he belongs!"

"Hmph," Lauralee replied. "If Reggie marries me and that horrible old man turns up, he just might climb into bed one night and find himself sharing it with kobolds. And if that doesn't frighten him into heart failure, I don't know what will. Better to find a way to be rid of him permanently, Carolyn; he has a fortune of his own, and his daughter will inherit all of it. Waste not, want not, I always say."

"Don't bicker, girls," Alison said absently. "We need to plan for this weekend party carefully. The difficulty, however, is that we *must* go into London for several days if we are to get proper costumes for this occasion. It will be a fancy-dress ball, after all. Now, are you quite certain your magics are firmly in place on your rivals? We cannot afford any slippage."

"Absolutely," Lauralee said, in a voice that allowed for no doubt. "Our spells are working flawlessly, and they are so subtle I doubt that anyone has noticed any changes in the other girls. No matter what they sound like to anyone else, the moment they are in Reggie's presence, they will be irritating. Their conversation will be inane, they'll talk too much, and their voices will be shrill. It isn't much of a change, just half an octave or so, but it does grate on his nerves."

"Whereas *we* make sure to pitch our voices low when we speak to him," Carolyn said smugly. "We don't talk too much, we get him to talk about things he likes, and we try to be soothing. The contrast alone has endeared us to him."

"Good. And after a week of nothing but high-pitched irritation around him, he will be all the happier to see you back," Alison said gaily. "Well, off to bed, girls! We have a journey to make in the morning!"

The sound of footsteps below marked the departure of Carolyn and her mother from Lauralee's room. Now fully awake, Eleanor listened to the sounds of her stepsister preparing for bed in the room below.

So they were going to be gone for a full week! She could scarcely believe her luck. A week without the extra chores, the extra laundry—there would be so much more she could get accomplished! If there was the slightest chance that she could get through all of the rest of the Major Arcana cards in their absence—

Well, perhaps not all of them, but surely one each day wasn't too much to try for.

She caught herself just in time. *Just be glad you have the peace to work in,* she told herself. *Don't try to jump ahead of yourself.*

Still, she *would* have a week alone, and after that, this ball couldn't possibly take place terribly soon. She vaguely remembered what she knew about the big country weekends at the homes of the wealthy and titled. These things took time, a great deal of time, to organize. There were orders for food to be given, substitutions for things that couldn't be obtained would have to be made, rooms prepared, invitations sent. So while that was going on, everyone in this household would be distracted, too. Surely if Alison was now Lady Devlin's especial friend, her ladyship would ask Alison to help with the preparations. Even if not, there would be so much concentration on the weekend that no one would pay a lot of attention to Eleanor, especially if she kept herself quite quiet and unobtrusive.

Perhaps the end of July would be the earliest that this weekend could take place. By then it was possible, just possible, that she would have enough understanding of magic and her Element to break free. She was coming nearer to it, she could sense it. She could *see* the bonds of Alison's spells now, and they were weakening. Like a prisoner rasping her bonds against the stone wall of her prison, she was wearing away at them. But she needed more power; she needed greater understanding of her Element, and the ability to call up an Elemental who would be more than a helpful little pet, or something that mostly would not offer advice, like the Salamanders.

One step at a time, she warned herself. *First, you have to learn, and you have to practice. Remember what the Hermit told you. Fire must respect you before it will serve with you.* She would see how much time during the next week that Sarah could spare, and spend every free moment practicing, reading, and finding her way into the realm of the Tarot to learn still more.

And somehow, keep Alison from finding out about any of it.

July 11, 1917
Longacre Park, Warwickshire

"My mother has gone insane," Reggie said flatly. "This business of holding a weekend *and* a fancy-dress ball is absolute folly." He stared across the breakfast table at Lady

Virginia, daring her to disagree. Breakfast was, as usual at Longacre, a matter of helping one's self from the sideboard, so the only people present were himself, Lady Virginia, and the Brigadier.

Lady Virginia sighed, and looked meditatively at a grilled tomato resting in lone splendor on her plate. "I would not put it quite so strongly, but for the most part, I admit I do find this plan of a weekend party and fancy-dress ball to be somewhat ill-advised."

"Ill-advised?" He shook his head. "My lady, have you any idea how much work the staff is already doing? A staff that is adequate for a few visitors, but is seriously undermanned for something like this?" He'd been fielding plaintive pleas already, mostly from the cook and her staff, who were trying to find a way to provide four fancy dinners under rationing, not to mention the afternoon teas, the buffet breakfasts, and the luncheons for the guests who would be spending the entire weekend. He was going to have to do some foraging among the neighbors and his friends, and scour the home farms for produce.

Fortunately, I have some contacts among the Yanks, who seem to be overburdened with provisions.

He didn't want to think about what this weekend was going to mean in terms of being personally besieged by marriage-minded maidens and mamas. They'd be coming from miles around for the ball.

Lady Virginia sighed. "Nevertheless, Reggie, I understand completely what is motivating her, and it is not entirely the urge to see you bound up in wedlock."

He gritted his teeth, and studiously buttered a piece of dark toast. "Not—entirely, you say." The thought of fielding all those women made his head ache. Or maybe his head was aching because of the way his jaw was clenched. Nevertheless, it was not something he could contemplate quietly.

The Brigadier, wisely, was keeping silent, pretending a polite deafness.

"No." His godmother looked up at the ceiling for a moment, as if searching for inspiration in the intricately carved plaster. "I think she has finally gotten over your father's death. I think she has realized that the world still goes on outside the gates of Longacre Park. And I think this is her first, rather rash step towards rejoining that world. Your aunt and I have both been attempting to coax her back out of her retired state. I should hate to see this fail to come off; I fear it might send her back into seclusion again."

Reggie stopped buttering his toast, and stared at Lady Virginia, struck dumb with first astonishment, then guilt. If that were true—

He needed another opinion on this, quickly. He turned to the second of his breakfast companions. "Brigadier? What do you think? You've known Mater for as long as anyone; you should be some sort of judge here."

The Brigadier, still erect, still fit, and still every inch the soldier despite his years and gray hair, coughed once, politely. "I wouldn't be so discourteous as to contradict a lady, but I also wouldn't even make an attempt at guessing what is going through any lady's mind, no matter how long I've known her. These are mysteries that a man dares to plumb at his peril." He raised one bushy eyebrow and nodded at Lady Virginia. "I leave that to the members of their own sex."

Lady Virginia smiled slightly. "I never thought you were a coward, Brigadier."

He lifted his hand to interrupt her—politely. "I was, in my time, considered a good strategist, my lady," he said, with a twinkle in his eye. "And a good strategist never attacks a fortified stronghold. Ever." He spread his empty hands in a gesture of conciliation. "Besides, I am at a disadvantage. My daughter-in-law and granddaughter will be invited for the ball. If they were to discover that I dared to be against it, however briefly, I will have to watch for arsenic in my brandy."

Reggie swallowed his groan. If it was, indeed, the case that this was the sign his mother was ready to move back into her old circles again—then how could he possibly object to something that would get his mother to do what he had been praying she would ever since his father's untimely death? She *couldn't* keep trying to lock the world outside away. It wasn't healthy. She'd turn into a Miss Havisham if she weren't careful.

But there was no denying the fact that this weekend party was a thinly disguised attempt to force him to make some sort of choice of fiancee and announce an engagement. If not announce an engagement *and* a wedding—at this point in the war there had been so many hasty marriages that virtually any young man who wanted or needed a special license could get one on a moment's notice. Not that he entirely blamed her on that score; he *was* the only heir, and he *was* going back to the Front when his leg healed—

—when his mind healed—

But dash it all, there wasn't one of these society fillies that he could stand being in the same room with for the course of a card-party! How was he to tolerate one day in, day out, for the rest of his life?

The mere thought took away his appetite, and he excused himself from the table, going out onto the terrace to stare unseeing down into the gardens. He had made some progress towards the goal that Lady Virginia had set for him; his shields were far more transparent now, and he had been making some small, tentative attempts at reading the currents of magic around him. As a result, he sensed it was her coming up behind him, long before she spoke.

She stood beside him, looking out onto the vista that had cost his distant ancestor a pretty penny to produce. "Sometimes I wonder if you hate me, Reggie," she said, in a voice that sounded tired.

He turned towards her with surprise. "Hate you? No! Why should I hate you?"

"Because I tell you all the uncomfortable truths you would rather not hear. It's a privilege of age. But that doesn't make it less painful to hear them, I'm sure." She made a little, annoyed sound in the back of her throat. "Not that I'm going to stop telling them to you."

"Not that I expect you to," he countered. He leaned on

the marble balustrade and looked out into the garden. "Mater wants me married. She wants it with a desperation that frightens me. I *don't* want a wife, or a fiancé, or anything like one. I won't insult you by claiming some noble motives, my lady, or pretending I want to spare some unknown girl grief when I go back to the Front; the simple fact is that I have not met one single young woman who would be 'suitable' in Mater's eyes who was not a dead bore, an empty-headed mannequin suited only for displaying expensive clothing, or—"

He almost said, "Or a hard-eyed chit who would wait just long enough for me to get onto the train to the Channel-ferry before collecting her lovers to populate my house at my expense," but decided that discretion was the better part there. Besides, Lady Virginia would want to know who he was talking about, and he didn't want to tell her.

"Or an opportunist more interested in my title and social connections than myself," he concluded, instead.

"Ah," said her ladyship, nodding wisely. "The Robinson girls."

"Among others." He laughed without humor. "They aren't the only ones by a stretch, but they are the most persistent at the moment. I think even their mother would be casting her cap at me, if she thought she could slip herself past Mater's eye."

Lady Virginia sighed. "I almost wish she would try; it might shake your mother's friendship with the creature. I know this is unreasonable of me, and I know that I should be happy for her to have a friend—but there is something about that woman *and* her girls that puts my back up."

Reggie knew what it was, even if Lady Virginia didn't. She would never admit it, never recognize it in herself, but Lady Virginia was a snob . . . the idea of someone whose money came from trade marrying into the aristocracy secretly outraged her. Well, it probably wouldn't outrage her if the girl was also a Master—but Mastery was another sort of aristocracy.

Or perhaps, as long as it's someone else's blue-blooded

family, and not hers, nor that of her friends, it wouldn't matter so much.

It was hardly her fault; it was the way she'd been raised. And he probably would not have noticed, if it hadn't been for that stupid not-quite-quarrel he'd had with Eleanor.

He sighed. He missed those conversations. He missed her company, her wit, her intelligence, and how she was kind without making him feel as if he owed her something for her kindness. He'd been down to the meadow several times, but she'd never again appeared. Either he had offended her so much that she was shunning his company, or else his timing was so exquisitely bad that she thought *he* was avoiding *her*—and as a result she had stopped coming.

Or else, and this was the likeliest, she was kept too busy for frivolous visits in the middle of the day to the meadow. It was summer, after all, and there were probably a thousand chores she was being made to do. Oh, it made him depressed to think about it, that fine, keen mind, shackled to some sort of menial work. It was like seeing a Derby winner hitched to a plow.

If only he could do something for her without insulting her further.

If only some of those empty-headed dolls his mother kept dragging about could have a fraction of her intelligence and personality.

"There will be young women you've never even seen at this weekend, Reggie," Lady Virginia said, breaking into his melancholy thoughts. "Perhaps—"

"Or perhaps not," he said, more harshly than he had intended, and tried to soften it with a sheepish smile. "I'll keep an open mind, my lady. I won't promise more than that."

There was one saving grace in all of this. With the weekend looming up, and all of the preparations that even Lady Virginia would have to help with, she wouldn't be pressuring him so much to take up his magic quickly.

A silver lining of sorts. These days, he would take whatever sliver of silver he could get.

"Exactly what sort of girl interests you, Reggie?" she

asked, out of the blue. "I've never been able to make you out. I must suppose you had your little flings—"

"Quite enough, with my debts honorably discharged," he replied, flippantly. "There is one thing to be said in favor of a girl who only expects money and presents from one; you always know where you are with her, and she always has someone waiting in the wings when you tire of her."

Lady Virginia winced. "Is that the prevailing attitude now?" she asked soberly. "In my day, there was at least a pretense of romance."

"We haven't time to waste on romance, my lady," he said flatly. "Not when—"

He didn't say it, but it was there, hanging in the air between them. *Not when in a week or two or three you can be just another grave in Flanders.*

She brooded down on the roses. "I expect there is a great deal to be said for knowing that if the—worst—happens, your current inamorata will simply shrug and move on to another when she sees your name in the papers. But those of your generation that live through this hideousness are coming out with scars of the heart and soul as well as the body, and I do not know what that will mean in the long run."

"Neither do I," he replied truthfully. "But you asked what sort of girl I find attractive—"

Involuntarily, the image of Eleanor, independent, clever, intelligent, entirely unsuitable Eleanor, flashed through his mind.

"Someone I can talk to, about *anything,*" he said, finally. "Someone who has the brains not only to understand what I'm talking about, but to hold up her side of the conversation. When you have the wherewithal to buy as much beauty as you want, it isn't as important. Mind, I'm not saying that I don't like a girl to be pretty, but—" He shrugged helplessly. "Never mind. It's hardly relevant."

"Surely at some point," Lady Virginia began, "you must have encountered—"

It was time to put an end to this, so he put up the one argument he knew there would be no getting around. "My lady, there's another condition, and it's one I cannot tell Mater. I watched how father struggled to keep Mater ignorant of his Elemental work, the difficulties and even heartache it caused for both of them, and I decided a long time ago that I won't marry anyone who isn't an Elemental Master in her own right. I must have someone I don't have to keep that sort of secret from, and how likely is that?"

There. That will silence her. He actually had sworn that—before the war—so he wasn't lying. Not that he ever expected to take up the wand of an Air Master again. Merely dropping some of his shields had been shudderingly difficult; he could not even think about working real magic again without bringing on an attack of panic.

Lady Virginia looked at him out of the corners of her eyes. "Perhaps more likely than you think."

He snorted. "They're not exactly thick on the ground," was all he said. He tried not to think of Peter Scott with raw envy. Curse the man—he had the perfect partner, a woman who was an Elemental Master, brilliant, self-sufficient, and a stunning, exotic beauty.

Not that Mater wouldn't drop dead on the spot if I brought home a half-breed Hindu.

She was the one woman he had ever met who could actually understand, really and truly, what the war did to a man, did to his soul. Maybe that was the biggest problem with the girls of his set. They didn't, and couldn't. None of *them* had volunteered as nurses or VAD girls in France or Belgium. None of them had the least idea of the things that lay inside his mind; none of them would ever want to know. They preferred to think of the war the way those first volunteers had, as a chance for glory, and if one must die, to die nobly. They didn't know and couldn't understand that there was nothing noble or glorious about those churned-over fields, the dead zones of mud and razor-wire. And if he tried to tell them, they would turn away in horror.

Doctor Maya knew, and didn't flinch from it. But how many like her were there?

"It has been my experience, limited though it is, that if you are really determined in that direction, the partner will find you when you are both ready," she said gravely. "But I am sure that makes me sound like some sort of mystic, so I will keep my opinions to myself. Just keep an open mind as you promised—and open eyes as well."

She retreated to the house, leaving him staring down at the garden, wondering bitterly if *anyone* who hadn't experienced the Front could ever understand what it did to someone inside.

We look, act, and talk like our old selves, but we've been damaged, each and every one of us, he thought. *We're scarred inside. Like rosebuds with canker-worms at their hearts. We look the same, but even if we live, we'll never blossom. And there is nothing that will change that. Nothing at all.*

24

July 15, 1917
Broom, Warwickshire

SUNSHINE AND FRESH AIR FLOODED the kitchen, and The Arrows was very peaceful without the Robinsons and Howse present. So peaceful, that Eleanor wondered what it would be like to live here like this forever—if somehow, the Robinsons would just never return.

"I've thought and I've reasoned, and I've looked," Sarah said aloud, startling Eleanor as she concentrated on a particularly obtuse paragraph about the Hanged Man card. "And much as I hate to admit that I'm wrong—well, I'm wrong."

Eleanor blinked, and stared at her mentor. Sarah was sitting cross-legged on the floor of the kitchen, staring down at a pile of stones with markings on them. *Runestones,* she called them, and she used them not only to try and give her some direction for the future, but to try and learn what was going on around her that might be hidden from her. If, for instance, someone was sick enough that he needed to see the medical doctor and not just depend on her herbal remedies. There were many country folk who still were suspicious of the doctor and veterinarian, and sometimes it took Sarah a deal of convincing to get them to go to either gentleman.

"Wrong about what?" Eleanor asked. It took a lot to get Sarah to admit she was wrong about *anything.* She was dreadfully stubborn that way.

Then again, she had every right to be.

"I've always said that the big house and the village haven't got much of anything to say to each other," Sarah replied sourly, still staring down at her stones. "Still, I knew it was an Air Master that chased off the revenants; I knew it couldn't be a local witch, no matter how powerful, when you told me about it, and I was right. It turns out she's a guest up there at Longacre, though, and it seems that she's staying the summer. And that changes everything."

"An Air Master?" Eleanor said, catching her breath. Oh, granted, it wasn't her Element, but *any* Master could help her—

More to the point, unlike, say, a constable or any other authority figure, any Elemental Master would know she was telling the truth about Alison and what Alison had done to her. She wouldn't have to try and convince an Elemental Master that she wasn't mad because she was talking about magic.

"That's what we've needed, what you've needed, to see if you can't get cut free of your stepmother and her wicked magic. And now, I've asked the cards, the bones, and the stones, and they're *all* saying you need to go up there and meet with that Air Master. In fact, they say if you don't, well—" she shook her head. "It'll be bad, that's all. Not just bad for you, either. The stones reckon Alison's got some wicked mischief going that's going to be a trouble no matter what steps are taken to stop her, but horrible bad if she isn't stopped." Sarah looked up, her face full of fear. "I can't tell what it is, but at a guess, she's let loose some kind of sickness; she's Earth, and that's the sort of thing they do when they go to the bad. Pestilence and plague." Sarah bit her lip. "Well, the stones say that if you work with that Air Master and get yourself cut free, Alison will fall, but if you don't, she'll use you somehow and put more power into whatever it is she's done, and the stones don't say how *much* worse it will be, but they're all showing their bad sides."

She felt as if hope and fear were at war inside her. Hope, because here was exactly what she needed. Fear, because how could she ever *get* what she needed with Alison's hearth-binding still holding her? "But—I can't get as far as Longacre," she protested. "And even if I could, I can't just stroll up to even the tradesman's entrance and ask to be introduced to the Air Master!" Even if she knew the Air Master's real name. Especially not looking like a servant. She knew better than to go to the front door—she'd be turned away in a heartbeat.

"Well, now, that's not necessarily true . . . because you only need to get inside those walls *once* and talk to her. After that, if she's worth anything, and the stones say she is, she'll come to you." Sarah gathered up the stones and poured them into a little leather bag. "And there *is* one night, coming up, when you can walk in the front door and be presented like you were to the manor born. Provided you're wearing a fancy dress." She tilted her head to one side. "Think about it. The night of that fancy dress ball. If your stepsisters are good enough to be invited, you surely are as well."

Eleanor's hand flew to her mouth. "Good gad!" she cried. "You're right, you're exactly right! But—" As quickly as her hopes rose, they dropped again. "Where am I going to get an invitation? Or a costume? Especially one that will look as if it belongs among people like that?"

"Ah, now, what about that attic of yours?" Sarah replied, with a lift of her brow. "I think we ought to take a look up there, first, before we think about any other possibilities. As for the invitation, you leave that up to me. I'll find a way to get you invited."

Eleanor wanted to protest that she'd been through all of the chests and had salvaged the only usable garments up there, but Sarah was already on her feet and marching towards the steps. With a sigh of resignation, Eleanor followed.

It was easier to move the chests with two of them, but it was rather disheartening to see what the moths and time had done to some of the once-beautiful gowns that had been inside them. Silk shattered and tore like wet tissue as they lifted gowns out; the satins had mostly discolored, beadwork fell off the bodices. But just as Eleanor turned away, even though there were older chests and clothes-presses waiting, certain that they had completely eliminated any possibility of finding anything, Sarah let out an exclamation of satisfaction.

"What?" Eleanor blurted, turning back.

Sarah held up a froth of flounces and lace. "I knew there should be one of these still good!" she exclaimed with satisfaction. "It's still a tale in the village, how the three girls from Broom went up to London and were the belles of the ball. The fellow who owned The Arrows before your father bought it was just as well-off; the wool-trade, d'ye see, that and The Arrows had been in his family since Great Harry's day. This is a ball-gown from the time of Victoria's coronation; all three of the daughters here went down to London on account of some aunt who married a title got them all manner of invitations. She got them into all the right circles and chaperoned them about for three weeks. It must have worked, since two of them got husbands out of the journey, and but the third never could settle on anyone, and ended up back here, taking care of her parents when they got old. That's who your father bought the house from, the daughter who never married."

Curious now, Eleanor made her way back to where Sarah was unpacking the petticoats that went with the gown. They, remarkably, were also still sound. The gown was stupefying to one used to the current narrow skirts and minimal (or in Eleanor's case, nonexistent) corseting. She couldn't imagine how much Venice lace had gone into trimming the row after row of flounces on the skirt. Twenty yards? Thirty? The neckline was low enough to make her blush; the puffy little flounced sleeves were as tiny as the skirt was huge. It was made of some sort of flounces of netting or gauzy stuff in a dark ivory tone over a slightly heavier skirt. Maybe it had once been pure white, and had aged to this color, but if so, it had done so uniformly.

"You'll look a rare treat," Sarah said, giving the gown a

good shake. "This is Indian cotton, from back in the day when it was dearer than silk."

"I'll look a rare Guy—" Eleanor retorted. But she reached out to touch the delicate lace, anyway, wondering wistfully if she really could fit into it.

A moment later, she found out, at Sarah's insistence. She was surprised to find that it fit her very well indeed.

"A good thing that they didn't reckon young girls should wear much but flowers or feathers, back in the day," Sarah said, looking very pleased. " 'Cause how I should manage jewels, I haven't a clue. We'll say you're little Princess Victoria herself. Here, I've got a nice rose-colored sash off that silk that went to bits, that'll take the place of the old one that's gone, a bit of cleaning, some flowers and a domino-mask—you leave it to me. Put your hair up, and a bit of glamorie, even Alison won't recognize you."

Eleanor looked down at herself, feeling a thrill of excitement. And it wasn't because she would finally find a possible mentor, or because this might be the chance to plead her case to an Elemental Master. No, there was only one thought in her head at the moment.

Reggie will be there. And he'll see me like this—not shabby.

"But how am I going to get there?" she asked, as it occurred to her that trying to walk up to Longacre in that dress was going to be in impossible proposition.

"I'll borrow a cart and horse and put a glamorie on them, too," Sarah said dismissively. "Make them look like a carriage. Wouldn't pass in daylight, but this will be after dark. I'll be your coachman, I'll hand you out, so nobody gets close enough to see through the glamorie."

"But—I *still* can't get as far as the manor!" she objected weakly. "Alison's bindings—I've tried stretching them, and they still only go as far as the meadow."

"You will be able to. Alison will have her hands full with her girls. She'll be trying to hide her nature from that Air Master, you can count on it. She'll be distracted by the ball. For an hour or two, and working together, we'll be able to stretch those bindings just far enough that night." Sarah sounded quite sure of herself, and Eleanor just gave in.

She had to be right. This was Eleanor's only chance to get some outside help.

She wanted to see Reggie, even if he didn't recognize her. Maybe *because* he wouldn't recognize her. Just once, she wanted to talk to him, and see him look at her the way he would look at any other girl that was his social equal.

She wanted—a memory. No matter what happened to her after that night, she wanted to have a memory of being a princess at a ball, dancing with a handsome knight, and allow herself to be just that little bit in love with him.

"You're right," she said, with a nod. "If we don't seize this opportunity, there may never be another one; we *have* to make it work."

July 17, 1917
London

Thanks to her friendship with Lady Devlin, the Savoy had put the Robinsons up in a better suite than usual; the girls didn't even have to share a room, which made for a little more peace and quiet. It certainly impressed Warrick Locke when he arrived on Alison's summons.

Alison saw no need to trouble herself with secrecy today; what could be more natural than a meeting with her solicitor since they both "happened" to be in London? The girls were at fittings for their costumes; nothing could be more respectable than having him come to her hotel suite in broad daylight with a briefcase full of papers. Howse was right in the next room, though she could have been in this one, if Alison had wished, and neither seen nor heard anything but her book. It had taken more than a year, but now Howse was nicely obedient to Alison's will and directions, yet still had enough freedom of thought that she performed all of her duties properly.

Just for the sake of verisimilitude, Locke had a stack of papers on the table. The fact that none of those papers concerned *her* was something no one else would ever find out. Some of them, however, concerned Eleanor, who was the central topic of their conversation. Eleanor was a loose end that Alison very much wanted tidied up before there was a wedding in the offing. It would be harder to dispose of her quietly when one was connected to the Fenyxes of Longacre Park.

But Locke still had no better plan than the old one, even though he'd had weeks to think of alternatives. Alison was extremely disappointed in him; normally he was full of ideas, but he seemed terribly fixated on this one. Perhaps it was because of his own personal obsessions, but if that was indeed the case, the sooner he got them under control, the better.

"I tell you, Warrick, no matter how much you like your plan to break that wretched girl's mind, it is too complicated," Alison objected. "What's more, it relies too much on that man of yours, as well as bringing in possible confederates. I know you trust him, but every time you add a person to a plan you double the chances of something being said or done at the wrong time and either ruining the whole thing or giving the plan away. Or worse still, you've added the danger of having your confederate decide to betray you."

Warrick Locke frowned. "Robbie has been working with me for a very long time now. Frankly, if you are concerned about him doing something other than what he has been ordered to do, I can tell you that in all the time that I have known him, he has never once had an original idea for himself."

"It's too complicated a plan," Alison countered, throttling down her rising irritation with him. "There are too many things that can go wrong, *including* that the wretched child just might be tougher-minded than you think. The closer I come to reaching my goals, the less I like complicated plans. I find that the more I have to lose, the less inclined I am to take chances on something that *might* work.

And the whole house of cards you wish to construct has far too many points of possible failure for my comfort."

"It's the only idea that has any chance at all of giving you the results you want," he replied, with ill grace. "If she dies, you lose, because the inheritance goes to the cousin. If she disappears, you lose, because until she's proven dead, you can't touch her money and when she's proven dead, the inheritance goes to the cousin. If she stays sane, and attains her majority, you lose, because sooner or later the trustees are going to want to see her to turn her fortune over to her and then there's no telling what will happen. If you injure her physically to the point that she can't care for herself, you still lose, because doctors will be involved, and someone will find out that you've been making a slave of her *and* making free with her inheritance. The only way you win is if you keep her alive and drive her so completely mad that she withdraws into herself and never comes out again. That means breaking her will, her spirit, and her mind, and there's only one way that I know for certain to do that. After all, it's not as if you can drop her down a hole and be done with her."

"Wait a moment—" she said, with a sudden surge of interest and a jolt of euphoria as his words caused an interesting image to flash across her mind. She caught and held that image; quickly extrapolated something from it, and then, smiled, slowly. "You just might have something, Warrick. You might just have solved the conundrum."

"Pardon?" He blinked at her, caught off-guard by her words.

"You said something very interesting. You said that I couldn't just drop her down a hole and be done with it." Her smile broadened. "But that just might be exactly what we want to do with her. There's more than one way to get the results we want from her."

Now he was completely confused, that much was very plain. "I thought the best plan was to break her mind."

"Be patient with me. What was the first spell I put on her? To bind her to the hearth. Correct?" She nodded as he frowned. "So this has kept her confined to the house and grounds. She can't go off on her own; that binding was intended to keep her from looking for help. But that same binding spell may serve us in another way. If she were to be taken away from the hearth, carried off somewhere, she would *have* to try and make her way back, no matter what obstacles were in her path. Or—? Do you remember how I constructed the bindings? Because I certainly do."

"I'm not sure I see where this is going, but I believe the geas you put on her forces her to try, and keep trying, to make her way back to The Arrows. And the longer she's away the more of her mind becomes obsessed with the need to return, until she can't even eat or sleep, she's so driven by and consumed with that need." Now his frown looked as if he was beginning to see the shape of something, but hadn't yet deciphered the puzzle she had set him.

She helped him out with some clues. "Warwickshire is full of abandoned coal mines. Lady Devlin was just complaining about one of them last week—it's collapsing, evidently, and causing subsidence on the property of one of her friends, spoiling a good meadow. Now suppose, just suppose, that we were to drop her down one of those, then report that she has gone missing, as we always intended to do. The first thing and only thing she would try to do is return to the hearth, driven by her growing obsession, and if we took care to drop her into one where she couldn't climb out, where the tunnels run from the entrance *towards* Broom, can you see what would happen?"

His frown deepened. "I—think so—"

Alison sat forward in her chair, leaning towards him. "She will have to follow the pull of the geas. Which means she would be forced to penetrate deeper into the mine, until she could go no further, without lights, without anything to help her." She nodded as his eyes widened with understanding. "Think of that; alone in the dark and possibly injured, she comes to a dead end. She can't retrace her steps, because the spell won't let her go back. She can't go on, because she's at a dead end. She's hungry, thirsty, and more and more of her mind is taken up with the obsession to return. Now, just to add something to ensure that we get the results we want, a mine is in the earth, and what's more, it's in *violated* earth, which means the Elementals associated with it are all of my sort. So if trying to claw her way through coal-bearing rock with her bare hands isn't enough to drive her mad, my little friends can take care of that problem by pushing her over the edge of sanity. Little monsters with glowing eyes appearing and vanishing in the dark, things gibbering and drooling on her, cold hands clutching at her, plucking at her clothing . . . it would take a stronger mind than *she* has to come out of that intact!"

"But you need to have her in your custody in order to keep control of her inheritance," Locke objected.

She was already prepared for the objection. "And I can do that. I merely wait a day or so, then nudge a rescue party to the right coal mine and allow them to find her. Fear, thirst, hunger, constant attack by gnomes and kobolds, and the geas—if she has any mind left after forty-eight hours of that, I will be shocked and amazed. By that time, I imagine the only thing we'll need to worry about is replacing her with a servant." She did sigh at that. It was getting impossible to find servants that weren't thieves, drunks, or both. With so many women getting much better wages and shorter hours by taking the places of men than they could ever obtain as servants, only the dregs were left.

On the other hand, once the business of Eleanor is settled, perhaps the answer would be simply to use magical coercions on whatever I can get. I pity any thief that tries to purloin anything from my house. Or perhaps she could take someone feeble-minded from the workhouse. The same coercions that kept Eleanor scrubbing and tending should work on the feeble-minded.

Locke gazed at her with astonishment. "My hat is off to you. I would not have thought of any of that. I hesitate to call anything a *perfect* plan, but this one is as close to perfect as a reasonable person could wish. I assume you'll put her to sleep to make her easier to handle?"

"Probably," Alison agreed. "I wouldn't even need to use a spell, if I didn't want to. A little chloroform on a sponge would do the trick."

"More reliably renewable than a spell, too," Locke murmured admiringly. "And costs nothing in power. You could even do it with your daughters; simply wait until the girl has gone to sleep, go up to her room, administer the sponge, and there will not even be a struggle."

She did not ask how he knew that. Presumably he had some experience in such matters.

"As I told you, I prefer simple plans," she replied, feeling so pleased with her own ideas that she was willing to be very pleasant to the man. "And it does occur to me that when this works, I'll be needing to find some place safe and secure to put the afflicted child. I scarcely intend to keep her at home; the present servant problem is bad enough without trying to find someone to care for and stand guard over a madwoman. I presume that you've been looking into such things?"

"Discreetly, I assure you, and mentioning no names," he responded immediately, and dug into his case for a file. "And here are the best places I found—*quite* discreet, very understanding about the need to keep someone alive and healthy, but once a patient is checked in, they don't ever emerge."

She smiled, and leaned over the table to examine the tastefully subdued brochures. On his own ground, Locke was knowledgeable and immensely helpful.

She would definitely keep him around a while longer.

Especially now that he realized she didn't *need* him to come up with better plans than he could. It would make him a little on edge, and anxious not to get on her bad side, because she was, after all, a most generous client.

July 18, 1917
Longacre Park, Warwickshire

Lady Devlin was a very old-fashioned hostess, and that meant she believed in doing things the old-fashioned way.

She was writing out every one of the invitations for the ball herself, since she no longer had a secretary to tend to such things for her. The estate manager could probably have done it for her, but she claimed that she was enjoying it. After a while, out of sheer guilt, Reggie elected to help her. His once-neat copperplate handwriting was gone all to hell, of course, with lack of practice, but it was good enough to address envelopes.

Which was tedious, but saved his mother the effort of writing out the addresses and allowed her to concentrate on the aesthetics of producing the invitations. They couldn't be printed, alas; perhaps the middle-class found invitations where one filled in missing names and dates acceptable, but no one of Lady Devlin's stature would even consider resorting to such a stratagem. Besides, many of them required a certain level of personalization in the form of a note.

It did allow him to sit down without looking like a malingerer. It also gave him a chance to find out who the girls were that would be pursuing him at this little hunt disguised as a party.

Roberta and Leva Cygnet; not much of a surprise there. They were already coming to teas and tennis-parties. "Mrs. Regina Towner," though—"Regina Towner?" he asked, casually. "Do I know the Towners?"

"An old friend from school," his mother replied, just as casually. *Right enough; mother's age, which means her daughter is probably my age . . . Mr. and Mrs Robert Tansy, Esq., and daughter. So Ginger will be in the howling pack. Good gad, I hope some of my lads come through. I need all the distractions I can muster, and Ginger likes to dance.* Some of the next few were innocuous enough. Then, "Lt. Commander Matthew Mann, the Hon. Mrs. Matthew Mann, Miss Mann." *Ah, good gad. The Brigadier's granddaughter, and Mama is an "Hon." I've never seen an "Hon." that wasn't on the hunt for a title for the family. Well, the Brigadier warned me.* "Viscountess Arabella Reed." One of Lady Virginia's friends, she was a chatterbox, but at least she didn't have any daughters.

Then, at last, the run of invitations that he hoped would save him—pilots-in-training at the school headquartered at Oxford, and lads he knew either were on leave or could get it. Even a cadet was a second lieutenant, and while Mamas were on the hunt for titles, daughters were easily distracted by officers' dress-uniforms.

Second Lt. Michael Freed, Second Lt. David Jackson, at Reading. Lt. Vincent Paul Mills, good gad, I hope he doesn't get shot to bits before this thing comes off; that handsome face will be even more of a distraction than his uniform. Captain Michael Dolbeare; good thing he's training the lads at Oxford; he's a got enough medals at this point to sink him if he fell in the river, and the girls can't resist the shiny. Lt. Allen McBain; arm in a sling, but even if he can't dance he's another handsome devil. That Scots burr, though; the girls will giggle over it and make him blush, which is entertaining as well as a distraction. Now the Oxford lot. Second Lt. John Oliver, Second Lt. Charles Goddard, Second Lt. Lyman Evans—at least they aren't losing a flying-student a day the way they were at the start of the war, or half my invitations would never get answered. Of course Turner had made sure that the names he had given Reggie were of the better students who had less chance of cracking up. That was a concern; ambulances were stationed at the students' fields because they were, by heaven, needed. The accident rate was appalling, the death-rate even more so. The Rumpetys killed more lads than combat did. *Thank God for the Gosport system.* Things had changed since he was a cadet; now there was a logical system in place for training. Still. Back in his day, there were always several dozen crashes a day when the weather permitted and the planes were up. Usually one cadet died a day, and several more were injured. *Not so bad now, though. Can't afford to lose that many in training, I suppose. Took those old men long enough to figure that out.*

He shook off the shakes that threatened him as he remembered some of those crashes . . . fortunately, his sojourn at the school as a cadet had been mercifully short. He already knew how to fly, and didn't take long to prove it.

Captain William Robert Howe. Can't do without him. He's bringing the band— Thanks to the Brigadier; this was a regular infantry band, though they had played for the RFC. That would give some of the PBI a thrill, coming up to a country house to play. Captain Howe was the officer in charge and the bandleader, all in one. And, the Brigadier claimed, single. Another alternate target for the husband-hunters. PBI he might be, and less glamorous than a pilot, but he was a captain.

Captain Steven Stewart, and he'd damned well better get leave. Steve had pledged on his life he'd come. Tommy had sworn he'd see to it. Tommy had incentive; was getting a case of whiskey from the Longacre cellars if Steve did make it.

Lt. Commander Geoffrey Cockburn, and if he puts his auto in the pond again, I'll make him go in after it. Captain Christopher Whitmore, and he had better not bring all that photographic paraphernalia with him. Both had been chums of his at college. Geoff was a tearaway, Chris studious, both still single and not at all unhandsome. Yet more fodder for the husband-hunters. With luck, he'd get a word with them ahead of time so they could help keep the harpies off.

"Here's the uniformed lot, Mater," he said, with relief, putting his stack beside the rest of the finished envelopes.

"Ah, good," she replied, absently. "Here, there's just a few more of the local people. Be a dear and do them, would you?"

Mrs. and Mrs. Donald Hinshaw, the vicar and his wife. Doctor and Mrs. Robert Sutherland. And then—

Mrs. Alison Robinson, Miss Danbridge, Miss Carolyn Danbridge, Miss Eleanor Robinson. . . .

Eleanor? For a moment, his mind went blank. Then it refocused again. Eleanor Robinson. *His* Eleanor?

She was that—woman's daughter? But how was that possible?

"Mater, who's this Eleanor Robinson?" he asked casually, or at least, as casually as he could manage.

"Oh, she's just dear Alison's stepdaughter," his mother

said, indifferently. "The vicar reminded me about her, or at least, I think it was the vicar. Someone did, anyway. She's supposed to be at Oxford, so I suppose she's a terrible bluestocking not to come home for the summer, but it wouldn't do not to invite her, even if she doesn't come."

She's supposed to be at Oxford? But— He felt as if he'd been poleaxed, he was so stunned. There was certainly no *monetary* reason why she shouldn't be at university—that woman spent money as freely as his own mother did, and it was common knowledge she was well-off, so there should be no trouble with the fees.

For that matter, given how Alison Robinson spent lavishly, why was Eleanor always so shabby-looking? Why did she have hands like a charwoman?

What was going on there?

And the next question. *How do I find out if I can't get near Eleanor in the first place?*

25

July 20, 1917
Longacre Park, Warwickshire

REGGIE HAD DECIDED ON CAROLYN as the most likely to let something about Eleanor drop—she clearly was not the more intelligent of the sisters (though neither of them were a match for their mother) but he still was going to tread very cautiously around her. He didn't want to alert any of the three to the fact that he knew their stepsister was somewhere in Broom. In fact, he didn't want to alert them to the fact that he had met her more than once. It had taken a great deal of willpower not to limp down to his motor and take it right to the door of The Arrows that day when he had addressed an invitation to her, and only the fact that so very much was ringing false had kept him from doing so. There was a great deal more than met the eye going on; he had a notion that he might eventually want Lady Virginia's help on this, but not until he had investigated all other courses of action himself.

A tennis match presented the best opportunity; his mother was playing against hers, and he brought her a lemonade as a pretext for sitting next to her. After some noncommittal chat, he managed to steer the conversation towards Oxford, and asked, as if in afterthought, "Oh—don't you have a sister there?"

She jerked as if she'd been stung by a bee, and stared at him, wide-eyed. If he hadn't known there was something wrong before this, he would have by her reaction. He knew guilt when he saw it. "A sister?"

"Eleanor?" he prompted. "It occurred to me that the only Robinsons in Broom had a daughter named Eleanor. Before the war, I remember talking to her about going to Oxford—she had her heart set on it, and was taking the examinations in order to qualify."

"Oh—*Eleanor!*" Her brittle laugh rang entirely false. "She's only my stepsister, not a real sister. I scarcely think of her at all, actually, we're practically strangers." Her smile was too bright, and she looked very nervous to him. He fancied that Eleanor was nowhere near as much of a stranger as she was pretending.

He smiled slightly, or rather, stretched his lips in something like a smile. "I suppose for form's sake we ought to invite her to the ball, too. It isn't done to leave out one sister of three. People might talk."

Again, that brittle laugh. "Oh, you can if you like, but *I* shouldn't trouble myself. She'd never come. She's a dreadful bluestocking, and she never even comes home on the vacs. I don't think she knows such things as balls exist. She *certainly* doesn't know how to dress. She'd never leave her—studies—for anything that frivolous."

He leaned back in his chair. He hadn't missed that moment of hesitation when she had sought for a word to describe what Eleanor was doing. He yawned. "Oh, well, in that case, if you think she won't feel slighted. The vicar suggested to Mater that she ought to be included on the guest list is all."

"Oh." The girl's voice grew hard, and just a touch cold. "The vicar, was it? No, I really shouldn't bother if I were you. I'll make sure Mother reminds the vicar of how much Eleanor dislikes leaving Oxford. I suppose she'll be a don, once they allow such things."

He made a sound like a laugh. "It's not as if there won't

be a surfeit of young ladies to dance with; too many of them are likely to be wallflowers as it is, unless I can bring some more cadets from the RFC up to scratch. I think we can do without her."

"So do I." She swiftly turned the subject to costumes, and whether he thought it would be too warm for eighteenth-century court dress. "Wouldn't an Empire gown be cooler?" she asked.

"I should think so," he replied. "And besides, it'd be deuced difficult to dance in those side-things that stick out—what-you-call-'ems—"

"Panniers," she said with immense satisfaction. "Lauralee wouldn't hear of anything but being Madame Pompadour, but *I* thought Empress Josephine would be far more elegant *and* cooler."

"Well, there I agree with you, but don't tell her that," he said, in a confidential tone of voice. "I'd rather dance with a girl who can move about in her costume than have to steer some wire contraption around the floor." She giggled and agreed. He thought he had effectively distracted her from the subject of her sister.

As he continued talking with her to make sure she had forgotten his question in her flutter of excitement about his attentions, he digested what he had learned. Well, now he knew this much, at least. He knew that Eleanor *was* Alison's stepdaughter, and he knew that they were, for some reason, keeping alive a fiction that she was at Oxford. It was clear that she wasn't—but the question was, what was she doing in Broom? His assumption that she had fallen on hard times was obviously wrong, but why was she dressed like an inferior servant and clearly doing menial labor?

He worried at the problem for the rest of the day, through tea, while he dressed for dinner and all through dinner. It made for a quiet meal, but his aunt more than made up for his silence, and his mother was so full of her entertainment plans that they didn't really notice that he wasn't talking much. How was it that neither the vicar nor the doctor were aware that "Eleanor is at Oxford" was a complete fiction? Surely, if she had been strolling around Broom, someone would have noticed and said something. And she certainly wasn't transporting herself to their meadow by magic carpet. None of this was making much sense.

After dinner he went out on the terrace with a drink; the Brigadier joined him as they watched the sun set; the sky ablaze with red, gold, and purple, the last rays of the setting sun making streaks across the horizon. It looked like a Turner painting.

"You would never know there was a war from here," the old man said at last, and Reggie thought he sounded wistful. "Must admit, I was dubious about this brouhaha your mother set her heart on, but—it won't be bad to forget for a little while, and pretend."

"Like children playing truant from school," Reggie replied, with bitter longing. "But it won't go away."

"But we can rest our minds from it for a little, surely, without feeling guilty." The Brigadier sipped his brandy. "We'll all put on our dominoes and pretend that outside the walls of Longacre it is 1912; we can even persuade ourselves for a little that our lost and absent friends are out there in the crowd, too. And as long as the masks are being worn, we can hold to the illusion. Is that so wrong?"

Yes, he wanted to say. *Yes, because the ones that haven't been killed by the idiotic strategies of old men fighting a war with last century's tactics are out there putting their lives at risk because those same old men are so certain that what they want is God's will that they won't admit they are wrong* or *that what they are doing is a hideous, horrible mistake.*

But he didn't say it. In part, because he knew that although the Brigadier agreed with him in his heart, he could never admit it aloud. And in part because it would only hurt that good old man further.

"Sometimes—one needs illusions," he said, carefully, and left it at that.

Illusions. So much of what was going on here was an illusion. Not just this country weekend and the ball, but everything on this side of the Channel. No one wanted to talk about the war anymore, or think about it even, except those who had been in it. The topics that seemed to obsess most people had nothing whatsoever to do with the war except as the war had caused the problems. And that drove him mad, sometimes. He wanted to wake them up, drag them forcibly down to the hospitals and *show* them the shell-shocked and the maimed, to *make* them care, force them to understand what this war was doing. Was he in the wrong, then, to want to break into the comfortable illusions and shout at them all, that their petty little concerns over their comforts, the shortage of servants, the rationed food, were selfish, self-centered and disgusting to him? That over there in France, that sound like thunder that came over the Channel when the wind was right, was the sound of people dying, and it was time they woke up and acknowledged it?

But he wanted to forget it too—part of him was so tired of it all that he was sick with longing for it to just stop, to go away, and take all his memories with it.

He turned his mind back to the problem of Eleanor with a feeling almost of relief. It was something to think about that was *not* the war, and part of him deeply sympathized with the Brigadier. Like those nights when he would lie in his bed at the hospital and recite poem after poem in his head to keep from thinking about what was out there in the dark, waiting for him to fall asleep. Because you could only think about the war and what it was doing to you and your mates for so long before you started going mad.

Eleanor Robinson should have been at Oxford, and was not, and it was not for lack of money in her family. And in fact, from all appearances, she was working as a servant. Why, oh why, had she not told him herself what was wrong? Pride?

For that matter, why had her father married a scheming creature like Alison?

She vamped him I suppose, like her daughters are trying to vamp me. I suppose if you've never been vamped before, it would be easy to succumb. When would that have been? He tried to reckon up the last time he had seen her. It was before the war, before he joined the RFC. So at some point between then and the start of the war, her father had remarried. He'd done some checking, and her father had died at some time around the first Christmas of the war. So why had his daughter not been at Oxford at that point? Had Alison persuaded the besotted new husband that it was unnecessary to give a girl a university education? Or had she pled the war as an excuse, claiming she needed Eleanor at home? Just how besotted had he been, to deny his only child her one dream? He must have been caught like a salmon in a net.

And then, just as the last of the sun sank below the horizon, it struck him. What if her father had altered his will in favor of the new wife before he went off to the war?

It was just the sort of thing that Alison would have insisted on, he was sure of it. Manipulative creature that she was, she would have promised, ever so sweetly, that she would take as good care of Eleanor as of her own daughters. So why shouldn't her dear new husband not change his will to make her sole inheritor? After all, leaving flighty young girls anything directly was generally a bad idea. Who could guess what they would do with their inheritance, and of course, there were always cads who would romance them for their money, then waste it and leave them penniless and deserted.

He stared into the growing darkness, as beside him, the Brigadier lit up a cigarette. The end of it glowed as he pursued that line of thought to its logical conclusion.

So, assume that was precisely what had happened. Then her father had died in the first months of the war, leaving her entirely at the mercy of her stepmother, a woman who clearly despised her. Then what? What was she doing here, dressed like a servant?

Well, what were her choices? To leave—and do what? She wasn't suited to anything but marriage, and if she'd had a sweetheart in the village, he doubted that she would have been so keen to go to university. There was a sad truth to her condition; she had no skills with which to support herself. She hadn't enough education to become a governess. She hadn't the money to train as a nurse, and although she could have gone as a VAD no one could really live on the tiny stipend that was allotted to the volunteers. In the beginning she wouldn't have had the stamina for a factory job, and the

Land Girls hadn't been formed until later. That would have left her with only one option. To remain at home at the mercy of her stepmother, who must have seen her as a ready source of free labor and put her to work as a servant.

Which explained why she was dressed like one.

Now, her own pride would have kept her hidden from the village. And her stepmother would never have admitted she had treated her own stepdaughter so shabbily. And so the fiction of "Eleanor is at Oxford" was born, with both sides of the situation eager to maintain it.

His left hand clutched at the stone balustrade, and he downed the last of his drink and set the glass down lest he inadvertently shatter it in his sudden fit of anger. Perhaps it was absurd to be so angry over what was, essentially, a teacup tragedy when there were so many greater tragedies in the wake of this war. She wasn't dead, after all, merely ill-used. She hadn't been struck by a stray bullet and paralyzed, not blown to pieces by a shell.

But feelings, he reminded himself, were not rational. And this shabby treatment of a girl who'd done nothing to earn it made him very, very angry.

He could see how it was that no one noticed that she was still here, especially if she herself took pains to conceal the fact. And no one ever really *looked* at anyone in servants' clothing. Especially not someone dressed as shabbily as Eleanor was. So on the rare occasions when she escaped her work for a little, so long as she kept her head down—which everyone would expect anyway out of a lower servant—no one would recognize her. He didn't recall that she had socialized much with the girls her age, anyway; it had been the boys that had congregated around his aeroplane that knew her best, boys who were all long gone in the first weeks of the War. Perhaps the adults—the adult women, anyway—might have noticed, but in those first weeks and months, they had more than enough cares of their own to preoccupy them. The longer the charade went on, the less likely it would be that anyone would see the face of the clever schoolgirl in the visage of the work-hardened young woman.

That had to be it.

The question now was—what could he do about it? And to that question he had no ready answer. For a start, how could he even get to her to talk to her? Helping her would mean prying her out of her imprisoning shell, the walls of The Arrows, and at the moment, he had no good idea of how to do that.

Once he did that, he also had no good idea of how to offer help without it seeming like charity and pity, and he had a fairly good idea of what she would think about charity and pity. At least, he thought he did.

"Penny for your thoughts," the Brigadier said, out of the darkness, startling him from his concentration.

"I'd have to give you ha'pence change, Brigadier," he replied, mendaciously. "I wasn't thinking about much."

The old man chuckled. "Let's go in, then," he suggested. "The damp isn't doing either of us any good."

"Probably not," he agreed. "I was thinking of going down to the village, anyway."

"And I'm for my book and bed," the Brigadier replied. "It's peaceful out here. I shall take my rest while I can get it."

They parted company on the terrace, Reggie limping his way down to the stable to get his motorcar. He decided that he would see what he could learn by steering the conversation in The Broom around to the Robinsons. It would be natural enough, what with The Arrows being almost directly across the street, and that would be a good place to start.

July 22, 1917
Broom, Warwickshire

Sarah looked so triumphant when Eleanor arrived just before midnight that Eleanor could not in good conscience deny her the pleasure of revealing whatever it was that had put that smug smile on her face. She hoped it was good news, because today had been particularly brutal. The amount of work that she'd been laden with would have laid her out four years ago. She'd almost been too tired to come here tonight, and really, all that had gotten her out the door was the promise of eventual freedom.

"It is a very good thing that no one would ever entrust you with a state secret, because you could never conceal the fact that you *had* a secret in the first place," she told her mentor, as she picked up her mother's notebook to begin her exercises, took a deep breath, and concentrated on getting her second wind. She and Sarah were focusing on one thing now; to extend the length of her "leash," so that she could attend the fancy-dress ball—though how she was going to get inside the doors of the manor at Longacre Park without an invitation, she had no notion. There was no chance that one would come for her now. Lauralee, Carolyn, and Alison had long since gotten theirs, and the girls took every chance they could get to take out the precious piece of cream-laid vellum and flourish it about. Their acquaintances—one could hardly call them "friends," anymore—in the village were eaten up with envy. The only other villagers who had gotten invitations were the vicar and his wife, and the doctor and his. With this alone, Alison had made it wordlessly clear how much higher her social stature was in the tiny circle of Broom. That, in fact, she had escaped the social circle of Broom for another, more rarified atmosphere.

She had, of course, cleverly feigned confusion to "discover" that no one else had achieved similar invitations, and unlike her daughters (who might be excused such behavior on the grounds of their callow youth) she did *not* make much of it after that initial flurry of exquisitely acted discomfiture. In this way, even though she had without doubt made some real enemies among the village elite, none of them would dare come out actively and openly against her. The ladies still came to her teas and her war-effort gatherings—though with all of the invitations up to the manor, those were becoming infrequent. But she presided over them with the absent air of a queen who has other concerns than the petty ones of her subjects.

Eleanor had hoped that somehow, someone would remember her existence and include her in the joint invitation, but no one had; it had read, "Mrs. Alison Robinson, Miss Danbridge, and Miss Carolyn Danbridge." Not even a hint of "Eleanor." She had almost given up at that moment, but it did occur to her that Sarah might know a way of slipping her in, somehow—or perhaps even was planning to *forge* an invitation. Granted she wouldn't be on the guest list, but perhaps no one would check that, or if they did, she could claim she was part of "Alison Robinson and daughters." Or perhaps Sarah meant for her to slip in through the gardens, though how she was to do that in an enormous ballgown eluded her.

She settled herself at Sarah's old, age-darkened kitchen table, her brazier in front of her, a Salamander already lying coiled in the coals without needing to be summoned.

"Here you are, just as I promised," Sarah said, handing over a plain envelope that contained a cream-laid vellum one that—no mistake—was identical to the one in Alison's middle desk-drawer. The outer one was addressed to Sarah, but the inner to Eleanor herself—

At an Oxford address. Somerville College, to be exact.

She gazed at it in blank astonishment. She already knew what it contained, of course. Her invitation to the ball. But—

"How—" was all she could manage.

Sarah actually winked. "I have my ways," she said. "A little word to—someone—who kindly reminded her ladyship that Miss Robinson was away at Oxford as the invitations were picked up to be given to the postman, so she rewrote the Robinson invitations on the spot. And then, a—fellow follower of the Ancient Ways, not an Elemental Master, who is—" She hesitated. "Well, I'll only say this. She has every reason to be at Somerville, and she chose Somerville because it is the women's college that has no religious requirements that might conflict with her own faith."

Eleanor gaped at her, feeling her eyes going rounder with every passing moment.

"Oh, don't look at me like that!" Sarah laughed. "I told you there were more of us than you'd ever guess! At any rate, she intercepted your invitation and reposted it to me. That's all. You are on the guest list and you have a genuine invitation. So if I were you, I would stop staring and get back to my exercises, or on the day, you won't be able to get as far as the front gate." She plucked the invitation from Eleanor's nerveless fingers. "And I'll keep that safe, here. No point in risking having it found, and you'll have to come to me to dress anyway. Now, it's time to work, not daydream."

It was difficult to concentrate on the tedious mechanics of a spell which amounted to telling something very stupid and slow, over and over, that a boundary wasn't where it had been originally set. Doing so when your arms and shoulders ached from all the fetching and carrying you'd done, and your legs from all the trips up and down the stairs, was even harder. Magic, she had come to understand, was largely a means by which the magician imposed her will on the world, and made the world conform to it.

That sounded very simple, and in theory, it was—or would be, if there was a simple world to deal with, and only one magician in it.

The problem was that there were a great many other things, a few of them also magical in nature, that were also imposing *their* will on the world. Ways had to be found to get the results one wanted with the least interference with everything else. Some interference was inevitable; meddling with things made ripples, and disturbed other things.

It wasn't just that one didn't want to disrupt other things that were going on out of courtesy—or fear of reprisal. It was that when one did interfere unduly, there were consequences. Everything one did magically had a cascading effect, like the little pebble that starts an avalanche. Sometimes, of course, one could stop the cascade before things became serious, but you had to be *aware* of consequences to do that. You had to look for the things you might change, and include them in your plan. You had to try and think of things that weren't obvious.

Consequences . . . and responsibilities. That called to mind the purview of the High Priest. The Magician. Most of all, the Hermit, who moved slowly and only after studying all the possible ramifications of his actions.

One of those ramifications was that when things were jarred into new patterns, there were sometimes—Things—that took notice; different creatures for each Element. The ones for Earth were the Trolls and Giants, for Fire, the Wyverns and Fire-drakes (entirely different species than true Dragons). For Water it was the Leviathans, and for Air the Wendigo. They were not very bright, but they were very powerful, very dangerous, and always, always hungry. What they "ate" was the life-force of magicians. One did not want to attract their notice. Even Alison moved cautiously to avoid attracting Trolls and Giants.

So the smaller one's "footprint" of influence was, the better.

Alison had gotten away with as much use of magic as she had because she had confined it mostly to one single person—Eleanor. Hedging one person in with spells did not make much of an effect on the rest of the world.

Now it was Eleanor's turn, and the best course of action now seemed to be to work on the spells already in existence. That meant, at the moment, persuading the spell that kept pulling her back to the hearth that it had never been meant to call her back when she went beyond the grounds of The Arrows—that instead its boundary was much farther. It would return to its previous state when she took her attention off it, of course, but that didn't happen at once, and in fact, the more she worked at this, the longer she had before it reverted.

The village was very quiet at this time of night. A dog barked out in the distance, and nearer at hand, the trees rustled as a breeze tumbled among their leaves. Inside there was only the pop and crackle of the small fire in the fireplace, and the sound of their breathing.

"I *think,*" Sarah said, when she had been working at her spell-casting for the better part of an hour, "that if we could just find a way to dig up your finger and destroy it, that would break the spell."

Eleanor slowly released the spell she had been manipulating; she could see it in her head, like a cat's cradle of lines of magical power. It remained as she had left it, and she turned her attention to Sarah, who was watching her with solemn eyes. They'd had this discussion before. "But you're still not sure," Eleanor said flatly. She looked across the table into Sarah's eyes, and saw what she expected to see. Once again, Sarah had attempted to unravel the complexities of the spells around Eleanor, and once again, she had not been able to decipher them.

Sarah shook her head. "I'm not powerful enough to read all those spells she's tangled up around you. I just can't keep them separate in my mind. I think destroying the finger would break them all, but there's a chance that destroying the finger would make them bind more tightly."

"I'm not willing to take that risk," she replied, with a frown. "If I can achieve the Sun, that's the card of freedom and problems solved, and it's a Fire card. I'll have the knowledge, the wisdom and the power to use Justice's sword, and I can cut myself free of the spell-bindings." She paused a moment, and added, "They say it's a simple card. If I can pass through it soon . . ."

She didn't specify what she meant by "soon." She had eight more cards to pass through before she reached the Sun. She had yet to face Death . . . or even the Hanged Man. Truth to be told she didn't want to face either, but it had to be done. The Hermit had not been as frightening or as difficult as she had thought, but the Wheel of Fortune had been terrifying. One wouldn't think that an abstract concept like that would be frightening, but—

But it hadn't been abstract. It had been the whole *world* up there, looming in a sky that was half storm and half calm, with terrible energies crackling through it all, and the realization that a single turn of the Wheel could set random factors into motion that could doom all her plans.

And even as she had gazed up at it in awe—for it had looked nothing at all like the card, except in that it was a wheel, or at least wheel-shaped—she had felt herself and all the world coming apart, then returning together again, in what she came to understand was a cycle of creation and destruction, of death and rebirth, and she had grasped things for that moment that she couldn't even begin to articulate now. But evidently she had grasped them correctly, for the huge, looming Wheel settled, and a little more knowledge and power settled into her mind, and she was given to understand that she had passed this test, too.

So it was understandable that at this moment she really didn't want to think what the Death card was going to be like. It would have been easier on her nerves if the card had been called Transfiguration, or something of the sort.

Sarah gave her an odd look. "This isn't the path I would have seen you taking," she said at last. "Your mother was always so impatient, the Fire in her wanting to take things quickly—"

"Which isn't always a good idea. I think perhaps this business of using the Tarot to teach me was the best thing that could have happened to me." Eleanor grimaced, and rubbed the joint of her right thumb with her left hand, easing a little ache there. "Much though *I* would like to make things happen faster, I'm learning about the strengths and weaknesses of the other three Elements as I go, and I hope that means I won't be as vulnerable."

She didn't have to say aloud what she was thinking—that if her mother had known more about the strengths and weaknesses of the antagonistic Element of Water, she might not have died. She knew Sarah was thinking the same thing by the faint expression of regret mixed with other emotions too fleeting to catch.

But one of them was pride—pride in the daughter who was, perhaps, a little wiser than her mother.

"You're learning," was all Sarah said.

"I bloody well hope so!" Eleanor snapped, with a little show of Fire temperament, quickly throttled before it could have any other effect. "And before you say it, I will say it for you. Back to work. We have only a fortnight, and I have a lot of progress to make before then."

Sarah only nodded.

I'll do it because I have to. There's no going back now.

26

August 7, 1917
Longacre Park, Warwickshire

ON JULY THE 30TH, THE British had begun a major offensive at Ypres; like most of Britain, Reggie only got wind that something was afoot when the "regrets" began to come in. And he hadn't thought much of it at first, until today.

Today the post was full of them.

One or two officers canceling would have been a fluke—all of them at once meant a big push. When even the band canceled by the morning post (momentarily throwing his mother into a state of despair until Lady Virginia came to the rescue, promising a small orchestra made up entirely of women), he had known that there was something truly major going on.

He and his old college chums Steve and Geoff had a sort of unwritten code; by the afternoon post, when both of them sent brief notes referring to Caesar's campaigns in Gaul along with their apologies, he had all the information he needed. And far more than he wanted.

The Brigadier and his mother had tried to keep it from him, of course, but by late afternoon it had been in all the papers. He'd managed to keep himself together long enough to send a hasty telegram to Michael Dolbeare to recruit more RFC cadets to make up the difference, pledging to cover their train fare if need be, which considerably calmed his mother down about the holes in her guest list. That had been going through the motions, actually, because if he had thought about it, he might have lost his temper with her. How could she be in such a state over a mere absence of male guests, when across the Channel all hell was breaking loose? Bad enough that other people were being so callous, but this was his own mother.

And he'd been all right until just before dinner, until it hit him, until it really sank in. Then the shakes had started.

He kept himself together until he managed to reach the safe haven of his rooms. He even managed to pull his own curtains closed, and shut and lock the door. Then the fear got hold of him by the throat and shook him like a dog, sending him to his knees, making him crawl into the darkest corner of the room, where he shivered and wept and choked back moans of terror. He couldn't even put two ideas together into a whole; he didn't even know *what* he was afraid of. He only knew that this vast, insensate, and ravenous beast that was the war was loose, and it was going to devour the entire world and there was nothing he could do to stop it. . . .

He had vaguely heard someone pacing outside his rooms, rattling the knob once or twice, but they left him alone, for which he was both grateful and felt betrayed at the same time. Grateful, because he could not bear anyone seeing him like this. Betrayed, because they were leaving him alone with this fear, this mind-killing, soul-shriveling fear—

And all he could do was huddle, and shake, as wave after wave of the terror engulfed him, then ebbed, only to return.

How long he was in there, he couldn't have told; only that some time after darkness fell, there was the sound of a key in the lock, and the unmistakable presence in the room of Lady Virginia.

She closed the door behind her; he heard the scratch of a match, and smelled the sharp sulfur as she lit candles.

"Reggie," she said, quite as calmly as if he was not huddled in a ball in the corner. "I am not Doctor Maya, but I am very old, and I have seen a very great deal in my time. And if you can manage to bring yourself here, I may be able to offer you some little comfort. I should come down there on the floor next to you, but my bones are not so young that they permit any such thing anymore."

Somehow, he managed to crawl out of that corner. Somehow he managed to get to her, and put his head on her knee like a spaniel, and croak out a few words. He wasn't even sure what he was saying, only that he was giving some shape to the fear that was devouring him alive.

"I cannot tell you that it will be all right, Reggie," she said gravely. "Because we both know that it will not. But if the Brigadier is correct, and I believe he is, then the enemy is as battle-weary and worn as we, and he has no flood of energetic Americans coming at last to help. It will not end soon—but it will end."

And she offered silence at the right moment, and a few more words of her own at the right moment, and slowly, he stopped shaking, the fear lost its grip on him, and the fog lifted from his mind until he could think again.

Only then did she call his man in, and he took his drugs and went into a mercifully dreamless sleep.

And *they* did not come for him in the night; he sensed no malign presence on the other side of his barrier of slumber, nor did he hear evil mutterings nor feel the suffocating weight on him of the darker creatures of Earth, trying to smother him in his sleep. It might have been the drugs, it might have been his new defenses, it might all have been due to Lady Virginia.

When he struggled up out of sleep late the next morning, it was with no sense of victory, though, and not even anything he could call hope. It was, if anything, a feeling that he might actually live through the despair. He still wasn't entirely sure he wanted to, but he felt as if he would, regardless of his current preferences.

It was the Brigadier who was with him the next time the fit took him, later that afternoon. They were outside, on the terrace, and his knees just gave out. The Brigadier got him to a seat, saying nothing, although he could not have missed how hard Reggie was shaking, nor the blank, dry-mouthed stare Reggie knew he must have. And the good old man stayed with him as he closed his eyes and fought the fear as best he could—which was about as effective as trying to fight the sea.

After the first wave ebbed a little, the Brigadier cleared his throat apologetically, and began talking, sounding a bit self-conscious, but determined, nevertheless.

He didn't actually talk *to* Reggie. Instead, he rambled on about commonplace things. He'd been down to Broom and met some of "the lads" at the Broom pub, and they were good fellows, to be sure. He thought there might be something in the manner of work he could put in the way of one or two of them that were at loose ends. It was a fine little village, and he'd also been to the estate village of Arrow, which was a credit to him and his mother. The estate manager wanted him to know that the crops were looking very good this year, and that someone wanted to bring in another gasworks, like the one that supplied Longacre and Broom, but this time on manor property. Filthy things, gasworks, but there was plenty of coal near here and that would mean there could be gas piped in to the village of Arrow as well, which might be worth the mess. Perhaps one of the clever RFC fellows could find a way to make a gasworks less filthy. "We have gas laid on," the Brigadier rumbled, "At my bungalow. Deuced convenient for cook. Thinking about electricity; they electrified my club in London last year, and it's better than gas. You ought to consider having the telephone brought up here, Reggie. Good for your mother; keep her connected to the rest of us. Have to go forward, my boy, can't live in the past, and if you try and stick in one spot the future will run over the top of you."

Not a word about the war, not a word about how he looked, and under the paralysis of fear that made his guts go to water, he knew he must look hellish. Not one word of reproach, though the poor old man must surely wonder—

Or perhaps not. Lady Virginia had said he'd been to the Front itself, to the hospitals where men were brought in, filthy, screaming, their wounds crawling with maggots, their minds as shattered as their bodies. Maybe he did understand.

But it was the commonplaces that were anchoring him, little by little, back in the simple present. The count of new calves, the state of the orchards, thoughts of gasworks and electricity, the talk down at the Broom.

It dragged him back out of the pit, though he could not have said how or why. It let him get his breath back, let him unclench his fists and his jaw, let him sit in the wake of what proved to be the last wave of fear and turned his shaking into the mere trembling of exhaustion. And when he was finally able to think again, let him turn back to the Brigadier with eyes that held sanity again.

The old man paused in his rambling; gave him a long, hard look, and sighed. "Ah. There you are. Her ladyship said you might get taken like that."

"Yes," Reggie said. "Thank you, sir." Only three words, but he put a world of gratitude in them, and the Brigadier flushed a little, and coughed self-deprecatingly.

"Think I can leave you now?" he asked.

Reggie nodded. "Work to do, sir; you reminded me of it yourself, just now."

The Brigadier nodded with evident relief. "Work! There's the ticket!" he said, with a shade too much enthusiasm, so much so that Reggie felt sorry for him. "You concentrate on work, my boy, it's the best thing for you. Keep your mind set on solid things." The Brigadier's determinedly cheerful expression made Reggie attempt a feeble smile of his own.

At least he doesn't think I'm feigning or malingering, he thought, as the Brigadier retired to the house. That meant a great deal—more, in fact, than he had expected. The Brigadier did not think less of him because he was shell-shocked. That helped.

Enough that he did muster enough strength to get to his own feet again, and go in search of his estate manager. Maybe the Brigadier was right after all. Maybe keeping himself occupied would work. It wasn't as if there wasn't a lot to be done. Guests would be arriving in two days.

There was only one way to find out.

August 11, 1917
Broom, Warwickshire

Poor Howse's hair was coming down from its careful arrangement on the top of her head; bits of it were straggling down in front of her ears, and her face was red and damp with exertion. She looked as if she was going to wilt at any moment, and Eleanor felt ready to scream.

Between the two of them, Lauralee and Carolyn could have used a dozen maids to get them into their costumes, instead of only two. Lauralee, in her Madame Pompadour garb, had petticoats and panniers, underskirts and overskirts, a corset that pushed her breasts up until they looked like a pair of hard little apples, and a bodice cut so low that they were threatening to pop out at any moment. Alison had taken one look at that particular part of the display and ordered that a fichu of lace be inserted and tacked in place to prevent a disaster—which meant more work, as Lauralee fidgeted and shrieked every time she thought a needle was passing too close to her skin. And when all that was taken care of, came the white, powdered wig, the patches to be pasted on, and all the rest of it.

Carolyn's guise of Empress Josephine looked deceptively simple, and at least it didn't require a winch to pull the lacings of her corset tight, but the requisite hairstyle with its Grecian-inspired diadem and tiny, tight-curled ringlets done up in imitation of ancient statues had

Howse nearly in despair. She had two burns on her hands from the curling tongs already, and there had been one accident that had caused Carolyn to slap the hapless maid, and which had left the bedroom reeking of scorched hair. Fortunately only the very ends had been scorched; Howse had been able to trim out the ruined bit to Carolyn's satisfaction.

Alison had elected to wear the strangest costume of all, so far as Eleanor was concerned—and it gave her the most peculiar and uneasy feeling when she saw it. Alison's costume was a hooded, black velvet gown, something like a monk's robe, but lined in scarlet satin. There was something embroidered on it in black silk—not a discernable pattern, more like symbols of some sort, but the black-on-black of the silk made it nearly impossible to tell *what* it was. Around her waist she wore a very odd belt, for all the world like a hangman's rope, but made of silk. A floor-length, black veil, edged in jet beads, went over everything, and an odd tiara of stars held the veil in place.

When Howse asked, timidly, who Alison was portraying, Alison had just smiled, and said, lightly, "The Queen of the Night, of course. From Mozart's opera *The Magic Flute.* I doubt anyone else will think of it, and there's value in novelty."

At least the costume didn't require any special wigs or hairstyles, nor did it require a full hour to put on. Even if she did look like Lady Death. . . .

Though it did make Eleanor wonder, was this Alison's ritual robe? Some people liked to wear such things, although they weren't necessary, and didn't contribute any to the efficacy of a spell, unless the wearer had put spells or protections into the robes before she put them on.

If so, Eleanor could hardly imagine the cheek to wear such a thing to a fancy-dress ball.

When the three of them finally sailed out the door, it was a distinct relief. They were motored away by Alison's escort, Warrick Locke, who himself was costumed as some sort of wizard. When they were safely in the automobile, Howse closed the door behind them.

"I have a headache," she declared, staring at Eleanor. "I am going to wait in Madame's room."

Eleanor shrugged. "I think that would be a good idea," she said, in a neutral voice. "They won't be back for hours, and you'll need to be ready when they return."

She, of course, knew exactly what Howse was going to do. She was going to nap on Alison's bed—much more comfortable than her own. Since this was exactly what Eleanor wanted her to do, she simply waited until she couldn't hear any more movement overhead, then went to the kitchen and knelt beside the hearthstone.

The flames of the fire flared up as she breathed the first words of her spell, and a half dozen Salamanders burst out of the heart of the fire to slither up her arms and entwine themselves around her neck.

Slowly, carefully, Eleanor insinuated herself into the complex weave of the binding spell. With a word here, and a tweak there, she stretched it, rearranged it, suggested to it that its territory was not merely this house and grounds, but the entire county. She felt the spell respond, sluggishly, but by no means as slowly as it had the first time she had done this. *Make this your boundary until midnight,* she suggested to it.

With a shake, like a reluctant dog, the spell grumbled, stretched, and settled into its new configurations. With a final word to hold the new shape in place, she came out of her half-trance, and got to her feet with a feeling of distinct triumph. A spell, properly speaking, was a *process* and not a *thing*—but the ones that Alison had set on her certainly felt like things—things with lives of their own, and rudimentary personalities. Unpleasant personalities, but that was only to be expected.

She cocked an ear to the rooms overhead, and heard nothing. Eagerness took over, and unwilling to wait another moment, she slipped the latch of the kitchen door and closed it behind herself, then flew out of the garden gate and down the street to Sarah's cottage.

Other than a couple of men entering the Broom pub, there wasn't anyone else about. However much excitement the ball had generated in the Robinson household, for the rest of the village this were no differences between tonight and any other Saturday. Which was just as well, since the last thing she wanted was a lot of coming and going that might disturb Howse's slumber.

Feeling excitement and anticipation rising in her and threatening to boil over, she ran for all she was worth. She had not dared, until this moment, truly to believe that she was going to be able to *do* this. So many things in her life had been taken or thwarted that she had been afraid to put too much hope into this moment—

—this moment when she would live, for a few hours, the life she *should* have had. When she would be herself, Miss Eleanor Robinson, not Ellie the maid-of-all-work, with nothing to look forward to but a lifetime of drudgery in the house that should have been hers.

She managed to control herself when she reached Sarah's door, enough so that she paused, caught her breath, and after a preliminary tap and the expected response of "Come!" she opened the door quite demurely.

Only to gasp with shock, surprise, and delight at the vision that met her widening eyes.

"Like it, do you?" Sarah asked, a twinkle in her eyes and a pardonably smug expression on her face. "Not a bad job, if I do say so myself. And I do!"

Arrayed on an improvised dressmaker's-form made of a broomstick and a stuffed sack, was every little girl's dream of a fairy dress, the sort of thing that bedazzled young eyes believe in when they see the Fairy Princess at the Christmas pantomine. Only this gown was real, and not cheap muslin and machine-lace.

It had been a sort of ivory the last time Eleanor saw it—now it was a soft rose pink. "How did you change the color?" she stammered.

Sarah rubbed the side of her nose, and looked suitably smug. "Do you know, there's an old spell in my grimoire that does just that? Temporary, of course, but temporary is all you need, and after I took some thought about it, it seemed to me that a fairy princess was a better costume choice than Princess Victoria. The wings I made; you know what I always tell you—it's easier to change what's there than make new. I expect there won't be another fairy princess in the lot; those girls have forgotten magic by now, and think they're too old for fairies. You'll look nothing like yourself."

Little bouquets of rosebuds ornamented the skirt, here and there, and a garland of them ran from the right shoulder to the left hip. A pair of tiny, pink gauze wings sprang from the shoulders in the back. Waiting on the table was a wreath of rosebuds to wear in her hair, and a pair of pink silk opera gloves to cover her work-roughened hands. The left, of course, had only three fingers.

"What am I going to do for shoes?" she asked, suddenly, aware that her clumsy and well-worn walking shoes would ruin the entire effect of this exquisite gown. "And stockings—"

"Ah, that's where a little more magic and illusion come in," Sarah replied, with a sly wink. "Strip to your shift, my girl. I have some work to do yet."

Sarah was as good as her word. A handful of rose-petals pressed against each shoe, a breath of magic and a muttered charm—and the square-toed, worn brown leather was magically transmuted to a pair of the most delicate silk slippers Eleanor had ever seen, with pink stockings that matched the gown taking the place of the much-darned cotton stockings she had been wearing. She couldn't see any flaw in the illusion, though if she closed her eyes she knew very well she was still wearing her old stockings and shoes. Which was not at all a bad thing; they might be worn nearly to bits, but they were comfortable, which was more than could be said of most fashionable shoes.

With that transformation complete, the dressing began, though it didn't take more than a fraction of the time it had taken to dress her stepsisters. Petticoats and gown went on over her old underclothing; Sarah re-attached the garland of roses, and then, with practiced fingers, put up her hair and pinned the wreath to it. She pulled on the gloves—and it was done.

"Well! If I were a little girl or a young man, I would be half in love with you!" Sarah exclaimed, as she shed her skirt and apron to don a pair of antique breeches and a rusty woolen uniform coat. She brushed her hands over herself from the top of her head to the soles of her feet, and Eleanor felt another breath of power flit by her—

And in Sarah's place was a solemn faced, gray-haired man, in rose-red livery sporting more braid and gold buttons than any general could boast. "There's your invitation," said Sarah's voice, coming from the man's mouth—a distinctly disorienting proposition. "He" pointed at the mantelpiece, where the precious envelope was held securely between two jam-jars full of water and rosebuds. "You get that invitation, take a look in the mirror in the corner there to make sure I haven't forgotten anything, while I get your 'carriage,' milady. And don't forget. Midnight is as late as you can go, because that's the longest I can hold the illusions."

A careful check of as much of herself as she could see in Sarah's tiny mirror that hung over her washstand seemed to indicate that Sarah had been her usual efficient self. There was nothing to strike a false note, and Eleanor began to feel quite shivery with anticipation when she heard the sound of a horse's hooves and a low whistle just outside Sarah's door. She seized the invitation and hurried outside.

She hesitated a moment at the door itself, since she was wider than the doorway now, but the wide skirt wasn't as difficult to maneuver as she had feared it would be. She got through without even catching the lace on her flounces.

And there, to her absolutely astonished gaze, was the sort of open carriage that—according to the pictures she had seen—the King used on state occasions, only a bit smaller. In the light coming from the two little lamps on either side of the driver's box, she could tell that it was rose-red in color, with gilded ornamentation. "Sarah" sat on the driver's box, and expertly handled the reins of the snow-white horse that was harnessed to this confection by rose-red and gilded traces.

"It's an old pony-cart and plow-horse I borrowed from a friend," "Sarah" said, laughing at Eleanor's expression. "Be careful getting in; it's nowhere near as padded as it looks to be."

She was careful getting in, feeling the old, worn wood under the glove on her hand where her eyes told her there was bright gilding and slick paint. The lines of the carriage conformed to the shape of the old pony-cart beneath the illusion—she knew from her studies that the less a magician had to *create,* the better an illusion was, and here was the proof of that.

"Sarah" chirruped to the horse, who moved out with brisk dignity. Eleanor kept her hands tightly folded in her lap with her hands atop the precious invitation. She wished it weren't dark. She really felt like a fairy princess. She wished that she could see, and yes, be seen. In this guise, she would be like a sort of pantomime character herself, and it would have been a great deal of fun to act that way.

But no one came out of or went into the pub or the inn as they passed, and no little face peered down out of a bedroom window to gape in surprise. Probably Sarah was using a little more magic to make sure no one saw them—understandable, if disappointing.

What would I have thought as a little girl, if I had looked out a window and seen a fairy princess passing by in her carriage? I'd have believed in fairies so firmly that nothing could have dissuaded me. Perhaps, then, it was just as well—because little girls now were facing the loss of fathers, brothers, uncles, and were in dire need of magic that she could not supply. To send one looking for a fairy to conjure back her lost papa or brother would have been intolerably cruel.

The horse broke into a trot once they were out of the village; where an old horse got that kind of energy, Eleanor couldn't guess. More magic? Or was the old fellow just feeling frisky in the cool of the evening? Whichever it was, the carriage rattled merrily down the road to Longacre Park, and in a much shorter time than Eleanor would have guessed, it turned in through the huge wrought-iron gates and rolled onto a smooth graveled driveway.

The manor loomed up at the top of a shallow rise ahead of them, all lit up for the grand occasion, with lanterns set out along the staircase to light the way up. Eleanor felt her stomach clench as she gazed up at the enormous structure, feeling suddenly altogether out of her class. How on earth did the Fenyxes keep that enormous barn of a building up? Did they have an army of servants? Was all of that truly just to support two people, Reggie and his mother?

You have every right to be here, she told herself sternly, as the carriage drew nearer and nearer to the broad double staircases leading down to the drive, each one curving down from the side. *You have an invitation, and what's more, you have more right to be here than Alison and her brats.*

By repeating this to herself, over and over, by the time they reached the bottom of the staircases, she had some of her composure back.

Or at least, the illusion of composure.

There was a liveried footman—or foot-*boy* would probably be more accurate—waiting beneath the twin lamps at the foot of the stairs. He didn't even blink when Sarah brought the carriage to a halt, even though most guests were arriving by motorcar. He simply waited while Sarah got down, opened the carriage door, and handed her out; then he took Eleanor's hand and directed her to the bottom of the stairs, as if he had been doing this sort of thing all his life.

Well, given how entire families in Broom and Arrow tended to go into service and stay in service to the Fenyx household, perhaps he had. But the fact that he was so very young told her something else—no matter how sheltered the great house was from the real world, the real world could still affect it profoundly. Longacre Park was as subject to compulsory conscription as any other place in this country. Reggie might have been the first to go to the war, but it seemed that every other able-bodied man here had followed.

Sarah drove the carriage away before the illusion could waver at all, leaving Eleanor alone on the paved landing at the bottom of the stairs. She looked up, uncertain as to what she should do. She seemed to be the only person arriving alone, which made her feel very self-conscious. The big doors at the top were both flung open wide. There was another man in livery at the top, and an older gentlemen in a black swallow-tail coat and stiff white shirt. Another footman, and the butler, she expected.

All right. It's now or never. Escorted or not, I have an invitation, and I belong.

She put on her pink silk domino mask, tying the ribbons behind her head, then carefully picked up the sides of her gown, and began the long climb towards those huge doors, and whatever fate held for her inside them.

27

August 11, 1917
Longacre Park, Warwickshire

SHE HANDED OVER HER INVITATION to the butler, who inspected it, and to her relief, merely nodded. She had been afraid he would announce her, and if Alison was anywhere within hearing distance. . . .

Instead, she stepped into—well, she wasn't entirely sure *what* to call this room. There could easily have been a second floor to this room, and there wasn't. The ceiling was somewhere up a full two stories—easily forty feet. It was surely another forty feet wide and twice that in length. There were enough candles burning in candelabra all around the walls to have supplied an entire chandler's shop, supplementing the gaslights.

There was only one name that suited this space—the Great Hall.

And it was full. In one corner, a small orchestra composed entirely of black-gowned women (most of them not young) played what sounded suspiciously like ragtime. Four years ago, either circumstance would have caused a scandal. But as Eleanor eased herself into the room, she overheard, almost immediately, the end of a conversation.

". . . and even the band called up, my dear! *So* fortunate that Lady Virginia was here!"

"They seem a bit—modern," came the doubtful reply.

The first speaker laughed. "But of course they're modern! They're Virginia's pet suffragette band! But if *I* had to choose between holding a ball with a suffragette orchestra or holding one with a gramophone, I know which one I would take! At least when one engages women, there is no danger of seeing them called over to France!"

The second woman turned her masked face in the direction of the orchestra with ever evidence of interest. "I have a hunt ball in the autumn—I wonder if—"

Eleanor was never to hear what the speaker wondered, for the eddies and swirls around the edge of the area of the dancing carried the speakers away.

If this had been a fairy tale, the moment that Eleanor had entered the Great Hall, all conversation would have ceased, and every head would have turned her way. The butler would have announced her—which would have been a disaster.

But this was not a fairy tale, and although she did excite a few admiring or unreadable glances, for the most part, people looked at her, did not recognize her, and dismissed her from their minds within a few moments. While her gown was certainly passable, it was neither so very different nor so very outstanding as to excite interest. She was indeed the only fairy princess, but other girls had wide pink dresses. And the deeper she went into the room, the more obvious it was that she was in an entirely different strata of society than she had ever been before.

And so were her stepsisters, though they might not yet realize it.

This was Society, old money, old titles, and though whatever dressmaker Alison went to might be able to counterfeit the look of these garments, there was a subtle difference between these costumes and the ones she had just aided Lauralee and Carolyn into. She suspected that a close examination would prove they did not hold up to the sort of careful scrutiny that maids who tended these clothes would bring to bear. And while ladies' maids did not precisely gossip to their mistresses, they did have subtle ways of making things known.

Alison and her progeny might be in for a rude awakening if they ever were invited to someone else's country weekend, and she insisted on maintaining the fiction that she, too was a member of their class.

But in the meantime, Eleanor's costume did not mark her out as anything unusual. She was by no means vivacious enough to attract attention by herself; the real beauties here were identifiable even behind their little domino masks.

This suited Eleanor very well. Her goal, after all, was to find the Elemental Master, and no one here was likely to make her task any easier by identifying that worthy for her. She only knew that the Master was female, and that only because she herself had seen the woman at work the night that the revenants were dispersed.

She worked her way towards the wall, and realized with a certain dismay that there was *another* room behind this one, nearly as large, that had been thrown open to the ball-attendees. This was not going to make her task any easier.

She resigned herself, with a pang of disappointment, to the realization that she was unlikely to see Reggie after all. The young women substantially outnumbered the young men here, and it was unlikely that he was going to have a single minute free. And her own, much more pressing task must take precedence if she was going to get herself free of her stepmother.

Somewhere in this swirling chaos of people she had to find the traces of Air magic that would inevitably be hovering about such a Master. And now she was very grateful that her study of magic had required her to understand the other three Elements as well as her own. She might not be able to use Air magic, but she could definitely sniff it out.

She was nearly at the doorway in the right-hand wall of the Great Hall when she caught the first "scent" of Air magic. Just a hint of blue at the corner of her vision, an unexpected breath of cold, and a touch of sharp, clean scent, like juniper or rosemary. But she was on it like a hound, and followed it into a drawing room.

This, too, was evidently open to the guests, older ladies and gentlemen who were so engrossed in their card games that they didn't even take any notice of her. She scanned the area for that hint of magic, but her quarry was none of them—then she got another hint of it, through another doorway, which led her into a hall, not so brightly lit. And, quite probably, *not* supposed to be open to the guests.

But the Air Master was a friend of the family and according to Sarah, a longterm visitor here, and probably had the run of the place. She would be allowed to go places where ordinary guests at the ball would be unwelcome.

Better and better. She must be on the right track.

And the breath of Air Magic was stronger now; she followed the scent down the darkened, shadow-haunted hall, and into—

—the library.

Here, for the first time since she had entered these doors, she found herself consumed with envy of the people who lived here. The Great Hall excited her not at all; she could only think of how it dwarfed everyone who set foot in it. That drawing room had been far too rich and opulent for her to feel comfortable in it, and besides that, the furnishings were antique, probably fragile, and without a doubt irreplaceable. But this room, with its floor-to-ceiling bookshelves crammed with volumes—*this,* she desired. And in fact, as she took a few hesitant steps into the dimly lit room, she forgot, for a moment, why she was here, in the sudden surge of acquisitive desire.

"I beg your pardon, miss, but the party is—"

She started, then froze, at the sound of the familiar drawl, and the exclamation was startled out of her. *"Reggie?"*

There was a creak of leather as the figure rose out of the depths of an armchair to her left, and limped towards her. "Eleanor?" came the incredulous reply. "Is that you?"

She jerked at the ends of the ribbon of her mask, and pulled it off. "Of course it's me! I have an invitation!" she replied, now full of indignation. What? Did he think she was so far beneath him that she shouldn't be here?

"Of course you do; I addressed it myself," was his answer, as he limped out of the shadows with both hands outstretched. While most of the young men here were in their uniforms, he was not. He had donned a costume for the occasion; with a feeling of shock, she recognized the Magician from the Tarot deck, but the colors were blue, silver and white rather than red, white and gold. "I waited in the reception line for what seemed like hours, but you never came, and I thought—your stepmother—"

"She doesn't know I'm here," Eleanor said, her growing anger erased by the surge of irrational joy she felt at his words. "She'd have stopped me if she'd known I was coming." She felt the coercion of Alison's spells suddenly uncoil, sealing her lips over anything else she might have said.

"I thought it was something like that," was Reggie's only reply, as he took both her hands in his and gazed down into her eyes. "Look, let's not talk about your dreadful stepmother, nor your conniving stepsisters, nor anything else unpleasant. Mater has put on a first-rate show, so let's enjoy it together." He smiled at her, with something of the charm of the old Reggie. "So long as I'm with a girl, even if Mater doesn't know who she is, she'll leave me alone. If she does, so will everyone else, and it has not yet become the fashion, thank the good Lord, for ladies to cut in on men while dancing. Do you dance?"

She was so caught in those earnest eyes that all she could do was stammer, "I—haven't, not for—a long time—"

"Good, because my knee is a torture. We'll go revolve a little for form's sake, then—how about the garden? Capability Brown, you know, and all lit up with fairy-lanterns for the occasion. Appropriate for a fairy princess."

She hardly knew what to say. This was the sort of thing out of her wildest dreams, the ones she knew better than to believe in.

He's just using me as a defense against the girls like

Carolyn and Lauralee— cautioned a bitter voice from her head.

But her heart replied, *Then why is he looking at me like that?* Because those pale eyes were warm with an emotion she did not yet dare to believe in, and he looked very much as if he would like to do more than simply look at her.

And sheer instinct made her nod, which evidently was answer enough for him. He took the domino from her nerveless hands, tied it back on, and tucked her right hand into the crook of his arm. "Let's go brave the throng."

This time, when they passed through the drawing room, the play stopped. Head turned in their direction, and as they crossed into the Great Hall, she sensed the whispers begin behind them.

And as if this had suddenly turned into a fairy tale, as they walked into the Great Hall, they were surrounded by a zone of silence, and all eyes turned towards them. Reggie ignored it; she felt her cheeks flushing, but held her head high, and tried to walk with dignity. He led her to the exact center of the room, as the musicians in the corner brought their current number to a swift conclusion. Once there, he swung her to face him, and the next thing she knew, she was turning in his arms around the floor to the strains of a waltz.

Ravaged knee or not, he was light on his feet. Not a brilliant dancer, but a competent one, and the gown she was wearing was practically made for waltzing in. With a heady feeling of euphoria, she surrendered to the moment and let him guide her three times around the floor while the musicians kept the tempo a little slower than usual. After all, wasn't this the sort of thing she had dreamed of doing? It felt like a dream. It had all the perfect unreality of a dream.

The musicians must have had a fine sense of just how long Reggie could dance; about the time she felt his steps faltering slightly, they brought the waltz to a close with a flourish.

Under cover of the polite applause to the orchestra, he

bent and whispered, "If that's enough for you, would you like to see the gardens?"

All she could do was nod; once again, as the orchestra began a new piece, he tucked her hand into the crook of his elbow and escorted her out of the Great Hall, into the room behind it—she got a glimpse of a long table set with huge arrangements of flowers and punch-bowls—and then out onto a terrace.

The view down into the gardens was breathtaking, but he didn't give her much chance to look at it. He drew her down the stairs into the gardens themselves, which had, as he had told her, been lit up with fairy-lanterns. The wave of perfume that washed over her told her that the roses for which Longacre was famous were in full bloom. He took her down one of the paths to a stone bench—still within sight of the terrace, but not a straight line-of-sight. She carefully arranged her skirt, and gingerly took a seat. With a sigh of relief, he sat beside her.

"I was horribly afraid I had offended you past forgiveness," were the first words out of his mouth. "I never meant to. When you didn't come back—"

"You went to the meadow?" she interrupted, hit again by one of those surges of irrational pleasure.

He nodded. "As soon as I could. And you didn't come back, so I thought you were angry with me."

"I couldn't—" that was all she could manage before Alison's coercions clamed down on her.

"Because you had work to do—I hoped that was all it was, but I was afraid I had been a boor." He sighed. "I am neither fish nor fowl, Eleanor. On the one hand, I was raised by my parents and the nannies they chose for me, who are of the opinion that education beyond reading, writing, and a little figuring is bad for females. On the other, I am heavily influenced by my godmother, who is an unrepentant suffragist, and by what I learned myself at Oxford. Sometimes, when I am not thinking, things escape from me that are parrotings of Mater, and I am always sorry when they do. I plead forgiveness. I never meant to slight the intelligence of women, and least of all yours."

She took off her domino and looked up at him gravely. "As long as you promise to remember that," she said. "And I hope—"

How do I warn him about Alison and the girls? She couldn't say anything directly, but—

"I hope you're also remember that intelligence is a weapon of sorts, and it isn't always used to good ends, and that signifies for women just as well as men. Maybe more," she added, thoughtfully, "Since women don't have a great many weapons at their disposal, and they are inclined to use the ones they have with skill and precision."

He blinked for a moment, as if taken aback by her words, then nodded. "Ah. I think I know what you are hinting at. The charming Alison Robinson and her two lovely daughters." His mouth tightened. "Eleanor, what hold have they over you? I cannot believe that *they* can come up here to tea and tennis on a daily basis in gowns of the latest mode while *you* clearly are working at manual labor and kept as shabbily as a tweenie in a miser's house, unless they have some power over you!"

Oh, how she wanted to tell him! She fought the constraints of the spell, but all she could manage to get out, through gritted teeth, was, "She's my guardian. I have no rights, and no say in my life."

"Until you come of age, and that can't be long," he replied, his eyes icy for a moment. "And then—you can depend on me, Eleanor. You can."

She felt her hands starting to tremble, and she clasped them together to hide it. He reached over and took her hands.

"Eleanor," he said, as she stiffened. "I would like to be more than just your friend. A great deal more."

She went hot, then cold, then hot again. "You don't mean that," she said, half begging, half accusing. "You can't mean that. I don't fit in with all this—" she took her hands out of his and waved vaguely at the manor behind her. "and I don't fit in with 'your people!' Can't you see that?" She shook her head violently. "You and I—it's impossible, surely you understand!"

He made a little sound of mingled amusement and disgust. "There is one thing that Mad Ross is right about. All this is going to change in the next few years, Eleanor, and change drastically, and most of those people back there haven't a clue. This war is putting an end to their world as they know it, though it was starting to crumble around the edges before that." He sniffed. "A bloodline isn't worth much if you can't keep the roof over your head patched. And I can name you a dozen men in my circle, men who are contemporaries of my father, who've married chorus beauties, actresses, their children's governesses—even their housekeepers! There will be more of that—and there will be women who had no men in their families survive this war, who will marry policemen, gardeners, tradesmen—or never marry or remarry at all. And as for the people my age—" he shook his head. "We've seen too much. We've learned too much, and most of it was bitter. I've been thinking about this a very great deal, ever since that big push at Ypres started." He took a very deep breath. "I came to the conclusion that if Mater was going to insist that I do my family duty, it was going to be on *my* terms, with a woman I could respect, with intelligence; someone who could *talk* with me."

Her hands were sweating. Nervously, to save her silk gloves, she pulled them off.

He recaptured her hands. "These hands, no matter what they work at, are not all of you, Eleanor—not even most of what you are. You are intelligent, kind, forgiving—I could go on for the next half hour and still not come to the end of your good points. No, perhaps you don't 'fit in' with all of that behind me. But 'all that' is going to have to change if it is going to survive at all in the coming years. I am going to have to change. I don't see any reason why that change shouldn't come in a way that accommodates you, and your own changes."

Now she was shaking. But it wasn't only because of what he was saying. No, for no reason that she could understand, Alison's coercions were tightening around her.

And so were the spells binding her to the hearth-stone.

This had come without real warning. Granted, she had spent too long searching for the Air Master, and now they were pulling on her insistently, but she couldn't understand why she hadn't had some sign before this.

She felt them, like a corset laced too tight, squeezing off breath, and making it hard to think. Soon, they would become uncomfortable.

Then painful. Then maddening—

"I won't ask you for any kind of a decision now, Eleanor," he was saying, as she felt her hands growing cold. "But I would like you to consider the possibility of seeing me as more than your friend. I would like to know that there is a chance for me in your future."

She wanted to pay *attention* to his words, but she couldn't. She felt the spells closing in on her. It was becoming hard to breathe; the tugging at her mind and body were growing intolerable. And she couldn't help herself. She began to shake, and she pulled her hands out of his and sprang to her feet in a single convulsive movement.

"Eleanor!" he exclaimed, as she whirled to face him, hoping he could see something of her inner struggle in her expression. "Eleanor, what's wrong? Please, I haven't offended you again—"

She shook her head, frantically, and wrapped her own hands around her throat, trying to force some last words out of it before she had to run—

But the words that came were not the ones she had expected.

"Reggie—" she heard herself gasping "—I love you!"

And then, she turned, and ran, leaving him calling after her. She couldn't even understand what he was saying at that point, the spells were tightening on her so painfully. He had no hope of catching her, lame as he was, of course. Sarah would be waiting—

—but she could not stop for Sarah.

No, she could not stop for anything.

All she could do was run, for as long as she was running in the right direction the bands of pain around her body, around her *mind,* would ease just enough to allow her to continue running. But if she stopped, even for a moment....

She did not take the road. The road was too long. She fled headlong and heedless through the grounds, across the long, empty lawn, and into the "wilderness" which was no wilderness at all, of course, only a carefully cultivated illusion of one. She couldn't think; not clearly anyway. Only fragments of thought lanced across the all-encompassing demand of Alison's spells.

Why was this happening?

She stumbled across a bridle-path that went in the right direction, and turned down it; her rose-wreath and garland were gone, and her hair was down all one side. Her sides ached, but the coercions were not letting up. A branch tangled with her skirt and she yanked it free without missing a step.

How had the coercions suddenly snapped into place?

There was a low stone wall in the way; she scrambled over it, and found herself in a meadow full of sheep that scattered before her, bleating indignation. She kept going; at least here there was enough light to see—

Why were the coercions so strong, suddenly?

Another low, stone wall; she left more of her gown on one of the stones. Dimly, she recognized the top of the Round Meadow where she had met Reggie so often, the upper end, where she normally couldn't go. At least she knew the way from here.

If the pain in her side and her head would let her. Her world narrowed to the pain and the next step, each step bringing her closer to The Arrows, closer to the end of the pain. The end of the pain—

Run!

Her breath rasped in her lungs, sending sharp, icy stabs into her chest. Her vision blurred and darkened; she felt branches lashing at her as she passed. But all she could think of was that she must, *must* get to The Arrows.

Run!

She felt hard, bare dirt and hard-packed gravel under

her feet. She was in the road to Broom. She didn't remember getting over the fence.

Run, run, run!

She stumbled into the side of one of the houses on High Street; caught herself, pushed herself off, and kept running.

There was Sarah's cottage, just ahead. Then past.

She tripped and fell, bruising hands and knees at the corner; shoved herself up and kept running. Here was the Broom Tavern.

Almost there—

She stumbled again and fell into the fence around the garden of the Arrows. She caught herself, and ran the last few yards completely blind, shoving open the garden gate, and falling inside, down onto the path, as the gate swung shut again behind her.

And the pain stopped.

The mental pain, anyway.

As she lay on the ground, gasping for breath in great, aching lungfuls, she discovered an entirely new source of very physical pain. Her palms and knees burned, her side felt as if someone had stuck a knife in her, and whenever she moved, she could feel deep scratches and bruises everywhere. And all she could do was to lie there and try to get her breath back, because she couldn't move in her current state if her life depended on it.

But she could think, at least—though not coherently. Whole thoughts, rather than fragments, but they came to her in no particular order as she lay on her back with her eyes closed, gasping.

Freed from the coercions, her mind raced. *I have to get cleaned up and changed. Alison and the girls will be coming home. I can't look like this—maybe I can disguise some of the scratches and bruises with kitchen ash. At least they won't be expecting me to still be awake.*

Sarah would, she hoped, surely know when the coercions had suddenly tightened around her, and would take the cart and horse back to its owners. Surely she wouldn't sit there all night.

Another thought, a bleak one this time. *I failed. I didn't find the Air Master—*

Why had there been that breath of Air Magic around Reggie?

Oh heavens—what did I say to Reggie? Did I really tell him I loved him? How could I have done that? What on earth possessed me? I don't—

But there the thought came to an abrupt halt, because she could not, in all truth, have finished it with *"I don't love him,"* because it wasn't true.

What was he saying to me? It had all gotten jumbled up in the coercions, in the headlong flight across the countryside. She couldn't remember any of it clearly.

Except she knew very well he hadn't said that he loved her.

But had he implied it? He'd asked if he could be more than a friend to her, she remembered that much.

The pain in her side ebbed a little, and with a groan, she pushed herself up off the ground. Her hands were tough, and little more than bruised, but her knees—well, her stockings were surely ruined, and the way they stuck to her knees argued for a bleeding scrape there.

I need to start a fire. The Salamanders can help heal this enough that it doesn't look fresh. I should sleep in the kitchen. . . .

In fact, she had a good idea that she was going to have to sleep in the kitchen whether she wanted to or not. She didn't think she could get up the stairs right now.

It was just a good thing that there was still some clean clothing, laundered and dried just yesterday, that was still waiting downstairs to be taken to her room. Everything that wasn't connected to the ball had been given short shrift in the last few days, and her own business had been last on the list of things to be done.

She got herself to her feet, and stumbled into the kitchen, shoving open the door with an effort. The fire leapt up to answer her unspoken call, and she put another log on it while she stripped off the rags that were all that was left of that wonderful gown, and, with intense regret, threw them on the fire. There was no point in leaving any evidence for anyone to find.

She drew a basin of water from the kitchen pump and cleaned off the dirt and the dried blood with soap and a wet towel. Both her knees were a mess, and there were scratches all over her body. She could hide her knees, but not the scratches on her face and arms.

Something had to be done about that.

When the fire was burning brightly, she called a swarm of Salamanders to wreath around her injuries. They'd only have burned someone who wasn't a Fire magician, and they couldn't heal things up completely, but what they could do was minimize the appearance of the scrapes and deep scratches, so that they looked days, rather than hours old.

Finally, she put on the clean clothing, spread out the pallet-bed, and fell onto it. She felt as if she wanted to weep. All that work—and for nothing! All she had done was to allow herself to be distracted by Reggie and betrayed by her emotions. She hadn't found the Air Master. She was no nearer to freeing herself than she had been this morning.

As for Reggie—if he dared to come looking for her here—Alison would want to know why, and then—

Unbidden, the image of the Wheel of Fortune card rose in her mind. A few hours ago, she had been up, up, up—now the Wheel had turned, and she had tumbled down, down, down—

The Wheel would turn again. She had to believe that. She had to.

Exhaustion, mental and physical overcame her while she was trying to convince herself of that, and she slept.

Only to be jolted awake by the impact of a delicately pointed toe on her own sore ribs.

She started out of sleep, and looked up, dumbly, to find that Alison, her daughters, and the odious Warrick Locke were all gazing down at her with expressions on their faces that made her heart turn to stone. And a scrap of lace and a single rosebud dangled from Alison's fingertips.

"Take care of her," Alison said to Locke, before Eleanor could say a word.

And before she could move, he had swooped down on her like a hawk on a mouse, a rag in one hand that he clamped over her nose and mouth. There was a sickly-sweet smell—

—and then, nothing.

28

August 12, 1917
Broom, Warwickshire

ALISON LOOKED DOWN AT THE unconscious and much-battered form of her stepdaughter, sprawled on top of the heap of ragged blankets that was her bed, and seethed with rage that she carefully kept from her expression. There was no point in letting everyone know how close she was to unleashing that rage. In fact, she was quite sure that it was her control, and not her anger, that frightened Locke. "I am very glad you were clever enough to see past her costume at the ball, Lauralee," she said, keeping her voice level. "And gladder still that you kept her from seeing you. She very nearly undid everything we have accomplished so far. Who could have guessed that idiot boy would have been attracted to *her?*"

Carolyn pouted. "What I want to know is, where did she get that dress?" Her expression, as well as her voice, was raw with envy. That would have been moderately interesting under other circumstances, as her mother would never have guessed she had a passion for pink, lace, and rosebuds. It was an exceedingly misplaced concern, given the situation.

"Light the lamp, Carolyn," was all Alison said. She was

not entirely in charity with her younger daughter at the moment. Carolyn continued to pout, but did as she was ordered.

"And how did she get in the door?" Lauralee added, her own voice hard with the same anger her mother was feeling.

"More to the point, how did she get *out* the door—this door?" Alison retorted, gesturing at the exit from the kitchen. "There are explanations for the rest—she could have found the dress in the attic, for instance, and she could have told the butler that she was with us in order to get into the ball. Didn't you say Reggie had asked about her, Carolyn?"

Carolyn blinked, as if the question caught her by surprise. "Well," she admitted reluctantly, "yes, but—"

"So she could easily have been on the guest list, and all she had to do was claim she misplaced her invitation. But *how* did she manipulate my coercive spells?" Alison glared down at the wretched girl. "That's what I want to know!"

"You have been concentrating on Reggie," Warrick Locke reminded her. "And you've been quite careful about working magic anywhere around Lady Virginia since her ladyship arrived. Between the two, your coercive spells may have weakened. It's just a very good thing for all of us that Lauralee spotted her, and that the rest of us were at the ball too."

"If you hadn't had Warrick along, *he* wouldn't have been able to shield Lady Virginia from sensing magic," Lauralee reminded her mother. "So you were able to redouble your coercions and force her back here. She didn't fight that, so possibly, as Mr. Locke says, it's only that your binding spells were weakening over time because you haven't been renewing them."

"Or possibly the girl is coming into her powers." Alison gritted her teeth. That was the one possibility that simply hadn't occurred to her up until this moment. And it was the one possibility that made her the angriest. "If that's the case, then there's no time to waste. We'll have to take her out to the nearest mine, the one closest to the Hoar Stones, and dump her there now instead of later. If she *is* becoming a Fire mage—her powers won't do her any good in there. Not underground, and not when my creatures are finished with her."

Oh, the miserable chit! She was forcing everything—and ruining what she hadn't forced!

"Alison," Locke said, warningly, pulling out his watch, and showing the face to her, "It's nearly five in the morning. We can't take her now. Someone will see us."

For one moment, Alison deeply regretted her rise in social status, because it would have been very relieving of her frustrations to curse like a fishwife right now. Locke was right, of course; none of the motors had anywhere to hide a bundled-up body, and the sun would be up by the time they got everything packed up and into the automobiles. It would have to wait until dark.

"How do you want to keep her unconscious?" Locke continued, now looking nervous. "I hate to advise against more chloroform, because it is dangerous, and there's an equal chance that I'd kill her or she'd come out of it—and you don't want her dead, that will do you no good at all—"

"I have something," Alison interrupted him. "It's a bit more precise."

She went upstairs to her room, and came back down with the morphia kit in both hands. It amused her slightly to see Locke's eyes bulge a little when he realized what it was. She readied the needle, pleased that she had learned to do all of this a long time ago. One of the few benefits of caring for the aged. . . .

"You surprise me," Locke said, finally, as she pulled a measured dose of the fluid into the chamber. "This is not something I would have expected you to possess." The look of shock still on his face made her raise an eyebrow.

"Don't be an idiot, Warrick," Lauralee snapped. "Mother's not an addict. She just believes in being prepared. She got that from our doctor in London ages ago. She told him it was because Eleanor had fits."

"And I pay him well enough to be incurious," Alison said, kneeling down at the girl's side, turning her arm over, and probing for a vein. "He noted it in his records as being for Eleanor, and it cost me a pretty penny, too. But you never know when you're going to need to keep someone quiet." She injected the fluid, and stood up. "There. That should keep her for quite some time. And it has the added benefit that, if she *is* coming into her powers, it will throw her right out of her body for a while, which should thoroughly disorient her."

She waved at Locke, who was just standing there, gaping at her. "Take the little wretch and bundle her out of sight somewhere."

"Where?" he asked, and she turned a furious face towards him.

"I don't care! You know this house well enough to find some place! I don't want anyone coming in here and stumbling over her, that's all!" She suppressed the urge to stamp her foot. Did she have to think of everything?

"The wash-house?" suggested Lauralee sweetly. "No one would look in there, and it will be handy for taking her out to the autos when we leave tonight."

They all looked to Alison, who nodded. Carolyn, she noted, was looking more and more calf-like. Stupid *and* sulky. Well, it was clear which of her daughters was the more useful.

Alison watched, lips pressed tightly together, as Locke picked up the girl, heaved her over his shoulder, and followed Lauralee out the kitchen door and into the dark and shadowy yard. There was a creak as the wash-house door opened, a soft thud, and the creak of the door again. Then a rattle as Lauralee shot home the bolt, locking Eleanor in. Wise little Lauralee, who was also taking no chances.

Lauralee led the way back in through the kitchen door, yawning, and in spite of the tension, Alison found herself yawning as well. "Mother, I am shattered—"

"We all are," Alison said, cutting her off, grimly. "This has been a less than successful night, and we are going to have to act quickly and resolutely to minimize the damage. We can't do that without sleep. *She* will keep. Warrick, you can take one of the spare bedrooms; at this point, with as much as we have at stake, I am willing to risk a little gossip."

Lauralee nodded, looking relieved. Carolyn walked up the first few stairs, and her sister followed, more slowly, burdened as she was by her elaborate costume.

"I *did* come to the ball with you," Locke pointed out meekly. "And it would only be hospitable to offer a place for me for the night, after such a late return."

"Do you think Reggie will come looking for her here?" Lauralee asked suddenly, turning back to look down at them with an expression of worry.

What with everything else that was going wrong—probably. "He might," Alison replied. "And we need to be prepared for that." She thought about it for a moment. "Our best bet may be to try and convince him that the girl he met was not Eleanor, but—Lauralee."

"Lauralee!" Carolyn exclaimed angrily, jealousy sharpening her tone. "Why Lauralee?"

"She's the nearest in size, he didn't set eyes on her once all evening, and the difference in hair-color can be explained with a wig," Alison replied, consigning Carolyn's hopes to the dustbin without a twinge. "Whereas you, dear, he danced with twice, so he knows very well that you weren't in the fairy princess costume. He can't possibly have *known* who Eleanor is; when would he ever have met her? It might work, and if it does, we'll have saved the situation. You can explain running away somehow. I leave it up to you to think of something."

"I will," Lauralee promised, and she turned to go back up the stairs. Her sister led the way, bristling and pouting at the same time.

"That one's going to be trouble," Locke warned. "She's going to let jealousy of her sister take precedence over everything else."

Alison sniffed. "She's the least of my worries. She'll behave herself now because this situation will fall to pieces if we don't all work together. And she'll behave herself later—because she knows what will happen if she doesn't."

"Oh?" Locke replied, looking skeptical.

She dropped the mask she habitually wore and let him see the true Alison Robinson, just for a moment. He shrank back, as she reinforced the revelation with her next words.

"I only *need* one daughter," she said, icily. "And I periodically remind them of that." She smiled as he nodded, trembling, and all but scrambled up the stairs to a guest room.

August 12, 1917
Elsewhere

At one moment, Eleanor had been surrounded by the last people on earth she wanted to see. She had started to get up, but Warrick Locke had pounced on her with a rag in one hand. He had covered her nose and mouth with it; she had been forced to breathe through it, tasting a sickly-sweet, unbearably thick aroma, and the next thing she knew she had been thrust into blackness. She seemed to fall forever, then there was a kind of electric jolt—

Now, she was *here*. The Tarot-world, with its flat, blue sky and its flat, green lawns. But this was a part of it she had never seen before. She stood inside a square of grass that was surrounded by hedges whose tops were well above her head. It all looked very measured and regular; too regular to be real.

"Where am I?" she said aloud, though she really only thought she was talking to herself.

But she wasn't alone. She heard something behind her, and turned. "You are in the center of a maze," said the Hermit, pushing back his cowl and setting his lantern down. He frowned, but at the hedges, not at her, his bushy gray brows knitting together. "You are in great danger; this is merely a reflection in this world of another reality that surrounds you."

At the moment, she didn't care what the maze was for. "I know I don't belong here," she said urgently. "And I know I'm in danger—but I didn't come here by myself, and I don't know how to get out! Is there any way you can help me?"

He looked directly into her eyes, and she saw a personality there—something she had not ever really seen with any of the other Tarot cards. "The Perfect Fool asks the unasked questions—" he said aloud. Then he changed.

He became—Fire. Fire incarnate. A sexless creature of insubstantial flame, gazing at her with penetrating blue eyes, eyes the color of a hot gas flame. His voice remained the same, however.

"I think we can dispense with this, child," he said, and with a casual gesture, the maze, the flat blue sky, the flat green earth, were all gone. In their place—a world of fire, fire which not only did not burn her, but which, when it touched her, felt like a cool caress. "You are not a Master, not yet—I am not compelled to obey you, nor required by mutual bargain."

She shook her head. "I know that," she replied, swallowing. "And I know I'll be studying all my life to really understand my powers. I was foolish to think I could Master all the cards in a few days, but—but I *think* I could have gotten enough to have broken free of Alison."

"You are in great danger," the Fire Elemental repeated. "And the maze we were in is nothing to the maze that holds you tight in tangles of magic."

"Yes I am," she agreed, shivering. "I don't think I can escape from this by myself. I need help. Will you, can you help me?"

"That depends," the Elemental said, measuringly. "You must show by your intelligence that you deserve help."

Fire—most difficult of the Elements. Dangerous to try and control. More dangerous to lie to. But win its loyalty—

"I have to break the coercions," she said flatly. "And I have to break free of *here,* and get back to the real world again."

But the Elemental simply regarded her gravely. Finally, "Or—?" he prompted.

Fire is the hardest to hold, most difficult to understand, like-

liest to rebel, and is impressed only by—intellect. This Elemental was showing remarkable patience by those standards. She pummeled her brain. What could she do to get out of the coercions? If she broke them, Alison would know. She'd already tried stretching them. What else was there? If she looked around herself a certain way, she could actually *see* them here, tangling around her in a rat's nest of bindings like—

She blinked, and looked again. *Like—a—maze—just as he told me.*

She took a deep breath. She couldn't solve the thing in the "real" world, but—here?

"What happens if I thread my way out of the coercions?" she asked the Fire Elemental.

He grinned broadly, and nodded, the flames that were his hair brightening. "Then her spells will no longer hold you, and yet, they will not be broken. So she will not be aware that her spells no longer hold you. But do you think you can solve this?"

"I have to," she replied grimly. "I'll see if wall-following will do it. It might take longer, but it's the surest."

She focused her concentration until the tangles of the spells that confined her became clear, concentrated further, willing the tangles to take on the tangible form of walls and passageways.

The magician imposes his will, his way of seeing on the Plane of Magic, and the Plane reflects what he wills. She couldn't will herself out of this, because the mind and will that had set the spells was stronger than she was. But she could force it to take on a semblance of something she could deal with.

She found herself at the heart of another maze. She didn't like the look of the walls that surrounded her, either; they were dark and repellent and she didn't want to touch them, but wall-following meant keeping one hand on either the left or the right-hand wall and following it, no matter what, and after a moment of thought, she put her hand on the left-hand wall, and stepped into the shadowy, intimidating darkness of the maze itself.

The Fire Elemental came with her, which surprised her a little, though it was heartening to have company. She hadn't expected it, and since he brought light with him, this meant she could actually see where she was going.

That was an advantage. Seeing the walls that made up the maze clearly was not an advantage.

They *felt* like something alive—but not pleasant. Faintly warm, pulsing, a touch slimy. But worse than the feel was the look; a suggestion of faces there, and not nice faces, either. She didn't ask if the walls were alive; that was fairly obvious. "Can they feel?" she asked instead.

"Oh yes," came the reply; grim, and with a dangerous edge to it.

"Are they in pain?" she continued. Not that she wanted to know—except that she did.

"Oh, yes," softly, yet somehow grimmer still.

She made another two turnings; the faces in the walls were set in frozen expressions of despair. "Can I free them?" she asked. Not that she wanted to, but—

But nothing should suffer if it doesn't have to.

The Fire Elemental stopped, looking at her with an expression of utter astonishment. "Why would you desire to do that?" he asked.

"Because if I can, I should," she replied, knowing that this was the right answer. Not the most expedient, and perhaps not the wisest, but the right answer. "This—this is wrong. If I can make it right, then it's my duty to. I have power, and power begets responsibility."

And the walls began to murmur.

She shivered at the sound, which carried something of the tone of those revenants in it. But the Fire Elemental straightened, and spread his arms wide, the little flamelets that danced over him rising from his outstretched limbs. "Hear, my lesser brothers of Earth? Do you hear this child of Flame? You are in thrall to a Dark Master of Earth. She is not bound to you; she has no responsibility to you, and yet—she would free you."

A single, enormous face formed on the wall immediately in front of her. The eyes were closed and remained closed;

she was just as glad. She had the feeling that if those eyes opened and looked at her, she'd be sick with fear.

It wasn't an ugly or deformed face; in fact the features were quite regular. But there was something about it that made her wish she wasn't looking at it. Something dark and cruel, something that loved pain, and was bargaining with her only because it had no choice.

"We hear," said the chorus of voices, which now came from the single face, although the lips didn't move. "Why?"

"Because," the Fire Elemental replied, with pride welling in every word, "she is *better* than your mistress."

The face in the wall did not react one way or another to this statement.

"How can I free you?" she asked, her voice trembling, yet determined.

"Break her defenses, and you will free us," came the reply, in a low and ugly rumble. "Swear that you will!"

Be very careful what you promise! came the thought. *This is the Elemental world, and words have more weight here than in the real world.* If she promised—and failed—there would be a different sort of price to pay, and there was no telling what that price would be, only that it could be very expensive.

And you do not *want to owe an unknown penalty to a negative Elemental.*

"I promise I will try," she said instead. "If you will give me the key to this place that holds me."

The face became very still for a moment, as if all of the creatures speaking through it were consulting with one another. Then it spoke again. "Follow the Tree," it said, "The counter-Tree. The Tree of Death."

And it faded back into the wall again, but Eleanor knew exactly what it meant—it was a riddle, probably given to her in that form because *she* had not promised to do anything but try, but not a very clever one. She was to trace the opposite path of the Tree of Life; fortunately, the Tree of Life happened to be one of the major Tarot layouts as well as the key to the Kabala, or she wouldn't have known what the face in the wall meant. Mentally she retraced her steps from the center of the maze, and realized with relief that she would only have to go back and change her last turning.

"Why are you here with me?" she asked, as she set out on the new pattern, greatly relieved that she was no longer going to have to touch those walls.

"Because, although I cannot help you directly, I have a function I *can* perform for you," he said, and tilted his head to the side, expectantly.

A function he can perform for me— Abruptly, she realized that he already *had.*

"You—you are an intermediary!" she exclaimed, stopping dead in her tracks. "You can negotiate with the other Elements!"

He nodded, gravely. "That is my function. And if you can make your way from this place—"

"I will," she replied, fiercely. "And when I do—I have some ideas."

A faint smile flickered over the being's face. "I rather thought as much," he said, and gestured. "Lead on."

She did; and something else occurred to her as she followed the path of the anti-Tree.

Alison had made a very grave mistake, by throwing her into this place, this state. She probably thought that she was imprisoning Eleanor further, and it must have been that Alison had drugged her. The opiates had a long history of being used to access occult states, which was why people who had no business *being* in such a state used them as "easy" ways to attain knowledge. Maybe Alison had assumed being drugged was going to make her easier to handle, and that would have been true, if she had not been learning discipline and control all this time, and if she had not already been traveling in the Tarot realm. And Alison was accustomed to thinking only in terms of *commanding* and *coercing* the creatures of her Element; it must not have even crossed her mind that Eleanor might find allies—or at least, something willing to bargain with her—here.

Alison would have done better to have bound and gagged her. If Eleanor got her way, Alison would live to regret that error.

But first, she still had to escape from the spell-maze, before Alison delivered her physical body to whatever fate the Earth Master had in mind.

August 12, 1917
Longacre Park, Warwickshire

By the time Reggie reacted to Eleanor's flight, it was too late. She was out of sight before he could get to his feet, and in the end, all he could find of her was the gloves she had left on the bench beside him.

He could not hope to find her, not now. He had no idea where she had run to—and even if he left the ball and went straight to The Arrows, what was he to do there? Force his way inside? Demand that they produce her? If her stepmother had gone to such lengths to hide her, there was no reason on earth why she should conjure the girl up simply because he demanded it.

Slowly and cautiously, Reg. The first one over the barricades is the first one shot.

With light and music and laughter spilling out of the doors and windows above him, he returned to the garden bench to try and make some sense of what had just happened. One moment, she had been talking with him, perfectly sensibly—the next, she was fleeing as if pursued by demons. And yet, it couldn't have been what *he* said that sent her running away, could it?

Hadn't she managed to choke out that she *loved* him before she ran?

Surely her stepmother's hold over her could not control her here, in the privacy of Longacre's gardens—

Unless—

He shook his head at the thought. No, surely not. Surely it was not possible that Alison Robinson was a magician.

Was it?

He was completely unwilling to drop his barricades now. If Alison Robinson was a magician—heaven alone only knew what she had set in motion to try and ensnare him for one of her daughters. There might be a spell just waiting for a break in his defenses.

By the time he found Lady Virginia just paying her farewells to her cronies as the guests began to depart, and got her to come down into the garden with him, the traces of—yes—*magic* were almost too faint for her to read. All she could say for certain was that both Earth magic of the darker sort and Fire magic had left a hint of "scent" behind.

"Back inside, please," his godmother said when she'd finished. "It's altogether too damp and chilly for my bones. Let's adjourn to the library; there should still be a fire there."

Somewhat reluctantly, he agreed. He still wanted to go tearing after Eleanor, but he knew that would be the wrong thing to do. He had no plan of action, and to go into this without a plan was asking for trouble.

The Earth—well, dark magic of some sort—he had expected. But who was the Fire? The only mages here were Air—

Unless—Eleanor?

When he spoke his thoughts aloud, incredulously, Lady Virginia only shrugged, as she extended her toes towards the library fire. "Magicians are always more vulnerable to magic than other folk," she pointed out. "If the girl *is* an Elemental Mage, then her stepmother would have an easier time of it in trying to control her. The hardest creature to affect by magic is someone who has none of it at all."

He fidgeted with the cane he had taken from the stand near the door, and longed to be able to pace as he used to at times like these. To think of poor Eleanor, down there, in that repellent woman's hands—

She looked at him sharply. "Reginald," she said, very slowly, "Are you in love with this girl?"

He would have thought it was obvious to a far less astute person than his godmother, but he replied, "Yes. Yes, I am."

"Your mother won't like it," Lady Virginia cautioned. "She's common."

"So are the Americans that keep marrying into the peerage," he snapped, feeling an entirely irrational surge of irritation. "And so are the other two girls, and Mater would have no trouble at all throwing me to one of them!"

"Ah, but the Americans have fortunes—large fortunes," his godmother retorted. "Even if the girl inherited, and there's no guarantee of that, she's prosperous, but no heiress. And Alison Robinson is in Burke's, so presumably so are her daughters."

"*Is* she?" he replied. "Someone with the name she's claiming is, but anyone can claim to be a member of a family one is never going to encounter. And I didn't find any mention of Carolyn, Lauralee, or either of Alison's marriages in Burke's, if she is who she claims to be."

"She was vetted by Alderscroft—" Lady Virginia began, and before she could continue, her jaw tightened. "Alderscroft, who would swear his second-best hunter was a member of the peerage if he thought it would serve the cause. I begin to smell a rat, Reginald. Alderscroft may have used her before, and certainly knows she lives in Broom, so he might have told her to keep an eye on *you*, without bothering to tell me about it, may I add. But it is as certain as the sun rising in the east that she decided to aggrandize herself as soon as she saw the situation. I *knew* there was something about that woman that I did not like."

"I may very well discover more you won't like before I'm through," Reggie said grimly.

"It wouldn't surprise me." Lady Virginia reached out and took his hand. "Please promise me that you will not go tearing down there this instant in your motor."

"I would *like* to—but I feel that would be a very bad notion," he replied with feeling. "I will go down there tomorrow. I might actually catch the girl myself, in which case, I will bundle her up here and put her in your hands. If there are coercions on her—you can deal with them."

"Against a creature like Alison Robinson? I should think so," his godmother told him, in a tone that would have been arrogant in anyone but a mage of her ability. "I'll open up your father's workroom and prepare it. Heaven knows I've used it often enough in the past. On *our* home ground, Reginald, it would take an army of mages to defeat us."

"If I can't find her immediately, I'll have to try subterfuge. And fortunately, I have an excuse." He smiled thinly. "I have these. And I will be looking for the girl who fits them."

He held up the pink silk gloves. Lady Virginia raised an eyebrow.

"Forgive my skepticism, Reginald, but virtually any girl whose hands aren't completely ruined could fit into a pair of silk gloves—"

"Oh, no. Not these," he retorted, and spread out the fingers of the left-hand glove. The *three* fingers.

Lady Virginia blinked. "Ah," she said. "Well, that puts a different complexion on things, doesn't it? Rather like Anne Boleyn's set of five."

"Rather like." He folded the gloves carefully and tucked them inside his tunic. "I'd like very much to see either Carolyn or Lauralee fit that glove."

"Hmm." Lady Virginia stared into the fire. "Be careful what you wish for. If the girls are like the mother, they might find a way, at whatever cost."

29

August 12, 1917
Elsewhere

"THESE WALLS—THEY REPRESENT SOMETHING. It wasn't just spells that Alison put to tie me to the hearth, was it?" she asked her companion, when the silence within the maze became unbearable.

"No; she has actually tied minor Elementals into the spells so that she did not have to renew them so often," the Fire creature replied. "This is why the maze appears to be a living thing. It actually is; more than one."

"Ugh." She shuddered, and glanced at the walls around them. Colored a sad brown, suggestions of faces continued to come and go. "Is that as nasty as I think it is?"

"Surely." The Fire creature regarded her soberly. "As certainly as you have been imprisoned by them, they have been imprisoned by Alison. They may be creatures of darkness, but they have spent the years as the bars of your cage."

The more she learned about Alison, the more she wanted to be free of her. If ever there was someone evil—

I am not really "here," she reminded herself. *This is like the Tarot world; my body is—well, wherever Alison put it. Perhaps the cellar. I must escape the maze and then—then wake up from whatever she did to me.* But she had to wonder, what would happen to the "real" Eleanor, if her—call it "spirit-self"—was hurt?

Her mother's notebooks hadn't covered that possibility.

And what would happen if she didn't get back to herself in a few hours? How long could her untenanted body sleep before life began to fade?

So strange—her body here felt real, felt solid, solid enough that her insides twisted with tension when she realized that she might be fighting against time as well as Alison.

She didn't really expect to be able to leave the maze unopposed. Just because she had managed to strike some kind of bargain with the maze itself, it did not follow that there were not more elemental Earth creatures here to block her passage. Probably they would try to intimidate her first, though.

Above her—vague darkness. They walked on a surface that was very like dead grass, and the only light here came from her companion. If ever there was a place of stagnation, this was it. The air was dry and acrid, with a faint scent of corruption. And the maze walls did not get any better the deeper she went.

And just as she had expected, once they were, by her accounting, roughly halfway through, she sensed something up ahead of her. When she turned the corner—there it was.

She might have mistaken it for a Brownie if she hadn't known better. It looked like exactly like a child's picture-book illustration of a Brownie in a red cap—but it was the cap that gave it away.

This was a Redcap, a vicious little gnome with an insatiable appetite for murder. It soaked its cap in the blood of its victims; hence the name. There was no point in even trying to negotiate with something like this; it was completely evil and absolutely treacherous.

And if she had not been studying all four Elements instead of just her own, she would never have known that.

She felt her eyes narrow as she stepped threateningly towards the Redcap. There was power welling up in her; she felt it rising inside, and she knew that if she had to strike at this thing, the power would answer her. There were only two ways to deal with a Redcap; make it run or destroy it. Turning your back on it would be fatal.

"Hello, daughter of Adam," the Recap said, wheedlingly, looking up at her with an entreating gaze. "I am lost, trapped here, like you. Won't you help me find the way out of this maze?"

"I think not, Redcap," she replied, before the Fire elemental could warn her. "I think you know the way out already. Don't you?"

The Redcap's face underwent a frightening transformation. Its eyes turned red, with a greenish glow to the pupils; it hunched over, hands fumbling at its belt for the knife it probably had hidden there, and it snarled, showing sharp, pointed teeth.

"Look out!" the Fire creature called, but she was already calling up fire herself, in the shape of her Salamanders. They appeared out of nowhere, as large as bloodhounds and fierce as lions, two of them, planting themselves between her and the Redcap, hissing.

The Redcap leapt back with a curse. It shook its fist at her, and ran off into the depths of the maze. Since it wasn't going the way she planned, she kept the Salamanders from chasing it.

When it was gone, they fawned around her like affectionate cats, rubbing up against her and butting their heads into her hands. The Fire creature regarded them with amusement.

"Under other circumstances," it said, "I would say that you have a remarkable way with animals. I am glad that you have won their loyalty."

"So am I," she replied fervently. "Should I keep them with us?"

"Definitely. I have no idea what might lie ahead of us, except that I cannot imagine that there will *not* be more trouble."

She just nodded. She doubted very much that the next

obstacle they encountered would be so obliging as to run away.

August 12, 1917
Longacre Park, Warwickshire

Reggie didn't sleep very much—but then, he hadn't expected to. And he had flown and fought on less rest than he'd gotten last night. He had gone over his plan so many times it was engraved in his mind—

Not that he really expected to find the Robinsons following *his* plan. No, he would just have to keep his wits about him and try to find a way to get to Eleanor. Once they were together, he didn't think that even Alison would try to oppose him taking her out.

She *could* summon a constable, he supposed—but he doubted that the Broom constable, old as he was, would do more than make a token effort to stop him. And once Eleanor was freed from whatever holds Alison had placed on her, the shoe would almost certainly be on the other foot. He suspected that she had some ugly tales to tell.

It was very hard, though, to have to rise, breakfast as usual—and wait. Wait, because if he went down at any time before, say, noon—no one would let him in. Certainly Eleanor was not permitted to answer the door. She hadn't before, when he'd called, and that was probably to keep her from being recognized by a visitor, or from blurting out a plea for help. If he arrived too early, no one would be awake, and he could hardly pound on the door and bellow at them to let him in. Not unless he *wanted* to tip his hand.

No, above all, he didn't want anyone to know what he was up to until it was too late to do anything about it.

The Robinsons had left about three—so they would not

be receiving visitors until noon at the earliest. So he would have to wait.

Except—if he was going to go into a confrontation with an Earth Master, his simple barricades were not going to suffice.

So after breakfast, with a feeling of fear that would have paralyzed him had he not been eaten alive with worry for Eleanor, he took a certain back staircase that his mother was not even aware existed, up to a room on the same floor as the servants' quarters. Except that this room connected with no other chamber in the house, and the door to the staircase was carved with sigils that would allow only an Elemental Master to see it.

It took a terrible effort for him to take each step upwards—because each step brought him nearer to the moment when he must give up his defenses and accept the power back into his hands—and with that power, open himself to attack. He was sweating by the time he reached the landing.

It was his father's old workroom, a corner room with tall windows on two sides, lined with books and cabinets for supplies on the other two, and with a floor of white marble inlaid with a magic circle in silver. And Lady Virginia was already there.

She was dressed for the occasion, in a loose, sky-blue robe of silk, with her ice-white hair in a single plait down her back. Curiously enough, this made her look younger, rather than older.

"I thought you might turn up," she said, as he closed the door to the staircase behind him. "So I didn't put up the wards yet."

He shivered, involuntarily. "If you had any idea how frightened I am—" Then he steeled himself, before the panic could rise up and choke him. "But I don't have a choice, do I?"

"Not if Alison Robinson is a Master—and all of the preliminary work I have done tells me she is," Lady Virginia replied grimly. "I believe—though I am not yet sure—that *she* is the one responsible for that plague of revenants outside your father's old shields. I can't imagine why she would set them on you, but I'm not very good at deciphering the plans of individuals with the kind of twisted soul capable of summoning something like that up in the first place."

Reggie nodded. Then he spoke the hardest words he had ever said in his life. "Tell me what to do, Godmother," he begged. "Help me, please. I need my powers back, and we don't have a great deal of time before I face her."

"Then *I* will need to force your shields open," she replied, jaw set. "And it won't be easy on you."

He bowed his head, with the feeling that he was baring his neck to the axe. "I never thought it would," he said, with miserable determination.

August 12, 1917
Elsewhere

The end of the maze was very near, and Eleanor had routed a good half-dozen nasty creatures that had tried to ambush her on the way. The worst had been the Night-mare; at least, so far. A truly dreadful black thing it was with far too many legs, all of them ending in talons rather than hooves, and long, white fangs. The Salamanders had not been able to attack it, and it had come charging straight at her—

And she had found herself with a flaming sword in her hands. She had no more idea of how to use it than how to fly—but slashing wildly at the Night-mare had made it shy sideways to avoid the attack, aborting its charge. It had stared at her with evil red eyes for a moment, then, like the Redcap, it had retreated into the depths of the maze.

"Interesting," her companion said, as she let the sword go, only to have it vanish into thin air the moment she loosed her hold on the hilt. "It appears that however Alison is controlling or coercing these creatures, it is not enough to make them face any sort of serious opposition. I believe she has completely underestimated you."

"I hope so!" Eleanor replied, as her Salamanders pressed up against her legs, one on either side of her.

Now she was one turn away from the exit to the maze, or so she thought. When she rounded this last corner, she should be free of the spells that bound her to the hearth of The Arrows.

But of course, Alison was not likely to let her go without a fight.

She turned the corner, and found herself facing every creature she had encountered thus far, and some new ones, all lined up across the exit-point to the maze.

August 12, 1917
Longacre Park, Warwickshire

Reggie emerged from the workroom feeling—unnerved. Unsettled? No, far too mild a word. Severely rattled, and definitely drained. Those hard-built barricades were gone, but he had yet to test the strength of his powers as an Air Master, because he did not want to alert Alison to the fact that those powers were back, and neither did Lady Virginia. Psychologically—

He was a wreck, for he had, in the space of a few hours, lived through and endured the sharp-focused memory of his ordeal after being shot down. The difference was, this time he had his godmother to guide him through it. This time, he had come out the other side still sane. Or at least, relatively so. But his nerves were raw, and fear surged and ebbed unexpectedly, making him wonder just how much control he could keep.

But they had run out of time. It was midafternoon by the time Lady Virginia allowed him to go, and some instinct warned him that Alison Robinson was going to do whatever she had planned for Eleanor very soon. He had to get down there *now*—or, he suspected, he would lose her forever.

His auto was waiting for him at the door, as he had requested before he went up to the workroom. He thanked heaven that she wasn't a temperamental beast; in fact, she might have been sensitive to his urgency, for she fired up at the first spark, all cylinders roaring like uncaged lions.

He threw the auto down the drive at a reckless pace, and kept it up right to the outskirts of Broom—but the moment he was within sight of the place, he throttled the racing engine down, and proceeded at what seemed to his raw nerves to be a crawl. This was not just to avoid knocking people down, it was because things had to *seem* normal. If Alison suspected anything, she could, and probably would, refuse him entrance.

It made him want to scream with impatience as he dawdled down the main street, smiling tightly, and waving at some of his cronies from the pub. Only one thought kept him steady; Alison did not know how much Eleanor had said to him. Nor did she know they already knew each other. So there should be no real reason in her mind to suspect how much Reggie already knew or guessed. She should not have felt the need to rush into a solution to the problem of Eleanor's escape.

Or so he hoped and prayed. There had been one good sign, anyway—Lady Virginia had been assiduously monitoring the area for signs of powerful magic ever since last night, and there had been nothing.

At long last he pulled up to the edge of the street beside The Arrows. He parked the beast right there, took out his cane, and limped to the front doorway to ring the bell.

It was answered by Carolyn, who looked startled and confused the moment she set eyes on him.

"Reggie!" she exclaimed, pushing a lock of hair out of

her eyes. "What a delightful surprise! We didn't expect you—"

"I know," he said, stretching his mouth in what he hoped was a genuine-looking smile. "But I had to come down here today. I know how clever you all are, and how you know just about everyone for miles around, and I was hoping you girls could help me solve a mystery."

"But—of course, please come in, I can't think what I'm doing, leaving you standing in the door like this." She laughed; was it his imagination, or did it ring false? "We're sending formal thank-you letters, of course, but since you are here, I must tell you that your ball was wonderful; I don't know when I've had a better time!"

"Actually, that's why I'm here," he said, seizing the opportunity with both hands as he stepped into the parlor at her direction. The Arrows was at least as old as the Broom; real, genuine Tudor construction. The place betrayed its age, with blackened beams, white-plaster walls, and very low ceilings that made him want to duck his head. "You see, I encountered someone at the ball, but she left before I got a chance to find out who she was, and I hoped you could help me with that."

"Me?" Carolyn turned towards him as he took a seat beside the fire, and he was sure he was not mistaken; there was a flush of guilt on her cheeks. He felt his gut tighten. "How could I help?"

"Indeed, as eager as we are to assist you in any way, Reggie, I don't know what we could do in this case," said Alison Robinson, gliding into the room, soundlessly. He didn't jump, but she had startled him, moving so quietly. There was something altogether snakelike about the way she moved. If he'd had hackles, they'd have been up. "There were dozens of young women at your ball, and all of them were masked for most of the evening."

"Ah," he said brightly. "But I think you might know this girl, and she has one very distinctive characteristic. You see, she wore these gloves—"

He held out the pink silk gloves to Alison, who examined them with a faint frown on her face. Right until the moment when she realized that the left-hand glove had only three fingers.

Then, she started, and paled for a moment, and he felt his heart leap in triumph. So, they *were* up to something! And they hadn't known Eleanor had left anything of herself behind.

"Actually, I believe you are correct," she said, recovering quickly and turning a bland face towards him, "I do know something about the girl who wore this glove. If you'll wait a moment—"

"I would wait a year if you could bring her to me," Reggie replied, his heartbeat quickening with nervous tension. Should he not have presented the gloves to Alison? Now she knew something was up, but did she guess how much he knew about Eleanor? Or rather—how little? *She can't be going to bring Eleanor. There's some trickery going on here.* But before he could think of anything else to say, Alison had carried the gloves away with her and Carolyn was babbling at him about the delights of the ball.

He tried, unsuccessfully, to get her onto any other subject, or at least to slow down the torrent of words. To no avail; it was clear that she was babbling out of sheer panic now, and nothing he said was going to penetrate the wall of fear she had around her. He sat on the edge of his seat, alive with tension, trying to listen past Carolyn's wall of words to what was going on in the next rooms. Was there the creak of a door, something slamming, a muffled exclamation? Was there the sound of a struggle?

"Here we are!" Alison said brightly, making him jump. "Here is your mysterious girl, Reggie—I am afraid that my Lauralee was playing a bit of a prank on you, pretending to be a stranger to you. Girlish high spirits and all—" She smiled thinly. "Of course, she didn't want to spoil the joke by allowing you to guess who she was, so she tells me she ran away from you in the garden."

Sure enough, behind Alison came Lauralee—but a very pale Lauralee, with her teeth clenched, though she tried to feign that she was completely normal. And she was wearing both gloves.

He stood as they both entered the room. "Lauralee!" he said, immediately on his guard, but hoping he wasn't showing it. "How could I not have recognized you?"

"I wore a wig," she said, her voice strained, her mouth stretched in something that looked nothing like a smile. "And I took care to disguise my voice." As he neared her, he saw that her pupils were very large, and heard a faint slur to her words, as if she was drugged.

Yes, there was no trickery; she wore the gloves. But he knew very well that the *last* time he had seen her, she had owned the usual number of fingers. Which must mean—

The thought made him sick. The girl must be mad. Or her mother. Or both.

Probably both.

He might have spared a moment to pity her, if such an act had not simply shown him that she was as ruthless as her mother. And fear of what they might be doing to Eleanor made him act in a way he probably wouldn't have, otherwise. He reached out and seized both her hands before she could prevent it, and gave the left one a squeeze.

She nearly fainted. And seeping blood stained the side of the glove, where she must have only now cut off the little finger of her left hand. He looked up at Alison's face, and saw that it was suffused with rage.

He had them. "I think—" he began—

And pain and blackness descended on him from behind.

August 12, 1917
Broom, Warwickshire

"Well, Carolyn, you have redeemed yourself in my eyes," Alison said, as Reggie crumpled to the floor. Carolyn stared first at him, then at her mother, wide-eyed, the poker she had used to hit him with still clutched in her nerveless fingers. "Oh, don't look at me like that, you haven't the strength to kill him! You have merely rendered him unconscious. Go and get my kit. I fear we will have two bundles to smuggle out after dark, not one."

She turned to Lauralee, who had reeled against the wall, whimpering with pain, cradling her injured left hand in her right. "I warned you to be sure that you had cauterized the wound properly *and* that the laudanum had taken effect before you came out of the kitchen!"

"I couldn't help it. He squeezed my hand, Mother," Lauralee replied, her voice faint and full of agony. "He broke open the wound—"

"So he knew all along. He came here looking for Eleanor, and he *knew* it was Eleanor behind the mask. This is worse than I thought." She stood rigid, rooted in thought, arms crossed over her chest, tapping one finger against her forearm. "That's it; the only hope we have is to take him to the Hoar Stones and make him forget her."

Lauralee blinked up at her mother through tears of pain. "Can you do that?"

"Well, I can make him forget a great deal, and her with it," Alison admitted. "I can erase, in general, every memory he has had since he came home. Then when he wakes, it will be up to you to convince him that he proposed marriage to you last night in the garden, and that he has been in love with you all along."

Carolyn, who had not yet moved, put the poker aside. "But won't that be a problem with his mother?" she faltered. "She wants him to marry within the peerage. That's what everyone was saying last night. And how do we explain that he was injured and his loss of memory?"

Alison shrugged. "We'll say we found him wandering and brought him back. It isn't as if there haven't been rumors about the steadiness of his mind." She frowned. This was getting more complicated by the moment, and dangerous, too. "We'll have to be quick, though. If he doesn't come back by morning—"

"His motorcar is here," Lauralee pointed out. "People

will know that. By now, everyone in the village knows that."

Alison gave vent to her feelings with a curse. Carolyn flinched. "Then one of us—me, I suppose—will have to drive our auto, and one of us will have to drive his."

"I'll drive it," Warrick Locke said from the stairs. "Here's your kit, Alison. It was still on the hall table." He handed her the morphia kit and looked down at the prone form of Reggie Fenyx with a lifted brow. "I hope you didn't damage him, Carolyn. Things could be cursed difficult if you have."

"So what if she did?" Alison retorted, filling a syringe and kneeling beside her victim. "It will make my job easier. Bloody hell. I *hate* complications—"

"Then let's plan this very carefully," Locke said, grimly, "Because this isn't just 'complications,' Alison. You've physically assaulted a man, and not just any man, but a peer, and not just any peer, but a genuine hero of the war. If he remembers what he came for, and what happened to him, the law is going to come into it, and I very much doubt I can get you out of it."

She turned to stare at him as she removed the needle from the vein in Reggie's arm. "You assume I haven't been in this position before."

"If you have, that was in London. In a part of London where people know better than to be curious," he said, coldly. "And you must have dealt with someone who was a nonentity. This is a tiny village, where everyone knows everyone else's business. And this is Captain Reginald Fenyx, baron. Have a care, Alison. This is dangerous."

She took a deep breath and held it to prevent herself from snapping at him. He was right. She needed his help.

The trouble was, it was going to cost her. Men like Warrick Locke could wait decades for an opportunity to get their hooks set in a target—and once they did, it was impossible to shake them off.

"So what do you suggest?" she asked, with feigned meekness.

"After dark, I pull Reggie's motor around to the old stable. You bundle him up in a blanket and bring him out; I'll put him in the passenger's side and wear his coat, goggles and cap myself. Don't try to hide him, I want people to see that there is someone with the driver, though not who. I'll take him straight to the Hoar Stones, leave him there, and drive his motor back along the route you'll be coming, where I'll abandon it in a ditch." Locke's eyes glittered as he spoke; there was no mistake, he enjoyed the part he was now playing, and he was going to get his pound of flesh out of it. "You'll bring the girl along and pick me up. We'll all go back to the Hoar Stones, drop the girl down the mine-shaft either before you do your work with Reggie, or afterwards, depending on how things work out. *You* will work your spell on his memories while *I* damage his clothing to make it look like he was in an accident. Everyone around here knows how he likes to drive like a demon. That will explain the crack on the head *and* the amnesia afterwards."

She had to admit, it was a brilliant plan. "Do we leave him with the motor?" she asked, reluctantly. She really didn't want him out of her sight, but—

"Yes, but we'll drive to that coaching-inn we stayed at, and one of us will go rushing in there to report the accident," Locke replied. "While people are milling about, we'll slip away, and there will be no connection between us and his condition. And as for Eleanor, she figures into the plan, too. We'll leave Eleanor's old coat, and perhaps a bundle of belongings in his auto, and once he's identified, no doubt someone will come around to ask why he was here. We'll say we never saw him, then identify the coat and the clothing. That will give us the excuse to send a search-party back in that area to look for her, once you're sure she's gone quite mad! Everyone will assume she eloped with him, or he persuaded her to go away with him, and without a doubt, everyone will assume the worst of her."

She ground her teeth, but smiled at him. Damn the man. It was a good plan, making the best possible use of all of the disasters that fate had thrown at them. "It will work," she conceded.

"It will do more than merely work," Locke said, raising his chin arrogantly. "It's the way to guarantee that one of your girls marries the boy. Don't you see? If Lady Devlin thinks that he and Eleanor were off together, unchaperoned, perhaps on their way to a wedding at the worst, or a clandestine liaison at the best, she'll be terrified that *you* will demand he marry Eleanor! Bad enough to tie her precious boy to a commoner, but one who's gone mad? And if instead, he's fixated on Lauralee and you give your consent, she'll be so relieved that you aren't making a fuss about the stepdaughter that you'll have no trouble getting her to agree to the wedding herself. She thinks you're gentry—poor, but blue blood. By the time she finds out differently, it will be too late. Especially if you hasten the wedding on the grounds of scandal, the war, or both."

He was right, curse him. Well, of course he was right. He was used to thinking in terms of blackmail. She hadn't much practice in that particular "art." She had always dealt with her enemies in much more direct ways—and with those from whom she wanted favors, by means much more arcane.

"What about me?" Carolyn mewed plaintively. "If Reggie's going to marry Lauralee, what about me?"

At that moment, Alison caught a glimpse of something avid in Locke's eyes, and knew what he was going to demand as *his* payment for all of this. After all, she would now control the Robinson fortune outright, once she was appointed guardian to a madwoman. Carolyn would stand to inherit all that; Lauralee wouldn't need it once she was Lady Devlin. Carolyn was pretty, soon to be wealthy, none-too-clever, and just as ruthless as Locke. She was a good match for him, by his way of thinking. He would not have to hide things from her, and she would be just as eager to cover up irregularities as he was.

"Oh, you'll have your wedding, too, Carolyn," she replied, with a little nod to Locke. "Just as splendid as Lauralee's. I'll see to that."

And she would see to it that the girl found Locke acceptable, too. After all, it was a great deal easier to put a death-curse on a man whose wife would do anything her mother said.

Because the clever Warrick Locke was getting too clever. And Alison Robinson had not gotten where she was now by allowing anyone to have a hold over her.

30

August 12, 1917
Elsewhere

ELEANOR STARED AT THE SMALL army of Earth Elementals facing them, and put one hand on the back of a Salamander to steady herself. There was no way that she could battle all of them—they'd overwhelm her by sheer numbers. Was it possible that she could call for more help?

Well, what do I lose by trying? She didn't close her eyes, but she did turn her focus inward, calling up from memory the glyphs and sigils that would bring one of the Great Elementals, many of whom had been worshipped as gods. At this point, she didn't particularly care which one, either; the only thing that she did stipulate in her mind was that she really didn't want to fight, not even these things—

As she traced the last sigil in her mind, the whole diagram suddenly flared in the air between her and the Earth creatures, hanging there like a fantastical fireworks display.

And beside her, she heard a swift intake of breath.

Her companion began to grow. His nimbus of flame flared out, engulfing her—but she felt nothing but a cool breeze on her skin, and smelled nothing but the faint scent of cinnamon and clove. He sprouted wings, too, and his head became bird-like—no, hawk-like—and when he stopped growing, at roughly twelve feet tall, she recognized him. Or at least, what he represented.

Horus, the Egyptian god of the rising sun, the son of Osiris and Isis.

She stared at him. Of all creatures, the least likely—

Or perhaps not. She had been working through a Tarot pack which employed many symbols out of ancient Egypt. Horus was as likely as any other, given that influence.

The Earth creatures stared at him as well, dumbfounded, as the flaming sigils faded away. He looked down at them, then turned his head to stare at Eleanor, wings flaring.

"Do you still want to negotiate with them?" came his mild voice. "I think you're in a better position now."

The Salamanders romped about his ankles as she looked up at him. "I'd rather not hurt anyone," she said, though a bit doubtfully. "If I can help it, that is."

"That's wise, here," he conceded. "There's no point in making more enemies than you have to. They have long memories, and hold grudges forever."

He turned to the Earth creatures. "Let us pass," he said, his voice taking on trumpet-like tones. "We would rather not harm you, but we will fight to escape if we must. You do not wish to fight us."

There was uneasy stirring from the line of Earth creatures, but no one moved. Finally the Redcap spoke up, sullenly.

"All right for you to say, but what about us? What happens when the Earth Master discovers you've slipped the trap? She'll have us then, for certain-sure!"

Horus clacked his beak impatiently. "And if we break her protections first? She'll be yours, then."

There were startled looks, then the creatures began talking urgently among themselves. Eleanor couldn't even begin to recognize what they all were; a good half of them hadn't been in any of her reading yet. They all looked like things out of nightmare. Including, of course, the Nightmare.

Horus waited patiently until the murmuring stopped, but if he had expected a direct answer, he didn't get one. Instead, the assembled creatures merely faded away into the shadows and the depths of the maze, leaving the path open.

Eleanor looked up at her protector, and he down at her. "That is as direct an answer as you will ever have from the likes of them," Horus said. "The way is open, for now—until they change their minds."

That was all she needed. She ran forward, out of the maze and into—

—darkness—

She realized, after a moment of light-headed giddiness that at least part of the darkness was because there was a blanket over her head. It was stifling, and she could hardly think, because she felt so—so intoxicated—

That's—because—I am— Alison had drugged her, as she had suspected, and there was still plenty of the stuff in her veins. She jounced along, lying on her side, two sets of feet poking into her, and the roar of an automobile engine near at hand. It was hard, so hard to think—even the fear that sat cold and primal in the pit of her soul was sluggish.

And her companion was gone, now that she was in the real world again. There was no one to advise her.

She fought her way through the glue that clogged her mind. Fire. Burning. She was outside Alison's spells, and in control of her own powers now. There must be something Fire could do!

Can—can I burn this stuff—out of me?

There had been some hints of that in her mother's notes, of a kind of healing that Fire Masters could do, that literally burned out disease and poison. This drug was poison in and of itself.

What did she have to lose? Alison was taking her away somewhere, and it was just lucky she'd broken free of the spell, because otherwise she'd be feeling the compulsions right now.

And at that thought, she felt a cold certainty steal over her, and with it, the fear woke out of its sluggish sleep to seize her heart. Alison knew that. So Alison was planning on it. Why?

She had to clear this poison out of her veins so she could think clearly!

She had only one thing to try. If she waited for the drug to wear off, it might be too late. She *had* to burn it out before Alison expected it to wear off. Because Alison certainly had Locke with her still, and perhaps Locke's brutish manservant, and there was no way she could escape them all.

Once again, she turned within, concentrating on another sigil, this time a simple one; just as well, because it kept slipping away from her as she felt herself floating away.

Ateh. Malkuth. Geteth. She had traced this thing a thousand times; each Name from her mother's notes attached to a particular stroke in the air with finger or wand. But now she traced it in her mind instead of the air, and muzzily tried to hold the image burning there.

It nearly escaped from her three times before she completed it, and tried to put purpose to it. Its intention was to purify. Could it purify her blood?

Only one way to find out. It seemed to flutter in her mind, like a bird, impatient to fly. It, at least, thought it had a purpose.

She set it free, and let go. If it didn't do what she wanted, there wouldn't be a second chance.

August 13, 1917
The Hoar Stones

"What did you do with him?" Alison asked, as Locke made his way up the path to the Hoar Stones behind her, with Eleanor slung over his shoulder like a bag of coal. She was impressed in spite of herself; she was accustomed to seeing

Locke leave all of the work to his servant, but it appeared he could manage quite a bit by himself. He'd certainly managed to bring Reggie Fenyx here on his own, and he was carrying Eleanor as if her weight was inconsequential.

"He's in the lee of the rocks, just outside the chamber," Locke replied. "He's still out cold. I thought you'd want to keep the chamber itself clear so you can work."

"Very wise. Leave the girl there as well," Alison said, absentmindedly; they were still a good thirty yards from the Hoar Stones, yet already she could feel its power drawing her. Had the work she'd done here last spring woken some ancient source of magic from a long slumber? Well, if that was so, all the better.

She reached out to the source of the power, greedily, and felt her lips stretching in a grin as it responded to her. Lovely, lovely Earth-born power; whatever purpose the Hoar Stones had been originally meant to serve, over the centuries there had been enough who had used it as a place of sacrifice that the ground here was as blood-soaked as the fields of Flanders. Blood spilled called power, and this sort of power was the kind that answered her hand the best.

She felt like a child in a sweet-shop, told to take what she wanted. Finally, she was going to have it *all!*

The power filled her, thick and intoxicating, with the hint of corruption she found so irresistible, and she moved into the chamber as if in a trance as Locke dumped Eleanor beside another bundle of blanket and clothing just outside it. It occurred to her then that Locke was probably stronger than he looked; Reggie Fenyx was no small man, and Locke had somehow manhandled him from the motor all the way up here.

Then again—Locke might have managed to rouse Reggie enough to get him to walk. Even unconscious, a clever use of magic could have gotten Reggie to stumble along in Locke's wake or in front of him. And if he damaged himself somewhat, well, so much the better; he'd *look* like someone who had been staggering about after an accident.

She put them both temporarily from her mind as Locke

and the girls joined her in the chamber. This was going to be a difficult piece of work, and she needed to concentrate on it.

Reggie lay quite still as Alison's henchman dumped someone beside him. The last thing he wanted any of them to know was that he was awake and aware and prepared to act—if feeling nauseous and half-crippled counted as being prepared to act. Little did any of them know that he'd been using his pain-medications for so long that he had built up a tolerance for opiates; the air moving around his face when the auto was in motion had served to arouse him, and the drive out into the country had given him long enough to get his brain more-or-less working again. When the man had mumbled some sort of half-learned charm over him, he'd felt the intent of it through the very minimal shields he had put up, and had acted the part of an automaton, staggering up the shadow-shrouded path in the man's wake. Unfortunately, he was without a cane, and the ground was anything but even. He didn't even want to think about the damage he had done to himself, trying to walk; he thought he'd felt something tear loose around his kneecap once. The pain of his knee had burned what was left of the drug out of him altogether, and he must have stumbled and fallen a dozen times. Evidently the man had expected that, because Locke just stopped whenever that happened, waited for Reggie to pick himself up, then led him on.

Reggie had been perfectly ready to fall over where the man pointed. By that time his head was perfectly clear, but it ached so much from what he presumed was a blow, and his knee was in such agony, that by the time he realized that he was alone among these ancient stones, it was too late to do anything about it. He could already hear someone coming up the same path. All he could do was feign unconsciousness and wait to see what happened next.

What happened was that Locke dumped someone else practically on top of him. Someone small, and very warm.

Eleanor?

He continued to lie quietly as the sound of the others moved off a little. The way he was positioned, he couldn't see anything anyway; his face was turned towards the megalithic stone, and the other person had been dropped behind him.

But he was sure it was Eleanor. It wasn't just the sense that it was her, or instinct. Logic said that was the likeliest—but why? What was Alison planning?

It was nothing good for either of them, but it was Eleanor he was worried about the most. He represented the means to a very large fortune, as well as a kind of life she clearly aspired to. If she got rid of him, she lost her access to that life; Lady Virginia would see to that. No, it made more sense, far more sense, for her to try and work some bedazzlement on his mind, to make him pliant and willing to marry one of her wretched daughters.

It was Eleanor that he was concerned about. He still didn't know how Eleanor factored into all this—except that she was now clearly an obstacle in the path to Alison's goals. He couldn't dismiss the idea that they meant to murder her—after all, who would notice? No one in Broom even gave her existence a second thought now.

Even more chilling was the thought that Alison might murder Eleanor in order to get the power she needed to control him.

And he was patently in no shape to take them on in a straight-on physical contest. He wasn't even sure he could manage a successful escape. The longer this situation dragged on, the less confident he became.

And on top of that, as bad as his physical condition already was, he knew it was rapidly deteriorating. Lying here on the ground was making his muscles stiffen, and there was no point in pretending otherwise, he had a concussion that wasn't getting any better either. His head pounded, and though he tried to think through the pain and the nausea, it was getting harder to put two coherent thoughts together with every passing moment; his mouth was dry, and a slow serpent of fear had begun crawling up his spine, making him feel weak and helpless.

He could sense power rising very near by—Earth power, and even though it only brushed by him in passing, the moment it touched him, he felt panic stifling him. He knew that sort of power—born of blood and death. He had met its like before.

When he had been buried in that trench.

Alison began chanting somewhere on the other side of the stones, her voice echoing strangely, and he sensed the power awakening and answering her call—

He felt a whimper rising in his throat—

And a small, warm hand clamped itself over his mouth.

"Shh," Eleanor breathed in his ear. "It's all right; try not to make a sound. Alison and the rest are busy right now. If we're very careful, we might be able to get away before they realize we're gone."

And go where? he thought wildly, but he knew she was right. Whatever Alison was up to, there was a point she'd be so preoccupied with controlling what she was raising that she should be oblivious to anything but what she was doing.

The only question was, could *he* even walk, much less run?

It's not as if I have a choice, he reminded himself. *It's run—somehow—or lie here and let her do whatever she's going to do.*

Even though fear was welling up inside him and making him want nothing more than to curl up where he was and hide inside himself. Trying to huddle inside himself was not an option now. Even if he had felt willing to let them do whatever they wanted to him, what were their plans for Eleanor? If he gave up to the fear, he would be abandoning her.

But the fear had a mind of its own, where he was concerned. Despite his efforts to resist it, and all the work that Lady Virginia had done with him, he felt it taking him over, paralyzing him, flooding his heart with chill, until there was nothing real for him except that fear. His control slipped to the edge of loss, and tremors shook his body.

And then the miracle occurred. Eleanor's hand moved down from his mouth to rest over his heart, and warmth began to spread from it.

Not just physical warmth, either—a psychic warmth that stopped his shaking, and drove the fear back, a wonderfully fierce passion that had no time for creeping terror. It was like magic—

No, it *was* magic! It was Fire magic, the complement and perfect partner to Air—Fire magic being directed by the sure hand of someone who, if she was not yet a Master, would certainly one day become one!

Before he could wonder where she had suddenly gotten that skill, a set of shields grew up around both of them; slowly, so slowly that at first he thought the perimeter of warming around him was some side-effect of the magic she was working on him. The he realized that she was building shields—not as he would have expected out of a Fire Mage, with a showy rush of upwelling, vibrant power, but slowly, as if beginning from the barest, glowing coals and building a fire by patiently feeding those coals a little air, a little fuel, straw by straw.

By that time he was no longer shaking; though his head still ached and he felt sick, his mind was clear again. Not that he wasn't afraid—and so was she, he sensed it in the rigidity of her body where it lay wedged against his, and the way she was trembling—but fear was no longer paralyzing him.

I need to help her—and it has to be just as subtle, so that we don't alert Alison to what we're doing.

First he needed to help her with those shields. Then—could he call a Sylph and sent it for help? Would one even come so near the poisonous, dark Earth power that Alison was raising?

He had to try; the nearest help was Lady Virginia, and the only way to get word to her was via an Air Elemental.

But it would be the first time he had called one since the crash. Would they even come to him anymore?

He's awake! That was more than Eleanor had hoped for; she hadn't even cared that he was shaking hard enough to rattle both of them. She'd been hearing bits about this "shellshock" business from Sarah, and it didn't surprise her at all that Reggie suffered from it—fine, so he was overwhelmed by fear. Well, she had the counter to fear, the weapon to drive it back. Fear couldn't stand against the fire of passion.

But one thing did surprise her. Before, it had been as if he was surrounded by an impenetrable wall that allowed nothing arcane to get in at him—but which was also opaque to his senses so that he never knew that she was a Fire Mage. Now—now he was open.

Open enough that she responded to his fear completely on instinct. She put her hand over his heart, and willed her power into him.

Fire—

Passion. Courage. Heart. Fire was all of these things and more, but these were the ones that were important now, to shore up his crumbling emotions and give him strength to find his feet again. She sensed it, she *knew* it; that was all he needed, just a little help—he *wanted* to fight his own fear, but he was so worn by it that he hadn't the strength. Very well; he should have some of hers.

And when she sensed he was no longer shaking, she went to work building shields around the two of them, starting with the merest trace of power, layering them up slowly, so that—she hoped—Alison wouldn't notice what was happening until it was too late.

It was after the first three or four layers had been constructed that she sensed another power joining hers.

She had never felt Air magic before, but even if her inner sight hadn't shown her the soft blue glow of it, she had no doubt of what it was; there was a lightness to it, the coolness of intellect, and a liveliness. Even as he layered in his own subtle shields, interleaving them with hers, she felt his magic feeding hers, Fire and Air mingling until the blending was far more powerful than the mere sum of both. And at that moment she felt her own courage rise.

She was terribly glad that he had joined her in creating the shields that surrounded them both, because when she finally threw off the blanket they had bundled her in and sat up, trusting that by this time Alison was so deeply involved in her own magics that she wouldn't notice anything else going on, what she saw made her lose her hard-won courage for a moment.

The very stones of this Neolithic monument were glowing a muddy, ugly yellow with Alison's newly raised power. Oh, not glowing to ordinary sight, but to the trained Inner Eye of a magician there was no mistake, none at all. This was an old, old power, and it answered to Alison slowly, but it was answering. And it was as dark a power as Alison could have wished.

She pulled the blanket off Reggie's head and tugged at his shoulder; as he sat up, much more slowly than she had, she didn't have to direct his attention to the stones. He saw it on his own.

He pulled her head towards his face, and put his mouth right up to her ear to whisper, "That's not good."

She nodded.

"We have to get out of here now," he continued, urgently. "Can help me get to my feet?"

She nodded harder.

She got to her feet—slowly, and with a great care for making sure she didn't break a twig or dislodge any rattling stones. But there was one thing that she she knew she *had* to do if they were going to walk out of here.

She had to find him some sort of support, a stick he could use as a cane. His knee could not possibly be in good shape right now.

Except, of course, that she couldn't actually see in the

shadow-shrouded woodlot, in the dark of night, to find any such thing.

All right. I need someone—or something—that can see.

With infinite care, she pushed out the shields on the forest-side of their protections, until they extended well into the undergrowth. Then she called a Salamander.

She stipulated that it was to be a very, very small Salamander, the kind that had first come to her, scarcely bigger than a tiny kitten. Alison hadn't noticed the little creatures when they were under her own roof; with luck, she wouldn't notice one now.

She had no fire for it, and this was far, far too close to inimical power. She wasn't sure any Fire Elemental would answer her here.

But her heart leapt when, without so much as a spark of real fire to feed from—it still came! It wreathed apprehensively around her wrists and through her fingers, every movement of it telling her that it was *not* happy to be near so much dark power. She soothed it as best she could, and tried to impress on its mind what she needed—a good, stout stick, sound and strong, and not too short.

It hesitated for a moment, regarding her with glowing yellow eyes, then darted off into the brush, coursing back and forth like a beagle on a scent, but staying within the protection of the shields. She knew when it had found what she had asked for by the way that it darted out of the brush towards her, then back in again. It wasn't going to talk to her, not here. Wise. Alison might well hear such a thing.

She followed it, treading very carefully, never putting her full weight on her foot until she knew there was nothing beneath it to make a sound that would betray them. For the first time, she was glad of her worn shoes; the soles were so thin she could easily feel what was under her feet. Pushing carefully through the undergrowth, she found the Salamander running up and down the length of the stick, which was a bit longer than the canes Reggie normally used—more like a quarterstaff. Well, that was not such a bad thing. It might make a better weapon at need, and the longer it was, the less likely it would be that Reggie would need to lean on her.

She dismissed the Salamander with her thanks—it was clearly growing terrified at the feel of the terrible Earth power outside the shields, and she didn't blame it. With infinite care, she pulled the stick out from the undergrowth, little by little, until, with a sigh of relief, she got it free.

She turned around with it in her grip in time to see something wispy, sinuous, and pale blue streaking away from Reggie's hands. She hadn't gotten a good enough look at it to tell what it was, but she hoped he was sending for help. She tiptoed back to him and handed him the stick. With a look of relief, he took it gladly and used it to get himself—with her help—to his feet.

"Now which way?" he whispered.

She shook her head. "I don't know!" she whispered back. "I never saw anything!"

She might not have been unconscious when she was brought here, but she had been bundled in a blanket. Truth to tell, she hadn't a clue which direction to go in.

Reggie clung to the rough staff Eleanor had found for him and tried to think. Had the path into this place been between those two flat stones he was facing now, or—

"Mother!" shrieked a young female voice behind him. *"They're awake! They're trying to sneak away!"*

Too late.

A soundless explosion of sickly yellow light impacted against their shields; he felt Eleanor react just in time to strengthen them, and a second later, he was reinforcing her. Fire magic was better for shields anyway; you couldn't wear away at Fire shields, the Fire just ate everything you threw at it. Even nasty stuff of the sort that Alison was throwing at them now; Fire just purified it, then consumed it. You could smother them, drown them, or blast through them if you were powerful enough, but you needed either to be extremely powerful in the first place, or to make an all-or-nothing commitment to the attack to do so, and Alison hadn't yet made that kind of attack.

Following directly on her attack came Alison herself, her face a mask of fury, with her solicitor Warrick Locke right beside her. He seemed to be unarmed, but she had a wicked-looking knife in one hand—a ritual blade, maybe, but it was also a real weapon, and he and Eleanor were unarmed. He gripped his stick like a quarterstaff, but he knew that he wouldn't be of much help with his leg ready to give out at any moment.

Real fire, physical fire, suddenly sprang up in a circle around them, following the line of the shields and setting fire to the undergrowth. It was a waist-high perimeter of flame that kept Alison and her minions from getting at her victims physically.

Reggie couldn't do exactly the same thing—but he *could* call a storm-wind, to lash at their adversaries with the branches of trees and bushes—and he did. Carolyn shrieked with indignation, and Warrick Locke ducked.

"Get them!" Alison shouted furiously over the howling wind, as her hair escaped from its pins and whipped in tendrils around her head, like the snakes of a Medusa.

Reggie expected another attack on their shields, and indeed, one came, a dull blow that actually drove the shields back a little. It didn't matter; the Elemental Fire devoured the rest of the attack, and the line of physical fire simply followed the shields, and Locke shook his head, when Alison gestured furiously at him.

And the glow of power faded a bit from the megaliths. He felt his heart leap—either she was losing control of it and it was sliding back into quiescence, or else she was draining it with her attacks. In either case, unless she found another source of power soon, she would be reduced to her own resources—

That was the moment when she seized Warrick Locke's wrist, shouted something incomprehensible—

And Locke screamed in fear and pain, falling to his knees, as he aged fifty years in a handful of seconds. A few seconds more, and Alison dropped his wrist, and the lifeless, withered hulk of what had been a man fell to the side, no longer moving.

Where did she get that? He knew what it was, in theory. Earth Masters healed—and so could harm. They grew—and so knew how to destroy. They could give life—and take it. It was what made them so dangerous when they went to the bad.

Shocked to the core, Reggie just stared.

Both her daughters were equally shocked, and as a consequence, didn't react quickly enough when their mother seized both of their wrists.

"No!" he shouted—not that he cared for them, and they had certainly been ready to consign *him* to whatever fate Alison had prepared for him, but no one should die like that—

But Alison was evidently not ready to kill her own flesh and blood. Quite.

Though the creatures she cast aside, first Carolyn, then Lauralee, were never going to attract anyone's attention again, except as objects of pity.

Alison turned towards them again, her eyes glowing with rage and power, her hands crooked into claws. And all around her, the stones were incandescent with terrible power.

She gestured with a crooked finger, and the earth rose in a wave and crushed out the physical fire over half of the periphery of the shields, leaving behind only the shields of Elemental Fire and Air themselves as protection.

Eleanor swallowed down fear and nausea, and tried to *think*. Their shields weren't going to hold, not for long, since they were feeding off nothing but her own strength. There had to be a way to stop her!

She held onto Reggie's arm, and backed up a step, so that he did the same. A slow, terrible smile stretched Alison's lips in a dreadful mockery of pleasure. She gestured again, and this time it was a horde of those horrible gnome-things that rose up out of the raw earth and flung themselves at the shields.

Eleanor gathered her wits, and called her Salamanders.

Once again, faithful and protective, they came, leaping out of the flames of the dying fires, dashing towards Alison's gnomes.

But they were joined by something Eleanor had never seen before; slender, sinuous things like legless dragons. They didn't seem to have much in the way of attacking ability, but whenever they whipped themselves around a Salamander, the Fire Elemental grew markedly larger or brighter—or both.

The Salamanders reached the line of gnomes, and this time, the gnomes didn't run.

There were more of them than there were Salamanders, and they swarmed the Fire Elementals, threatening to pull them down. But whatever the Salamanders came into contact with burst into flame.

The Salamanders weren't getting off unscathed, however; the gnomes had heavy clubs and spears, and they were perfectly prepared to use them.

Then a dozen of them got through, and Reggie lurched forwards to interpose himself between them and her. Two frantic Salamanders raced towards them, and a Sylph, a delicate, winged creature, suddenly popped into existence, hovering in midair. The Salamanders got one each, and the fairy-like being might have looked delicate, but she accounted for the other four with her bow and arrows.

But not before two of the got to Reggie, and while he was fending one off with his staff, the second ducked under a blow and smashed into Reggie's bad knee with his club.

Reggie toppled over with a choked-off cry of agony, as the winged girl filled the evil creature with three swift arrows in succession.

With a wordless cry of fury, Eleanor reached for more power—in what might have been an unexpected place. Not to the physical fires being extinguished by more gnomes, but down—down past the layer of Earth where Alison's power lay, down past the planet's stony skin, down into the place where the Earth itself gave way to Fire, and the molten rock showed which of the Powers was stronger—

"No!" It was Alison's turn to shout, as she concentrated all of her anger and fury on Eleanor.

The fury began to take shape, rising out of the earth before them.

A Giant.

Not the sort that Jack had met at the top of his beanstalk. That Giant, uncouth as he had been, was a paragon of intelligence and sophistication next to this thing.

It was made of the earth that it rose from. Near-shapeless, it had a blob of rancid clay for a head, with two holes gouged out for eyes, at the bottom of each of which glowed the same, sickly-yellow light as suffused the stones. A misshapen lump defined a nose, and beneath that, was an empty yawn of a mouth. It had no neck to speak of; the head seemed to grow directly from the moss-covered, massive shoulders. And as yet, it had no discernable arms or legs—

That changed in a moment; a club-like arm with undifferentiated mitten-hands reached out, snatched up a battling gnome and Salamander together, and tossed them both into its gaping maw, devouring them both with a single gulp.

It grew a trifle, and reached out for another pair of fighters—

Horrified, Eleanor looked away for a moment—and caught sight of Alison.

Her stepmother was transfixed by the battle; partly because she was pouring everything she had into her creation, and partly in mesmerized pleasure at the carnage.

But she had forgotten something.

She had dropped her additional protections, relying only on her old, unaugmented shields.

And Eleanor now knew how to unweave those—she had used the same key on her shields as she had on the spells binding Eleanor to the hearthstone.

Reggie had struggled to his good knee and was staring in horror at the giant, shaking in every limb, his eyes wide. She grabbed his arm and shook it. He wrenched his gaze away from the giant and looked up at her. His face was so pale he looked like a corpse.

"We have one chance!" she shouted, over the bass growls of the giant. "Help me!"

From somewhere, he dragged up the final dregs of his courage. Life came back into his eyes.

"Her shields!" she cried, "Forget about the giant—drop *our* shields, then come in, Air and Fire together, and follow my lead—

He nodded; he dropped the staff and she crouched beside him; they clasped hands and let their own shields go.

Alison howled in triumph; the giant echoed it, and wrenched himself up further out of the earth.

Alison's shields flickered as she let the last of her concentration slip from them.

And together, a single melded lance of Fire and Air struck at the weakest point, blasting it away—and the shields unraveled.

Alison faltered, and took a single step back. The loss of her shields confused her for one vital moment.

And the giant turned, wrenching its body completely out of the ground. It stared at her for several long seconds; her eyes widened, as she realized in that instant that she was unprotected—

—and that all around her were creatures she had forced to obey her with whatever weapon came to hand. Creatures who saw her momentarily unprotected.

Like the giant that she had just created out of earth and blood and pain.

She looked up at it with her mouth open. It looked down at her.

And then, it fell upon her, burying her alive in a mound of freshly-turned soil before she could make a sound.

The last of the gnomes swarmed over the mound, burying themselves into the ground where she had been.

And suddenly, there was silence—except for the mindless whimpering of the two creatures that had once been Carolyn and Lauralee.

Reggie sank slowly to the ground, his teeth gritted against the agony of his ruined knee—slowly, only because Eleanor caught him as he fell and eased him down. That took the last of *her* strength, and all she could do was to hold him as the remaining Salamanders curled around them both, keeping them warm and protected, and wait for dawn, help, or both.

Epilogue

November 25, 1917
Somerville College
Oxford University

SOME OF THE GIRLS THOUGHT the little studies in Somerville College were cramped and shabby. Then again, some of the girls were accustomed to the kind of accommodation one found at Longacre Park . . . for Eleanor, even if the study had been the size and bleakness of her garret room at The Arrows, it still would have been paradise. A raw November wind rattled the windows, but she had a fine fire going (and before long, someone with less access to wood or a more slender budget for coal would be around to "borrow" a log or two). One of the scouts had managed tea and toast; Eleanor had jam and butter from Sarah by parcel this morning. All was right with the world.

Eleanor poured her visitor another cup of tea with a feeling of unreality. It still seemed an impossibility that she was here, settled in Oxford, a student at last in Somerville College.

"So," asked Doctor Maya, stirring honey from the Longacre hives into her tea in lieu of unobtainable sugar. "How are you enjoying life as a student of literature?"

"It's incredible," Eleanor replied. "I keep thinking I'm

going to wake up in my bed in the garret and it will all have been a dream."

"And the studies?" Maya persisted, giving her a penetrating look. "They're going well?"

Eleanor laughed; she knew what Maya was thinking. That Reggie's proximity would be a powerful distraction. Little did she know that he was harder on her than her tutor, and she was harder on herself than both of them put together. "I think my generation is going to be a trial to those who follow us," she told the doctor. "Those of us who are *here* are determined to prove that we can be as valuable as the ones who left to become VADs or do some other sort of war-work. And when Oxford grants us degrees—*which they will*—we are going to be among the first in line to demand ours. Compared to what Alison kept me at, this is light duty." She sighed, but it was with content. "And compared to how I've been living at The Arrows, this place is a delight. Reggie keeps us both supplied with wood for the fireplaces from Longacre, and with other things, too. I find I can get a lot of help when I need it in trade for an egg or a jar of honey."

Maya *tsk*ed wryly. "You're a regular black-marketeer. I'll have to demand a bribe of some of those eggs to keep quiet, I'm afraid. They can't be had for any price in London."

Eleanor laughed. She was doing a lot of that these days.

She didn't remember much past Alison's demise. She'd been drained almost to fainting, and Reggie *was* unconscious when Lady Virginia appeared like an avenging angel and carried them both off to Longacre. Lady Devlin hadn't known what to think—at first she had, with some bewilderment, tentatively welcomed Eleanor as the hitherto-unknown stepdaughter of her friend Alison Robinson.

Then the situation rapidly unraveled. It had been decided to say *nothing* about Alison, Warrick Locke, and the girls; the farmer upon whose land the Hoar Stones stood had found the autos, the body of Locke, and the two near-witless sisters. Constables digging in the churned-up earth had turned up the body of Alison, but other than that, no one could make heads or tails of why the four were out there in the first place, nor what had turned two young women into withered hags nor what had destroyed Locke. And, once Peter Almsley intervened on behalf of the War Office, country constables being what they were, it was decided that it was best not to ask too many more questions that couldn't be answered. It was all written up that Locke had murdered Alison and buried her body, and that the shock had prematurely aged her daughters, who had killed Locke in a fit of insanity.

This was more than scandal, this was sensation, and Eleanor suddenly found herself unwelcome at Longacre Park.

However, she was well on her feet by this time, and The Arrows was *hers.* Rightfully hers, as she found out when the lawyers came to see her. She didn't even need to lift a finger to do anything to help Carolyn and Lauralee if she chose not—

But she was not hard-hearted enough to throw them onto the state. Since they were clearly not fit to stand trial, they were currently being cared for in an institution for the criminally insane—comfortably, at Eleanor's insistence and expense.

Reggie's knee was shattered past all hope. Eleanor had met Maya when Lady Virginia had insisted that only Maya could or should tend to Reggie's injuries, and she and the doctor had hit it off immediately. Doctor Maya had done her best, but it was clear to her, and to the army surgeon who came to examine him, that he would never fly in combat again. Flying an aeroplane—at least, the current models—required having two good arms and legs.

So he as soon as he had gotten a cast on the leg, he had put in for a transfer to the Oxford branch of the Royal Flying Corps training school. He'd been accepted, of course; with a record like his, they'd have been insane not to accept him. So he was here when Eleanor had enrolled for her first year as a university student, reading literature. Here, there was no Lady Devlin to have to placate, and they could meet as often as they liked, which was generally every day.

"You haven't announced an engagement?" Maya asked.

Eleanor shook her head, twisting the ring that Reggie had "unofficially" given her. "I want to have finished my studies and passed my vivas, even if they won't give me a degree yet. And by then, maybe Lady Devlin will have come around to the idea of having me as a daughter-in-law."

Maya grimaced. "I'm sorry to hear that she's being an obstruction. Fortunately, that was not a problem in my case."

But Eleanor only shrugged. "She can't help how she was brought up," she pointed out. "And besides . . . we have an ally. Or two, actually."

Maya raised her eyebrows, as Eleanor carefully buttered a piece of toast. "I knew about Lady Virginia; she was fairly obvious, because if nothing else, she would want Reggie to marry another Master. Who else?"

"The Brigadier." She blushed; the old fellow had been amazingly kind to her, and for the life of her, she didn't know why. Maybe it was just because he was fond of Reggie, and Reggie was clearly as blissfully happy in her presence as she was in his. "He's on our side, too. And I think he has—well, a kind of secret weapon. I think he's started to court Lady Devlin, and if he is, she'll find it hard to be against something that he's for."

"Really!" Doctor Maya laughed. "Well, the sly old fox! He knew about Devlin being a Master, you know—one of the few people who aren't mages who ever do find out about us. I don't think he ever let Reggie know that he knew, but he's an old crony of Alderscroft, and that's where it all started. And it was partly his doing that Devlin met Reggie's mother in the first place. I don't know the details, but he introduced them at some point."

"Ah," Eleanor replied thoughtfully. "That explains a great deal." She took a sip of her tea. "At any rate, my magical studies are coming along well, too. My tutor thinks that the Tarot approach is a good one, so we're keeping on with it. And Reggie says that's another reason not to rush into a marriage; he says that before we even think about settling down, *I* need to have a firm control on my powers. Because children with Masters on both sides tend to be precocious when it comes to magic."

She flushed a little; Maya pretended not to notice. "Talking about children already, is he?" she said, nodding. "In that case, I don't think I need to go and interrogate him about his intentions!"

Eleanor flushed deeper. "Oh no, he's sound, definitely sound," she said, laughing and fanning her cheeks. "In fact, he's my best help aside from my official tutor. We have special permission to work at the Bodleian. The Vice-Principal doesn't like it, but since the Principal is another Elemental Master, she doesn't say much, she just glares at us when she sees us in public together." She shrugged. "She means well, and so I don't care. I've only been here for this term, and she has no idea what kind of student I am; she may think I'm here only so I can be near Reggie. As soon as she realizes I'm serious about my studies, she'll probably stop acting like a Mother Superior."

Maya looked at her watch. "Well, I should love to make a longer visit, but I can't if I'm to catch the train. No, don't get up!" she urged, when Eleanor started to rise. "I can find my own way out, and the weather is hideous. You get back to your books. And keep that lad out of trouble. I had to scold him for trying to do too much again."

When Maya was gone, Eleanor settled back in her chair, with *Hamlet* wedged open in front of her, and a Salamander wrapped around her feet, keeping them warm. If someone had waved a magic wand and given her three wishes, this was exactly where she would have wished to be. The only flaw in life was Lady Devlin's opposition to having a "commoner" as her daughter-in-law—

Which is next to no problem at all, she thought, warming the tea again by asking another Salamander to pop out of the fireplace and wrap himself around the pot. *Compared to unweaving Alison's spells.*

Besides, she wanted time. She and Reggie had scarcely

known each other. Not that she didn't love him! But love was not entirely rational. She was not going to be Lady Devlin all over again, either. This was going to be a marriage of partners.

Whether Reggie entirely understood this yet, or not.

"And," she said aloud, "whether he's comfortable with it or not."

A movement in the fireplace made her glance at it to see two bright blue eyes looking back at her. *"Just remember, daughter of Eve,"* said the Phoenyx who was her chief magical tutor, and evidently a friend of Horus, *"If you need a negotiator, you always have one at your disposal."*

Eleanor burst into laughter that she could not stop until her irritated neighbor knocked on the wall to make her quiet down.

MERCEDES LACKEY

The Novels of Valdemar

Exile's Valor

Once a heroic captain in the army of Karse, Valdemar's traditional enemy, Alberich became one of Valdemar's Heralds. Despite prejudice against him, he becomes the personal protector of young Queen Selenay. But can he protect her from the dangers of her own heart?

"*A must for Valdemar fans.*"
—Booklist

0-7564-0206-9

To Order Call: 1-800-788-6262

DAW 24

MERCEDES LACKEY

THE GATES OF SLEEP

The *Elemental Masters* Series

Evil portents have warned that Marina Roeswood will be killed by the hand of her own aunt before her eighteenth birthday. Hidden in rural Cornwall, Marina has no knowledge of the dark curse that shadows her life. Will her half-trained magic prove powerful enough to overturn this terrible prophecy of death?

0-7564-0101-1

"A wonderful example of a new look at an old theme."—*Publishers Weekly*

And don't miss the first book of
The Elemental Masters:
The Serpent's Shadow
0-7564-0061-9

To Order Call: 1-800-788-6262

DAW 23